OTTO PENZLI
AMERICAN MYS

THE GREENE MURDER CASE

S. S. Van Dine was the pen name of Willard Huntington Wright (1888-1939), an American art critic and novelist. He was an important figure in avant-garde cultural circles in pre-WWI New York, and he created the immensely popular fictional detective Philo Vance, a sleuth and aesthete who first appeared in books in the 1920s, then in movies and on the radio.

Otto Penzler, the creator of American Mystery Classics, is also the founder of the Mysterious Press (1975); Mysterious-Press.com (2011), an electronic-book publishing company; and New York City's Mysterious Bookshop (1979). He has won a Raven, the Ellery Queen Award, two Edgars (for the *Encyclopedia of Mystery and Detection*, 1977, and *The Lineup*, 2010), and lifetime achievement awards from NoirCon and *The Strand Magazine*. He has edited more than 70 anthologies and written extensively about mystery fiction.

THE GREENE MURDER CASE

S. S.
VAN DINE

Introduction by
OTTO
PENZLER

AMERICAN
MYSTERY
CLASSICS

Penzler Publishers
New York

Published in 2024 by Penzler Publishers
58 Warren Street, New York, NY 10007
penzlerpublishers.com

Distributed by W. W. Norton

Cover image: Andy Ross
Cover design: Mauricio Diaz

Paperback ISBN 978-1-61316-569-0
Hardcover ISBN 978-1-61316-568-3
eBook ISBN 978-1-61316-570-6

Library of Congress Control Number: 2024930327

Printed in the United States of America

9 8 7 6 5 4 3 2 1

INTRODUCTION

THE APPEARANCE of Philo Vance as an amateur sleuth in the Roaring Twenties had an enormous impact on the history of the mystery genre, providing the American Golden Age of the detective story with a figure whose popularity equaled or exceeded that of the British writers who established it. While the first books created by S. S. Van Dine became a bestselling sensation, not everyone jumped onto the bandwagon in praise of the erudite aesthete who helped the New York City Police Department solve crimes.

"Rotten, aren't they?" wrote one observer of the New York literary scene. "I can't abide that Philo Vance. A nincompoop. Don't see why they've made such a hit. We've a dozen better detective novels on our list but all of them together haven't sold as many copies as one of those damned Van Dine thrillers."

Those harsh words were penned by none other than Willard Huntington Wright (1888-1939), a successful journalist, editor, and art critic who pseudonymously wrote the Van Dine novels, presumably referring to the Charles Scribner's Sons mystery catalogue in which his books held a regular place of honor.

With the creation of Philo Vance in *The Benson Murder Case* (1926), Van Dine's ensuing novels were enormous bestsellers until readers gravitated to the more realistic novels of Dashiell Hammett and those who followed. Although Mary Roberts Rinehart enjoyed greater sales than Van Dine—indeed, than any mystery writers in the world through the 1920s and 1930s—they were novels of suspense, heavily infused with romance and humor, rather than detective stories.

Born in Charlottesville, Virginia, the son of Annie Van Vranken and Archibald Davenport Wright, Willard was educated at St. Vincent and Pomona Colleges in California and Harvard University and studied art in Munich and Paris.

Wright worked as a literary and art critic for several publications, beginning with the *Los Angeles Times* in 1907. He was editor in chief of *Smart Set*, where he met H. L. Mencken and George Jean Nathan; the three authors collaborated on *Europe after 8:15* (1913), a series of sketches on European night life. Wright's first novel, *The Man of Promise* (1916), received some critical acclaim but little financial reward. In 1907 he married Katharine Belle Boynton; they had one daughter and were divorced in 1930, after which he married Eleanor Pulapaugh.

Never enjoying robust health, Wright had a rigid work schedule as columnist, editor, and aspiring fiction writer and suffered a severe breakdown in 1923, after which he was confined to bed for more than two years with a heart ailment. Forbidden to become excited or to engage in scholarly studies, he read detective novels, amassing a library of more than 2,000 volumes. Believing that he could do as well as the past masters of the form, he decided to improve on their art by writing for a different audience—a more intelligent, better-educated one. Because of his past attempts at serious scholarship (he had written critiques of modern painting, and on Nietzsche for the *Encyclopaedia Britannica*), he feared ridicule if he turned to writing detective novels and thus adopted a pseudonym. Using an old family name (Van Dyne) and the abbreviation of "steamship" as his initials, he outlined three Vance novels and brought them to the greatest of all editors—Maxwell Perkins at Scribner's. Each outline was 10,000 words long and contained every character and plot element necessary to give the prospective publisher a clear-cut concept of the finished work. They were eagerly accepted. Van Dine then enlarged them to 30,000 words in a second draft, complete except for dialogue, mood, and more complete characterization. The third and final draft was more than twice as long as the second draft and required virtually no editing. His posthumous final book, *The Winter Murder Case* (1939), was published from the second draft.

The books became overwhelming successes, making the previously debt-ridden author wealthy, and his snobbish detective soon became the most popular literary sleuth in the world. Because of all the magazine serializations, book club sales, original editions, reprints, foreign editions, and motion pictures, it is safe to suggest that Van Dine's income was probably one of the largest of any author in the world during the decade preceding his death; yet he left an estate of only $13,000.

Like Vance, Van Dine enjoyed his wealth, living in a luxurious penthouse, dining at the finest restaurants, drinking the costliest wines, wearing expensive clothes, and spending his prodigious income as quickly as possible. Like Vance, too, Van Dine was a sophisticated poseur, able to talk intelligently—and condescendingly—about a wide variety of topics.

Van Dine was the editor of *The Great Detective Stories* (1927), an anthology published under his real name. His introduction to this volume is one of the classics of detective fiction scholarship. His article "Twenty Rules for Writing Detective Stories," which first appeared in *The American Magazine* in 1928, is a complete guidebook for dealing fairly with the reader, even though it is constricting.

Although his rules sometimes inhibited creativity, Van Dine strictly imposed them on his own books and his series detective. Philo Vance had clearly been influenced by Lord Peter Wimsey and H.C. Bailey's Reggie Fortune, just as he then influenced the authors who created the character of Ellery Queen, notably with an affected English accent, esoteric knowledge, and speech pattern.

Like his creator, Vance is a dilettante who constantly injects his knowledge of the most arcane subjects, particularly those relating to art, music, philosophy, and religion, into murder investigations.

The aristocratic amateur detective is able to help solve murder cases for his best friend, District Attorney Markham. Sergeant Heath of the New York City Police Department initially dislikes Vance for his pomposity and affectations, his nonchalant and whimsical manner, and his long-winded, pedantic lectures on subjects that have no relation to the matter at hand, but later learns to respect and befriend him.

Apparently amused, Vance constantly smiles cynically even in the grimmest situations. Like Wright, the detective attended Harvard and several European universities, indulging his taste for knowledge, especially art. His interest in psychology directed him into the field of crime detection as an avocation, where he is eager to test his theories about human personalities.

Just under six feet tall, slim, and graceful, Vance has cool gray eyes, a straight, slender nose, and a thin-lipped mouth that almost suggests cruelty as well as irony. A disciple of Nietzsche, he is not above killing someone when it becomes obvious that the law will be unable to punish a murderer that he has tracked down.

Vance appears in twelve adventures, each with a similar title: *The ---- Murder Case*, the missing word being precisely six letters in all but *The Gracie Allen Murder Case*, an exception he made for his friend.

His exploits were recorded by Van Dine, Vance's lawyer and friend who accompanied him on his investigations and recorded them, much as Dr. Watson did for Sherlock Holmes. The first was *The Benson Murder Case*, based loosely on the actual 1920 murder of Joseph Elwell. In the novel, wealthy businessman Alvin Benson is shot to death in his luxury New York City apartment and Vance deduces the murderer almost immediately but seems to enjoy the plight of Markham and Heath as they employ circumstantial evidence to successively fix the guilt on five different people.

Although Vance finds it more difficult to finger the guilty party in the classic locked room murder situation in *The "Canary" Murder Case*, Vance again finds it amusing to let Markham and Heath flounder until he uses psychology to trap the killer, but only at the very end of the tale. Before he is convinced that he has identified the murderer, Vance admits, "My mental darkness is Egyptian, Stygian, Cimmerian—I'm in a perfect Erebus of tenebrosin."

He has delved into the brutal murder of the vamp Margaret Odell, who had received the sobriquet of "Canary" as a result of a part she had played in "an elaborate ornithological ballet in the Follies." Like *Benson*, this novel also was based on a real-life murder, the strangulation of a popular showgirl of the day, though there is little resemblance of the circumstances between the two crimes.

The Greene Murder Case (1928) diverges from the first two books in that they involved a single murder (the second killing in *"Canary"* was merely a byproduct) in which Vance had to match wits with a murderer in the upper stratus of New York's financial elite, while his third novel presented a virtual bloodbath. Vance described it as a "palimpsest of horror," "a history of the Greene holocaust," and "a heinous plot against the Greene family."

We quickly learn that someone entered the Greene mansion on East 53rd Street, overlooking the East River, and shot two sisters, one of whom was killed instantly and the other in critical condition. The theory of a burglary gone wrong becomes a mockery once Vance begins to analyze it, much to the annoyance of Markham who nonetheless asks his friend to work on the case with him. More bodies pile up in the Greene pogrom until Vance brings down the murderer in an unexpected physical confrontation.

The Greene Murder Case was the richest and most complex case that Van Dine had written to that time and sales skyrocketed as it sold more copies than *Benson* and *"Canary"* combined.

The enormous success of the book and its highly visual content made it a candidate for film and Paramount again cast one of its contract actors, the dapper William Powell, to play the detective, as he had in *"Canary"* earlier in the same year (1929).

Powell was perfect for the role and embraced it, having become fond of the Vance character, describing him as a "smooth fellow. Nice to be as intelligent as Vance, eh? But with all his suave, cynical exterior, he has a warm heart. He feels a real sympathy for those bereft by the murders he so deftly solves."

Jean Arthur, who went on to become a major film star, mainly in comedic roles, appeared in *The "Canary" Murder Case* against type as a floozy Follies actress. After her first Philo Vance film and her second, she had been the daughter of a doomed family menaced by the titular villain in *The Mysterious Dr. Fu Manchu* (1929).

Eight years later, Paramount remade *The Greene Murder Case* as *A Night of Mystery* (1937) with Grant Richards cast as Vance. Unknown to film, he had been recruited from the U.S. Government's WPA Federal Theatre Project. As is common with remakes, the film suffered badly when compared with the original.

Fortunately for readers, the text of this detective novel is the original, taken from a first edition of the book, to be enjoyed as it was by millions in the 1920s—and ever after.

Otto Penzler
New York
January 2024

THE GREENE MANSION, NEW YORK, AS IT APPEARED AT THE
TIME OF THE NOTORIOUS GREENE MURDER CASE

From an old woodcut by Lowell L. Balcum.

THE GREENE MURDER CASE

S. S. VAN DINE

Murder most foul, as in the best it is;
But this most foul, strange and unnatural.
　　　　　　　　　　—Hamlet.

TO
NORBERT L. LEDERER
Αγαθή δέ παράφασίς έστιν έταίρου

CHARACTERS OF THE BOOK

PHILO VANCE

JOHN F.-X. MARKHAM
>District Attorney of New York County.

MRS. TOBIAS GREENE
>The mistress of the Greene mansion.

JULIA GREENE
>The eldest daughter.

SIBELLA GREENE
>Another daughter.

ADA GREENE
>The youngest daughter.

CHESTER GREENE
>The elder Son.

REX GREENE
>The younger Son.

DR. ARTHUR VON BLON
>The Greene family physician.

SPROOT
>The Greene butler.

GERTRUDE MANNHEIM
>The cook.

HEMMING
>The senior maid.

BARTON
>The junior maid.

MISS CRAVEN
>Mrs. Greene's nurse.

CHIEF INSPECTOR O'BRIEN
>Of the Police Department of New York City.

WILLIAM M. MORAN

    Commanding officer of the Detective Bureau.

ERNEST HEATH

    Sergeant of the Homicide Bureau.

SNITKIN

    Detective of the Homicide Bureau.

BURKE

    Detective of the Homicide Bureau.

CAPTAIN ANTHONY P. JERYM

    Bertillon expert.

CAPTAIN DUBOIS

    Finger-print expert.

DR. EMANUEL DOREMUS

    Medical Examiner.

DR. DRUMM

    An official Police Surgeon.

MARIE O'BRIEN

    A Police nurse.

SWACKER

    Secretary to the District Attorney.

CURRIE

    Vance's valet.

CHAPTER I

A DOUBLE TRAGEDY

(Tuesday, November 9; 10 a. m.)

IT HAS long been a source of wonder to me why the leading criminological writers—men like Edmund Lester Pearson, H. B. Irving, Filson Young, Canon Brookes, William Bolitho, and Harold Eaton—have not devoted more space to the Greene tragedy; for here, surely, is one of the outstanding murder mysteries of modern times—a case practically unique in the annals of latter-day crime. And yet I realize, as I read over my own voluminous notes on the case, and inspect the various documents relating to it, how little of its inner history ever came to light, and how impossible it would be for even the most imaginative chronicler to fill in the hiatuses.

The world, of course, knows the external facts. For over a month the press of two continents was filled with accounts of this appalling tragedy; and even the bare outline was sufficient to gratify the public's craving for the abnormal and the spectacular. But the inside story of the catastrophe surpassed even the wildest flights of public fancy; and, as I now sit down to divulge those facts for the first time, I am oppressed with a feeling akin to unreality, although I was a witness to most of them and hold in my possession the incontestable records of their actuality.

Of the fiendish ingenuity which lay behind this terrible crime, of the warped psychological motives that inspired it, and of the strange hidden sources of its technic, the world is completely ignorant. Moreover, no explanation has ever been given of the analytic steps that led to its solution. Nor have the events attending the mechanism of that solution—events in themselves highly dramatic and unusual—ever been recounted. The public believes that the termination of the case was a result of the usual police methods of investigation; but this is because the public is unaware of many of the vital factors of the crime itself, and because both the Police Department and the District Attorney's office have, as if by tacit agreement, refused to make known the entire truth—whether for fear of being disbelieved or merely because there are certain things so terrible that no man wishes to talk of them, I do not know.

The record, therefore, which I am about to set down is the first complete and unedited history of the Greene holocaust.[*] I feel that now the truth should be known, for it is history, and one should not shrink from historical facts. Also, I believe that the credit for the solution of this case should go where it belongs.

The man who elucidated the mystery and brought to a close that palimpsest of horror was, curiously enough, in no way officially connected with the police; and in all the published accounts of the murder his name was not once mentioned. And yet, had it not been for him and his novel methods of criminal deduction, the heinous plot against the Greene family would have been conclusively successful. The police in their researches

---

[*] It is, I hope, unnecessary for me to state that I have received official permission for my task.

were dealing dogmatically with the evidential appearances of the crime, whereas the operations of the criminal were being conducted on a plane quite beyond the comprehension of the ordinary investigator.

This man who, after weeks of sedulous and disheartening analysis, eventually ferreted out the source of the horror, was a young social aristocrat, an intimate friend of John F.-X. Markham, the District Attorney. His name I am not at liberty to divulge, but for the purposes of these chronicles I have chosen to call him Philo Vance. He is no longer in this country, having transferred his residence several years ago to a villa outside of Florence; and, since he has no intention of returning to America, he has acceded to my request to publish the history of the criminal cases in which he participated as a sort of *amicus curiæ*. Markham also has retired to private life; and Sergeant Ernest Heath, that doughty and honest officer of the Homicide Bureau who officially handled the Greene case for the Police Department, has, through an unexpected legacy, been able to gratify his life's ambition to breed fancy wyandottes on a model farm in the Mohawk Valley. Thus circumstances have made it possible for me to publish my intimate records of the Greene tragedy.

A few words are necessary to explain my own participation in the case. (I say "participation," though, in reality, my rôle was that of passive spectator.) For several years I had been Vance's personal attorney. I had resigned from my father's law firm—Van Dine, Davis & Van Dine—in order to devote myself exclusively to Vance's legal and financial needs, which, by the way, were not many. Vance and I had been friends from our undergraduate days at Harvard, and I found in my new duties as his legal agent and monetary steward a sinecure combined with many social and cultural compensations.

Vance at that time was thirty-four years old. He was just under six feet, slender, sinewy, and graceful. His chiselled regular features gave his face the attraction of strength and uniform modelling, but a sardonic coldness of expression precluded the designation of handsome. He had aloof gray eyes, a straight, slender nose, and a mouth suggesting both cruelty and asceticism. But, despite the severity of his lineaments—which acted like an impenetrable glass wall between him and his fellows—, he was highly sensitive and mobile; and, though his manner was somewhat detached and supercilious, he exerted an undeniable fascination over those who knew him at all well.

Much of his education had been acquired in Europe, and he still retained a slight Oxonian accent and intonation, though I happen to be aware that this was no affectation: he cared too little for the opinions of others to trouble about maintaining any pose. He was an indefatigable student. His mind was ever eager for knowledge, and he devoted much of his time to the study of ethnology and psychology. His greatest intellectual enthusiasm was art, and he fortunately had an income sufficient to indulge his passion for collecting. It was, however, his interest in psychology and his application of it to individual behaviorism that first turned his attention to the criminal problems which came under Markham's jurisdiction.

The first case in which he participated was, as I have recorded elsewhere, the murder of Alvin Benson.[*] The second was the seemingly insoluble strangling of the famous Broadway beauty, Margaret Odell.[†] And in the late fall of the same year came the Greene tragedy. As in the two former cases, I kept a complete record of this new investigation. I possessed myself of every available document, making verbatim copies of those claimed for the

[*] "The Benson Murder Case" (Scribners, 1926).
[†] "The 'Canary' Murder Case" (Scribners, 1927).

police archives, and even jotted down the numerous conversations that took place in and out of conference between Vance and the official investigators. And, in addition, I kept a diary which, for elaborateness and completeness, would have been the despair of Samuel Pepys.

The Greene murder case occurred toward the end of Markham's first year in office. As you may remember, the winter came very early that season. There were two severe blizzards in November, and the amount of snowfall for that month broke all local records for eighteen years. I mention this fact of the early snows because it played a sinister part in the Greene affair: it was, indeed, one of the vital factors of the murderer's scheme. No one has yet understood, or even sensed, the connection between the unseasonable weather of that late fall and the fatal tragedy that fell upon the Greene household; but that is because all of the dark secrets of the case were not made known.

Vance was projected into the Benson murder as the result of a direct challenge from Markham; and his activities in the Canary case were due to his own expressed desire to lend a hand. But pure coincidence was responsible for his participation in the Greene investigation. During the two months that had elapsed since his solution of the Canary's death Markham had called upon him several times regarding moot points of criminal detection in connection with the routine work of the District Attorney's office; and it was during an informal discussion of one of these problems that the Greene case was first mentioned.

Markham and Vance had long been friends. Though dissimilar in tastes and even in ethical outlook, they nevertheless respected each other profoundly. I have often marvelled at the friendship of these two antipodal men; but as the years went by I came more and more to understand it. It was as if they were drawn together by those very qualities which each realized—perhaps with a certain repressed regret—were lacking in his own nature. Markham was forthright, brusque, and, on occasion, domineering, taking life with grim and serious concern, and following the dictates of his legal conscience in the face of every obstacle: honest, incorruptible, and untiring. Vance, on the other hand, was volatile, debonair, and possessed of a perpetual Juvenalian cynicism, smiling ironically at the bitterest realities, and consistently fulfilling the rôle of a whimsically disinterested spectator of life. But, withal, he understood people as profoundly as he understood art, and his dissection of motives and his shrewd readings of character were—as I had many occasions to witness—uncannily accurate. Markham apprehended these qualities in Vance, and sensed their true value.

It was not yet ten o'clock of the morning of November the 9th when Vance and I, after motoring to the old Criminal Courts Building on the corner of Franklin and Centre Streets, went directly to the District Attorney's office on the fourth floor. On that momentous forenoon two gangsters, each accusing the other of firing the fatal shot in a recent pay-roll hold-up, were to be cross-examined by Markham; and this interview was to decide the question as to which of the men would be charged with murder and which held as a State's witness. Markham and Vance had discussed the situation the night before in the lounge-room of the Stuyvesant Club, and Vance had expressed a desire to be present at the examination. Markham had readily assented, and so we had risen early and driven down-town.

The interview with the two men lasted for an hour, and Vance's disconcerting opinion was that neither was guilty of the actual shooting.

"Y' know, Markham," he drawled, when the sheriff had returned the prisoners to the Tombs, "those two Jack Sheppards are quite sincere: each one thinks he's telling the truth. *Ergo*, neither of 'em fired the shot. A distressin' predicament. They're obvious gallows-birds—born for the gibbet; and it's a beastly shame not to be able to round out their destinies in proper fashion. . . . I say, wasn't there another participant in the hold-up?"

Markham nodded. "A third got away. According to these two, it was a well-known gangster named Eddie Maleppo."

"Then Eduardo is your man."*

Markham did not reply, and Vance rose lazily and reached for his ulster.

"By the by," he said, slipping into his coat, "I note that our upliftin' press bedecked its front pages this morning with headlines about a pogrom at the old Greene mansion last night. Wherefore?"

Markham glanced quickly at the clock on the wall, and frowned.

"That reminds me. Chester Greene called up the first thing this morning and insisted on seeing me. I told him eleven o'clock."

"Where do *you* fit in?" Vance had taken his hand from the door-knob, and drew out his cigarette-case.

"I don't!" snapped Markham. "But people think the District Attorney's office is a kind of clearinghouse for all their troubles. It happens, however, that I've known Chester Greene a long time—we're both members of the Marylebone Golf Club—and so I must listen to his plaint about what was obviously an attempt to annex the famous Greene plate."

---

* This was subsequently proved correct. Nearly a year later Maleppo was arrested in Detroit, extradited to New York, and convicted of the murder. His two companions had already been successfully prosecuted for robbery. They are now serving long terms in Sing Sing.

"Burglary—eh, what?" Vance took a few puffs on his cigarette. "With two women shot?"

"Oh, it was a miserable business! An amateur, no doubt. Got in a panic, shot up the place, and bolted."

"Seems a dashed curious proceeding." Vance abstractedly re-seated himself in a large armchair near the door. "Did the antique cutlery actually disappear?"

"Nothing was taken. The thief was evidently frightened off before he made his haul."

"Sounds a bit thick, don't y' know.—An amateur thief breaks into a prominent home, casts a predat'ry eye on the dining-room silver, takes alarm, goes up-stairs and shoots two women in their respective boudoirs, and then flees. . . . Very touchin' and all that, but unconvincin'. Whence came this caressin' theory?"

Markham was glowering, but when he spoke it was with an effort at restraint.

"Feathergill was on duty last night when the call was relayed from Headquarters, and accompanied the police to the house. He agrees with their conclusions."*

"Nevertheless, I could bear to know why Chester Greene is desirous of having polite converse with you."

Markham compressed his lips. He was not in cordial mood that morning, and Vance's flippant curiosity irked him. After a moment, however, he said grudgingly:

"Since the attempted robbery interests you so keenly, you may, if you insist, wait and hear what Greene has to say."

"I'll stay," smiled Vance, removing his coat. "I'm weak; just can't resist a passionate entreaty. . . . Which one of the Greenes is Chester? And how is he related to the two deceased?"

"There was only one murder," Markham corrected him in a

---

* Amos Feathergill was then an Assistant District Attorney. He later ran on the Tammany ticket for assemblyman, and was elected.

tone of forbearance. "The oldest daughter—an unmarried woman in her early forties—was killed instantly. A younger daughter, who was also shot, has, I believe, a chance of recovery."

"And Chester?"

"Chester is the elder son, a man of forty or thereabouts. He was the first person on the scene after the shots had been fired."

"What other members of the family are there? I know old Tobias Greene has gone to his Maker."

"Yes, old Tobias died about twelve years ago. But his wife is still living, though she's a helpless paralytic. Then there are—or rather were—five children: the oldest, Julia; next, Chester; then another daughter, Sibella, a few years under thirty, I should say; then Rex, a sickly, bookish boy a year or so younger than Sibella; and Ada, the youngest—an adopted daughter twenty-two or three, perhaps."

"And it was Julia who was killed, eh? Which of the other two girls was shot?"

"The younger—Ada. Her room, it seems, is across the hall from Julia's, and the thief apparently got in it by mistake while making his escape. As I understand it, he entered Ada's room immediately after firing on Julia, saw his error, fired again, and then fled, eventually going down the stairs and out the main entrance."

Vance smoked a while in silence.

"Your hypothetical intruder must have been deuced confused to have mistaken Ada's bedroom door for the staircase, what? And then there's the query: what was this anonymous gentleman, who had called to collect the plate, doing above-stairs?"

"Probably looking for jewellery." Markham was rapidly losing patience. "*I* am not omniscient." There was irony in his inflection.

"Now, now, Markham!" pleaded Vance cajolingly. "Don't be

vindictive. Your Greene burglary promises several nice points in academic speculation. Permit me to indulge my idle whims."

At that moment Swacker, Markham's youthful and alert secretary, appeared at the swinging door which communicated with a narrow chamber between the main waiting-room and the District Attorney's private office.

"Mr. Chester Greene is here," he announced.

CHAPTER II

THE INVESTIGATION OPENS

(Tuesday, November 9; 11 a. m.)

WHEN CHESTER Greene entered it was obvious he was under a nervous strain; but his nervousness evoked no sympathy in me. From the very first I disliked the man. He was of medium height and was bordering on corpulence. There was something soft and flabby in his contours; and, though he was dressed with studied care, there were certain signs of overemphasis about his clothes. His cuffs were too tight; his collar was too snug; and the colored silk handkerchief hung too far out of his breast pocket. He was slightly bald, and the lids of his close-set eyes projected like those of a man with Bright's disease. His mouth, surmounted by a close-cropped blond moustache, was loose; and his chin receded slightly and was deeply creased below the under lip. He typified the pampered idler.

When he had shaken hands with Markham, and Vance and I had been introduced, he seated himself and meticulously inserted a brown Russian cigarette in a long amber-and-gold holder.

"I'd be tremendously obliged, Markham," he said, lighting

his cigarette from an ivory pocket-lighter, "if you'd make a personal investigation of the row that occurred at our diggin's last night. The police will never get anywhere the way they're going about it. Good fellows, you understand—the police. But . . . well, there's something about this affair—don't know just how to put it. Anyway, I don't like it."

Markham studied him closely for several moments.

"Just what's on your mind, Greene?" The other crushed out his cigarette, though he had taken no more than half a dozen puffs, and drummed indecisively on the arm of his chair.

"Wish I knew. It's a rum affair—damned rum. There's something back of it, too—something that's going to raise the very devil if we don't stop it. Can't explain it. It's a feeling I've got."

"Perhaps Mr. Greene is psychic," commented Vance, with a look of bland innocence.

The man swung about and scrutinized Vance with aggressive condescension. "Tosh!" He brought out another Russian cigarette, and turned again to Markham: "I do wish you'd take a peep at the situation."

Markham hesitated. "Surely you've some reason for disagreeing with the police and appealing to me."

"Funny thing, but I haven't." (It seemed to me Greene's hand shook slightly as he lit his second cigarette.) "I simply know that my mind rejects the burglar story automatically."

It was difficult to tell if he were being frank or deliberately hiding something. I did feel, however, that some sort of fear lurked beneath his uneasiness; and I also got the impression that he was far from being heart-broken over the tragedy.

"It seems to me," declared Markham, "that the theory of the burglar is entirely consistent with the facts. There have been many other cases of a housebreaker suddenly taking alarm, losing his head, and needlessly shooting people."

Greene rose abruptly and began pacing up and down.

"I can't argue the case," he muttered. "It's beyond all that, if you understand me." He looked quickly at the District Attorney with staring eyes. "Gad! It's got me in a cold sweat."

"It's all too vague and intangible," Markham observed kindly. "I'm inclined to think the tragedy has upset you. Perhaps after a day or two——"

Greene lifted a protesting hand.

"It's no go. I'm telling you, Markham, the police will never find their burglar. I feel it—here." He mincingly laid a manicured hand on his breast.

Vance had been watching him with a faint suggestion of amusement. Now he stretched his legs before him and gazed up at the ceiling.

"I say, Mr. Greene—pardon the intrusion on your esoteric gropings—but do you know of any one with a reason for wanting your two sisters out of the way?"

The man looked blank for a moment.

"No," he answered finally; "can't say that I do. Who, in Heaven's name, would want to kill two harmless women?"

"I haven't the groggiest notion. But, since you repudiate the burglar theory, and since the two ladies were undoubtedly shot, it's inferable that some one sought their demise; and it occurred to me that you, being their brother and domiciled *en famille*, might know of some one who harbored homicidal sentiments toward them."

Greene bristled, and thrust his head forward. "I know of no one," he blurted. Then, turning to Markham, he continued wheedlingly: "If I had the slightest suspicion, don't you think I'd come out with it? This thing has got on my nerves. I've been mulling over it all night, and it's—it's bothersome, frightfully bothersome."

Markham nodded non-committally, and rising, walked to the window, where he stood, his hands behind him, gazing down on the gray stone masonry of the Tombs.

Vance, despite his apparent apathy, had been studying Greene closely; and, as Markham turned to the window, he straightened up slightly in his chair.

"Tell me," he began, an ingratiating note in his voice; "just what happened last night? I understand you were the first to reach the prostrate women."

"I was the first to reach my sister Julia," retorted Greene, with a hint of resentment. "It was Sproot, the butler, who found Ada unconscious, bleeding from a nasty wound in her back."

"Her back, eh?" Vance leaned forward, and lifted his eyebrows. "She was shot from behind, then?"

"Yes." Greene frowned and inspected his fingernails, as if he too sensed something disturbing in the fact.

"And Miss Julia Greene: was she too shot from behind?"

"No—from the front."

"Extr'ordin'ry!" Vance blew a ring of smoke toward the dusty chandelier. "And had both women retired for the night?"

"An hour before. . . . But what has all that got to do with it?"

"One never knows, does one? However, it's always well to be in possession of these little details when trying to run down the elusive source of a psychic seizure."

"Psychic seizure be damned!" growled Greene truculently. "Can't a man have a feeling about something without——?"

"Quite—quite. But you've asked for the District Attorney's

assistance, and I'm sure he would like a few data before making a decision."

Markham came forward and sat down on the edge of the table. His curiosity had been aroused, and he indicated to Greene his sympathy with Vance's interrogation.

Greene pursed his lips, and returned his cigarette-holder to his pocket.

"Oh, very well. What else do you want to know?"

"You might relate for us," dulcetly resumed Vance, "the exact order of events after you heard the first shot. I presume you did hear the shot."

"Certainly I heard it—couldn't have helped hearing it. Julia's room is next to mine, and I was still awake. I jumped into my slippers and pulled on my dressing-gown; then I went out into the hall. It was dark, and I felt my way along the wall until I reached Julia's door. I opened it and looked in—didn't know who might be there waiting to pop me—and I saw her lying in bed, the front of her nightgown covered with blood. There was no one else in the room, and I went to her immediately. Just then I heard another shot which sounded as if it came from Ada's room. I was a bit muzzy by this time—didn't know what I'd better do; and as I stood by Julia's bed in something of a funk—oh, I was in a funk all right . . ."

"Can't say that I blame you," Vance encouraged him.

Greene nodded. "A damned ticklish position to be in. Well, anyway, as I stood there, I heard some one coming down the stairs from the servants' quarters on the third floor, and recognized old Sproot's tread. He fumbled along in the dark, and I heard him enter Ada's door. Then he called to me, and I hurried over. Ada was lying in front of the dressing-table; and Sproot and I lifted her on the bed. I'd gone a bit weak in the knees; was expecting any minute to hear another shot—don't know why. Anyway, it didn't come; and then I heard Sproot's voice at the hall telephone calling up Doctor Von Blon."

"I see nothing in your account, Greene, inconsistent with the theory of a burglar," observed Markham. "And furthermore, Feathergill, my assistant, says there were two sets of confused footprints in the snow outside the front door."

Greene shrugged his shoulders, but did not answer.

"By the by, Mr. Greene,"—Vance had slipped down in his chair and was staring into space—"you said that when you looked into Miss Julia's room you saw her in bed. How was that? Did you turn on the light?"

"Why, no!" The man appeared puzzled by the question. "The light was on."

There was a flutter of interest in Vance's eyes.

"And how about Miss Ada's room? Was the light on there also?"

"Yes."

Vance reached into his pocket, and, drawing out his cigarette-case, carefully and deliberately selected a cigarette. I recognized in the action an evidence of repressed inner excitement.

"So the lights were on in both rooms. Most interestin'."

Markham, too, recognized the eagerness beneath his apparent indifference, and regarded him expectantly.

"And," pursued Vance, after lighting his cigarette leisurely, "how long a time would you say elapsed between the two shots?"

Greene was obviously annoyed by this cross-examination, but he answered readily.

"Two or three minutes—certainly no longer."

"Still," ruminated Vance, "after you heard the first shot you rose from your bed, donned slippers and robe, went into the hall, felt along the wall to the next room, opened the door cautiously, peered inside, and then crossed the room to the bed—all this, I gather, before the second shot was fired. Is that correct?"

"Certainly it's correct."

"Well, well! As you say, two or three minutes. Yes, at least that. Astonishin'!" Vance turned to Markham. "Really, y' know, old man, I don't wish to influence your judgment, but I rather think you ought to accede to Mr. Greene's request to take a hand in this investigation. I too have a psychic feeling about the case. Something tells me that your eccentric burglar will prove an *ignis fatuus.*"

Markham eyed him with meditative curiosity. Not only had Vance's questioning of Greene interested him keenly, but he knew, as a result of long experience, that Vance would not have made the suggestion had he not had a good reason for doing so. I was in no wise surprised, therefore, when he turned to his restive visitor and said:

"Very well, Greene, I'll see what I can do in the matter. I'll probably be at your house early this afternoon. Please see that every one is present, as I'll want to question them."

Greene held out a trembling hand. "The domestic roster—family and servants—will be complete when you arrive."

He strode pompously from the room.

Vance sighed. "Not a nice creature, Markham—not at all a nice creature. I shall never be a politician if it involves an acquaintance with such gentlemen."

Markham seated himself at his desk with a disgruntled air.

"Greene is highly regarded as a social—not a political—decoration," he said maliciously. "He belongs to your totem, not mine."

"Fancy that!" Vance stretched himself luxuriously. "Still, it's you who fascinate him. Intuition tells me he is not overfond of me."

"You did treat him a bit cavalierly. Sarcasm is not exactly a means of endearment."

"But, Markham old thing, I wasn't pining for Chester's affection."

"You think he knows, or suspects, something?"

Vance gazed through the long window into the bleak sky beyond.

"I wonder," he murmured. Then: "Is Chester, by any chance, a typical representative of the Greene family? Of recent years I've done so little mingling with the élite that I'm woefully ignorant of the East Side nabobs."

Markham nodded reflectively.

"I'm afraid he is. The original Greene stock was sturdy, but the present generation seems to have gone somewhat to pot. Old Tobias the Third—Chester's father—was a rugged and, in many ways, admirable character. He appears, however, to have been the last heir of the ancient Greene qualities. What's left of the family has suffered some sort of disintegration. They're not exactly soft, but tainted with patches of incipient decay, like fruit that's lain on the ground too long. Too much money and leisure, I imagine, and too little restraint. On the other hand, there's a certain intellectuality lurking in the new Greenes. They all seem to have good minds, even if futile and misdirected. In fact, I think you underestimate Chester. For all his banalities and effeminate mannerisms, he's far from being as stupid as you regard him."

"*I* regard Chester as stupid! My dear Markham! You wrong me abominably. No, no. There's nothing of the anointed ass about our Chester. He's shrewder even than you think him. Those œdematous eyelids veil a pair of particularly crafty eyes.

Indeed, it was largely his studied pose of fatuousness that led me to suggest that you aid and abet in the investigation."

Markham leaned back and narrowed his eyes.

"What's in your mind, Vance?"

"I told you. A psychic seizure—same like Chester's subliminal visitation."

Markham knew, by this elusive answer, that for the moment Vance had no intention of being more definite; and after a moment of scowling silence he turned to the telephone.

"If I'm to take on this case, I'd better find out who has charge of it and get what preliminary information I can."

He called up Inspector Moran, the commanding officer of the Detective Bureau. After a brief conversation he turned to Vance with a smile.

"Your friend, Sergeant Heath, has the case in hand. He happened to be in the office just now, and is coming here immediately."*

In less than fifteen minutes Heath arrived. Despite the fact that he had been up most of the night, he appeared unusually alert and energetic. His broad, pugnacious features were as imperturbable as ever, and his pale-blue eyes held their habitual penetrating intentness. He greeted Markham with an elaborate, though perfunctory, handshake; and then, seeing Vance, relaxed his features into a good-natured smile.

"Well, if it isn't Mr. Vance! What have you been up to, sir?"

Vance rose and shook hands with him.

---

* It was Sergeant Ernest Heath, of the Homicide Bureau, who had been in charge of both the Benson and the Canary cases; and, although he had been openly antagonistic to Vance during the first of these investigations, a curious good-fellowship had later grown up between them. Vance admired the Sergeant's dogged and straightforward qualities; and Heath had developed a keen respect—with certain reservations, however—for Vance's abilities.

"Alas, Sergeant, I've been immersed in the terracotta orna-mentation of Renaissance facades, and other such trivialities, since I saw you last.* But I'm happy to note that crime is picking up again. It's a deuced drab world without a nice murky murder now and then, don't y' know."

Heath cocked an eye, and turned inquiringly to the District Attorney. He had long since learned how to read between the lines of Vance's badinage.

"It's this Greene case, Sergeant," said Markham.

"I thought so." Heath sat down heavily, and inserted a black cigar between his lips. "But nothing's broken yet. We're round-ing up all the regulars, and looking into their alibis for last night. But it'll take several days before the check-up's complete. If the bird who did the job hadn't got scared before he grabbed the swag, we might be able to trace him through the pawnshops and fences. But something rattled him, or he wouldn't have shot up the works the way he did. And that's what makes me think he may be a new one at the racket. If he is, it'll make our job hard-er." He held a match in cupped hands to his cigar, and puffed furiously. "What did you want to know about the prowl, sir?"

Markham hesitated. The Sergeant's matter-of-fact assump-tion that a common burglar was the culprit disconcerted him.

"Chester Greene was here," he explained presently; "and he seems convinced that the shooting was not the work of a thief. He asked me, as a special favor, to look into the matter."

Heath gave a derisive grunt.

"Who but a burglar in a panic would shoot down two women?"

"Quite so, Sergeant." It was Vance who answered. "Still, the lights were turned on in both rooms, though the women had

---

* Vance, after reading proof of this sentence, requested me to make mention here of that beautiful volume, "Terra Cotta of the Italian Renaissance," recently published by the National Terra Cotta Society, New York.

gone to bed an hour before; and there was an interval of several minutes between the two shots."

"I know all that." Heath spoke impatiently. "But if an ama-choor did the job, we can't tell exactly what did happen up-stairs there last night. When a bird loses his head——"

"Ah! There's the rub. When a thief loses his head, d' ye see, he isn't apt to go from room to room turning on the lights, even assuming he knows where and how to turn them on. And he certainly isn't going to dally around for several minutes in a black hall between such fantastic operations, especially after he has shot some one and alarmed the house, what? It doesn't look like panic to me; it looks strangely like design. Moreover, why should this precious amateur of yours be cavorting about the boudoirs up-stairs when the loot was in the dining-room below?"

"We'll learn all about that when we've got our man," countered Heath doggedly.

"The point is, Sergeant," put in Markham, "I've given Mr. Greene my promise to look into the matter, and I wanted to get what details I could from you. You understand, of course," he added mollifyingly, "that I shall not interfere with your activities in any way. Whatever the outcome of the case, your department will receive entire credit."

"Oh, that's all right, sir." Experience had taught Heath that he had nothing to fear in the way of lost *kudos* when working with Markham. "But I don't think, in spite of Mr. Vance's ideas, that you'll find much in the Greene case to warrant attention."

"Perhaps not," Markham admitted. "However, I've committed myself, and I think I'll run out this afternoon and look over the situation, if you'll give me the lie of the land."

"There isn't much to tell." Heath chewed on his cigar cogi-tatingly. "A Doctor Von Blon—the Greene family physician—

phoned Headquarters about midnight. I'd just got in from an up-town stick-up call, and I hopped out to the house with a couple of the boys from the Bureau. I found the two women, like you know, one dead and the other unconscious—both shot. I phoned Doc Doremus,* and then looked the place over. Mr. Feathergill came along and lent a hand; but we didn't find much of anything. The fellow that did the job musta got in by the front door some way, for there was a set of footprints in the snow coming and going, besides Doctor Von Blon's. But the snow was too flaky to get any good impressions. It stopped snowing along about eleven o'clock last night; and there's no doubt that the prints belonged to the burglar, for no one else, except the doctor, had come or gone after the storm."

"An amateur housebreaker with a front-door key to the Greene mansion," murmured Vance. "Extr'ordin'ry!"

"I'm not saying he had a key, sir," protested Heath. "I'm simply telling you what we found. The door mighta been unlatched by mistake; or some one mighta opened it for him."

"Go on with the story, Sergeant," urged Markham, giving Vance a reproving look.

"Well, after Doc Doremus got there and made an examination of the older woman's body and inspected the younger one's wound, I questioned all the family and the servants—a butler, two maids, and a cook. Chester Greene and the butler were the only ones who had heard the first shot, which was fired about half past eleven. But the second shot roused old Mrs. Greene— her room adjoins the younger daughter's. The rest of the household had slept through all the excitement; but this Chester fellow had woke 'em all up by the time I got there. I talked to all of 'em, but nobody knew anything. After a coupla hours I left a

---

* Doctor Emanuel Doremus, the Chief Medical Examiner.

man inside and another outside, and came away. Then I set the usual machinery going; and this morning Captain Dubois went over the place the best he could for finger-prints. Doc Doremus has got the body for an autopsy, and we'll get a report to-night. But there'll be nothing helpful from that quarter. She was fired on from in front at close range—almost a contact shot. And the other woman—the young one—was all powder-marked, and her nightgown was burnt. She was shot from behind.—That's about all the dope."

"Have you been able to get any sort of a statement from the younger one?"

"Not yet. She was unconscious last night, and this morning she was too weak to talk. But the doctor—Von Blon—said we could probably question her this afternoon. We may get something out of her, in case she got a look at the bird before he shot her."

"That suggests something to me, Sergeant." Vance had been listening passively to the recital, but now he drew in his legs, and lifted himself a little. "Did any member of the Greene household possess a gun?"

Heath gave him a sharp look.

"This Chester Greene said he had an old .32 revolver he used to keep in a desk drawer in his bedroom."

"Oh, did he, now? And did you see the gun?"

"I asked him for it, but he couldn't find it. Said he hadn't seen it for years, but that probably it was around somewheres. Promised to dig it up for me to-day."

"Don't hang any fond hopes on his finding it, Sergeant." Vance looked at Markham musingly. "I begin to comprehend the basis of Chester's psychic perturbation. I fear he's a crass materialist after all. . . . Sad, sad."

"You think he missed the gun, and took fright?"

"Well—something like that . . . perhaps. One can't tell. It's deuced confusin'." He turned an indolent eye on the Sergeant. "By the by, what sort of gun did your burglar use?"

Heath gave a gruff, uneasy laugh.

"You score there, Mr. Vance. I've got both bullets—thirty-twos, fired from a revolver, not an automatic. But you're not trying to intimate——"

"Tut, tut, Sergeant. Like Goethe, I'm merely seeking for more illumination, if one may translate *Licht*——"

Markham interrupted this garrulous evasion.

"I'm going to the Greene house after lunch, Sergeant. Can you come along?"

"Sure I can, sir. I was going out anyway."

"Good." Markham brought forth a box of cigars. "Meet me here at two. . . . And take a couple of these *Perfectos* before you go."

Heath selected the cigars, and put them carefully into his breast pocket. At the door he turned with a bantering grin.

"You coming along with us, Mr. Vance—to guide our erring footsteps, as they say?"

"Nothing could keep me away," declared Vance.

CHAPTER III

AT THE GREENE MANSION

(Tuesday, November 9; 2.30 p. m.)

THE GREENE mansion—as it was commonly referred to by
New Yorkers—was a relic of the city's *ancien régime*. It had stood
for three generations at the eastern extremity of 53d Street, two
of its oriel windows actually overhanging the murky waters of
the East River. The lot upon which the house was built extended
through the entire block—a distance of two hundred feet—and
had an equal frontage on the cross-streets. The character of the
neighborhood had changed radically since the early days; but the
spirit of commercial advancement had left the domicile of the
Greenes untouched. It was an oasis of idealism and calm in the
midst of moiling commercial enterprise; and one of the stipulations in old Tobias Greene's last will and testament had been
that the mansion should stand intact for at least a quarter of a
century after his death, as a monument to him and his ancestors.
One of his last acts on earth was to erect a high stone wall about
the entire property, with a great double iron gateway opening
on 53d Street and a postern-gate for tradesmen giving on 52d
Street.

The mansion itself was two and a half stories high, surmounted by gabled spires and chimney clusters. It was what architects call, with a certain intonation of contempt, a "château flamboyant"; but no derogatory appellation could detract from the quiet dignity and the air of feudal traditionalism that emanated from its great rectangular blocks of gray limestone. The house was sixteenth-century Gothic in style, with more than a suspicion of the new Italian ornament in its parts; and the pinnacles and shelves suggested the Byzantine. But, for all its diversity of detail, it was not flowery, and would have held no deep attraction for the Freemason architects of the Middle Ages. It was not "bookish" in effect; it exuded the very essence of the old.

In the front yard were maples and clipped evergreens, interspersed with hydrangea and lilac-bushes; and at the rear was a row of weeping willows overhanging the river. Along the herring-bone-bond brick walks were high quickset hedges of hawthorn; and the inner sides of the encircling wall were covered with compact espaliers. To the west of the house an asphalt driveway led to a double garage at the rear—an addition built by the newer generation of Greenes. But here too were boxwood hedgerows which cloaked the driveway's modernity.

As we entered the grounds that gray November afternoon an atmosphere of foreboding bleakness seemed to have settled over the estate. The trees and shrubs were all bare, except the evergreens, which were laden with patches of snow. The trellises stood stripped along the walls, like clinging black skeletons; and, save for the front walk, which had been hastily and imperfectly swept, the grounds were piled high with irregular snowdrifts. The gray of the mansion's masonry was almost the color of the brooding overcast sky; and I felt a premonitory chill of eeriness pass over me as we mounted the shallow steps that led to the high front door, with its pointed pediment above the deeply arched entrance.

Sproot, the butler—a little old man with white hair and a heavily seamed capriform face—admitted us with silent, funereal dignity (he had evidently been apprised of our coming); and we were ushered at once into the great gloomy drawing-room whose heavily curtained windows overlooked the river. A few moments later Chester Greene came in and greeted Markham fulsomely. Heath and Vance and me he included in a single supercilious nod.

"Awfully good of you to come, Markham," he said, with nervous eagerness, seating himself on the edge of a chair and taking out his cigarette-holder. "I suppose you'll want to hold an inquisition first. Whom'll I summon as a starter?"

"We can let that go for the moment," said Markham. "First, I'd like to know something concerning the servants. Tell me what you can about them."

Greene moved restlessly in his chair, and seemed to have difficulty lighting his cigarette.

"There's only four. Big house and all that, but we don't need much help. Julia always acted as housekeeper, and Ada looked after the Mater.—To begin with, there's old Sproot. He's been butler, seneschal, and majordomo for us for thirty years. Regular family retainer—kind you read about in English novels—devoted, loyal, humble, dictatorial, and snooping. And a damned nuisance, I may add. Then there are two maids—one to look after the rooms and the other for general service, though the women monopolize her, mostly for useless fiddle-faddle. Hemming, the older maid, has been with us ten years. Still wears corsets and fit-easy shoes. Deep-water Baptist, I believe—excruciatingly devout. Barton, the other maid, is young and flighty: thinks she's irresistible, knows a little *table-d'hôte* French, and is the kind that's constantly expecting the males of the family to kiss her behind the door. Sibella picked her out—she's just the kind Sibella would pick out. Been adorning our house and shirking the hard work for about two years. The cook's a stodgy German woman, a typical *Hausfrau*—voluminous bosoms and number-ten feet. Puts in all her spare time writing to distant nieces and nephews in the upper reaches of the Rhine basin somewhere; and boasts that the most fastidious person could eat off her kitchen floor, it's that clean; though I've never tried it. The old man engaged her a year before he died; gave orders she was to remain as long as she liked.—There you have the personnel of the backstairs. Of course, there is a gardener who loafs about the lawn in summer. He hibernates in a speak-easy up Harlem way."

"No chauffeur?"

"A nuisance we dispense with. Julia hated motor-cars, and Rex is afraid to travel in them—squeamish lad, Rex. I drive my own racer, and Sibella's a regular Barney Oldfield. Ada drives, too, when the Mater isn't using her and Sibella's car is idle.—So endeth."

Markham had been making notes as Greene rambled along with his information. At length he put out the cigar he had been smoking.

"Now, if you don't mind, I want to look over the house."

Greene rose with alacrity and led the way into the main lower hall—a vaulted, oak-panelled entrance containing two large carved Flemish tables of the Sambin school, against opposite walls, and several Anglo-Dutch crown-back chairs. A great Daghestan rug stretched along the parqueted floor, its faded colors repeated in the heavy draperies of the archways.

"We have, of course, just come from the drawing-room,"

explained Greene, with a pompous air. "Back of it, down the hall"—he pointed past the wide marble stairway—"was the governor's library and den—what he called his *sanctum sanctorum*. Nobody's been in it for twelve years. The Mater has kept it locked up ever since the old man died. Sentiment of some kind; though I've often told her she ought to clean the place out and make a billiard-room of it. But you can't move the Mater, once she's got an idea in her head. Try it some time when you're looking for heavy exercise."

He walked across the hall and pulled aside the draperies of the archway opposite to the drawing-room.

"Here's the reception-room, though we don't use it much nowadays. Stuffy, stiff place, and the flue doesn't draw worth a damn. Every time we've built a fire here, we've had to have the cleaners in to remove the soot from the tapestries." He waved his cigarette-holder toward two beautiful Gobelins. "Back there, through those sliding doors, is the dining-room; and farther on are the butler's pantry and the kitchen where one may eat off the floor. Care to inspect the culinary department?"

"No, I think not," said Markham. "And I'll take the kitchen floor for granted.—Now, can we look at the second floor?"

We ascended the main stairs, which led round a piece of marble statuary—a Falguière figure, I think—, and emerged into the upper hall facing the front of the house where three large close-set windows looked out over the bare trees.

The arrangement of the rooms on the second floor was simple and in keeping with the broad foursquare architecture of the house; but for the sake of clarification I am embodying in this record a rough diagram of it; for it was the disposition of these rooms that made possible the carrying out of the murderer's hideous and unnatural plot.

There were six bedrooms on the floor—three on either side of the hall, each occupied by a member of the family. At the front of the house, on our left, was the bedroom of Rex Greene, the younger brother. Next to it was the room occupied by Ada Greene; and at the rear were Mrs. Greene's quarters, separated from Ada's by a fair-sized dressing-room through which the two apartments communicated. It will be seen from the diagram that Mrs. Greene's room projected beyond the main western elevation of the house, and that in the L thus formed was a small balustraded stone porch with a narrow flight of stairs, set against the house, leading to the lawn below. French doors opened upon this porch from both Ada's and Mrs. Greene's rooms.

On the opposite side of the hall were the three rooms occupied by Julia, Chester, and Sibella, Julia's room being at the front of the house, Sibella's at the rear, and Chester's in the centre. None of these rooms communicated with the other. It might also be noted that the doors to Sibella's and Mrs. Greene's rooms were just behind the main staircase, whereas Chester's and Ada's were directly at the head of the stairs, and Julia's and Rex's farther toward the front of the house. There was a small linen closet between Ada's room and Mrs. Greene's; and at the rear of the hall were the servants' stairs.

Chester Greene explained this arrangement to us briefly, and then walked up the hall to Julia's room.

"You'll want to look in here first, I imagine," he said, throwing open the door. "Nothing's been touched—police orders. But I can't see what good all that stained bed-linen is to any one. It's a frightful mess."

The room was large and richly furnished with sage-green satin-upholstered furniture of the Marie Antoinette period. Opposite to the door was a canopied bedstead on a dais; and several dark blotches on the embroidered linen gave mute evidence of the tragedy that had been enacted there the night before.

Vance, after noting the disposition of the furniture, turned his gaze upon the old-fashioned crystal chandelier.

"Were those the lights that were on when you found your sister last night, Mr. Greene?" he asked casually.

The other nodded with surly annoyance.

"And where, may I ask, is the switch?"

"Behind the end of that cabinet." Greene indifferently indicated a highly elaborated *armoire* near the door.

"Invisible—eh, what?" Vance strolled to the *armoire* and looked behind it. "An amazin' burglar!" Then he went up to Markham and spoke to him in a low voice.

After a moment Markham nodded.

"Greene," he said, "I wish you'd go to your room and lie down on the bed just as you were last night when you heard the shot. Then, when I tap on the wall, get up and do everything you did last night—in just the way you did it. I want to time you."

The man stiffened, and gave Markham a look of resentful protestation.

"Oh, I say——!" he began. But almost at once he shrugged compliance and swaggered from the room, closing the door behind him.

Vance took out his watch, and Markham, giving Greene time to reach his room, rapped on the wall. For what seemed an interminable time we waited. Then the door opened slightly, and Greene peered round the casing. Slowly his eyes swept the room; he swung the door further ajar, stepped inside hesitantly, and moved to the bed.

"Three minutes and twenty seconds," announced Vance.

"Most disquietin'. . . . What do you imagine, Sergeant, the intruder was doing in the interim of the two shots?"

"How do I know?" retorted Heath. "Probably groping round the hall outside looking for the stairs."

"If he'd groped that length of time he'd have fallen down 'em."

Markham interrupted this discussion with a suggestion that we take a look at the servants' stairway down which the butler had come after hearing the first shot.

"We needn't inspect the other bedrooms just yet," he added, "though we'll want to see Miss Ada's room as soon as the doctor thinks it's advisable. When, by the way, will you know his decision, Greene?"

"He said he'd be here at three. And he's a punctual beggar—a regular fiend for efficiency. He sent a nurse over early this morning, and she's looking after Ada and the Mater now."

"I say, Mr. Greene," interposed Vance, "was your sister Julia in the habit of leaving her door unlocked at night?"

Greene's jaw dropped a little, and his eyes opened wider.

"By Jove—no! Now that you mention it . . . she always locked herself in."

Vance nodded absently, and we passed out into the hall. A thin, swinging baize door hid the servants' stairwell at the rear, and Markham pushed it open.

"Nothing much here to deaden the sound," he observed.

"No," agreed Greene. "And old Sproot's room is right at the head of the steps. He's got good ears, too—too damned good sometimes."

We were about to turn back, when a high-pitched querulous voice issued from the partly open door on our right.

"Is that you, Chester? What's all this disturbance? Haven't I had enough distraction and worry——?"

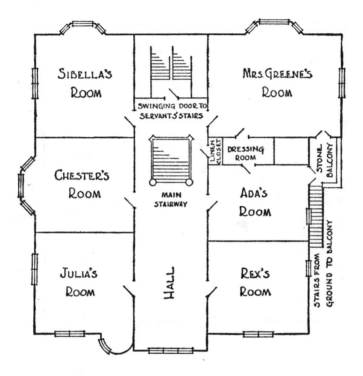

PLAN OF SECOND FLOOR.

(For the sake of simplification all bathrooms, clothes-closets, fireplaces, etc., have been omitted.)

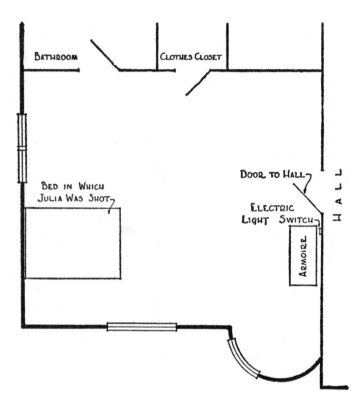

PLAN OF JULIA'S BEDROOM.

Greene had gone to his mother's door and put his head inside.

"It's all right, Mater," he said irritably. "It's only the police nosing around."

"The police?" Her voice was contemptuous. "What do they want? Didn't they upset me enough last night? Why don't they go and look for the villain instead of congregating outside my door and annoying me?—So, it's the police." Her tone became vindictive. "Bring them in here at once, and let *me* talk to them. The police, indeed!"

Greene looked helplessly at Markham, who merely nodded; and we entered the invalid's room. It was a spacious chamber, with windows on three sides, furnished elaborately with all manner of conflicting objects. My first glance took in an East Indian rug, a buhl cabinet, an enormous gilded Buddha, several massive Chinese chairs of carved teak-wood, a faded Persian tapestry, two wrought-iron standard lamps, and a red-and-gold lacquered high-boy. I looked quickly at Vance, and surprised an expression of puzzled interest in his eyes.

In an enormous bed, with neither head-piece nor foot-posts, reclined the mistress of the house, propped up in a semi-recumbent attitude on a sprawling pile of varicolored silken pillows. She must have been between sixty-five and seventy, but her hair was almost black. Her long, chevaline face, though yellowed and wrinkled like ancient parchment, still radiated an amazing vigor: it reminded me of the portraits I had seen of George Eliot. About her shoulders was drawn an embroidered Oriental shawl; and the picture she presented in the setting of that unusual and diversified room was exotic in the extreme. At her side sat a rosy-cheeked imperturbable nurse in a stiff white uniform, making a singular contrast to the woman on the bed.

Chester Greene presented Markham, and let his mother take

the rest of us for granted. At first she did not acknowledge the introduction, but, after appraising Markham for a moment, she gave him a nod of resentful forbearance and held out to him a long bony hand.

"I suppose there's no way to avoid having my home overrun in this fashion," she said wearily, assuming an air of great toleration. "I was just endeavoring to get a little rest. My back pains me so much to-day, after all the excitement last night. But what do I matter—an old paralyzed woman like me? No one considers me anyway, Mr. Markham. But they're perfectly right. We invalids are of no use in the world, are we?"

Markham muttered some polite protestation, to which Mrs. Greene paid not the slightest attention. She had turned, with seemingly great difficulty, to the nurse.

"Fix my pillows, Miss Craven," she ordered impatiently, and then added, in a whining tone: "Even you don't give a thought to my comfort." The nurse complied without a word. "Now, you can go in and sit with Ada until Doctor Von Blon comes.—How is the dear child?" Suddenly her voice had assumed a note of simulated solicitude.

"She's much better, Mrs. Greene." The nurse spoke in a colorless, matter-of-fact tone, and passed quietly into the dressing-room.

The woman on the bed turned complaining eyes upon Markham.

"It's a terrible thing to be a cripple, unable to walk or even stand alone. Both my legs have been hopelessly paralyzed for ten years. Think of it, Mr. Markham: I've spent ten years in this bed and that chair"—she pointed to an invalid's chair in the alcove—"and I can't even move from one to the other unless I'm lifted bodily. But I console myself with the thought that I'm not long for this world; and I try to be patient. It wouldn't be so bad, though, if my children were only more considerate. But I suppose I expect too much. Youth and health give little thought to the old and feeble—it's the way of the world. And so I make the best of it. It's my fate to be a burden to every one."

She sighed and drew the shawl more closely about her.

"You want to ask me some questions perhaps? I don't see what I can tell you that will be of any help, but I'm only too glad to do whatever I can. I haven't slept a wink, and my back has been paining me terribly as a result of all this commotion. But I'm not complaining."

Markham had stood looking at the old lady sympathetically. Indeed, she was a pitiful figure. Her long invalidism and solitude had warped what had probably been a brilliant and generous mind; and she had now become a kind of introspective martyr, with an exaggerated sensitiveness to her affliction. I could see that Markham's instinct was to leave her immediately with a few consoling words; but his sense of duty directed him to remain and learn what he could.

"I don't wish to annoy you more than is absolutely necessary, madam," he said in a kindly voice. "But it might help considerably if you permitted me to put one or two questions."

"What's a little annoyance, more or less?" she asked. "I've long since become used to it. Ask me anything you choose."

Markham bowed with Old World courtesy. "You are very kind, madam." Then, after a moment's pause: "Mr. Greene tells me you did not hear the shot that was fired in your oldest daughter's room, but that the shot in Miss Ada's room wakened you."

"That is so." She nodded slowly. "Julia's room is a considerable distance away—across the hall. But Ada always leaves the doors open between her room and mine in case I should need anything in the night. Naturally the shot in her room wakened me. . . . Let me see. I must have just fallen to sleep. My back was giving me a great deal of trouble last night; I had suffered all day with it, though I of course didn't tell any of the children about it. Little they care how their paralyzed old mother suffers. . . . And then, just as I had managed to doze off, there came the report, and I was wide awake again—lying here helpless, unable to move, and wondering what awful thing might be going to happen to me. And no one came to see if I was all right; no one thought of me, alone and defenseless. But then, no one ever thinks of me."

"I'm sure it wasn't any lack of consideration, Mrs. Greene," Markham assured her earnestly. "The situation probably drove everything momentarily from their minds except the two victims of the shooting.—Tell me this: did you hear any other sounds in Miss Ada's room after the shot awakened you?"

"I heard the poor girl fall—at least, it sounded like that."

"But no other noises of any kind? No footsteps, for instance?"

"Footsteps?" She seemed to make an effort to recall her impressions. "No; no footsteps."

"Did you hear the door into the hall open or close, madam?" It was Vance who put the question.

The woman turned her eyes sharply and glared at him.

"No, I heard no door open or close."

"That's rather queer, too, don't you think?" pursued Vance. "The intruder must have left the room."

"I suppose he must have, if he's not there now," she replied acidly, turning again to the District Attorney. "Is there anything else you'd care to know?"

Markham evidently had perceived the impossibility of eliciting any vital information from her.

"I think not," he answered; then added: "You of course heard the butler and your son here enter Miss Ada's room?"

"Oh, yes. They made enough noise doing it—they didn't consider my feelings in the least. That fuss-budget, Sproot, actually cried out for Chester like a hysterical woman; and, from the way he raised his voice over the telephone, one would have thought Doctor Von Blon was deaf. Then Chester had to rouse the whole house for some unknown reason. Oh, there was no peace or rest for me last night, I can tell you! And the police tramped around the house for hours like a drove of wild cattle. It was positively disgraceful. And here was I—a helpless old woman—entirely neglected and forgotten, suffering agonies with my spine."

After a few commiserating banalities Markham thanked her for her assistance, and withdrew. As we passed out and walked toward the stairs I could hear her calling out angrily: "Nurse! Nurse! Can't you hear me? Come at once and arrange my pillows. What do you mean by neglecting me this way . . . ?"

The voice trailed off mercifully as we descended to the main hall.

CHAPTER IV

THE MISSING REVOLVER

(Tuesday, November 9; 3 p. m.)

"The Mater's a crabbed old soul," Greene apologized offhandedly when we were again in the drawing-room. "Always grousing about her doting offspring.—Well, where do we go from here?"

Markham seemed lost in thought, and it was Vance who answered.

"Let us take a peep at the servants and hearken to their tale: Sproot for a starter."

Markham roused himself and nodded, and Greene rose and pulled a silken bell-cord near the archway. A minute later the butler appeared and stood at obsequious attention just inside the room. Markham had appeared somewhat at sea and even uninterested during the investigation, and Vance assumed command.

"Sit down, Sproot, and tell us as briefly as possible just what occurred last night."

Sproot came forward slowly, his eyes on the floor, but remained standing before the centre-table.

"I was reading Martial, sir, in my room," he began, lifting his gaze submissively, "when I thought I heard a muffled shot. I wasn't quite sure, for the automobiles in the street back-fire quite loud at times; but at last I said to myself I'd better investigate. I was in negligé, if you understand what I mean, sir; so I slipped on my bath-robe and came down. I didn't know just where the noise had come from; but when I was half-way down the steps, I heard another shot, and this time it sounded like it came from Miss Ada's room. So I went there at once, and tried the door. It was unlocked, and when I looked in I saw Miss Ada lying on the floor—a very distressing sight, sir. I called to Mr. Chester, and we lifted the poor young lady to the bed. Then I telephoned to Doctor Von Blon."

Vance scrutinized him.

"You were very courageous, Sproot, to brave a dark hall looking for the source of a shot in the middle of the night."

"Thank you, sir," the man answered, with great humility. "I always try to do my duty by the Greene family. I've been with them——"

"We know all that, Sproot." Vance cut him short. "The light was on in Miss Ada's room, I understand, when you opened the door."

"Yes, sir."

"And you saw no one, or heard no noise? No door closing, for instance?"

"No, sir."

"And yet the person who fired the shot must have been somewhere in the hall at the same time you were there."

"I suppose so, sir."

"And he might well have taken a shot at you, too."

"Quite so, sir." Sproot seemed wholly indifferent to the danger he had escaped. "But what will be, will be, sir—if you'll pardon my saying so. And I'm an old man——"

"Tut, tut! You'll probably live a considerable time yet—just how long I can't, of course, say."

"No, sir." Sproot's eyes gazed blankly ahead. "No one understands the mysteries of life and death."

"You're somewhat philosophic, I see," drily commented Vance. Then: "When you phoned to Doctor Von Blon, was he in?"

"No, sir; but the night nurse told me he'd be back any minute, and that she'd send him over. He arrived in less than half an hour."

Vance nodded. "That will be all, thank you, Sproot.—And now please send me *die gnädige Frau Köchin.*"

"Yes, sir." And the old butler shuffled from the room.

Vance's eyes followed him thoughtfully.

"An inveiglin' character," he murmured.

Greene snorted. "*You* don't have to live with him. He'd have said 'Yes, sir,' if you'd spoken to him in Walloon or Volapük. A sweet little playmate to have snooping round the house twenty-four hours a day!"

The cook, a portly, phlegmatic German woman of about forty-five, named Gertrude Mannheim, came in and seated herself on the edge of a chair near the entrance. Vance, after a moment's keen inspection of her, asked:

"Were you born in this country, Frau Mannheim?"

"I was born in Baden," she answered, in flat, rather guttural tones. "I came to America when I was twelve."

"You have not always been a cook, I take it." Vance's voice had a slightly different intonation from that which he had used with Sproot.

At first the woman did not answer.

"No, sir," she said finally. "Only since the death of my husband."

"How did you happen to come to the Greenes?"

Again she hesitated. "I had met Mr. Tobias Greene: he knew my husband. When my husband died there wasn't any money. And I remembered Mr. Greene, and I thought——"

"I understand." Vance paused, his eyes in space. "You heard nothing of what happened here last night?"

"No, sir. Not until Mr. Chester called up the stairs and said for us to get dressed and come down."

Vance rose and turned to the window overlooking the East River.

"That's all, Frau Mannheim. Be so good as to tell the senior maid—Hemming, isn't she?—to come here."

Without a word the cook left us, and her place was presently taken by a tall, slatternly woman, with a sharp, prudish face and severely combed hair. She wore a black, one-piece dress, and heelless vici-kid shoes; and her severity of mien was emphasized by a pair of thick-lensed spectacles.

"I understand, Hemming," began Vance, reseating himself before the fireplace, "that you heard neither shot last night, and learned of the tragedy only when called by Mr. Greene."

The woman nodded with a jerky, emphatic movement.

"I was spared," she said, in a rasping voice. "But the tragedy, as you call it, had to come sooner or later. It was an act of God, if you ask *me.*"

"Well, we're not asking you, Hemming; but we're delighted to have your opinion.—So God had a hand in the shooting, eh?"

"He did that!" The woman spoke with religious fervor. "The Greenes are an ungodly, wicked family." She leered defiantly at Chester Greene, who laughed uneasily. "'For I shall rise up against them, saith the Lord of hosts—the name, the remnant, and son, and daughter, and nephew'—only there ain't no nephew—'and I will sweep them with the besom of destruction, saith the Lord.'"

Vance regarded her musingly.

"I see you have misread Isaiah. And have you any celestial information as to who was chosen by the Lord to personify the besom?"

The woman compressed her lips. "Who knows?"

"Ah! Who, indeed? . . . But to descend to temporal things: I assume you weren't surprised at what happened last night?"

"I'm never surprised at the mysterious workin's of the Almighty."

Vance sighed. "You may return to your Scriptural perusings, Hemming. Only, I wish you'd pause *en route* and tell Barton we crave her presence here."

The woman rose stiffly and passed from the room like an animated ramrod.

Barton came in, obviously frightened. But her fear was insufficient to banish completely her instinctive coquetry. A certain coyness showed through the alarmed glance she gave us, and one hand automatically smoothed back the chestnut hair over her ear. Vance adjusted his monocle.

"You really should wear Alice blue, Barton," he advised her seriously. "Much more becoming than cerise to your olive complexion."

The girl's apprehensiveness relaxed, and she gave Vance a puzzled, kittenish look.

"But what I particularly wanted you to come here for," he went on, "was to ask you if Mr. Greene has ever kissed you."

"Which—Mr. Greene?" she stammered, completely disconcerted.

Chester had, at Vance's question, jerked himself erect in his chair and started to splutter an irate objection. But articulation failed him, and he turned to Markham with speechless indignation.

The corners of Vance's mouth twitched. "It really doesn't matter, Barton," he said quickly.

"Aren't you going to ask me any questions about—what happened last night?" the girl asked, with obvious disappointment.

"Oh! Do you know anything about what happened?"

"Why, no," she admitted. "I was asleep——"

"Exactly. Therefore, I sha'n't bother you with questions." He dismissed her good-naturedly.

"Damn it, Markham, I protest!" cried Greene, when Barton had left us. "I call this—this gentleman's levity rotten-bad taste—damme if I don't!"

Markham, too, was annoyed at the frivolous line of interrogation Vance had taken.

"I can't see what's to be gained by such futile inquiries," he said, striving to control his irritation.

"That's because you're still holding to the burglar theory," Vance replied. "But if, as Mr. Greene thinks, there is another explanation of last night's crime, then it's essential to acquaint ourselves with the conditions existing here. And it's equally essential not to rouse the suspicions of the servants. Hence, my apparent irrelevancies. I'm trying to size up the various human factors we have to deal with; and I think I've done uncommonly well. Several rather interesting possibilities have developed."

Before Markham could reply Sproot passed the archway and opened the front door to some one whom he greeted respectfully. Greene immediately went into the hall.

"Hallo, doc," we heard him say. "Thought you'd be along pretty soon. The District Attorney and his *entourage* are here, and they'd like to talk to Ada. I told 'em you said it might be all right this afternoon."

"I'll know better when I've seen Ada," the doctor replied. He passed on hurriedly, and we heard him ascending the stairs.

"It's Von Blon," announced Greene, returning to the drawing-room. "He'll let us know anon how Ada's coming along." There was a callous note in his voice, which, at the time, puzzled me.

"How long have you known Doctor Von Blon?" asked Vance.

"How long?" Greene looked surprised. "Why, all my life. Went to the old Beekman Public School with him. His father—old Doctor Veranus Von Blon—brought all the later Greenes into the world; family physician, spiritual adviser, and all that sort of thing, from time immemorial. When Von Blon, senior, died we embraced the son as a matter of course. And young Arthur's a shrewd lad, too. Knows his pharmacopoeia. Trained by the old man, and topped off his medical education in Germany."

Vance nodded negligently.

"While we're waiting for Doctor Von Blon, suppose we have a chat with Miss Sibella and Mr. Rex. Your brother first, let us say."

Greene looked to Markham for confirmation; then rang for Sproot.

Rex Greene came immediately upon being summoned.

"Well, what do you want now?" he asked, scanning our faces with nervous intensity. His voice was peevish, almost whining, and there were certain overtones in it which recalled the fretful complaining voice of Mrs. Greene.

"We merely want to question you about last night," answered Vance soothingly. "We thought it possible you could help us."

"What help can I give you?" Rex asked sullenly, slumping into a chair. He gave his brother a sneering look. "Chester's the only one round here who seems to have been awake."

Rex Greene was a short, sallow youth with narrow, stooping shoulders and an abnormally large head set on a neck which appeared almost emaciated. A shock of straight hair hung down over his bulging forehead, and he had a habit of tossing it back with a jerky movement of the head. His small, shifty eyes, shielded by enormous tortoise-rimmed glasses, seemed never to be at rest; and his thin lips were constantly twitching as with a *tic douloureux*. His chin was small and pointed, and he held it drawn in, emphasizing its lack of prominence. He was not a pleasant spectacle, and yet there was something in the man—an overdeveloped studiousness, perhaps—that gave the impression of unusual potentialities. I once saw a juvenile chess wizard who had the same cranial formations and general facial cast.

Vance appeared introspective, but I knew he was absorbing every detail of the man's appearance. At length he laid down his cigarette, and focussed his eyes languidly on the desk-lamp.

"You say you slept throughout the tragedy last night. How do you account for that remarkable fact, inasmuch as one of the shots was fired in the room next to yours?"

Rex hitched himself forward to the edge of his chair, and turned his head from side to side, carefully avoiding our eyes.

"I haven't tried to account for it," he returned, with angry resentment; but withal he seemed unstrung and on the defensive. Then he hurried on: "The walls in this house are pretty thick anyway, and there are always noises in the street. . . . Maybe my head was buried under the covers."

"You'd certainly have buried your head under the covers if you'd heard the shot," commented Chester, with no attempt to disguise his contempt for his brother.

Rex swung round, and would have retorted to the accusation had not Vance put his next question immediately.

"What's your theory of the crime, Mr. Greene? You've heard all the details and you know the situation."

"I thought the police had settled on a burglar." The youth's eyes rested shrewdly on Heath. "Wasn't that your conclusion?"

"It was, and it is," declared the Sergeant, who, until now, had preserved a bored silence. "But your brother here seems to think otherwise."

"So Chester thinks otherwise." Rex turned to his brother with an expression of feline dislike. "Maybe Chester knows all about it." There was no mistaking the implication in his words.

Vance once more stepped into the breach.

"Your brother has told us all he knows. Just at present we're concerned with how much *you* know." The severity of his manner caused Rex to shrink back in his chair. His lips twitched more violently, and he began fidgeting with the braided frog of his smoking-jacket. I noticed then for the first time that he had short rachitic hands with bowed and thickened phalanges.

"You are sure you heard no shot?" continued Vance ominously.

"I've told you a dozen times I didn't!" His voice rose to a falsetto, and he gripped the arms of his chair with both hands.

"Keep calm, Rex," admonished Chester. "You'll be having another of your spells."

"To hell with you!" the youth shouted. "How many times have I got to tell them I don't know anything about it?"

"We merely want to make doubly sure on all points," Vance told him pacifyingly. "And you certainly wouldn't want your sister's death to go unavenged through any lack of perseverance on our part."

Rex relaxed slightly, and took a deep inspiration.

"Oh, I'd tell you anything I knew," he said, running his tongue over his dry lips. "But I always get blamed for everything that happens in this house—that is, Ada and I do. And as for avenging Julia's death: that doesn't appeal to me nearly so much as punishing the dog that shot Ada. She has a hard enough time of it here under normal conditions. Mother keeps her in the house waiting on her as if she were a servant."

Vance nodded understandingly. Then he rose and placed his hand sympathetically on Rex's shoulder. This gesture was so unlike him I was completely astonished; for, despite his deep-seated humanism, Vance seemed always ashamed of any outward show of feeling, and sought constantly to repress his emotions.

"Don't let this tragedy upset you too much, Mr. Greene," he said reassuringly. "And you may be certain that we'll do everything in our power to find and punish the person who shot Miss Ada.—We won't bother you any more now."

Rex got up almost eagerly and drew himself together.

"Oh, that's all right." And with a covertly triumphant glance at his brother, he left the room.

"Rex is a queer bird," Chester remarked, after a short silence. "He spends most of his time reading and working out abstruse problems in mathematics and astronomy. Wanted to stick a telescope through the attic roof, but the Mater drew the line. He's an unhealthy beggar, too. I tell him he doesn't get enough fresh air, but you see his attitude toward me. Thinks I'm weak-minded because I play golf."

"What were the spells you spoke about?" asked Vance. "Your brother looks as if he might be epileptic."

"Oh, no; nothing like that; though I've seen him have convulsive seizures when he got in a specially violent tantrum. He gets excited easily and flies off the handle. Von Blon says it's hyper-neurasthenia—whatever that is. He goes ghastly pale when he's worked up, and has a kind of trembling fit. Says things he's sorry for afterward. Nothing serious, though. What he needs is exercise—a year on a ranch roughing it, without his infernal books and compasses and T-squares."

"I suppose he's more or less a favorite with your mother." (Vance's remark recalled a curious similarity of temperament between the two I had felt vaguely as Rex talked.)

"More or less." Chester nodded ponderously. "He's the pet in so far as the Mater's capable of petting any one but herself. Anyway, she's never ragged Rex as much as the rest of us."

Again Vance went to the great window above the East River, and stood looking out. Suddenly he turned.

"By the by, Mr. Greene, did you find your revolver?" His tone had changed; his ruminative mood had gone.

Chester gave a start, and cast a swift glance at Heath, who had now become attentive.

"No, by Gad, I haven't," he admitted, fumbling in his pocket for his cigarette-holder. "Funny thing about that gun, too. Always kept it in my desk drawer—though, as I told this gentleman when he mentioned it"—he pointed his holder at Heath as if the other had been an inanimate object—"I don't remember actually having seen it for years. But, even so, where the devil could it have gone? Damme, it's mysterious. Nobody round here would touch it. The maids don't go in the drawers when they're cleaning the room—I'm lucky if they make the bed and dust the top of the furniture. Damned funny what became of it."

"Did you take a good look for it to-day, like you said?" asked Heath, thrusting his head forward belligerently. Why, since he held to the burglar theory, he should assume a bulldozing manner, I couldn't imagine. But whenever Heath was troubled, he was aggressive; and any loose end in an investigation troubled him deeply.

"Certainly, I looked for it," Chester replied, haughtily indignant. "I went through every room and closet and drawer in the house. But it's completely disappeared. . . . Probably got thrown out by mistake in one of the annual house-cleanings."

"That's possible," agreed Vance. "What sort of a revolver was it?"

"An old Smith & Wesson .32." Chester appeared to be trying to refresh his memory. "Mother-of-pearl handle: some scroll-engraving on the barrel—I don't recall exactly. I bought it fifteen years ago—maybe longer—when I went camping one summer in the Adirondacks. Used it for target practice. Then I got tired of it, and stuck it away in a drawer behind a lot of old cancelled checks."

"Was it in good working order then?"

"As far as I know. Fact is, it worked stiff when I got it, and I had the sear filed down, so it was practically a hair-trigger affair. The slightest touch sent it off. Better for shooting targets that way."

"Do you recall if it was loaded when you put it away?"

"Couldn't say. Might have been. It's been so long——"

"Were there any cartridges for it in your desk?"

"Now, that I can answer you positively. There wasn't a loose cartridge in the place."

Vance reseated himself.

"Well, Mr. Greene, if you happen to run across the revolver you will, of course, let Mr. Markham or Sergeant Heath know."

"Oh, certainly. With pleasure." Chester's assurance was expressed with an air of magnanimity.

Vance glanced at his watch.

"And now, seeing that Doctor Von Blon is still with his patient, I wonder if we could see Miss Sibella for a moment."

Chester got up, obviously relieved that the subject of the revolver had been disposed of, and went to the bell-cord beside the archway. But he arrested his hand in the act of reaching for it.

"I'll fetch her myself," he said, and hurried from the room.

Markham turned to Vance with a smile.

"Your prophecy about the non-reappearance of the gun has, I note, been temporarily verified."

"And I'm afraid that fancy weapon with the hair-trigger never will appear—at least, not until this miserable business is cleaned up." Vance was unwontedly sober; his customary levity had for the moment deserted him. But before long he lifted his eyebrows mockingly, and gave Heath a chaffing look.

"Perchance the Sergeant's predacious neophyte made off with the revolver—became fascinated with the scrollwork, or entranced with the pearl handle."

"It's quite possible the revolver disappeared in the way Greene said it did," Markham submitted. "In any event, I think you unduly emphasized the matter."

"Sure he did, Mr. Markham," growled Heath. "And, what's more, I can't see that all this repartee with the family is getting us anywheres. I had 'em all on the carpet last night when the shooting was hot; and I'm telling you they don't know nothing about it. This Ada Greene is the only person round here I want to talk to. There's a chance she can give us a tip. If her lights were on when the burglar got in her room, she maybe got a good look at him."

"Sergeant," said Vance, shaking his head sadly, "you're getting positively morbid on the subject of that mythical burglar."

Markham inspected the end of his cigar thoughtfully.

"No, Vance. I'm inclined to agree with the Sergeant. It appears to me that you're the one with the morbid imagination. I let you inveigle me into this inquiry too easily. That's why I've kept in the background and left the floor to you. Ada Greene's our only hope of help here."

"Oh, for your trusting, forthright mind!" Vance sighed and shifted his position restlessly. "I say, our psychic Chester is taking a dashed long time to fetch Sibella."

At that moment there came a sound of footsteps on the marble stairs, and a few seconds later Sibella Greene, accompanied by Chester, appeared in the archway.

CHAPTER V

HOMICIDAL POSSIBILITIES

(Tuesday, November 9; 3.30 p. m.)

SIBELLA ENTERED with a firm, swinging gait, her head held
high, her eyes sweeping the assemblage with bold interrogation.
She was tall and of slender, athletic build, and, though she was
not pretty, there was a cold, chiselled attractiveness in her lineaments that held one's attention. Her face was at once vivid and
intense; and there was a hauteur in her expression amounting
almost to arrogance. Her dark, crisp hair was bobbed but not
waved, and the severity of its lines accentuated the overdecisive
cast of her features. Her hazel eyes were wide-spaced beneath
heavy, almost horizontal eyebrows; her nose was straight and
slightly prominent, and her mouth was large and firm, with a
suggestion of cruelty in its thin lips. She was dressed simply, in
a dark sport suit cut extremely short, silk-wool stockings of a
heather mixture, and low-heeled mannish Oxfords.

Chester presented the District Attorney to her as an old acquaintance, and permitted Markham to make the other intro-
ductions.

"I suppose you know, Mr. Markham, why Chet likes you," she

said, in a peculiarly plangent voice. "You're one of the few persons at the Marylebone Club that he can beat at golf."

She seated herself before the centre-table, and crossed her knees comfortably.

"I wish you'd get me a cigarette, Chet." Her tone made the request an imperative.

Vance rose at once and held out his case.

"Do try one of these *Régies*, Miss Greene," he urged in his best drawing-room manner. "If you say you don't like them, I shall immediately change my brand."

"Rash man!" Sibella took a cigarette and permitted Vance to light it for her. Then she settled back in her chair and gave Markham a quizzical look. "Quite a wild party we pulled here last night, wasn't it? We've never had so much commotion in the old mansion. And it was just my luck to sleep soundly through it all." She made an aggrieved *moue*. "Chet didn't call me till it was all over. Just like him—he has a nasty disposition."

Somehow her flippancy did not shock me as it might have done in a different type of person. But Sibella struck me as a girl who, though she might feel things keenly, would not permit any misfortune to get the better of her; and I put her apparent callousness down to a dogged, if perverted, courageousness.

Markham, however, resented her attitude.

"One cannot blame Mr. Greene for not taking the matter lightly," he reproved her. "The brutal murder of a defenseless woman and the attempted murder of a young girl hardly come under the head of diversion."

Sibella looked at him reproachfully. "You know, Mr. Markham, you sound exactly like the Mother Superior of the stuffy convent I was confined in for two years." She became suddenly grave. "Why draw a long face over something that's happened and can't be helped? Anyway, Julia never sought to brighten her little corner. She was always crabbed and faultfinding, and her good deeds wouldn't fill a book. It may be unsisterly to say it, but she's not going to be missed so dreadfully. Chet and I are certainly not going to pine away."

"And what about the brutal shooting of your other sister?" Markham was with difficulty controlling his indignation.

Sibella's eyelids narrowed perceptibly, and the lines of her face became set. But she erased the expression almost at once.

"Well, Ada's going to recover, isn't she?" Despite her effort, she was unable to keep a certain hardness out of her voice. "She'll have a nice long rest, and a nurse to wait on her. Am I expected to weep copiously because of baby sister's escape?"

Vance, who had been closely watching this clash between Sibella and Markham, now took a hand in the conversation.

"My dear Markham, I can't see what Miss Greene's sentiments have to do with the matter. Her attitude may not be strictly in accord with the prescribed conduct for young ladies on such occasions, but I feel sure she has excellent reasons for her point of view. Let us give over moralizing, and seek Miss Greene's assistance instead."

The girl darted him an amused, appreciative glance; and Markham made a gesture of indifferent acquiescence. It was plain that he regarded the present inquiry as of little importance.

Vance gave the girl an engaging smile.

"It's really my fault, Miss Greene, that we are intruding here," he apologized. "It was I, d' ye see, that urged Mr. Markham to look into the case after your brother had expressed his disbelief in the burglar theory."

She nodded understandingly. "Oh, Chet sometimes has excellent hunches. It's one of his very few merits."

"You, too, I gather, are sceptical in regard to the burglar?"

"Sceptical?" She gave a short laugh. "I'm downright suspicious. I don't know any burglars, though I'd dearly love to meet one; but I simply can't bring my flighty brain to picture them going about their fascinating occupation the way our little entertainer did last night."

"You positively thrill me," declared Vance. "Y' see, our minority ideas coincide perfectly."

"Did Chet give you any intelligible explanation for his opinion?" she asked.

"I'm afraid not. He was inclined to lay his feelings to metaphysical causes. His conviction was due, I took it, to some kind of psychic visitation. He knew, but could not explain: he was sure, but had no proof. It was most indefinite—a bit esoteric, in fact."

"I'd never suspect Chet of spiritualistic leanings." She shot her brother a tantalizing look. "He's really deadly commonplace, when you get to know him."

"Oh, cut it, Sib," objected Chester irritably. "You yourself had a spasm this morning when I told you the police were hotfooting it after a burglar."

Sibella made no answer. With a slight toss of the head she leaned over and threw her cigarette into the grate.

"By the by, Miss Greene"—Vance spoke casually—"there has been considerable mystery about the disappearance of your brother's revolver. It has completely vanished from his desk drawer. I wonder if you have seen it about the house anywhere."

At his mention of the gun Sibella stiffened slightly. Her eyes took on an expression of intentness, and the corners of her mouth lifted into a faintly ironical smile.

"Chet's revolver has gone, has it?" She put the question colorlessly, as if her thoughts were elsewhere. "No . . . I haven't seen it." Then, after a momentary pause: "But it was in Chet's desk last week."

Chester heaved himself forward angrily.

"What were you doing in my desk last week?" he demanded.

"Don't wax apoplectic," the girl said carelessly. "I wasn't looking for love missives. I simply couldn't imagine you in love, Chet. . . ." The idea seemed to amuse her. "I was only looking for that old emerald stick-pin you borrowed and never returned."

"It's at the club," he explained sulkily.

"Is it, really! Well, I didn't find it anyway; but I did see the revolver.—Are you quite sure it's gone?"

"Don't be absurd," the man growled. "I've searched everywhere for it. . . . Including your room," he added vengefully.

"Oh, you would! But why did you admit having it in the first place?" Her tone was scornful. "Why involve yourself unnecessarily?"

Chester shifted uneasily.

"This gentleman"—he again pointed impersonally to Heath—"asked me if I owned a revolver, and I told him 'yes.' If I hadn't, some of the servants or one of my loving family would have told him. And I thought the truth was best."

Sibella smiled satirically.

"My older brother, you observe, is a model of all the old-fashioned virtues," she remarked to Vance. But she was obviously *distraite*. The revolver episode had somewhat shaken her self-assurance.

"You say, Miss Greene, that the burglar idea does not appeal to you." Vance was smoking languidly with half-closed eyes. "Can you think of any other explanation for the tragedy?"

The girl raised her head and regarded him calculatingly.

"Because I don't happen to believe in burglars that shoot women and sneak away without taking anything, it doesn't mean that I can suggest alternatives. I'm not a policewoman—though I've often thought it would be jolly good sport—and I had a vague idea it was the business of the police to run down criminals.—You don't believe in the burglar either, Mr. Vance, or you wouldn't have followed up Chet's hunch. Who do *you* think ran amuck here last night?"

"My dear girl!" Vance raised a protesting hand. "If I had the foggiest idea I wouldn't be annoying you with impertinent questions. I'm plodding with leaden feet in a veritable bog of ignorance."

He spoke negligently, but Sibella's eyes were clouded with suspicion. Presently, however, she laughed gaily and held out her hand.

"Another *Régie, monsieur.* I was on the verge of becoming serious; and I simply mustn't become serious. It's so frightfully boring. Besides, it gives one wrinkles. And I'm much too young for wrinkles."

"Like Ninon de L'Enclos, you'll aways be too young for wrinkles," rejoined Vance, holding a match to her cigarette. "But perhaps you can suggest, without becoming too serious, some one who might have had a reason for wanting to kill your two sisters."

"Oh, as for that, I'd say we'd all come under suspicion. We're not an ideal home circle, by any means. In fact, the Greenes are a queer collection. We don't love one another the way a perfectly nice and proper family should. We're always at each other's throats, bickering and fighting about something or other. It's rather a mess—this ménage. It's a wonder to me murder hasn't been done long before. And we've all got to live here until 1932, or go it on our own; and, of course, none of us could make a decent living. A sweet paternal heritage!"[*]

She smoked moodily for a few moments.

"Yes, any one of us had ample reason to be murderously inclined toward all the others. Chet there would strangle me now if he didn't think the nervous aftermath of the act would spoil his golf—wouldn't you, Chet dear? Rex regards us all as inferiors, and probably considers himself highly indulgent and altruistic not to have murdered us all long ago. And the only reason mother hasn't killed us is that she's paralyzed and can't manage it. Julia, too, for that matter, could have seen us all boiled in oil without turning a hair. And as for Ada"—her brows contracted and an extraordinary ferocity crept into her eyes—"she'd dearly love to see us all exterminated. She's not really one of us, and she hates us. Nor would I myself have any scruples about doing away with the rest of my fond family. I've thought of it often, but I could never decide on a nice thorough method." She flicked her cigarette ash on the floor. "So there you are. If you're looking for possibilities you have them galore. There's no one under this ancestral roof who couldn't qualify."

Though her words were meant to be satirical, I could not help feeling that a sombre, terrible truth underlay them. Vance, though apparently listening with amusement, had, I knew, been absorbing every inflection of her voice and play of expression, in an effort to relate the details of her sweeping indictment to the problem in hand.

"At any rate," he remarked offhandedly, "you are an amazingly frank young woman. However, I sha'n't recommend your arrest

[*] Sibella was here referring to Tobias Greene's will, which stipulated not only that the Greene mansion should be maintained intact for twenty-five years, but that the legatees should live out the estate during that time or become disinherited.

just yet. I haven't a particle of evidence against you, don't y' know. Annoyin', ain't it?"

"Oh, well," sighed the girl, in mock disappointment, "you may pick up a clew later on. There'll probably be another death or two around here before long. I'd hate to think the murderer would give up the job with so little really accomplished."

At this point Doctor Von Blon entered the drawing-room. Chester rose to greet him, and the formalities of introduction were quickly over. Von Blon bowed with reserved cordiality; but I noted that his manner to Sibella, while pleasant, was casual in the extreme. I wondered a little about this, but I recalled that he was an old friend of the family and probably took many of the social amenities for granted.

"What have you to report, doctor?" asked Markham. "Will we be able to question the young lady this afternoon?"

"I hardly think there'd be any harm in it," Von Blon returned, seating himself beside Chester. "Ada has only a little reaction fever now, though she's suffering from shock, and is pretty weak from loss of blood."

Doctor Von Blon was a suave, smooth-faced man of forty, with small, almost feminine features and an air of unwavering amiability. His urbanity struck me as too artificial—"professional" is perhaps the word—and there was something of the ambitious egoist about him. But I was far more attracted than repelled by him.

Vance watched him attentively as he spoke. He was more anxious even than Heath, I think, to question the girl.

"It was not a particularly serious wound, then?" Markham asked.

"No, not serious," the doctor assured him; "though it barely missed being fatal. Had the shot gone an inch deeper it would have torn across the lung. It was a very narrow escape."

"As I understand it," interposed Vance, "the bullet travelled transversely over the left scapular region."

Von Blon inclined his head in agreement.

"The shot was obviously aimed at the heart from the rear," he explained, in his soft, modulated voice. "But Ada must have turned slightly to the right just as the revolver exploded; and the bullet, instead of going directly into her body, ploughed along the shoulder-blade at the level of the third dorsal vertebra, tore the capsular ligament, and lodged in the deltoid." He indicated the location of the deltoid on his own left arm.

"She had," suggested Vance, "apparently turned her back on her assailant and attempted to run away; and he had followed her and placed the revolver almost against her back.—Is that your interpretation of it, doctor?"

"Yes, that would seem to be the situation. And, as I said, at the crucial moment she veered a little, and thus saved her life."

"Would she have fallen immediately to the floor, despite the actual superficiality of the wound?"

"It's not unlikely. Not only would the pain have been considerable, but the shock must be taken into account. Ada—or, for that matter, any woman—might have fainted at once."

"And it's a reasonable presumption," pursued Vance, "that her assailant would have taken it for granted that the shot had been fatal."

"We may readily assume that to be the case."

Vance smoked a moment, his eyes averted.

"Yes," he agreed, "I think we may assume that.—And another point suggests itself. Since Miss Ada was in front of the dressing-table, a considerable distance from the bed, and since the weapon was held practically against her, the encounter would seem to take on the nature of a deliberate attack, rather than a haphazard shot fired by some one in a panic."

Von Blon looked shrewdly at Vance, and then turned a questioning gaze upon Heath. For a moment he was silent, as if weighing his reply, and when he spoke it was with guarded reserve.

"Of course, one might interpret the situation that way. Indeed, the facts would seem to indicate such a conclusion. But, on the other hand, the intruder might have been very close to Ada; and the fact that the bullet entered her left shoulder at a particularly vital point may have been the purest accident."

"Quite true," conceded Vance. "However, if the idea of premeditation is to be abrogated, we must account for the fact that the lights were on in the room when the butler entered immediately after the shooting."

Von Blon showed the keenest astonishment at this statement.

"The lights were on? That's most remarkable!" His brow crinkled into a perplexed frown, and he appeared to be assimilating Vance's information. "Still," he argued, "that very fact may account for the shooting. If the intruder had entered a lighted room he may have fired at the occupant lest his description be given to the police later."

"Oh, quite!" murmured Vance. "Anyway, let us hope we'll learn the explanation when we've seen and spoken to Miss Ada."

"Well, why don't we get to it?" grumbled Heath, whose ordinarily inexhaustible store of patience had begun to run low.

"You're so hasty, Sergeant," Vance chided him. "Doctor Von Blon has just told us that Miss Ada is very weak; and anything we can learn beforehand will spare her just so many questions."

"All I want to find out," expostulated Heath, "is if she got a look at the bird that shot her and can give me a description of him."

"That being the case, Sergeant, I fear you are doomed to have your ardent hopes dashed to the ground."

Heath chewed viciously on his cigar; and Vance turned again to Von Blon.

"There's one other question I'd like to ask, doctor. How long was it after Miss Ada had been wounded before you examined her?"

"The butler's already told us, Mr. Vance," interposed Heath impatiently. "The doctor got here in half an hour."

"Yes, that's about right." Von Blon's tone was smooth and matter-of-fact. "I was unfortunately out on a call when Sproot phoned, but I returned about fifteen minutes later, and hurried right over. Luckily I live near here—in East 48th Street."

"And was Miss Ada still unconscious when you arrived?"

"Yes. She had lost considerable blood. The cook, however, had put a towel-compress on the wound, which of course helped."

Vance thanked him and rose.

"And now, if you'll be good enough to take us to your patient, we'll be very grateful."

"As little excitement as possible, you understand," admonished Von Blon, as he got up and led the way up-stairs.

Sibella and Chester seemed undecided about accompanying us; but as I turned into the hall I saw a look of interrogation flash between them, and a moment later they too joined us in the upper hall.

CHAPTER VI

AN ACCUSATION

(Tuesday, November 9; 4 p. m.)

ADA GREENE's room was simply, almost severely, furnished; but there was a neatness about it, combined with little touches of feminine decoration, that reflected the care its occupant had bestowed upon it. To the left, near the door that led into the dressing-room communicating with Mrs. Greene's chamber, was a single mahogany bed of simple design; and beyond it was the door that opened upon the stone balcony. To the right, beside the window, stood the dressing-table; and on the amber-colored Chinese rug before it there showed a large irregular brown stain where the wounded girl had lain. In the centre of the right wall was an old Tudor fireplace with a high oak-panelled mantel.

As we entered, the girl in the bed looked at us inquisitively, and a slight flush colored her pale cheeks. She lay on her right side, facing the door, her bandaged shoulder supported by pillows, and her left hand, slim and white, resting upon the blue-figured coverlet. A remnant of her fear of the night before seemed still to linger in her blue eyes.

Doctor Von Blon went to her and, sitting down on the edge

of the bed, placed his hand on hers. His manner was at once protective and impersonal.

"These gentlemen want to ask you a few questions, Ada," he explained, with a reassuring smile; "and as you were so much stronger this afternoon I brought them up. Do you feel equal to it?"

She nodded her head wearily, her eyes on the doctor.

Vance, who had paused by the mantel to inspect the hand-carving of the quadræ, now turned and approached the bed.

"Sergeant," he said, "if you don't mind, let me talk to Miss Greene first."

Heath realized, I think, that the situation called for tact and delicacy; and it was typical of the man's fundamental bigness that he at once stepped aside.

"Miss Greene," said Vance, in a quiet, genial voice, drawing up a small chair beside the bed, "we're very anxious to clear up the mystery about last night's tragedy; and, as you are the only person who is in a position to help us, we want you to recall for us, as nearly as you can, just what happened."

The girl took a deep breath.

"It—it was awful," she said weakly, looking straight ahead. "After I had gone to sleep—I don't know just what time—something woke me up. I can't tell you what it was; but all of a sudden I was wide awake, and the strangest feeling came over me. . . ." She closed her eyes, and an involuntary shudder swept her body. "It was as though some one were in the room, threatening me. . . ." Her voice faded away into an awed silence.

"Was the room dark?" Vance asked gently.

"Pitch-dark." Slowly she turned her eyes to him. "That's why I was so frightened. I couldn't see anything, and I imagined there was a ghost—or evil spirit—near me. I tried to call out, but I couldn't make a sound. My throat felt dry and—and stiff."

"Typical constriction due to fright, Ada," explained Von Blon. "Many people can't speak when they're frightened.—Then what happened?"

"I lay trembling for a few minutes, but not a sound came from anywhere in the room. Yet I knew—I *knew*—somebody, or something, that meant to harm me was here. . . . At last I forced myself to get up—very quietly. I wanted to turn on the lights—the darkness frightened me so. And after a while I was standing up beside the bed here. Then, for the first time, I could see the dim light of the windows; and it made things seem more real somehow. So I began to grope my way toward the electric switch there by the door. I had only gone a little way when . . . a hand . . . touched me. . . ."

Her lips were trembling, and a look of horror came into her wide-open eyes.

"I—I was so stunned," she struggled on, "I hardly know what I did. Again I tried to scream, but I couldn't even open my lips. And then I turned and ran away from the—the thing—toward the window. I had almost reached it when I heard some one coming after me—a queer, shuffling sound—and I knew it was the end. . . . There was an awful noise, and something hot struck the back of my shoulder. I was suddenly nauseated; the light of the window disappeared, and I felt myself sinking down—deep. . . ."

When she ceased speaking a tense silence fell on the room. Her account, for all its simplicity, had been tremendously graphic. Like a great actress she had managed to convey to her listeners the very emotional essence of her story.

Vance waited several moments before speaking.

"It was a frightful experience!" he murmured sympathetically. "I wish it wasn't necess'ry to worry you about details, but there are several points I'd like to go over with you."

She smiled faintly in appreciation of his considerateness, and waited.

"If you tried hard, do you think you could recall what wakened you?" he asked.

"No—there wasn't any sound that I can remember."

"Did you leave your door unlocked last night?"

"I think so. I don't generally lock it."

"And you heard no door open or close—anywhere?"

"No; none. Everything in the house was perfectly still."

"And yet you knew that some one was in the room. How was that?" Vance's voice, though gentle, was persistent.

"I—don't know . . . and yet there must have been something that told me."

"Exactly! Now try to think." Vance bent a little nearer to the troubled girl. "A soft breathing, perhaps—a slight gust of air as the person moved by your bed—a faint odor of perfume . . . ?"

She frowned painfully, as if trying to recall the elusive cause of her dread.

"I can't think—I can't remember." Her voice was scarcely audible. "I was so terribly frightened."

"If only we could trace the source!" Vance glanced at the doctor, who nodded understandingly, and said:

"Obviously some association whose stimulus went unrecognized."

"Did you feel, Miss Greene, that you knew the person who was here?" continued Vance. "That is to say, was it a familiar presence?"

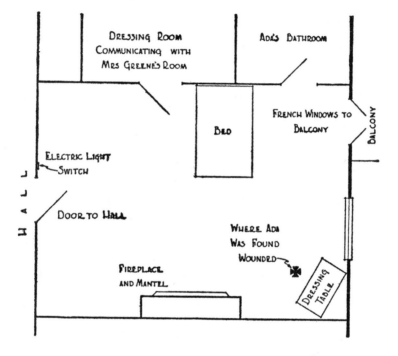

PLAN OF ADA'S BEDROOM.

"I don't know exactly. I only know I was afraid of it."

"But you heard it move toward you after you had risen and fled toward the window. Was there any familiarity in the sound?"

"No!" For the first time she spoke with emphasis. "It was just footsteps—soft, sliding footsteps."

"Of course, any one might have walked that way in the dark, or a person in bedroom slippers. . . ."

"It was only a few steps—and then came the awful noise and burning."

Vance waited a moment.

"Try very hard to recall those steps—or rather your impression of them. Would you say they were the steps of a man or a woman?"

An added pallor overspread the girl's face; and her frightened eyes ran over all the occupants of the room. Her breathing, I noticed, had quickened; and twice she parted her lips as if to speak, but checked herself each time. At last she said in a low tremulous voice:

"I don't know—I haven't the slightest idea."

A short, high-strung laugh, bitter and sneering, burst from Sibella; and all eyes were turned in amazed attention in her direction. She stood rigidly at the foot of the bed, her face flushed, her hands tightly clinched at her side.

"Why don't you tell them you recognized my footsteps?" she demanded of her sister in biting tones. "You had every intention of doing so. Haven't you got courage enough left to lie—you sobbing little cat?"

Ada caught her breath and seemed to draw herself nearer to the doctor, who gave Sibella a stern, admonitory look.

"Oh, I say, Sib! Hold your tongue." It was Chester who broke the startled silence that followed the outbreak.

Sibella shrugged her shoulders and walked to the window; and Vance again turned his attention to the girl on the bed, continuing his questioning as if nothing had happened.

"There's one more point, Miss Greene." His tone was even gentler than before. "When you groped your way across the room toward the switch, at what point did you come in contact with the unseen person?"

"About half-way to the door—just beyond that centre-table."

"You say a hand touched you. But how did it touch you? Did it shove you, or try to take hold of you?"

She shook her head vaguely.

"Not exactly. I don't know how to explain it, but I seemed to walk into the hand, as though it were outstretched—reaching for me."

"Would you say it was a large hand or a small one? Did you, for instance, get the impression of strength?"

There was another silence. Again the girl's respiration quickened, and she cast a frightened glance at Sibella, who stood staring out into the black, swinging branches of the trees in the side yard.

"I don't know—oh, I don't know!" Her words were like a stifled cry of anguish. "I didn't notice. It was all so sudden—so horrible."

"But try to think," urged Vance's low, insistent voice. "Surely you got some impression. Was it a man's hand, or a woman's?"

Sibella now came swiftly to the bed, her cheeks very pale, her eyes blazing. For a moment she glared at the stricken girl; then she turned resolutely to Vance.

"You asked me down-stairs if I had any idea as to who might have done the shooting. I didn't answer you then, but I'll answer you now. I'll tell you who's guilty!" She jerked her head toward the bed, and pointed a quivering finger at the still figure lying there. "There's the guilty one—that snivelling little outsider, that sweet angelic little snake in the grass!"

So incredible, so unexpected, was this accusation that for a time no one in the room spoke. A groan burst from Ada's lips, and she clutched at the doctor's hand with a spasmodic movement of despair.

"Oh, Sibella—how could you!" she breathed.

Von Blon had stiffened, and an angry light came into his eyes. But before he could speak Sibella was rushing on with her illogical, astounding indictment.

"Oh, she's the one who did it! And she's deceiving you just as she's always tried to deceive the rest of us. She hates us—she's hated us ever since father brought her into this house. She resents us—the things we have, the very blood in our veins. Heaven knows what blood's in hers. She hates us because she isn't our equal. She'd gladly see us all murdered. She killed Julia first, because Julia ran the house and saw to it that she did something to earn her livelihood. She despises us; and she planned to get rid of us."

The girl on the bed looked piteously from one to the other of us. There was no resentment in her eyes; she appeared stunned and unbelieving, as if she doubted the reality of what she had heard.

"Most interestin'," drawled Vance. It was his ironic tone, more than the words themselves, that focussed all eyes on him. He had been watching Sibella during her tirade, and his gaze was still on her.

"You seriously accuse your sister of doing the shooting?" He spoke now in a pleasant, almost friendly, voice.

"I do!" she declared brazenly. "She hates us all."

"As far as that goes," smiled Vance, "I haven't noticed a superabundance of love and affection in any of the Greene family." His tone was without offense. "And do you base your accusation on anything specific, Miss Greene?"

"Isn't it specific enough that she wants us all out of the way, that she thinks she would have everything—ease, luxury, freedom—if there wasn't any one else to inherit the Greene money?"

"Hardly specific enough to warrant a direct accusation of so heinous a character.—And by the by, Miss Greene, just how would you explain the method of the crime if called as a witness in a court of law? You couldn't altogether ignore the fact that Miss Ada herself was shot in the back, don't y' know?"

For the first time the sheer impossibility of the accusation seemed to strike Sibella. She became sullen; and her mouth settled into a contour of angry bafflement.

"As I told you once before, I'm not a policewoman," she retorted. "Crime isn't *my* specialty."

"Nor logic either apparently." A whimsical note crept into Vance's voice. "But perhaps I misinterpret your accusation. Did you mean to imply that Miss Ada shot your sister Julia, and that some one else—party or parties unknown, I believe the phrase is—shot Miss Ada immediately afterward—in a spirit of vengeance, perhaps? A *crime à quatre mains*, so to speak?"

Sibella's confusion was obvious, but her stubborn wrath had in no wise abated.

"Well, if that was the way it happened," she countered malevolently, "it's a rotten shame they didn't do the job better."

"The blunder may at least prove unfortunate for somebody," suggested Vance pointedly. "Still, I hardly think we can seriously entertain the double-culprit theory. Both of your sisters, d' ye see, were shot with the same gun—a .32 revolver—within a few minutes of each other. I'm afraid that we'll have to be content with one guilty person."

Sibella's manner suddenly became sly and calculating.

"What kind of a gun was yours, Chet?" she asked her brother.

"Oh, it was a .32, all right—an old Smith & Wesson revolver." Chester was painfully ill at ease.

"Was it, indeed? Well, that's that." She turned her back on us and went again to the window.

The tension in the room slackened, and Von Blon leaned solicitously over the wounded girl and rearranged the pillows.

"Every one's upset, Ada," he said soothingly. "You mustn't worry about what's happened. Sibella'll be sorry to-morrow and make amends. This affair has got on everybody's nerves."

The girl gave him a grateful glance, and seemed to relax under his ministrations.

After a moment he straightened up and looked at Markham.

"I hope you gentlemen are through—for to-day, at least."

Both Vance and Markham had risen, and Heath and I had followed suit; but at that moment Sibella strode toward us again.

"Wait!" she commanded imperiously. "I've just thought of something. Chet's revolver! I know where it went.—*She* took it." Again she pointed accusingly at Ada. "I saw her in Chet's room the other day, and I wondered then why she was snooping about there." She gave Vance a triumphant leer. "That's specific, isn't it?"

"What day was this, Miss Greene?" As before, his calmness seemed to counteract the effect of her venom.

"What day? I don't remember exactly. Last week some time."

"The day you were looking for your emerald pin, perhaps?"

Sibella hesitated; then said angrily: "I don't recall. Why should I remember the exact time? All I know is that, as I was passing down the hall, I glanced into Chet's room—the door was half open—and I saw *her* in there . . . by the desk."

"And was it so unusual to see Miss Ada in your brother's room?" Vance spoke without any particular interest.

"She never goes into any of our rooms," declared Sibella. "Except Rex's, sometimes. Julia told her long ago to keep out of them."

Ada gave her sister a look of infinite entreaty.

"Oh, Sibella," she moaned; "what have I ever done to make you dislike me so?"

"What have you done!" The other's voice was harsh and strident, and a look almost demoniacal smouldered in her levelled eyes. "Everything! Nothing! Oh, you're clever—with your quiet, sneaky ways, and your patient, hangdog look, and your goody-goody manner. But you don't pull the wool over *my* eyes. You've been hating all of us ever since you came here. And you've been waiting for the chance to kill us, planning and scheming—you vile little——"

"Sibella!" It was Von Blon's voice that, like the lash of a whip, cut in on this unreasoned tirade. "That will be enough!" He moved forward, and glanced menacingly into the girl's eyes. I was almost as astonished at his attitude as I had been at her wild words. There was a curious intimacy in his manner—an implication of familiarity which struck me as unusual even for a family physician of his long and friendly standing. Vance noticed it too, for his eyebrows went up slightly and he watched the scene with intense interest.

"You've become hysterical," Von Blon said, without lowering his minatory gaze. "You don't realize what you've been saying."

I felt he would have expressed himself far more forcibly if strangers had not been present. But his words had their effect.

Sibella dropped her eyes, and a sudden change came over her. She covered her face with her hands, and her whole body shook with sobs.

"I'm—sorry. I was mad—and silly—to say such things."

"You'd better take Sibella to her room, Chester." Von Blon had resumed his professional tone. "This business has been too much for her."

The girl turned without another word and went out, followed by Chester.

"These modern women—all nerves," Von Blon commented laconically. Then he placed his hand on Ada's forehead. "Now, young lady, I'm going to give you something to make you sleep after all this excitement."

He had scarcely opened his medicine-case to prepare the draught when a shrill, complaining voice drifted clearly to us from the next room; and for the first time I noticed that the door of the little dressing-room which communicated with Mrs. Greene's quarters was slightly a jar.

"What's all the trouble now? Hasn't there been enough disturbance already without these noisy scenes in my very ear? But it doesn't matter, of course, how much *I* suffer. . . . Nurse! Shut those doors into Ada's room. You had no business to leave them open when you knew I was trying to get a little rest. You did it on purpose to annoy me. . . . And nurse! Tell the doctor I must see him before he goes. I have those stabbing pains in my spine again. But who thinks about me, lying here paralyzed——?"

The doors were closed softly, and the fretful voice was cut off from us.

"She could have had the doors closed a long time ago if she'd really wanted them closed," said Ada wearily, a look of distress on her drawn white face. "Why, Doctor Von, does she always pretend that every one deliberately makes her suffer?"

Von Blon sighed. "I've told you, Ada, that you mustn't take your mother's tantrums too seriously. Her irritability and complaining are part of her disease."

We bade the girl good-by, and the doctor walked with us into the hall.

"I'm afraid you didn't learn much," he remarked, almost apologetically. "It's most unfortunate Ada didn't get a look at her assailant." He addressed himself to Heath. "Did you, by the way, look in the dining-room wall-safe to make sure nothing was missing? You know, there's one there behind the big niello over the mantel."

"One of the first places we inspected." The Sergeant's voice was a bit disdainful. "And that reminds me, doc: I want to send a man up in the morning to look for finger-prints in Miss Ada's room."

Von Blon agreed amiably, and held out his hand to Markham.

"And if there's any way I can be of service to you or the police," he added pleasantly, "please call on me. I'll be only too glad to help. I don't see just what I can do, but one never knows."

Markham thanked him, and we descended to the lower hall. Sproot was waiting to help us with our coats, and a moment later we were in the District Attorney's car ploughing our way through the snowdrifts.

CHAPTER VII

VANCE ARGUES THE CASE

(Tuesday, November 9; 5 p. m.)

IT WAS nearly five o'clock when we reached the Criminal Courts Building. Swacker had lit the old bronze-and-china chandelier of Markham's private office, and an atmosphere of eerie gloom pervaded the room.

"Not a nice family, Markham old dear," sighed Vance, lying back in one of the deep leather-upholstered chairs. "Decidedly not a nice family. A family run to seed, its old vigor vitiated. If the heredit'ry sires of the contempor'ry Greenes could rise from their sepulchres and look in upon their present progeny, my word! what a jolly good shock they'd have! . . . Funny thing how these old families degenerate under the environment of ease and idleness. There are the Wittelsbachs, and the Romanoffs, and the Julian-Claudian house, and the Abbassid dynasty—all examples of phyletic disintegration. . . . And it's the same with nations, don't y' know. Luxury and unrestrained indulgence are corruptin' influences. Look at Rome under the soldier emperors, and Assyria under Sardanapalus, and Egypt under the later Ramessids, and the Vandal African empire under Gelimer. It's very distressin'."

"Your erudite observations might be highly absorbing to the social historian," grumbled Markham, with an undisguised show of irritability; "but I can't say they're particularly edifying, or even relevant, in the present circumstances."

"I wouldn't be too positive on that point," Vance returned easily. "In fact, I submit, for your earnest and profound consideration, the temperaments and internal relationships of the Greene clan, as pointers upon the dark road of the present investigation. . . . Really, y' know"—he assumed a humorsome tone—"it's most unfortunate that you and the Sergeant are so obsessed with the idea of social justice and that sort of thing; for society would be much better off if such families as the Greenes were exterminated. Still, it's a fascinatin' problem—most fascinatin'."

"I regret I can't share your enthusiasm for it." Markham spoke with asperity. "The crime strikes me as sordid and commonplace. And if it hadn't been for your interference I'd have sent Chester Greene on his way this morning with some tactful platitudes. But you had to intercede, with your cryptic innuendoes and mysterious head-waggings; and I foolishly let myself be drawn into it. Well, I trust you had an enjoyable afternoon. As for myself, I have three hours' accumulated work before me."

His complaint was an obvious suggestion that we take ourselves off; but Vance showed no intention of going.

"Oh, I sha'n't depart just yet," he announced, with a bantering smile. "I couldn't bring myself to leave you in your present state of grievous error. You need guidance, Markham; and I've quite made up my mind to pour out my flutterin' heart to you and the Sergeant."

Markham frowned. He understood Vance so well that he knew the other's levity was only superficial—that, indeed, it cloaked some particularly serious purpose. And the experience of a long, intimate friendship had taught him that Vance's actions—however unreasonable they might appear—were never the result of an idle whim.

"Very well," he acquiesced. "But I'd be grateful for an economy of words."

Vance sighed mournfully.

"Your attitude is so typical of the spirit of breathless speed existing in this restless day." He fixed an inquisitive gaze on Heath. "Tell me, Sergeant: you saw the body of Julia Greene, didn't you?"

"Sure, I saw it."

"Was her position in the bed a natural one?"

"How do I know how she generally laid in bed?" Heath was restive and in bad humor. "She was half sitting up, with a coupla pillows under her shoulders, and the covers pulled up."

"Nothing unusual about her attitude?"

"Not that I could see. There hadn't been a struggle, if that's what you mean."

"And her hands: were they outside or under the covers?"

Heath looked up, mildly astonished.

"They were outside. And, now that you mention it, they had a tight hold on the spread."

"Clutching it, in fact?"

"Well, yes."

Vance leaned forward quickly.

"And her face, Sergeant? Had she been shot in her sleep?"

"It didn't look that way. Her eyes were wide open, staring straight ahead."

"Her eyes were open and staring," repeated Vance, a note of

eagerness coming into his voice. "What would you say her expression indicated? Fear? Horror? Surprise?"

Heath regarded Vance shrewdly. "Well, it mighta been any one of 'em. Her mouth was open, like as if she was surprised at something."

"And she was clutching the spread with both hands." Vance's look drifted into space. Then slowly he rose and walked the length of the office and back, his head down. He halted in front of the District Attorney's desk, and leaned over, resting both hands on the back of a chair.

"Listen, Markham. There's something terrible and unthinkable going on in that house. No haphazard unknown assassin came in by the front door last night and shot down those two women. The crime was planned—thought out. Some one lay in wait—some one who knew his way about, knew where the light-switches were, knew when every one was asleep, knew when the servants had retired—knew just when and how to strike the blow. Some deep, awful motive lies behind that crime. There are depths beneath depths in what happened last night— obscure fetid chambers of the human soul. Black hatreds, unnatural desires, hideous impulses, obscene ambitions are at the bottom of it; and you are only playing into the murderer's hands when you sit back and refuse to see its significance."

His voice had a curious hushed quality, and it was difficult to believe that this was the habitually debonair and cynical Vance.

"That house is polluted, Markham. It's crumbling in decay— not material decay, perhaps, but a putrefaction far more terrible. The very heart and essence of that old house is rotting away. And all the inmates are rotting with it, disintegrating in spirit and mind and character. They've been polluted by the very atmosphere they've created. This crime, which you take so lightly, was inevitable in such a setting. I only wonder it was not more terrible, more vile. It marked one of the tertiary stages of the general dissolution of that abnormal establishment."

He paused, and extended his hand in a hopeless gesture.

"Think of the situation. That old, lonely, spacious house, exuding the musty atmosphere of dead generations, faded inside and out, run down, dingy, filled with ghosts of another day, standing there in its ill-kept grounds, lapped by the dirty waters of the river. . . . And then think of those six ill-sorted, restless, unhealthy beings compelled to live there in daily contact for a quarter of a century—such was old Tobias Greene's perverted idealism. And they've lived there, day in and day out, in that mouldy miasma of antiquity—unfit to meet the conditions of any alternative, too weak or too cowardly to strike out alone; held by an undermining security and a corrupting ease; growing to hate the very sight of one another, becoming bitter, spiteful, jealous, vicious; wearing down each other's nerves to the raw; consumed with resentment, aflame with hate, thinking evil—complaining, fighting, snarling. . . . Then, at last, the breaking-point—the logical, ineluctable figuration of all this self-feeding, ingrowing hatred."

"All of that is easy to understand," agreed Markham. "But, after all, your conclusion is wholly theoretic, not to say literary.— By what tangible links do you connect last night's shooting with the admittedly abnormal situation at the Greene mansion?"

"There are no tangible links—that's the horror of it. But the joinders are there, however shadowy. I began to sense them the minute I entered the house; and all this afternoon I was reaching for them blindly. But they eluded me at every turn. It was like a house of mazes and false passages and trapdoors and reeking oubliettes: nothing normal, nothing sane—a house in a nightmare, peopled by strange, abnormal creatures, each reflecting the subtle, monstrous horror that broke forth last night and went prowling about the old hallways. Didn't you sense it? Didn't you see the vague shape of this abomination continually flash out and disappear as we talked to these people and watched them battling against their own hideous thoughts and suspicions?"

Markham moved uneasily and straightened a pile of papers before him. Vance's unwonted gravity had affected him.

"I understand perfectly what you mean," he said. "But I don't see that your impressions bring us any nearer to a new theory of the crime. The Greene mansion is unhealthy—that's granted—and so, no doubt, are the people in it. But I'm afraid you've been oversusceptible to its atmosphere. You talk as if last night's crime were comparable to the poisoning orgies of the Borgias, or the Marquise de Brinvilliers affair, or the murder of Drusus and Germanicus, or the suffocation of the York princes in the Tower. I'll admit the setting is consonant with that sort of stealthy, romantic crime; but, after all, housebreakers and bandits are shooting people senselessly every week throughout the country, in very much the same way the two Greene women were shot."

"You're shutting your eyes to the facts, Markham," Vance declared earnestly. "You're overlooking several strange features of last night's crime—the horrified, astounded attitude of Julia at the moment of death; the illogical interval between the two shots; the fact that the lights were on in both rooms; Ada's story of that hand reaching for her; the absence of any signs of a forced entry——"

"What about those footprints in the snow?" interrupted Heath's matter-of-fact voice.

"What about them, indeed?" Vance wheeled about. "They're as incomprehensible as the rest of this hideous business. Some one walked to and from the house within a half-hour of the crime; but it was some one who knew he could get in quietly and without disturbing any one."

"There's nothing mysterious about that," asserted the practical Sergeant. "There are four servants in the house, and any one of 'em could've been in on the job."

Vance smiled ironically.

"And this accomplice in the house, who so generously opened the front door at a specified hour, failed to inform the intruder where the loot was, and omitted to acquaint him with the arrangement of the house; with the result that, once he was inside, he went astray, overlooked the dining-room, wandered up-stairs, went groping about the hall, got lost in the various bedrooms, had a seizure of panic, shot two women, turned on the lights by switches hidden behind the furniture, made his way down-stairs without a sound when Sproot was within a few feet of him, and walked out the front door to freedom! . . . A strange burglar, Sergeant. And an even stranger inside accomplice.—No; your explanation won't do—decidedly it won't do." He turned back to Markham. "And the only way you'll ever find the true explanation for those shootings is by understanding the unnatural situation that exists in the house itself."

"But we know the situation, Vance," Markham argued patiently. "I'll admit it's an unusual one. But it's not necessarily criminal. Antagonistic human elements are often thrown together; and a mutual hate is generated as a result. But mere hate is rarely a motive for murder; and it certainly does not constitute evidence of criminal activity."

"Perhaps not. But hatred and enforced propinquity may breed all manner of abnormalities—outrageous passions, abominable evils, devilish intrigues. And in the present case there are any number of curious and sinister facts that need explaining——"

"Ah! Now you're becoming more tangible. Just what are these facts that call for explanation?"

Vance lit a cigarette and sat down on the edge of the table.

"For instance, why did Chester Greene come here in the first place and solicit your help? Because of the disappearance of the gun? Maybe; but I doubt if it is the whole explanation. And what about the gun itself? Did it disappear? Or did Chester secrete it? Deuced queer about that gun. And Sibella said she saw it last week. But did she see it? We'll know a lot more about the case when we can trace the peregrinations of that revolver.— And why did Chester hear the first shot so readily, when Rex, in the next room to Ada's, says he failed to hear the second shot?— And that long interval between the two reports will need some explaining.—And there's Sproot—the multilingual butler who happened to be reading Martial—Martial, by all that's holy!— when the grim business took place, and came directly to the scene without meeting or hearing any one.—And just what significance attaches to the pious Hemming's oracular pronouncements about the Lord of hosts smiting the Greenes as he did the children of Babylon? She has some obscure religious notion in her head—which, after all, may not be so obscure.—And the German cook: there's a woman with, as we euphemistically say, a past. Despite her phlegmatic appearance, she's not of the servant class; yet she's been feeding the Greenes dutifully for over a dozen years. You recall her explanation of how she came to the Greenes? Her husband was a friend of old Tobias's; and Tobias gave orders she was to remain as cook as long as she desired. She needs explaining, Markham—and a dashed lot of it.—And Rex, with his projecting parietals and his wambly body and his periodic fits. Why did he get so excited when we questioned him? He certainly didn't act like an innocent and uncomprehending spectator of an attempted burglary.—And again I mention the lights. Who turned them on, and why? And in both rooms! In Julia's room *before* the shot was fired, for she evidently saw the assassin and understood his purpose; and in Ada's room, *after* the shooting! Those are facts which fairly shriek for explanation; for without an explanation they're mad, irrational, utterly incredible.—And why wasn't Von Blon at home in the middle of the night when Sproot phoned him? And how did it happen he nevertheless arrived so promptly? Coincidence? . . . And, by the by, Sergeant: was that double set of footprints like the single spoor of the doctor's?"

"There wasn't any way of telling. The snow was too flaky."

"It probably doesn't matter particularly, anyhow." Vance again faced Markham and resumed his recapitulation. "And then there are the points of difference in these two attacks. Julia was shot from the front when she was in bed, whereas Ada was shot in the back after she had risen from bed, although the murderer had ample time to go to her and take aim while she was still lying down. Why did he wait silently until the girl got up and approached him? How did he dare wait at all after he had killed Julia and alarmed the house? Does that strike you as panic? Or as cool-headedness?—And how did Julia's door come to be unlocked at that particular time? That's something I especially want clarified.—And perhaps you noticed, Markham, that Chester himself went to summon Sibella to the interview in the drawing-room, and that he remained with her a considerable time. Why, now, did he send Sproot for Rex, and fetch Sibella personally? And why the delay? I yearn for an explanation of what passed between them before they eventually appeared.—And why was Sibella so definite that there wasn't a burglar, and yet so evasive when we asked her to suggest a counter-theory? What underlay her satirical frankness when she held up each member of the Greene household, including herself, as a possible suspect?—And then there are the details of Ada's story. Some of them are amazing, incomprehensible, almost fabulous. There was no apparent sound in the room; yet she was conscious of a menacing presence. And that outstretched hand and the shuffling footsteps—we simply must have an explanation of those things. And her hesitancy about saying whether she thought it was a man or a woman; and Sibella's evident belief that the girl thought it was she. That wants explaining, Markham.—And Sibella's hysterical accusation against Ada. What lay behind that?—And don't forget that curious scene between Sibella and Von Blon when he reproached her for her outburst. That was devilish odd. There's some intimacy there—*ça saute aux yeux.* You noticed how she obeyed him. And you doubtless observed, too, that Ada is rather fond of the doctor: snuggled up to him figuratively during the performance, opened her eyes on him wistfully, looked to him for protection. Oh, our little Ada has flutterings in his direction. And yet he adopts the hovering professional-bedside manner of a high-priced medico toward her, whereas he treats Sibella very much as Chester might if he had the courage."

Vance inhaled deeply on his cigarette.

"Yes, Markham, there are many things that must be satisfactorily accounted for before I can believe in your hypothetical burglar."

Markham sat for a while, engrossed in his thoughts.

"I've listened to your Homeric catalogue, Vance," he said at length, "but I can't say that it inflames me. You've suggested a number of interesting possibilities, and raised several points that might bear looking into. However, the only potential weight of your argument lies in an accumulation of items which, taken separately, are not particularly impressive. A plausible answer might be found for each one of them. The trouble is, the integers of your summary are without a connecting thread, and consequently must be regarded as separate units."

"That legal mind of yours!" Vance rose and paced up and down. "An accumulation of queer and unexplained facts centring about a crime is no more impressive than each separate item in the total! Well, well! I give up. I renounce all reason. I fold up my tent like the Arabs and as silently steal away." He took up his coat. "I leave you to your fantastic, delirious burglar, who walks without keys into a house and steals nothing, who knows where electric switches are hidden but can't find a staircase, who shoots women and then turns up the lights. When you find him, my dear Lycurgus, you should, in all humaneness, send him to the psychopathic ward. He's quite unaccountable, I assure you."

Markham, despite his opposition, had not been unimpressed. Vance unquestionably had undermined to some extent his belief in a housebreaker. But I could readily understand why he was reluctant to abandon this theory until it had been thoroughly tested. His next words, in fact, explained his attitude.

"I'm not denying the remote possibility that this affair may go deeper than appears. But there's too little to go on at present to warrant an investigation along other than routine lines. We can't very well stir up an ungodly scandal by raking the members of a prominent family over the coals, when there's not a scintilla of evidence against any one of them. It's too unjust and dangerous a proceeding. We must at least wait until the police have finished their investigation. Then, if nothing develops, we can again take inventory and decide how to proceed. . . . How long, Sergeant, do you figure on being busy?"

Heath took his cigar from his mouth and regarded it thoughtfully.

"That's hard to say, sir. Dubois'll finish up his finger-printing to-morrow, and we're checking up on the regulars as fast as we can. Also, I've got two men digging up the records of the Greene servants. It may take a lot of time, and it may go quick. Depends on the breaks we get."

Vance sighed.

"And it was such a neat, fascinatin' crime! I've rather been looking forward to it, don't y' know, and now you talk of prying into the early amours of serving-maids and that sort of thing. It's most disheartenin'."

He buttoned his ulster about him and walked to the door.

"Ah, well, there's nothing for me to do while you Jasons are launched on your quaint quest. I think I'll retire and resume my translation of Delacroix's 'Journal.'"

But Vance was not destined then to finish this task he had had in mind so long. Three days later the front pages of the country's press carried glaring head-lines telling of a second grim and unaccountable tragedy at the old Greene mansion, which altered the entire character of the case and immediately lifted it into the realm of the foremost *causes célèbres* of modern times. After this second blow had fallen all ideas of a casual burglar were banished. There could no longer be any doubt that a hidden death-dealing horror stalked through the dim corridors of that fated house.

CHAPTER VIII

THE SECOND TRAGEDY

(Friday, November 12; 8 a. m.)

THE DAY after we had taken leave of Markham at his office the rigor of the weather suddenly relaxed. The sun came out, and the thermometer rose nearly thirty degrees. Toward night of the second day, however, a fine, damp snow began to fall, spreading a thin white blanket over the city; but around eleven the skies were again clear.

I mention these facts because they had a curious bearing on the second crime at the Greene mansion. Footprints again appeared on the front walk; and, as a result of the clinging softness of the snow, the police also found tracks in the lower hall and on the marble stairs.

Vance had spent Wednesday and Thursday in his library reading desultorily and checking Vollard's catalogue of Cézanne's water-colors. The three-volume edition of the "Journal de Eugène Delacroix"* lay on his writing-table; but I noticed that he did not so much as open it. He was restless and distracted, and his long silences at dinner (which we ate together in the living-room be-

---

* E. Plon, Nourrit et Cie., Paris, 1893.

fore the great log fire) told me only too clearly that something was perturbing him. Moreover, he had sent notes cancelling several social engagements, and had given orders to Currie, his valet and domestic factotum, that he was "out" to callers.

As he sat sipping his cognac at the end of dinner on Thursday night, his eyes idly tracing the forms in the Renoir *Beigneuse* above the mantel, he gave voice to his thoughts.

"'Pon my word, Van, I can't shake the atmosphere of that damnable house. Markham is probably right in refusing to take the matter seriously—one can't very well chivy a bereaved family simply because I'm oversensitive. And yet"—he shook himself slightly—"it's most annoyin'. Maybe I'm becoming weak and emotional. What if I should suddenly go in for Whistlers and Böcklins! Could you endure it? *Miserere nostri!* . . . No, it won't come to that. But—dash it all!—that Greene murder is haunting my slumbers like a lamia. And the business isn't over yet. There's a horrible incompleteness about what's already occurred. . . ."

It was scarcely eight o'clock on the following morning when Markham brought us the news of the second Greene tragedy. I had risen early, and was having my coffee in the library when Markham came in, brushing past the astonished Currie with only a curt nod.

"Get Vance out right away—will you, Van Dine?" he began, without even a word of greeting. "Something serious has happened."

I hastened to fetch Vance, who grumblingly slipped into a camel's-hair dressing-gown and came leisurely into the library.

"My dear Markham!" he reproached the District Attorney. "Why pay your social calls in the middle of the night?"

"This isn't a social call," Markham told him tartly. "Chester Greene has been murdered."

"Ah!" Vance rang for Currie, and lighted a cigarette. "Coffee for two and clothes for one," he ordered, when the man appeared. Then he sank into a chair before the fire and gave Markham a waggish look. "That same unique burglar, I suppose. A perseverin' lad. Did the family plate disappear this time?"

Markham gave a mirthless laugh.

"No, the plate's intact; and I think we can now eliminate the burglar theory. I'm afraid your premonitions were correct—damn your uncanny faculty!"

"Pour out your heart-breakin' story." Vance, for all his levity, was extraordinarily interested. His moodiness of the past two days had given way to an almost eager alertness.

"It was Sproot who phoned the news to Headquarters a little before midnight. The operator in the Homicide Bureau caught Heath at home, and the Sergeant was at the Greene house inside of half an hour. He's there now—phoned me at seven this morning. I told him I'd hurry out, so I didn't get many details over the wire. All I know is that Chester Greene was fatally shot last night at almost the exact hour that the former shootings occurred—a little after half past eleven."

"Was he in his own room at the time?" Vance was pouring the coffee which Currie had brought in.

"I believe Heath did mention he was found in his bedroom."

"Shot from the front?"

"Yes, through the heart, at very close range."

"Very interestin'. A duplication of Julia's death, as it were." Vance became reflective. "So the old house has claimed another victim. But why Chester? . . . Who found him, incidentally?"

"Sibella, I think Heath said. Her room, you remember, is next to Chester's; and the shot probably roused her. But we'd better be going."

"Am I invited?"

"I wish you would come." Markham made no effort to hide his desire to have the other accompany him.

"Oh, I had every intention of doing so, don't y' know." And Vance left the room abruptly to get dressed.

It took the District Attorney's car but a few minutes to reach the Greene mansion from Vance's house in East 38th Street. A patrolman stood guard outside the great iron gates, and a plain-clothes man lounged on the front steps beneath the arched doorway.

Heath was in the drawing-room talking earnestly to Inspector Moran, who had just arrived; and two men from the Homicide Bureau stood by the window awaiting orders. The house was peculiarly silent: no member of the family was to be seen.

The Sergeant came forward at once. His usual ruddiness of complexion was gone and his eyes were troubled. He shook hands with Markham, and then gave Vance a look of friendly welcome.

"You had the right dope, Mr. Vance. Somebody's ripping things wide open here; and it isn't swag they're after."

Inspector Moran joined us, and again the handshaking ceremony took place.

"This case is going to stir things up considerably," he said. "And we're in for an unholy scandal if we don't clean it up quickly."

The worried look in Markham's eyes deepened.

"The sooner we get to work, then, the better. Are you going to lend a hand, Inspector?"

"There's no need, I think," Moran answered quietly. "I'll leave the police end entirely with Sergeant Heath; and now that you—and Mr. Vance—are here, I'd be of no use." He gave Vance a pleasant smile, and made his adieus. "Keep in touch with me, Sergeant, and use all the men you want."*

When he had gone Heath gave us the details of the crime.

At about half past eleven, after the family and the servants had retired, the shot was fired. Sibella was reading in bed at the time and heard it distinctly. She rose immediately and, after listening for several moments, stole up the servants' stairs—the entrance to which was but a few feet from her door. She wakened the butler, and the two of them then went to Chester's room. The door was unlocked, and the lights in the room were burning. Chester Greene was sitting, slightly huddled, in a chair near the desk. Sproot went to him, but saw that he was dead, and immediately left the room, locking the door. He then telephoned to the police and to Doctor Von Blon.

"I got here before Von Blon did," Heath explained. "The doctor was out again when the butler phoned, and didn't get the message till nearly one o'clock. I was damn glad of it, because it gave me a chance to check up on the footprints outside. The minute I turned in at the gate I could see that somebody had come and gone, the same as last time; and I whistled for the man on the beat to guard the entrance until Snitkin arrived. Then I came on in, keeping along the edge of the walk; and the first thing I noticed when the butler opened the door was a little puddle of water on the rug in the hall. Somebody had recently tracked the soft snow in. I found a coupla other puddles in the hall, and there were some wet imprints on the steps leading up-stairs . Five minutes later Snitkin gave me the signal from the street, and I put him to work on the footprints outside. The

---

* Inspector William M. Moran, who died last summer, had been the commanding officer of the Detective Bureau for eight years. He was a man of rare and unusual qualities, and with his death the New York Police Department lost one of its most efficient and trustworthy officials. He had formerly been a well-known up-State banker who had been forced to close his doors during the 1907 panic.

tracks were plain, and Snitkin was able to get some pretty accurate measurements."

After Snitkin had been put to work on the footprints, the Sergeant, it seemed, went up-stairs to Chester's room and made an examination. But he found nothing unusual, aside from the murdered man in the chair, and after half an hour descended again to the dining-room, where Sibella and Sproot were waiting. He had just begun his questioning of them when Doctor Von Blon arrived.

"I took him up-stairs," said Heath, "and he looked at the body. He seemed to want to stick around, but I told him he'd be in the way. So he talked to Miss Greene out in the hall for five or ten minutes, and then left."

Shortly after Doctor Von Blon's departure two other men from the Homicide Bureau arrived, and the next two hours were spent in interrogating the members of the household. But nobody, except Sibella, admitted even hearing the shot. Mrs. Greene was not questioned. When Miss Craven, the nurse, who slept on the third floor, was sent in to her, she reported that the old lady was sleeping soundly; and the Sergeant decided not to disturb her. Nor was Ada awakened: according to the nurse, the girl had been asleep since nine o'clock.

Rex Greene, however, when interviewed, contributed one vague and, as it seemed, contradictory bit of evidence. He had been lying awake, he said, at the time the snowfall ceased, which was a little after eleven. Then, about ten minutes later, he had imagined he heard a faint shuffling noise in the hall and the sound of a door closing softly. He had thought nothing of it, and only recalled it when pressed by Heath. A quarter of an hour afterward he had looked at his watch. It was then twenty-five minutes past eleven; and very soon after that he had fallen asleep.

"The only queer thing about his story," commented Heath, "is the time. If he's telling the tale straight, he heard this noise and the door shutting twenty minutes or so before the shot was fired. And nobody in the house was up at that time. I tried to shake him on the question of the exact hour, but he stuck to it like a leech. I compared his watch with mine, and it was O. K. Anyhow, there's nothing much to the story. The wind mighta blown a door shut, or he mighta heard a noise out in the street and thought it was in the hall."

"Nevertheless, Sergeant," put in Vance, "if I were you I'd file Rex's story away for future meditation. Somehow it appeals to me."

Heath looked up sharply and was about to ask a question; but he changed his mind and said merely: "It's filed." Then he finished his report to Markham.

After interrogating the occupants of the house he had gone back to the Bureau, leaving his men on guard, and set the machinery of his office in operation. He had returned to the Greene mansion early that morning, and was now waiting for the Medical Examiner, the finger-print experts, and the official photographer. He had given orders for the servants to remain in their quarters, and had instructed Sproot to serve breakfast to all the members of the family in their own rooms.

"This thing's going to take work, sir," he concluded. "And it's going to be touchy going, too."

Markham nodded gravely, and glanced toward Vance, whose eyes were resting moodily on an old oil-painting of Tobias Greene.

"Does this new development help co-ordinate any of your former impressions?" he asked.

"It at least substantiates the feeling I had that this old house reeks with a deadly poison," Vance replied. "This thing is like a witches' sabbath." He gave Markham a humorous smile. "I'm beginning to think your task is going to take on the nature of exorcising devils."

Markham grunted.

"I'll leave the magic potions to you. . . . Sergeant, suppose we take a look at the body before the Medical Examiner gets here."

Heath led the way without a word. When we reached the head of the stairs he took a key from his pocket and unlocked the door of Chester's room. The electric lights were still burning—sickly yellow disks in the gray daylight which filtered in from the windows above the river.

The room, long and narrow, contained an anachronistic assortment of furniture. It was a typical man's apartment, with an air of comfortable untidiness. Newspapers and sports magazines cluttered the table and desk; ash-trays were everywhere; an open cellaret stood in one corner; and a collection of golf-clubs lay on the tapestried Chesterfield. The bed, I noticed, had not been slept in.

In the centre of the room, beneath an old-fashioned cut-glass chandelier, was a Chippendale "knee-hole" desk, beside which stood a sleepy-hollow chair. It was in this chair that the body of Chester Greene, clad in dressing-gown and slippers, reclined. He was slumped a little forward, the head turned slightly back and resting against the tufted upholstery. The light from the chandelier cast a spectral illumination on his face; and the sight of it laid a spell of horror on me. The eyes, normally prominent, now seemed to be protruding from their sockets in a stare of unutterable amazement; and the sagging chin and flabby parted lips intensified this look of terrified wonder.

Vance was studying the dead man's features intently.

"Would you say, Sergeant," he asked, without looking up, "that Chester and Julia saw the same thing as they passed from this world?"

Heath coughed uneasily.

"Well," he admitted, "something surprised them, and that's a fact."

"Surprised them! Sergeant, you should thank your Maker that you are not cursed with an imagination. The whole truth of this fiendish business lies in those bulbous eyes and that gaping mouth. Unlike Ada, both Julia and Chester saw the thing that menaced them; and it left them stunned and aghast."

"Well, we can't get any information outa *them.*" Heath's practicality as usual was uppermost.

"Not oral information, certainly. But, as Hamlet put it, murder, though it have no tongue, will speak with most miraculous organ."

"Come, come, Vance. Be tangible." Markham spoke with acerbity. "What's in your mind?"

"'Pon my word, I don't know. It's too vague." He leaned over and picked up a small book from the floor just beneath where the dead man's hand hung over the arm of the chair. "Chester apparently was immersed in literature at the time of his taking off." He opened the book casually. "'Hydrotherapy and Constipation.' Yes, Chester was just the kind to worry about his colon. Some one probably told him that intestinal stasis interfered with the proper stance. He's no doubt clearing the asphodel from the Elysian fields at the present moment preparat'ry to laying out a golf-course."

He became suddenly serious.

"You see what this book means, Markham? Chester was sitting here reading when the murderer came in. Yet he did not so much as rise or call out. Furthermore, he let the intruder stand directly in front of him. He did not even lay down his book, but sat back in his chair relaxed. Why? Because the murderer was some one Chester knew—and trusted! And when the gun was suddenly brought forth and pointed at his heart, he was too astounded to move. And in that second of bewilderment and unbelief the trigger was pulled and the bullet entered his heart."

Markham nodded slowly, in deep perplexity, and Heath studied the attitude of the dead man more closely.

"That's a good theory," the Sergeant conceded finally. "Yes, he musta let the bird get right on top of him without suspecting anything. Same like Julia did."

"Exactly, Sergeant. The two murders constitute a most suggestive parallel."

"Still and all, there's one point you're overlooking." Heath's brow was roughened in a troubled frown. "Chester's door mighta been unlocked last night, seeing as he hadn't gone to bed, and so this person coulda walked in without any trouble. But Julia, now, was already undressed and in bed; and she always locked her door at night. Now, how would you say this person with the gun got into Julia's room, Mr. Vance?"

"There's no difficulty about that. Let us say, as a tentative hypothesis, that Julia had disrobed, switched off the lights, and climbed into her queenly bed. Then came a tap on the door—perhaps a tap she recognized. She rose, put on the lights, opened the door, and again repaired to her bed for warmth while she held parley with her visitor. Maybe—who knows?—the visitor sat on the edge of the bed during the call. Then suddenly the visitor produced the revolver and fired, and made a hurried exit, forgetting to switch the lights off. Such a theory—though I don't insist on the details—would square neatly with my idea regarding Chester's caller."

"It may've been like you say," admitted Heath dubiously. "But why all the hocus-pocus when it came to shooting Ada? That job was done in the dark."

"The rationalistic philosophers tell us, Sergeant"—Vance became puckishly pedantic—"that there's a reason for everything, but that the finite mind is woefully restricted. The altered technic of our elusive culprit when dealing with Ada is one of the things that is obscure. But you've touched a vital point. If we could discover the reason for this reversal of our *inconnu's* homicidal tactics, I believe we'd be a lot forrader in our investigation."

Heath made no reply. He stood in the centre of the room running his eye over the various objects and pieces of furniture. Presently he stepped to the clothes-closet, pulled open the door, and turned on a pendant electric light just inside. As he stood gloomily peering at the closet's contents there was a sound of heavy footsteps in the hall and Snitkin appeared in the open door. Heath turned and, without giving his assistant time to speak, asked gruffly:

"How did you make out with those footprints?"

"Got all the dope here." Snitkin crossed to the Sergeant, and held out a long Manila envelope. "There wasn't no trouble in checking the measurements and cutting the patterns. But they're not going to be a hell of a lot of good, I'm thinking. There's ten million guys more or less in this country who coulda made 'em."

Heath had opened the envelope and drawn forth a thin white cardboard pattern which looked like an inner sole of a shoe.

"It wasn't no pigmy who made this print," he remarked.

"That's the catch in it," explained Snitkin "The size don't mean nothing much, for it ain't a shoe-track. Those footprints were made by galoshes, and there's no telling how much bigger they were than the guy's foot. They mighta been worn over a

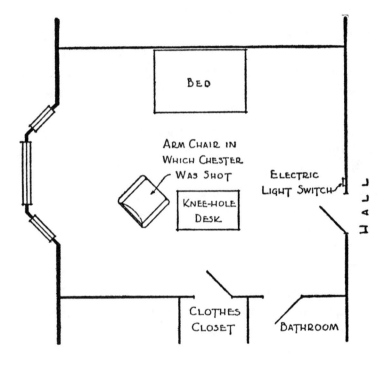

CHESTER'S BEDROOM.

shoe anywheres from a size eight to a size ten, and with a width anywheres from an A to a D."

Heath nodded with obvious disappointment.

"You're sure about 'em being galoshes?" He was reluctant to let what promised to be a valuable clew slip away.

"You can't get around it. The rubber tread was distinct in several places, and the shallow, scooped heel stood out plain as day. Anyhow, I got Jerym* to check up on my findings."

Snitkin's gaze wandered idly to the floor of the clothes-closet.

"Those are the kind of things that made the tracks." He pointed to a pair of high arctics which had been thrown carelessly under a boot-shelf. Then he leaned over and picked up one of them. As his eye rested on it he gave a grunt. "This looks like the size, too." He took the pattern from the Sergeant's hand and laid it on the sole of the overshoe. It fitted as perfectly as if the two had been cut simultaneously.

Heath was startled out of his depression.

"Now, what in hell does that mean!"

Markham had drawn near.

"It might indicate, of course, that Chester went out somewhere last night late."

"But that don't make sense, sir," objected Heath. "If he'd wanted anything at that hour of the night he'd have sent the butler. And, anyway, the shops in this neighborhood were all closed by that time, for the tracks weren't made till after it had stopped snowing at eleven."

"And," supplemented Snitkin, "you can't tell by the tracks

---

* Captain Anthony P. Jerym was one of the shrewdest and most painstaking criminologists of the New York Police Department. Though he had begun his career as an expert in the Bertillon system of measurements, he later specialized in footprints—a subject which he had helped to elevate to an elaborate and complicated science. He had spent several years in Vienna studying Austrian methods, and had developed a means of scientific photography for footprints which gave him rank with such men as Londe, Burais, and Reiss.

whether the guy that made 'em left the house and came back, or came to the house and went away, for there wasn't a single print on top of the other."

Vance was standing at the window looking out.

"That, now, is a most interestin' point, Sergeant," he commented. "I'd file it away along with Rex's story for prayerful consideration." He sauntered back to the desk and looked at the dead man thoughtfully. "No, Sergeant," he continued; "I can't picture Chester donning gum-shoes and sneaking out into the night on a mysterious errand. I'm afraid we'll have to find another explanation for those footprints."

"It's damn funny, just the same, that they should be the exact size of these galoshes."

"If," submitted Markham, "the footprints were not Chester's, then we're driven to the assumption that the murderer made them."

Vance slowly took out his cigarette-case.

"Yes," he agreed, "I think we may safely assume that."

CHAPTER IX

THE THREE BULLETS

(Friday, November 12; 9 a. m.)

At this moment Doctor Doremus, the Medical Examiner, a brisk, nervous man with a jaunty air, was ushered in by one of the detectives I had seen in the drawing-room. He blinked at the company, threw his hat and coat on a chair, and shook hands with every one.

"What are your friends trying to do, Sergeant?" he asked, eying the inert body in the chair. "Wipe out the whole family?" Without waiting for an answer to his grim pleasantry he went to the windows and threw up the shades with a clatter. "You gentlemen all through viewing the remains? If so, I'll get to work."

"Go to it," said Heath. Chester Greene's body was lifted to the bed and straightened out. "And how about the bullet, doc? Any chance of getting it before the autopsy?"

"How'm I going to get it without a probe and forceps? I ask you!" Doctor Doremus drew back the matted dressing-gown and inspected the wound. "But I'll see what I can do." Then he straightened up and cocked his eye facetiously at the Sergeant. "Well, I'm waiting for your usual query about the time of death."

"We know it."

"Hah! Wish you always did. This fixing the exact time by looking over a body is all poppycock anyway. The best we fellows can do is to approximate it. *Rigor mortis* works differently in different people. Don't ever take me too seriously, Sergeant, when I set an exact hour for you.—However, let's see. . . ."

He ran his hands over the body on the bed, unflexed the fingers, moved the head, and put his eye close to the coagulated blood about the wound. Then he teetered on his toes, and squinted at the ceiling.

"How about ten hours? Say, between eleven-thirty and midnight. How's that?"

Heath laughed good-naturedly.

"You hit it, doc—right on the head."

"Well, well! Always was a good guesser." Doctor Doremus seemed wholly indifferent.

Vance had followed Markham into the hall.

"An honest fellow, that archiater of yours. And to think he's a public servant of our beneficent government!"

"There are many honest men in public office," Markham reproved him.

"I know," sighed Vance. "Our democracy is still young. Give it time."

Heath joined us, and at the same moment the nurse appeared at Mrs. Greene's door. A querulous dictatorial voice issued from the depths of the room behind her.

" . . . And you tell whoever's in charge that I want to see him—right away, do you understand! It's an outrage, all this commotion and excitement, with me lying here in pain trying to get a little rest. Nobody shows me any consideration."

Heath made a grimace and looked toward the stairs; but Vance took Markham's arm.

"Come, let's cheer up the old lady."

As we entered the room, Mrs. Greene, propped up as usual in bed with a prismatic assortment of pillows, drew her shawl primly about her.

"Oh, it's you, is it?" she greeted us, her expression moderating. "I thought it was those abominable policemen making free with my house again. . . . What's the meaning of all this disturbance, Mr. Markham? Nurse tells me that Chester has been shot. Dear, dear! If people must do such things, why do they have to come to my house and annoy a poor helpless old woman like me? There are plenty of other places they could do their shooting in." She appeared deeply resentful at the fact that the murderer should have been so inconsiderate as to choose the Greene mansion for his depredations. "But I've come to expect this sort of thing. Nobody thinks of *my* feelings. And if my own children see fit to do everything they can to annoy me, why should I expect total strangers to show me any consideration?"

"When one is bent on murder, Mrs. Greene," rejoined Markham, stung by her callousness, "one doesn't stop to think of the mere inconvenience his crime may cause others."

"I suppose not," she murmured self-pityingly. "But it's all the fault of my children. If they were what children ought to be, people wouldn't be breaking in here trying to murder them."

"And unfortunately succeeding," added Markham coldly.

"Well, that can't be helped." She suddenly became bitter. "It's their punishment for the way they've treated their poor old mother, lying here for ten long years, hopelessly paralyzed. And do you think they try to make it easy for me? No! Here I must stay, day after day, suffering agonies with my spine; and they never give me a thought." A sly look came into her fierce old eyes. "But they think about me sometimes. Oh, yes! They think how nice it would be if I were out of the way. Then they'd get all my money. . . ."

"I understand, madam," Markham put in abruptly, "that you were asleep last night at the time your son met his death."

"Was I? Well, maybe I was. It's a wonder, though, that some one didn't leave my door open just so I'd be disturbed."

"And you know no one who would have any reason to kill your son?"

"How should I know? Nobody tells me anything. I'm a poor neglected, lonely old cripple. . . ."

"Well, we won't bother you any further, Mrs. Greene." Markham's tone held something both of sympathy and consternation.

As we descended the stairs the nurse reopened the door we had just closed after us, and left it ajar, no doubt in response to an order from her patient.

"Not at all a nice old lady," chuckled Vance, as we entered the drawing-room. "For a moment, Markham, I thought you were going to box her ears."

"I admit I felt like it. And yet I couldn't help pitying her. However, such utter self-concentration as hers saves one a lot of mental anguish. She seems to regard this whole damnable business as a plot to upset her."

Sproot appeared obsequiously at the door.

"May I bring you gentlemen some coffee?" No emotion of any kind showed on his graven wrinkled face. The events of the past few days seemed not to have affected him in any degree.

"No, we don't want coffee, Sproot," Markham told him brusquely. "But please be good enough to ask Miss Sibella if she will come here."

"Very good, sir."

The old man shuffled away, and a few minutes later Sibella strolled in, smoking a cigarette, one hand in the pocket of her vivid-green sweater-jacket. Despite her air of nonchalance her face was pale, its whiteness contrasting strongly with the deep crimson rouge on her lips. Her eyes, too, were slightly haggard; and when she spoke her voice sounded forced, as if she were playing a role against which her spirit was at odds. She greeted us blithely enough, however.

"Good morning, one and all. Beastly auspices for a social call." She sat down on the arm of a chair and swung one leg restlessly. "Some one certainly has a grudge against us Greenes. Poor old Chet! He didn't even die with his boots on. Felt bedroom slippers! What an end for an outdoor enthusiast!—Well, I suppose I'm invited here to tell my story. Where do I begin?" She rose, and throwing her half-burned cigarette into the grate, seated herself in a straight-backed chair facing Markham, folding her sinewy, tapering hands on the table before her.

Markham studied her for several moments.

"You were awake last night, reading in bed, I understand, when the shot was fired in your brother's room."

"Zola's 'Nana,' to be explicit. Mother told me I shouldn't read it; so I got it at once. It was frightfully disappointing, though."

"And just what did you do after you heard the report?" continued Markham, striving to control his annoyance at the girl's flippancy.

"I put my book down, got up, donned a kimono, and listened for several minutes at the door. Not hearing anything further, I peeked out. The hall was dark, and the silence felt a bit spooky. I knew I ought to go to Chet's room and inquire, in a sisterly fashion, about the explosion; but, to tell you the truth, Mr. Markham, I was rather cowardly. So I went—oh, well, let the truth prevail: I *ran* up the servants' stairs and routed out our Admirable Crichton; and together we investigated. Chet's door was unlocked, and the fearless Sproot opened it. There sat Chet, looking as if he'd seen a ghost; and somehow I knew he was dead. Sproot went in and touched him, while I waited; and then we went down to the dining-room. Sproot did some phoning, and afterward made me some atrocious coffee. A half-hour or so later this gentleman"—she inclined her head toward Heath—"arrived, looking distressingly glum, and very sensibly refused a cup of Sproot's coffee."

"And you heard no sound of any kind before the shot?"

"Not a thing. Everybody had gone to bed early. The last sound I heard in this house was mother's gentle and affectionate voice telling the nurse she was as neglectful as the rest of us, and to bring her morning tea at nine sharp, and not to slam the door the way she always did. Then peace and quiet reigned until half past eleven, when I heard the shot in Chet's room."

"How long was this interregnum of quietude?" asked Vance.

"Well, mother generally ends her daily criticism of the family around ten-thirty; so I'd say the quietude lasted about an hour."

"And during that time you do not recall hearing a slight shuffling sound in the hall? Or a door closing softly?"

The girl shook her head indifferently, and took another cigarette from a small amber case she carried in her sweater-pocket.

"Sorry, but I didn't. That doesn't mean, though, that people couldn't have been shuffling and shutting doors all over the place. My room's at the rear, and the noises on the river and in

52d Street drown out almost anything that's going on in the front of the house."

Vance had gone to her and held a match to her cigarette.

"I say, you don't seem in the least worried."

"Oh, why worry?" She made a gesture of resignation. "If anything is to happen to me, it'll happen, whatever I do. But I don't anticipate an immediate demise. No one has the slightest reason for killing me—unless, of course, it's some of my former bridge partners. But they're all harmless persons who wouldn't be apt to take extreme measures."

"Still"—Vance kept his tone inconsequential—"no one apparently had any reason for harming your two sisters or your brother."

"On that point I couldn't be altogether lucid. We Greenes don't confide in one another. There's a beastly spirit of distrust in this ancestral domain. We all lie to each other on general principles. And as for secrets! Each member of the family is a kind of Masonic Order in himself. Surely there's some reason for all these shootings. I simply can't imagine any one indulging himself in this fashion for the mere purpose of pistol practice."

She smoked a moment pensively, and went on:

"Yes, there must be a motive back of it all—though for the life of me I can't suggest one. Of course Julia was a vinegary, unpleasant person, but she went out very little, and worked off her various complexes on the family. And yet, she may have been leading a double life for all I know. When these sour old maids break loose from their inhibitions I understand they do the most utterly utter things. But I just can't bring my mind to picture Julia with a bevy of jealous Romeos." She made a comical grimace at the thought. "Ada, on the other hand, is what we used to call in algebra an unknown quantity. No one but dad knew where she came from, and he would never tell. To be sure, she doesn't get much time to run around—mother keeps her too busy. But she's young and good-looking in a common sort of way"—there was a tinge of venom in this remark—"and you can't tell what connections she may have formed outside the sacred portals of the Greene mansion.—As for Chet, no one seemed to love him passionately. I never heard anybody say a good word for him but the golf pro at the club, and that was only because Chet tipped him like a *parvenu*. He had a genius for antagonizing people. Several motives for the shooting might be found in his past."

"I note that you've changed your ideas considerably in regard to the culpability of Miss Ada." Vance spoke incuriously.

Sibella looked a little shamefaced.

"I did get a bit excited, didn't I?" Then a defiance came into her voice. "But just the same, she doesn't belong here. And she's a sneaky little cat. She'd dearly love to see us all nicely murdered. The only person that seems to like her is cook; but then, Gertrude's a sentimental German who likes everybody. She feeds half the stray cats and dogs in the neighborhood. Our rear yard is a regular pound in summer."

Vance was silent for a while. Suddenly he looked up.

"I gather from your remarks, Miss Greene, that you now regard the shootings as the acts of some one from the outside."

"Does any one think anything else?" she asked, with startled anxiety. "I understand there were footprints in the snow both times we were visited. Surely they would indicate an outsider."

"Quite true," Vance assured her, a bit overemphatically, obviously striving to allay whatever fears his queries may have aroused in her. "Those footprints undeniably indicate that the intruder entered each time by the front door."

"And you are not to have any uneasiness about the future, Miss Greene," added Markham. "I shall give orders to-day to have a strict guard placed over the house, front and rear, until there is no longer the slightest danger of a recurrence of what has taken place here."

Heath nodded his unqualified approbation.

"I'll arrange for that, sir. There'll be two men guarding this place day and night from now on."

"How positively thrilling!" exclaimed Sibella; but I noticed a strange reservation of apprehension in her eyes.

"We won't detain you any longer, Miss Greene," said Markham, rising. "But I'd greatly appreciate it if you would remain in your room until our inquiries here are over. You may, of course, visit your mother."

"Thanks awf'ly, but I think I'll indulge in a little lost beauty sleep." And she left us with a friendly wave of the hand.

"Who do you want to see next, Mr. Markham?" Heath was on his feet, vigorously relighting his cigar.

But before Markham could answer Vance lifted his hand for silence, and leaned forward in a listening attitude.

"Oh, Sproot!" he called. "Step in here a moment."

The old butler appeared at once, calm and subservient, and waited with a vacuously expectant expression.

"Really, y' know," said Vance, "there's not the slightest need for you to hover solicitously amid the draperies of the hallway while we're busy in here. Most considerate and loyal of you; but if we want you for anything we'll ring."

"As you desire, sir."

Sproot started to go, but Vance halted him.

"Now that you're here you might answer one or two questions."

"Very good, sir."

"First, I want you to think back very carefully, and tell me if you observed anything unusual when you locked up the house last night."

"Nothing, sir," the man answered promptly. "If I had, I would have mentioned it to the police this morning."

"And did you hear any noise or movement of any kind after you had gone to your room? A door closing, for instance?"

"No, sir. Everything was very quiet."

"And what time did you actually go to sleep?"

"I couldn't say exactly, sir. Perhaps about twenty minutes past eleven, if I may venture to make a guess."

"And were you greatly surprised when Miss Sibella woke you up and told you a shot had been fired in Mr. Chester's room?"

"Well, sir," Sproot admitted, "I was somewhat astonished, though I endeavored to conceal my emotions."

"And doubtless succeeded admirably," said Vance dryly. "But what I meant was this: did you not anticipate something of the kind happening again in this house, after the other shootings?"

He watched the old butler sharply, but the man's lineaments were as arid as a desert and as indecipherable as an expanse of sea.

"If you will pardon me, sir, for saying so, I don't know precisely what you mean," came the colorless answer. "Had I anticipated that Mr. Chester was to be done in, so to speak, I most certainly would have warned him. It would have been my duty, sir."

"Don't evade my question, Sproot." Vance spoke sternly. "I asked you if you had any idea that a second tragedy might follow the first."

"Tragedies very seldom come singly, sir, if I may be permitted to say so. One never knows what will happen next. I try not to anticipate the workings of fate, but I strive to hold myself in readiness——"

"Oh, go away, Sproot—go quite away," said Vance. "When I crave vague rhetoric I'll read Thomas Aquinas."

"Yes, sir." The man bowed with wooden courtesy, and left us.

His footsteps had scarcely died away when Doctor Doremus strode in jauntily.

"There's your bullet, Sergeant." He tossed a tiny cylinder of discolored lead on the drawing-room table. "Nothing but dumb luck. It entered the fifth intercostal space and travelled diagonally across the heart, coming out in the post-axillary fold at the anterior border of the trapezius muscle, where I could feel it under the skin; and I picked it out with my pen-knife."

"All that fancy language don't worry me," grinned Heath, "so long's I got the bullet."

He picked it up and held it in the palm of his hand, his eyes narrowed, his mouth drawn into a straight line. Then, reaching into his waistcoat pocket, he took out two other bullets, and laid them beside the first. Slowly he nodded, and extended the sinister exhibits to Markham.

"There's the three shots that were fired in this house," he said. "They're all .32-revolver bullets—just alike. You can't get away from it, sir: all three people here were shot with the same gun."

CHAPTER X

THE CLOSING OF A DOOR

(Friday, November 12; 9.30 a. m.)

As HEATH spoke Sproot passed down the hall and opened the front door, admitting Doctor Von Blon.

"Good morning, Sproot," we heard him say in his habitually pleasant voice. "Anything new?"

"No, sir, I think not." The reply was expressionless. "The District Attorney and the police are here.—Let me take your coat, sir."

Von Blon glanced into the drawing-room, and, on seeing us, halted and bowed. Then he caught sight of Doctor Doremus, whom he had met on the night of the first tragedy.

"Ah, good morning, doctor," he said, coming forward. "I'm afraid I didn't thank you for the assistance you gave me with the young lady the other night. Permit me to make amends."

"No thanks needed," Doremus assured him. "How's the patient getting on?"

"The wound's filling in nicely. No sepsis. I'm going up now to have a look at her." He turned inquiringly to the District Attorney. "No objection, I suppose."

"None whatever, doctor," said Markham. Then he rose quickly.

"We'll come along, if you don't mind. There are a few questions I'd like to ask Miss Ada, and it might be as well to do it while you're present."

Von Blon gave his consent without hesitation.

"Well, I'll be on my way—work to do," announced Doremus breezily. He lingered long enough, however, to shake hands with all of us; and then the front door closed on him.

"We'd better ascertain if Miss Ada has been told of her brother's death," suggested Vance, as we went up the stairs. "If not, I think that task logically devolves on you, doctor."

The nurse, whom Sproot had no doubt apprised of Von Blon's arrival, met us in the upper hall and informed us that, as far as she knew, Ada was still ignorant of Chester's murder.

We found the girl sitting up in bed, a magazine lying across her knees. Her face was still pale, but a youthful vitality shone from her eyes, which attested to the fact that she was much stronger. She seemed alarmed at our sudden appearance, but the sight of the doctor tended to reassure her.

"How do you feel this morning, Ada?" he asked with professional geniality. "You remember these gentlemen, don't you?"

She gave us an apprehensive look; then smiled faintly and bowed.

"Yes, I remember them. . . . Have they—found out anything about—Julia's death?"

"I'm afraid not." Von Blon sat down beside her and took her hand. "Something else has happened that you will have to know, Ada." His voice was studiously sympathetic. "Last night Chester met with an accident——"

"An accident—oh!" Her eyes opened wide, and a slight tremor passed over her. "You mean. . . ." Her voice quavered and broke. "I know what you mean! . . . Chester's dead!"

Von Blon cleared his throat and looked away.

"Yes, Ada. You must be brave and not let it—ah—upset you too much. You see———"

"He was shot!" The words burst from her lips, and a look of terror overspread her face. "Just like Julia and me." Her eyes stared straight ahead, as if fascinated by some horror which she alone could see.

Von Blon was silent, and Vance stepped to the bed.

"We're not going to lie to you, Miss Greene," he said softly. "You have guessed the truth."

"And what about Rex—and Sibella?"

"They're all right," Vance assured her. "But why did you think your brother had met the same fate as Miss Julia and yourself?"

She turned her gaze slowly to him.

"I don't know—I just felt it. Ever since I was a little girl I've imagined horrible things happening in this house. And the other night I felt that the time had come—oh, I don't know how to explain it; but it was like having something happen that you'd been expecting."

Vance nodded understandingly.

"It's an unhealthy old house; it puts all sorts of weird notions in one's head. But, of course," he added lightly, "there's nothing supernatural about it. It's only a coincidence that you should have felt that way and that these disasters should actually have occurred. The police, y' know, think it was a burglar."

The girl did not answer, and Markham leaned forward with a reassuring smile.

"And we are going to have two men guarding the house all the time from now on," he said, "so that no one can get in who hasn't a perfect right to be here."

"So you see, Ada," put in Von Blon, "you have nothing to worry about any more. All you have to do now is to get well."

But her eyes did not leave Markham's face.

"How do you know," she asked, in a tense anxious voice, "that the—the person came in from the outside?"

"We found his footprints both times on the front walk."

"Footprints—are you sure?" She put the question eagerly.

"No doubt about them. They were perfectly plain, and they belonged to the person who came here and tried to shoot you.— Here, Sergeant"—he beckoned to Heath—"show the young lady that pattern."

Heath took the Manila envelope from his pocket and extracted the cardboard impression Snitkin had made. Ada took it in her hand and studied it, and a little sigh of relief parted her lips.

"And you notice," smiled Vance, "he didn't have very dainty feet."

The girl returned the pattern to the Sergeant. Her fear had left her, and her eyes cleared of the vision that had been haunting them.

"And now, Miss Greene," went on Vance, in a matter-of-fact voice, "we want to ask a few questions. First of all: the nurse said you went to sleep at nine o'clock last night. Is that correct?"

"I pretended to, because nurse was tired and mother was complaining a lot. But I really didn't go to sleep until hours later."

"But you didn't hear the shot in your brother's room?"

"No. I must have been asleep by then."

"Did you hear anything before that?"

"Not after the family had gone to bed and Sproot had locked up."

"Were you awake very long after Sproot retired?"

The girl pondered a moment, frowning.

"Maybe an hour," she ventured finally. "But I don't know."

"It couldn't have been much over an hour," Vance pointed out; "for the shot was fired shortly after half past eleven.—And you heard nothing—no sound of any kind in the hall?"

"Why, no." The look of fright was creeping back into her face. "Why do you ask?"

"Your brother Rex," explained Vance, "said he heard a faint shuffling sound and a door closing a little after eleven."

Her eyelids drooped, and her free hand tightened over the edge of the magazine she was holding.

"A door closing. . . ." She repeated the words in a voice scarcely audible. "Oh! And Rex heard it?" Suddenly she opened her eyes and her lips fell apart. A startled memory had taken possession of her—a memory which quickened her breathing and filled her with alarm. "I heard that door close, too! I remember it now. . . ."

"What door was it?" asked Vance, with subdued animation. "Could you tell where the sound came from?"

The girl shook her head.

"No—it was so soft. I'd even forgotten it until now. But I heard it! . . . Oh, what did it mean?"

"Nothing probably." Vance assumed an air of inconsequentiality calculated to alleviate her fears. "The wind doubtless."

But when we left her, after a few more questions, I noticed that her face still held an expression of deep anxiety.

Vance was unusually thoughtful as we returned to the drawing-room.

"I'd give a good deal to know what that child knows or suspects," he murmured.

"She's been through a trying experience," returned Markham. "She's frightened, and she sees new dangers in everything. But she couldn't suspect anything, or she'd be only too eager to tell us."

"I wish I were sure of that."

The next hour or so was occupied with interrogating the two maids and the cook. Markham cross-examined them thoroughly not only concerning the immediate events touching upon the two tragedies, but in regard to the general conditions in the Greene household. Numerous family episodes in the past were gone over; and when his inquiries were finished he had obtained a fairly good idea of the domestic atmosphere. But nothing that could be even remotely connected with the murders came to light. There had always been, it transpired, an abundance of hatred and ill-feeling and vicious irritability in the Greene mansion. The story that was unfolded by the servants was not a pleasant one; it was a record—scrappy and desultory, but none the less appalling—of daily clashes, complainings, bitter words, sullen silences, jealousies and threats.

Most of the details of this unnatural situation were supplied by Hemming, the older maid. She was less ecstatic than during the first interview, although she interspersed her remarks with Biblical quotations and references to the dire fate which the Lord had seen fit to visit upon her sinful employers. Nevertheless, she painted an arresting, if overcolored and prejudiced, picture of the life that had gone on about her during the past ten years. But when it came to explaining the methods employed by the Almighty in visiting his vengeance upon the unholy Greenes, she became indefinite and obscure. At length Markham let her go after she had assured him that she intended to remain at her post of duty—to be, as she expressed it, "a witness for the Lord" when his work of righteous devastation was complete.

Barton, the younger maid, on the other hand, announced, in

no uncertain terms, that she was through with the Greenes forever. The girl was genuinely frightened, and, after Sibella and Sproot had been consulted, she was paid her wages and told she could pack her things. In less than half an hour she had turned in her key and departed with her luggage. Such information as she left behind her was largely a substantiation of Hemming's outpourings. She, though, did not regard the two murders as the acts of an outraged God. Hers was a more practical and mundane view.

"There's something awful funny going on here," she had said, forgetting for the moment the urge of her coquettish spirits. "The Greenes are queer people. And the servants are queer, too—what with Mr. Sproot reading books in foreign languages, and Hemming preaching about fire and brimstone, and cook going around in a sort of trance muttering to herself and never answering a civil question.—And such a family!" She rolled her eyes. "Mrs. Greene hasn't got any heart. She's a regular old witch, and she looks at you sometimes as though she'd like to strangle you. If I was Miss Ada I'd have gone crazy long ago. But then, Miss Ada's no better than the rest. She acts nice and gentle-like, but I've seen her stamping up and down in her room looking like a very devil; and once she used language to me what was that bad I put my fingers in my ears. And Miss Sibella's a regular icicle—except when she gets mad, and then she'd kill you if she dared, and laugh about it. And there's been something funny about her and Mr. Chester. Ever since Miss Julia and Miss Ada were shot they've been talking to each other in the sneakiest way when they thought no one was looking. And this Doctor Von Blon what comes here so much: he's a deep one. He's been in Miss Sibella's room with the door shut lots of times when she wasn't any more sick than you are. And Mr. Rex, now. He's a

queer man, too. I get the creeps every time he comes near me."
She shuddered by way of demonstration. "Miss Julia wasn't as
queer as the rest. She just hated everybody and was mean."

Barton had rambled on loquaciously with all the thoughtless
exaggeration of a gossip who felt herself outraged; and Markham
had not interrupted her. He was trying to dredge up some nug-
get from the mass of her verbal silt; but when at last he sifted
it all down there remained nothing but a few shining grains of
scandal.

The cook was even less enlightening. Taciturn by nature, she
became almost inarticulate when approached on the subject of
the crime. Her stolid exterior seemed to cloak a sullen resentment at the fact that she should be questioned at all. In fact,
as Markham patiently pressed his examination, the impression
grew on me that her lack of responsiveness was deliberately
defensive, as if she had steeled herself to reticency. Vance, too,
sensed this attitude in her, for, during a pause in the interview, he
moved his chair about until he faced her directly.

"Frau Mannheim," he said, "the last time we were here you
mentioned the fact that Mr. Tobias Greene knew your husband,
and that, because of their acquaintance, you applied for a position here when your husband died."

"And why shouldn't I?" she asked stubbornly. "I was poor, and
I didn't have any other friends."

"Ah, friends!" Vance caught up the word. "And since you were
once on friendly terms with Mr. Greene, you doubtless know
certain things about his past, which may have some bearing on
the present situation; for it is not at all impossible, d' ye see, that
the crimes committed here during the past few days are connected with matters that took place years ago. We don't know

this, of course, but we'd be very much gratified if you would try to help us in this regard."

As he was speaking the woman had drawn herself up. Her hands had tightened as they lay folded in her lap, and the muscles about her mouth had stiffened.

"I don't know anything," was her only answer.

"How," asked Vance evenly, "do you account for the rather remarkable fact that Mr. Greene gave orders that you were to remain here as long as you cared to?"

"Mr. Greene was a very kind and generous man," she asserted, in a flat, combative voice. "Some there were that thought him hard, and accused him of being unjust; but he was always good to me and mine."

"How well did he know Mr. Mannheim?"

There was a pause, and the woman's eyes looked blankly ahead.

"He helped my husband once, when he was in trouble."

"How did he happen to do this?"

There was another pause, and then:

"They were in some deal together—in the old country." She frowned and appeared uneasy.

"When was this?"

"I don't remember. It was before I was married."

"And where did you first meet Mr. Greene?"

"At my home in New Orleans. He was there on business—with my husband."

"And, I take it, he befriended you also."

The woman maintained a stubborn silence.

"A moment ago," pursued Vance, "you used the phrase 'me and mine.'—Have you any children, Mrs. Mannheim?"

For the first time during the interview her face radically changed expression. An angry gleam shone in her eyes.

"No!" The denial was like an ejaculation.

Vance smoked lethargically for several moments.

"You lived in New Orleans until the time of your employment in this house?" he finally asked.

"Yes."

"And your husband died there?"

"Yes."

"That was thirteen years ago, I understand.—How long before that had it been since you had seen Mr. Greene?"

"About a year."

"So that would be fourteen years ago."

An apprehension, bordering on fear, showed through the woman's morose calmness.

"And you came all the way to New York to seek Mr. Greene's help," mused Vance. "Why were you so confident that he would give you employment after your husband's death?"

"Mr. Greene was a very good man," was all she would say.

"He had perhaps," suggested Vance, "done some other favor for you which made you think you could count on his generosity—eh, what?"

"That's neither here nor there." Her mouth closed tightly.

Vance changed the subject.

"What do you think about the crimes that have been committed in this house?"

"I don't think about them," she mumbled; but the anxiety in her voice belied the assertion.

"You surely must hold some opinion, Mrs. Mannheim, having been here so long." Vance's intent gaze did not leave the woman.

"Who, do you think, would have had any reason for wanting to harm these people?"

Suddenly her self-control gave way.

"Du lieber Herr Jesus! I don't know—I don't know!" It was like a cry of anguish. "Miss Julia and Mr. Chester maybe—*gewiss,* one could understand. They hated everybody; they were hard, unloving. But little Ada—*der süsse Engel!* Why should they want to harm her!" She set her face grimly, and slowly her expression of stolidity returned.

"Why, indeed?" A note of sympathy was evident in Vance's voice. After a pause he rose and went to the window. "You may return to your room now, Frau Mannheim," he said, without turning. "We sha'n't let anything further happen to little Ada."

The woman got up heavily and, with an uneasy glance in Vance's direction, left the room.

As soon as she was out of hearing Markham swung about.

"What's the use of raking up all this ancient history?" he demanded irritably. "We're dealing with things that have taken place within the past few days; and you waste valuable time trying to find out why Tobias Greene hired a cook thirteen years ago."

"There's such a thing as cause and effect," offered Vance mildly. "And frequently there's a dashed long interval between the two."

"Granted. But what possible connection can this German cook have with the present murders?"

"Perhaps none." Vance strode back across the room, his eyes on the floor. "But, Markham old dear, nothing appears to have any connection with this debacle. And, on the other hand, everything seems to have a possible relationship. The whole house is steeped in vague meanings. A hundred shadowy hands are pointing to the culprit, and the moment you try to determine the direction the hands disappear. It's a nightmare. Nothing means anything; therefore, anything may have a meaning."

"My dear Vance! You're not yourself." Markham's tone was one of annoyance and reproach. "Your remarks are worse than the obscure ramblings of the sibyls. What if Tobias Greene did have dealings with one Mannheim in the past? Old Tobias indulged in numerous shady transactions, if the gossip of twenty-five or thirty years ago can be credited.* He was forever scurrying to the ends of the earth on some mysterious mission, and coming home with his pockets lined. And it's common knowledge that he spent considerable time in Germany. If you try to dig up his past for possible explanations for the present business, you'll have your hands full."

"You misconstrue my vagaries," returned Vance, pausing before the old oil-painting of Tobias Greene over the fireplace. "I repudiate all ambition to become the family historian of the Greenes. . . . Not a bad head on Tobias," he commented, adjusting his monocle and inspecting the portrait. "An interestin' character. Dynamic forehead, with more than a suggestion of the scholar. A rugged, prying nose. Yes, Tobias no doubt fared forth on many an adventurous quest. A cruel mouth, though—rather sinister, in fact. I wish the whiskers permitted one a view of the chin. It was round, with a deep cleft, I'd say—the substance of which Chester's chin was but the simulacrum."

"Very edifying," sneered Markham. "But phrenology leaves me cold this morning.—Tell me, Vance: are you laboring under some melodramatic notion that old Mannheim may have been resurrected and returned to wreak vengeance on the Greene

---

* I remember, back in the nineties, when I was a schoolboy, hearing my father allude to certain picturesque tales of Tobias Greene's escapades.

progeny for wrongs done him by Tobias in the dim past? I can't see any other reason for the questions you put to Mrs. Mannheim. Don't overlook the fact, however, that Mannheim's dead."

"I didn't attend the funeral." Vance sank lazily again in his chair.

"Don't be so unutterably futile," snapped Markham. "What's going through your head?"

"An excellent figure of speech! It expresses my mental state perfectly. Numberless things are 'going through my head.' But nothing remains there. My brain's a veritable sieve."

Heath projected himself into the discussion.

"My opinion is, sir, that the Mannheim angle of this affair is a washout. We're dealing with the present, and the bird that did this shooting is somewheres around here right now."

"You're probably right, Sergeant," conceded Vance. "But—my word!—it strikes me that every angle of the case—and, for that matter, every cusp, arc, tangent, parabola, sine, radius, and hyperbole—is hopelessly inundated."

CHAPTER XI

A PAINFUL INTERVIEW

(Friday, November 12; 11 a. m.)

MARKHAM GLANCED impatiently at his watch.

"It's getting late," he complained, "and I have an important appointment at noon. I think I'll have a go at Rex Greene, and then leave matters in your hands for the time being, Sergeant. There's nothing much to be done here now, and your routine work must be gone through with."

Heath got up gloomily.

"Yes; and one of the first things to be done is to go over this house with a fine-tooth comb for that revolver. If we could find that gun we'd be on our way."

"I don't want to damp your ardor, Sergeant," drawled Vance, "but something whispers in my ear that the weapon you yearn for is going to prove dashed elusive."

Heath looked depressed; he was obviously of Vance's opinion.

"A hell of a case this is! Not a lead—nothing to get your teeth in."

He went to the archway and yanked the bell-cord viciously. When Sproot appeared he almost barked his demand that Mr.

Rex Greene be produced at once; and he stood looking truculently after the retreating butler as if longing for an excuse to
follow up his order with violence.

Rex came in nervously, a half-smoked cigarette hanging from
his lips. His eyes were sunken; his cheeks sagged, and his short
splay fingers fidgeted with the hem of his smoking-jacket, like
those of a man under the influence of hyoscine. He gave us a
resentful, half-frightened gaze, and planted himself aggressively
before us, refusing to take the seat Markham indicated. Suddenly he demanded fiercely:

"Have you found out yet who killed Julia and Chester?"

"No," Markham admitted; "but we've taken every precaution
against any recurrence. . . ."

"Precaution? What have you done?"

"We've stationed a man both front and rear——"

A cackling laugh cut him short.

"A lot of good that'll do! The person who's after us Greenes
has a key. He has a key, I tell you! And he can get in whenever he
wants to, and nobody can stop him."

"I think you exaggerate a little," returned Markham mildly.
"In any case, we hope to put our hands on him very soon. And
that's why I've asked you here again—it's quite possible that you
can help us."

"What do I know?" The man's words were defiant, and he
took several long inhalations on his cigarette, the ashes of which
fell upon his jacket unnoticed.

"You were asleep, I understand, when the shot was fired last
night," went on Markham's quiet voice; "but Sergeant Heath
tells me you were awake until after eleven and heard noises in
the hall. Suppose you tell us just what happened."

"Nothing happened!" Rex blurted. "I went to bed at half past ten, but I was too nervous to sleep. Then, some time later, the moon came out and fell across the foot of the bed; and I got up and pulled down the shade. About ten minutes later I heard a scraping sound in the hall, and directly afterward a door closed softly——"

"Just a moment, Mr. Greene," interrupted Vance. "Can you be a little more definite about that noise? What did it sound like?"

"I didn't pay any attention to it," was the whining reply. "It might have been almost anything. It was like some one laying down a bundle, or dragging something across the floor; or it might have been old Sproot in his bedroom slippers, though it didn't sound like him—that is, I didn't associate him with the sound when I heard it."

"And after that?"

"After that? I lay awake in bed ten or fifteen minutes longer. I was restless and—and expectant; so I turned on the lights to see what time it was, and smoked half a cigarette——"

"It was twenty-five minutes past eleven, I understand."

"That's right. Then a few minutes later I put out the light, and must have gone right to sleep."

There was a pause, and Heath drew himself up aggressively.

"Say, Greene: know anything about fire-arms?" He shot the question out brutally.

Rex stiffened. His lips sagged open, and his cigarette fell to the floor. The muscles of his thin jowls twitched, and he glared menacingly at the Sergeant.

"What do you mean?" The words were like a snarl; and I noticed that his whole body was quivering.

"Know what became of your brother's revolver?" pursued Heath relentlessly, thrusting out his jaw.

Rex's mouth was working in a paroxysm of fury and fear, but he seemed unable to articulate.

"Where have you got it hidden?" Again Heath's voice sounded harshly.

"Revolver? . . . Hidden? . . ." At last Rex had succeeded in formulating his words. "You—filthy rotter! If you've got any idea that I have the revolver, go up and tear my room apart and look for it—and be damned to you!" His eyes flashed, and his upper lip lifted over his teeth. But there was fright in his attitude as well as rage.

Heath had leaned forward and was about to say something further, when Vance quickly rose and laid a restraining hand on the Sergeant's arm. He was too late, however, to avoid the thing he evidently hoped to forestall. What Heath had already said had proved sufficient stimulus to bring about a terrible reaction in his victim.

"What do I care what that unspeakable swine says?" he shouted, pointing a palsied finger at the Sergeant. Oaths and vituperation welled shrilly from his twitching lips. His insensate wrath seemed to pass all ordinary bounds. His enormous head was thrust forward like a python's; and his face was cyanosed and contorted.

Vance stood poised, watching him alertly; and Markham had instinctively moved back his chair. Even Heath was startled by Rex's inordinate malignity.

What might have happened I don't know, had not Von Blon at that moment stepped swiftly into the room and placed a restraining hand on the youth's shoulder.

"Rex!" he said, in a calm, authoritative voice. "Get a grip on yourself. You're disturbing Ada."

The other ceased speaking abruptly; but his ferocity of manner did not wholly abate. He shook off the doctor's hand angrily and swung round, facing Von Blon.

"What are you interfering for?" he cried. "You're always meddling in this house, coming here when you're not sent for, and nosing into our affairs. Mother's paralysis is only an excuse. You've said yourself she'll never get well, and yet you keep coming, bringing her medicine and sending bills." He gave the doctor a crafty leer. "Oh, you don't deceive me. I know why you come here! It's Sibella!" Again he thrust out his head and grinned shrewdly. "She'd be a good catch for a doctor, too—wouldn't she? Plenty of money——"

Suddenly he halted. His eyes did not leave Von Blon, but he shrank back and the twitching of his face began once more. A quivering finger went up; and as he spoke his voice rose excitedly.

"But Sibella's money isn't enough. You want ours along with hers. So you're arranging for her to inherit all of it. That's it—that's it! *You're* the one who's been doing all this. . . . Oh, my God! You've got Chester's gun—you took it! And you've got a key to the house—easy enough for you to have one made. That's how you got in."

Von Blon shook his head sadly and smiled with rueful tolerance. It was an embarrassing moment, but he carried it off well.

"Come, Rex," he said quietly, like a person speaking to a refractory child. "You've said enough——"

"Have I!" cried the youth, his eyes gleaming unnaturally. "You knew Chester had the revolver. You went camping with him the summer he got it—he told me so the other day, after Julia was killed." His beady little eyes seemed to stare from his head; a spasm shook his emaciated body; and his fingers again began worrying the hem of his jacket.

Von Blon stepped swiftly forward and, putting a hand on each of his shoulders, shook him.

"That'll do, Rex!" The words were a sharp command. "If you carry on this way, we'll have to lock you up in an institution."

The threat was uttered in what I considered an unnecessarily brutal tone; but it had the desired effect. A haunting fear showed in Rex's eyes. He seemed suddenly to go limp, and he docilely permitted Von Blon to lead him from the room.

"A sweet specimen, that Rex," commented Vance. "Not a person one would choose for a boon companion. Aggravated macrocephalia—cortical irritation. But I say, Sergeant; really, y' know, you shouldn't have prodded the lad so."

Heath grunted.

"You can't tell me that guy don't know something. And you can bet your sweet life I'm going to search his room damn good for that gun."

"It appears to me," rejoined Vance, "he's too flighty to have planned the massacre in this house. He might blow up under pressure and hit somebody with a handy missile; but I doubt if he'd lay any deep schemes and bide his time."

"He's good and scared about something," persisted Heath morosely.

"Hasn't he cause to be? Maybe he thinks the elusive gunman hereabouts will chose him as the next target."

"If there *is* another gunman, he showed damn bad taste not picking Rex out first." It was evident the Sergeant was still smarting under the epithets that had so recently been directed at him.

Von Blon returned to the drawing-room at this moment, looking troubled.

"I've got Rex quieted," he said. "Gave him five grains of luminal. He'll sleep for a few hours and wake up penitent. I've rarely seen him quite as violent as he was to-day. He's supersensitive—cerebral neurasthenia; and he's apt to fly off the handle. But he's never dangerous." He scanned our faces swiftly. "One of you gentlemen must have said something pretty severe."

Heath looked sheepish. "I asked him where he'd hid the gun."

"Ah!" The doctor gave the Sergeant a look of questioning reproach. "Too bad! We have to be careful with Rex. He's all right so long as he isn't opposed too strongly. But I don't just see, sir, what your object could have been in questioning him about the revolver. You surely don't suspect him of having had a hand in these terrible shootings."

"You tell me who did the shootings, doc," retorted Heath pugnaciously, "and then I'll tell you who I *don't* suspect."

"I regret that I am unable to enlighten you." Von Blon's tone exuded its habitual pleasantness. "But I can assure you Rex had no part in them. They're quite out of keeping with his pathologic state."

"That's the defense of half the high-class killers we get the goods on," countered Heath.

"I see I can't argue with you." Von Blon sighed regretfully, and turned an engaging countenance in Markham's direction. "Rex's absurd accusations puzzled me deeply, but, since this officer admits he practically accused the boy of having the revolver, the situation becomes perfectly clear. A common form of instinctive self-protection, this attempting to shift blame on others. You can see, of course, that Rex was merely trying to turn suspicion upon me so as to free himself. It's unfortunate, for he and I were always good friends. Poor Rex!"

"By the by, doctor," came Vance's indolent voice; "that point about your being with Mr. Chester Greene on the camping-trip when he first secured the gun: was that correct? Or was it merely a fancy engendered by Rex's self-protective instinct?"

Von Blon smiled with faultless urbanity and, putting his head a little on one side, appeared to recall the past.

"It may be correct," he admitted. "I was once with Chester on a camping-trip. Yes, it's quite likely—though I shouldn't like to state it definitely. It was so long ago."

"Fifteen years, I think, Mr. Greene said. Ah, yes—a long time ago. *Eheu! fugaces, Postume, Postume, labuntur anni.* It's very depressin'. And do you recall, doctor, if Mr. Greene had a revolver along on that particular outing?"

"Since you mention it, I believe I do recall his having one, though again I should choose not to be definite on the subject."

"Perhaps you may recollect if he used it for target practice." Vance's tone was dulcet and uneager. "Popping away at tree-boles and tin cans and what not, don't y' know."

Von Blon nodded reminiscently.

"Ye-es. It's quite possible. . . ."

"And you yourself may have done a bit of desult'ry popping, what?"

"To be sure, I may have." Von Blon spoke musingly, like one recalling childish pranks. "Yes, it's wholly possible."

Vance lapsed into a disinterested silence, and the doctor, after a moment's hesitation, rose.

"I must be going, I'm afraid." And with a gracious bow he started toward the door. "Oh, by the way," he said, pausing, "I almost forgot that Mrs. Greene told me she desired to see you gentlemen before you went. Forgive me if I suggest that it might be wise to humor her. She's something of a dowager, you know, and her invalidism has made her rather irritable and exacting."

"I'm glad you mentioned Mrs. Greene, doctor." It was Vance

who spoke. "I've been intending to ask you about her. What is the nature of her paralysis?"

Von Blon appeared surprised.

"Why, a sort of paraplegia dolorosa—that is, a paralysis of the legs and lower part of the body, accompanied by severe pains due to pressure of the indurations on the spinal cord and nerves. No spasticity of the limbs has supervened, however. Came on very suddenly without any premonitory symptoms about ten years ago—probably the result of transverse myelitis. There's nothing really to be done but to keep her as comfortable as possible with symptomatic treatment, and to tone up the heart action. A sixtieth of strychnine three times a day takes care of the circulation."

"Couldn't by any chance be a hysterical akinesia?"

"Good Lord, no! There's no hysteria." Then his eyes widened in amazement. "Oh, I see! No; there's no possibility of recovery, even partial. It's organic paralysis."

"And atrophy?"

"Oh, yes. Muscular atrophy is now pronounced."

"Thank you very much." Vance lay back with half-closed eyes.

"Oh, not at all.—And remember, Mr. Markham, that I always stand ready to help in any way I can. Please don't hesitate to call on me." He bowed again, and went out.

Markham got up and stretched his legs.

"Come; we've been summoned to appear." His facetiousness was a patent effort to shake off the depressing gloom of the case.

Mrs. Greene received us with almost unctuous cordiality.

"I knew you'd grant the request of a poor old useless cripple," she said, with an appealing smile; "though I'm used to being ignored. No one pays any attention to my wishes."

The nurse stood at the head of the bed arranging the pillows beneath the old lady's shoulders.

"Is that comfortable now?" she asked.

Mrs. Greene made a gesture of annoyance.

"A lot you care whether I'm comfortable or not! Why can't you let me alone, nurse? You're always disturbing me. There was nothing wrong with the pillows. And I don't want you in here now anyway. Go and sit with Ada."

The nurse drew a long, patient breath, and went silently from the room, closing the door behind her.

Mrs. Greene reverted to her former ingratiating manner.

"No one understands my needs the way Ada does, Mr. Markham. What a relief it will be when the dear child gets well enough to care for me again! But I mustn't complain. The nurse does the best she knows how, I suppose.—Please sit down, gentlemen . . . yet what wouldn't I give if I could only stand up the way you can. No one realizes what it means to be a helpless paralytic."

Markham did not avail himself of the invitation, but waited until she had finished speaking and then said:

"Please believe that you have my deepest sympathy, madam. . . . You sent for me, Doctor Von Blon said."

"Yes!" She looked at him calculatingly. "I wanted to ask you a favor."

She paused, and Markham bowed but did not answer.

"I wanted to request you to drop this investigation. I've had enough worry and disturbance as it is. But *I* don't count. It's the family I'm thinking of—the good name of the Greenes." A note of pride came into her voice. "What need is there to drag us through the mire and make us an object of scandalous gossip for the *canaille?* I want peace and quiet, Mr. Markham. I won't be here much longer; and why should my house be overrun with policemen just because Julia and Chester have suffered their just deserts for neglecting me and letting me suffer here alone? I'm an old woman and a cripple, and I'm deserving of a little consideration."

Her face clouded, and her voice became harsh.

"You haven't any right to come here and upset my house and annoy me in this outrageous fashion! I haven't had a minute's rest since all this excitement began, and my spine is paining me so I can hardly breathe." She took several stertorous breaths, and her eyes flashed indignantly. "I don't expect any better treatment from my children—they're hard and thoughtless. But you, Mr. Markham—an outsider, a stranger: why should you want to torture me with all this commotion? It's outrageous—inhuman!"

"I am sorry if the presence of the officers of the law in your house disturbs you," Markham told her gravely; "but I have no alternative. When a crime has been committed it is my duty to investigate, and to use every means at my disposal to bring the guilty person to justice."

"Justice!" The old lady repeated the word scornfully. "Justice has already been done. I've been avenged for the treatment I've received these many years, lying here helpless."

There was something almost terrifying in the woman's cruel and unrelenting hatred of her children, and in the cold-blooded satisfaction she seemed to take in the fact that two of them had been punished by death. Markham, naturally sympathetic, revolted against her attitude.

"However much gratification you may feel at the murder of your son and daughter, madam," he said coldly, "it does not release me from my duty to find the murderer.—Was there anything else you wished to speak to me about?"

For a while she sat silent, her face working with impotent passion. The gaze she bent on Markham was almost ferocious.

But presently the vindictive vigilance of her eyes relaxed, and she drew a deep sigh.

"No; you may go now. I have nothing more to say. And, anyway, who cares about an old helpless woman like me? I should have learned by this time that nobody thinks of my comfort, lying here all alone, unable to help myself—a nuisance to every one. . . ."

Her whining, self-pitying voice followed us as we made our escape.

"Y' know, Markham," said Vance, as we came into the lower hall, "the Empress Dowager is not entirely devoid of reason. Her suggestion is deserving of consideration. The clarion voice of duty may summon you to this quest, but—my word!—whither shall one quest? There's nothing sane in this house— nothing that lends itself to ordin'ry normal reason. Why not take her advice and chuck it? Even if you learn the truth, it's likely to prove a sort of Pyrrhic vict'ry. I'm afraid it'll be more terrible than the crimes themselves."

Markham did not deign to answer; he was familiar with Vance's heresies, and he also knew that Vance himself would be the last person to throw over an unsolved problem.

"We've got something to go on, Mr. Vance," submitted Heath solemnly, but without enthusiasm. "There's those foot-tracks, for instance; and we've got the missing gun to find. Dubois is up-stairs now taking finger-prints. And the reports on the servants'll be coming along soon. There's no telling what'll turn up in a few days. I'll have a dozen men working on this case before night."

"Such zeal, Sergeant! But it's in the atmosphere of this old house—not in tangible clews—that the truth lies hidden. It's somewhere in these old jumbled rooms; it's peering out from dark corners and from behind doors. It's here—in this very hall, perhaps."

His tone was fraught with troubled concern, and Markham looked at him sharply.

"I think you're right, Vance," he muttered. "But how is one to get at it?"

"'Pon my soul, I don't know. How does one get at spectres, anyway? I've never had much intimate intercourse with ghosts, don't y' know."

"You're talking rubbish!" Markham jerked on his overcoat, and turned to Heath. "You go ahead, Sergeant; and keep in touch with me. If nothing develops from your inquiries, we'll discuss the next step."

And he and Vance and I went out to the waiting car.

CHAPTER XII

A MOTOR RIDE

(November 12—November 25)

THE INQUIRY was pushed according to the best traditions of the Police Department. Captain Carl Hagedorn, the firearms expert,* made a minute scientific examination of the bullets. The same revolver, he found, had fired all three shots: the peculiar rifling told him this; and he was able to state that the revolver was an old Smith & Wesson of a style whose manufacture had been discontinued. But, while these findings offered substantiation to the theory that Chester Greene's missing gun was the one used by the murderer, they added nothing to the facts already established or suspected. Deputy Inspector Conrad Brenner, the burglartools expert,† had conducted an exhaustive examination of the scene for evidential signs of a forced entrance, but had found no traces whatever of a housebreaker.

Dubois and his assistant Bellamy—the two leading finger-

---

* Captain Hagedorn was the expert who supplied Vance with the technical data in the Benson murder case, which made it possible for him to establish the height of the murderer.
† It was Inspector Brenner who examined and reported on the chiselled jewel-box in the "Canary" murder case.

print authorities of the New York Police Department—went so far as to take finger-prints of every member of the Greene household, including Doctor Von Blon; and these were compared with the impressions found in the hallways and in the rooms where the shootings had occurred. But when this tedious process was over not an unidentified print remained; and all those that had been found and photographed were logically accounted for.

Chester Greene's galoshes were taken to Headquarters and turned over to Captain Jerym, who carefully compared them with the measurements and the patterns made by Snitkin. No new fact concerning them, however, was discovered. The tracks in the snow, Captain Jerym reported, had been made either by the galoshes given him or by another pair of the exact size and last. Beyond this statement he could not, he said, conscientiously go.

It was established that no one in the Greene mansion, with the exception of Chester and Rex, owned galoshes; and Rex's were number seven—three sizes smaller than those found in Chester's clothes-closet. Sproot used only storm-rubbers, size eight; and Doctor Von Blon, who affected gaiters in winter, always wore rubber sandals during stormy weather.

The search for the missing revolver occupied several days. Heath turned the task over to men trained especially in this branch of work, and supplied them with a search-warrant in case they should meet with any opposition. But no obstacle was put in their way. The house was systematically ransacked from basement to attic. Even Mrs. Greene's quarters were subjected to a search. The old lady had at first objected, but finally gave her consent, and even seemed a bit disappointed when the men had finished. The only room that was not gone over was Tobias Greene's library. Owing to the fact that Mrs. Greene had never let the key go out of her possession, and had permitted no one to enter the room since her husband's death, Heath decided not to force the issue when she refused pointblank to deliver the key. Every other nook and corner of the house, however, was combed by the Sergeant's men. But no sign of the revolver rewarded their efforts.

The autopsies revealed nothing at variance with Doctor Doremus's preliminary findings. Julia and Chester had each died instantaneously from the effects of a bullet entering the heart, shot from a revolver held at close range. No other possible cause of death was present in either body; and there were no indications of a struggle.

No unknown or suspicious person had been seen near the Greene mansion on the night of either murder, although several people were found who had been in the neighborhood at the time; and a bootmaker, who lived on the second floor of the Narcoss Flats in 53d Street, opposite to the house, stated that he had been sitting at his window, smoking his bedtime pipe, during the time of both shootings, and could swear that no one had passed down that end of the street.

However, the guard which had been placed over the Greene mansion was not relaxed. Men were on duty day and night at both entrances to the estate, and every one entering or leaving the premises was closely scrutinized. So close a watch was kept that strange tradesmen found it inconvenient and at times difficult to make ordinary deliveries.

The reports that were turned in concerning the servants were unsatisfactory from the standpoint of detail; but all the facts unearthed tended to eliminate each subject from any possible connection with the crimes. Barton, the younger maid, who had quitted the Greene establishment the morning after the second tragedy, proved to be the daughter of respectable working people living in Jersey City. Her record was good, and her companions all appeared to be harmless members of her own class.

Hemming, it turned out, was a widow who, up to the time of her employment with the Greenes, had kept house for her husband, an iron-worker, in Altoona, Pa. She was remembered even there among her former neighbors as a religious fanatic who had led her husband sternly and exultantly in the narrow path of enforced rectitude. When he was killed by a furnace explosion she declared it was the hand of God striking him down for some secret sin. Her associates were few: they were in the main members of a small congregation of East Side Anabaptists.

The summer gardener of the Greenes—a middle-aged Pole named Krimski—was discovered in a private saloon in Harlem, well under the benumbing influence of synthetic whiskey—a state of beatific lassitude he had maintained, with greater or lesser steadfastness, since the end of summer. He was at once eliminated from police consideration.

The investigation into the habits and associates of Mrs. Mannheim and Sproot brought nothing whatever to light. Indeed, the habits of these two were exemplary, and their contacts with the outside world so meagre as to be regarded almost as non-existent. Sproot had no visible friends, and his acquaintances were limited to an English valet in Park Avenue and the tradespeople of the neighborhood. He was solitary by nature, and what few recreations he permitted himself were indulged in unaccompanied. Mrs. Mannheim had rarely left the premises of the Greene house since she had taken up her duties there at the time of her husband's death, and apparently knew no one in New York outside of the household.

These reports dashed whatever hopes Sergeant Heath may

have harbored of finding a solution to the Greene mystery by way of a possible accomplice in the house itself.

"I guess we'll have to give up the idea of an inside job," he lamented one morning in Markham's office a few days after the shooting of Chester Greene.

Vance, who was present, eyed him lazily.

"I shouldn't say that, don't y' know, Sergeant. On the contr'ry, it was indubitably an inside job, though not just the variety you have in mind."

"You mean you think some member of the family did it?"

"Well—perhaps: something rather along that line." Vance drew on his cigarette thoughtfully. "But that's not exactly what I meant. It's a situation, a set of conditions—an atmosphere, let us say—that's guilty. A subtle and deadly poison is responsible for the crimes. And that poison is generated in the Greene mansion."

"A swell time I'd have trying to arrest an atmosphere—or a poison either, for the matter of that," snorted Heath.

"Oh, there's a flesh-and-blood victim awaiting your manacles somewhere, Sergeant—the agent, so to speak, of the atmosphere."

Markham, who had been conning the various reports of the case, sighed heavily, and settled back in his chair.

"Well, I wish to Heaven," he interposed bitterly, "that he'd give us some hint as to his identity. The papers are at it hammer and tongs. There's been another delegation of reporters here this morning."

The fact was that rarely had there been in New York's journalistic history a case which had so tenaciously seized upon the public imagination. The shooting of Julia and Ada Greene had been treated sensationally but perfunctorily; but after Chester

Greene's murder an entirely different spirit animated the newspaper stories. Here was something romantically sinister—something which brought back forgotten pages of criminal history.
Columns were devoted to accounts of the Greene family history.
Genealogical archives were delved into for remote titbits. Old
Tobias Greene's record was raked over, and stories of his early life became the common property of the man in the street.
Pictures of all the members of the Greene family accompanied
these spectacular tales; and the Greene mansion itself, photographed from every possible angle, was used regularly to illus-
trate the flamboyant accounts of the crimes so recently perpetrated there.

The story of the Greene murders spread over the entire country, and even the press of Europe found space for it. The tragedy,
taken in connection with the social prominence of the family
and the romantic history of its progenitors, appealed irresistibly
to the morbidity and the snobbery of the public.

It was natural that the police and the District Attorney's office should be hounded by the representatives of the press; and
it was also natural that both Heath and Markham should be
sorely troubled by the fact that all their efforts to lay hands on
the criminal had come to naught. Several conferences had been
called in Markham's office, at each of which the ground had
been carefully reploughed; but not one helpful suggestion had
been turned up. Two weeks after the murder of Chester Greene
the case began to take on the aspect of a stalemate.

During that fortnight, however, Vance had not been idle. The
situation had caught and held his interest, and not once had he

---

* Among the famous cases mentioned as being in some manner comparable to the
Greene shootings were the mass murders of Landru, Jean-Baptiste Troppmann, Fritz
Haarmann, and Mrs. Belle Gunness; the tavern murders of the Benders; the Van der
Linden poisonings in Holland; the Bela Kiss tin-cask stranglings; the Rugeley murders
of Doctor William Palmer; and the beating to death of Benjamin Nathan.

dismissed it from his mind since that first morning when Chester Greene had applied to Markham for help. He said little about the case, but he had attended each of the conferences; and from his casual comments I knew he was both fascinated and perplexed by the problem it presented.

So convinced was he that the Greene mansion itself held the secret to the crimes enacted there that he had made it a point to call at the house several times without Markham. Markham, in fact, had been there but once since the second crime. It was not that he was shirking his task. There was, in reality, little for him to do; and the routine duties of his office were particularly heavy at that time.*

Sibella had insisted that the funerals of Julia and Chester be combined in one service, which was held in the private chapel of Malcomb's Undertaking Parlors. Only a few intimate acquaintances were notified (though a curious crowd gathered outside the building, attracted by the sensational associations of the obsequies); and the interment at Woodlawn Cemetery was strictly private. Doctor Von Blon accompanied Sibella and Rex to the chapel, and sat with them during the services. Ada, though improving rapidly, was still confined to the house; and Mrs. Greene's paralysis of course made her attendance impossible, although I doubt if she would have gone in any case, for when the suggestion was made that the services be held at home she had vetoed it emphatically.

It was on the day after the funeral that Vance paid his first unofficial visit to the Greene mansion. Sibella received him without any show of surprise.

---

* The famous impure-milk scandal was then to the fore, and the cases were just appearing on the court calendar. Also, at that time, there was an anti-gambling campaign in progress in New York; and the District Attorney's office had charge of all the prosecutions.

"I'm so glad you've come," she greeted him, almost gaily. "I knew you weren't a policeman the first time I saw you. Imagine a policeman smoking *Régie* cigarettes! And I'm dying for some one to talk to. Of course, all the people I know avoid me now as they would a pestilence. I haven't had an invitation since Julia passed from this silly life. Respect for the dead, I believe they call it. And just when I most need diversion!"

She rang for the butler and ordered tea.

"Sproot makes much better tea than he does coffee, thank Heaven!" she ran on, with a kind of nervous detachment. "What a sweet day we had yesterday! Funerals are hideous farces. I could hardly keep a straight face when the officiating reverend doctor began extolling the glories of the departed. And all the time— poor man—he was eaten up with morbid curiosity. I'm sure he enjoyed it so much that he wouldn't complain if I entirely forgot to send him a check for his kind words. . . ."

The tea was served, but before Sproot had withdrawn Sibella turned to him pettishly.

"I simply can't stand any more tea. I want a Scotch high-ball." She lifted her eyes to Vance inquiringly, but he insisted that he preferred tea; and the girl drank her high-ball alone.

"I crave stimulation these days," she explained airily. "This moated grange, so to speak, is getting on my young and fretful nerves. And the burden of being a celebrity is quite overwhelming. I really have become a celebrity, you know. In fact, all the Greenes are quite famous now. I never imagined a mere murder or two could give a family such positively irrational prominence. I'll probably be in Hollywood yet."

She gave a laugh which struck me as a trifle strained.

"It's just too jolly! Even mother is enjoying it. She gets all the papers and reads every word that's written about us—which is a blessing, let me tell you. She's almost forgotten to find fault; and I haven't heard a word about her spine for days. The Lord tempers the wind—or is it something about an ill wind I'm trying to quote? I always get my classical references confused. . . ."

She ran on in this flippant vein for half an hour or so. But whether her callousness was genuine or merely a brave attempt to counteract the pall of tragedy that hung over her I couldn't make out. Vance listened, interested and amused. He seemed to sense a certain emotional necessity in the girl to relieve her mind; but long before we went away he had led the conversation round to commonplace matters. When we rose to go Sibella insisted that we come again.

"You're so comforting, Mr. Vance," she said. "I'm sure you're not a moralist; and you haven't once condoled with me over my bereavements. Thank Heaven, we Greenes have no relatives to swoop down on us and bathe us in tears. I'm sure I'd commit suicide if we had."

Vance and I called twice more within the week, and were received cordially. Sibella's high spirits were always the same. If she felt the horror that had descended so suddenly and unexpectedly upon her home, she managed to hide it well. Only in her eagerness to talk freely and in her exaggerated efforts to avoid all sign of mourning did I sense any effects on her of the terrible experience she had been through.

Vance on none of his visits referred directly to the crimes; and I became deeply puzzled by his attitude. He was trying to learn something—of that I was positive. But I failed to see what possible progress he could make by the casual methods he was pursuing. Had I not known him better I might have suspected him of being personally interested in Sibella; but such a notion I dismissed simultaneously with its formulation. I noticed, however, that after each call he became unaccountably pensive; and one evening, after we had had tea with Sibella, he sat for an hour before the fire in his living-room without turning a page of the volume of da Vinci's "Trattato della Pittura" which lay open before him.

On one of his visits to the Greene mansion he had met and talked with Rex. At first the youth had been surly and resentful of our presence; but before we went away he and Vance were discussing such subjects as Einstein's general-relativity theory, the Moulton-Chamberlin planetesimal hypothesis, and Poincaré's science of numbers, on a plane quite beyond the grasp of a mere layman like myself. Rex had warmed up to the discussion in an almost friendly manner, and at parting had even offered his hand for Vance to shake.

On another occasion Vance had asked Sibella to be permitted to pay his respects to Mrs. Greene. His apologies to her—which he gave a semiofficial flavor—for all the annoyance caused by the police immediately ingratiated him in the old lady's good graces. He was most solicitous about her health, and asked her numerous questions regarding her paralysis—the nature of her spinal pains and the symptoms of her restlessness. His air of sympathetic concern drew from her an elaborate and detailed jeremiad.

Twice Vance talked to Ada, who was now up and about, but with her arm still in a sling. For some reason, however, the girl appeared almost *farouche* when approached by him. One day when we were at the house Von Blon called, and Vance seemed to go out of his way to hold him in conversation.

As I have said, I could not fathom his motive in all this apparently desultory social give-and-take. He never broached the subject of the tragedies except in the most indirect way; he appeared, rather, to avoid the topic deliberately. But I did notice that, however casual his manner, he was closely studying every one in the house. No nuance of tone, no subtlety of reaction, escaped him. He was, I knew, storing away impressions, analyzing minute phases of conduct, and probing delicately into the psychological mainsprings of each person he talked to.

We had called perhaps four or five times at the Greene mansion when an episode occurred which must be recounted here in order to clarify a later development of the case. I thought little of it at the time, but, though seemingly trivial, it was to prove of the most sinister significance before many days had passed. In fact, had it not been for this episode there is no telling to what awful lengths the gruesome tragedy of the Greenes might have gone; for Vance—in one of those strange mental flashes of his which always seemed wholly intuitive but were, in reality, the result of long, subtle reasoning—remembered the incident at a crucial moment, and related it swiftly to other incidents which in themselves appeared trifling, but which, when co-ordinated, took on a tremendous and terrible importance.

During the second week following Chester Greene's death the weather moderated markedly. We had several beautiful clear days, crisp, sunshiny, and invigorating. The snow had almost entirely disappeared, and the ground was firm, without any of the slush that usually follows a winter thaw. On Thursday Vance and I called at the Greene mansion earlier than on any previous visit, and we saw Doctor Von Blon's car parked before the gate.

"Ah!" Vance observed. "I do hope the family Paracelsus is not departing immediately. The man lures me; and his exact relationship to the Greene family irks my curiosity."

Von Blon, as a matter of fact, was preparing to go as we entered the hallway. Sibella and Ada, bundled in their furs, stood just behind him; and it was evident that they were accompanying him.

"It was such a pleasant day," explained Von Blon, somewhat disconcertedly, "I thought I'd take the girls for a drive."

"And you and Mr. Van Dine must come with us," chimed in Sibella, smiling hospitably at Vance. "If the doctor's temperamental driving affects your heart action, I promise to take the wheel myself. I'm really an expert chauffeur."

I surprised a look of displeasure on Von Blon's face; but Vance accepted the invitation without demur; and in a few moments we were riding across town, comfortably installed in the doctor's big Daimler, with Sibella in front, next to the driver's seat, and Ada between Vance and me in the tonneau.

We went north on Fifth Avenue, entered Central Park, and, emerging at the 72d Street entrance, headed for Riverside Drive. The Hudson River lay like a sheet of blue-grass below us, and the Jersey palisades in the still clear air of early afternoon were as plainly etched as a Degas drawing. At Dyckman Street we went up Broadway, and turned west on the Spuyten Duyvil Road to Palisade Avenue overlooking the old wooded estates along the water. We passed through a private roadway lined with hedges, turned inland again to Sycamore Avenue, and came out on the Riverdale Road. We drove through Yonkers, up North Broadway into Hastings, and then skirted the Longue Vue Hill. Beyond Dobbs Ferry we entered the Hudson Road, and at Ardsley again turned west beside the Country Club golf-links, and came out on the river level. Beyond the Ardsley Station a narrow dir"'t road ran up the hill along the water; and, instead of following the main highway to the east, we continued up this little-used road, emerging on a kind of plateau of wild pasture-land.

A mile or so farther on—about midway between Ardsley and Tarrytown—a small dun hill, like a boulder, loomed directly in our path. When we came to the foot of it, the road swung sharply to the west along a curved promontory. The turn was narrow and dangerous, with the steep upward slope of the hill on one side and the precipitous, rocky descent into the river on the other. A flimsy wooden fence had been built along the edge of the drop, though what possible protection it could be to a reckless or even careless driver I could not see.

As we came to the outermost arc of the little detour Von Blon brought the car to a stop, the front wheels pointing directly toward the precipice. A magnificent vista stretched before us. We could look up and down the Hudson for miles. And there was a sense of isolation about the spot, for the hill behind us completely shut off the country inland.

We sat for several moments taking in the unusual view. Then Sibella spoke. Her voice was whimsical, but a curious note of defiance informed it.

"What a perfectly ripping spot for a murder!" she exclaimed, leaning over and looking down the steep slope of the bluff. "Why run the risk of shooting people when all you have to do is to take them for a ride to this snug little shelf, jump from the car, and let them topple—machine and all—over the precipice? Just another unfortunate auto accident—and no one the wiser! . . . Really, I think I'll take up crime in a serious way."

I felt a shudder pass over Ada's body, and I noticed that her face paled. Sibella's comments struck me as particularly heartless and unthinking in view of the terrible experience through which her sister had so recently passed. The cruelty of her words evidently struck the doctor also, for he turned toward her with a look of consternation.

Vance glanced quickly at Ada, and then attempted to banish the embarrassment of the tense silence by remarking lightly:

"We refuse to take alarm, however, Miss Greene; for no one, d' ye see, could seriously consider a criminal career on a day as perfect as this. Taine's theory of climatic influences is most comfortin' in moments like this."

Von Blon said nothing, but his reproachful eyes did not leave Sibella's face.

"Oh, let us go back!" cried Ada pitifully, nestling closer under the lap-robe, as if the air had suddenly become chill.

Without a word Von Blon reversed the machine; and a moment later we were on our way back to the city.

CHAPTER XIII

THE THIRD TRAGEDY

(November 28 and November 30)

THE FOLLOWING Sunday evening, November 28, Markham invited Inspector Moran and Heath to the Stuyvesant Club for an informal conference. Vance and I had dined with him and were present when the two police officials arrived. We retired to Markham's favorite corner of the club's lounge-room; and soon a general discussion of the Greene murders was under way.

"I'm rather amazed," said the Inspector, his voice even quieter than usual, "that nothing has turned up to focus the inquiry. In the average murder case there are numerous lines to be explored, even if the right one is not hit upon immediately. But in this affair there appears to be nothing whatever on which to concentrate."

"That fact in itself, I should say," rejoined Vance, "constitutes a distinguishing characteristic of the case which shouldn't be overlooked, don't y' know. It's a clew of vital importance, and if only we could probe its significance I think we'd be on our way toward a solution."

"A fine clew that is!" grumbled Heath. "'What clew have you

got, Sergeant?' asks the Inspector. 'Oh, a bully clew,' says I. 'And what is it?' asks the Inspector. 'The fact that there ain't *nothing* to go on!' says I."

Vance smiled.

"You're so literal, Sergeant! What I was endeavoring to express, in my purely laic capacity, was this: when there are no clews in a case—no *points de départ,* no tell-tale indications—one is justified in regarding everything as a clew—or, rather, as a factor in the puzzle. To be sure, the great difficulty lies in fitting together these apparently inconsequential pieces. I rather think we've at least a hundred clews in our possession; but none of them has any meaning so long as it's unrelated to the others. This affair is like one of those silly word-puzzles where all the letters are redistributed into a meaningless jumble. The task for the solver is to rearrange them into an intelligible word or sentence."

"Could you name just eight or ten of those hundred clews for me?" Heath requested ironically. "I sure would like to get busy on something definite."

"You know 'em all, Sergeant." Vance refused to fall in with the other's bantering manner. "I'd say that practically everything that has happened since the first alarm reached you might be regarded as a clew."

"Sure!" The Sergeant had lapsed again into sullen gloom. "The footprints, the disappearance of the revolver, that noise Rex heard in the hall. But we've run all those leads up against a blank wall."

"Oh, those things!" Vance sent a ribbon of blue smoke upward. "Yes, they're clews of a kind. But I was referring more specifically to the conditions existing at the Greene mansion—the organisms of the environment there—the psychological elements of the situation."

"Don't get off again on your metaphysical theories and esoteric hypotheses," Markham interjected tartly. "We've either got to find a practical *modus operandi*, or admit ourselves beaten."

"But, Markham old man, you're beaten on the face of it unless you can put your chaotic facts into some kind of order. And the only way you'll be able to do that is by a process of prayerful analysis."

"You give me some facts that've got some sense to 'em," challenged Heath, "and I'll put 'em together soon enough."

"The Sergeant's right," was Markham's comment. "You'll admit that as yet we haven't any significant facts to work with."

"Oh, there'll be more."

Inspector Moran sat up, and his eyes narrowed.

"What do you mean by that, Mr. Vance?" It was obvious that the remark had struck some chord of agreement in him.

"The thing isn't over yet." Vance spoke with unwonted sombreness. "The picture's unfinished. There's more tragedy to come before the monstrous canvas is rounded out. And the hideous thing about it is that there's no way of stopping it. Nothing now can halt the horror that's at work. It's got to go on."

"You feel that, too!" The Inspector's voice was off its normal pitch. "By God! This is the first case I've ever had that frightened me."

"Don't forget, sir," argued Heath, but without conviction, "that we got men watching the house day and night."

"There's no security in that, Sergeant," asserted Vance. "The killer is already in the house. He's part of the deadly atmosphere of the place. He's been there for years, nourished by the toxins that seep from the very stones of the walls."

Heath looked up.

"A member of the family? You said that once before."

"Not necessarily. But some one who has been tainted by the perverted situation that grew out of old Tobias's patriarchal ideas."

"We might manage to put some one in the house to keep an eye on things," suggested the Inspector. "Or, there's a possibility of prevailing upon the members of the family to separate and move to other quarters."

Vance shook his head slowly.

"A spy in the house would be useless. Isn't every one there a spy now, watching all the others, and watching them with fear and suspicion? And as for dispersing the family: not only would you find old Mrs. Greene, who holds the purse-strings, an adamantine obstacle, but you'd meet all manner of legal complications as a result of Tobias's will. No one gets a dollar, I understand, who doesn't remain in the mansion until the worms have ravaged his carcass for a full quarter of a century. And even if you succeeded in scattering the remnants of the Greene line, and locked up the house, you wouldn't have stamped out the killer. And there'll be no end of this thing until a purifying stake has been driven through his heart."

"Are you going in now for vampirism, Vance?" The case had exacerbated Markham's nerves. "Shall we draw an enchanted ring around the house and hang garlic on the door?"

Markham's extravagant comment of harassed discouragement seemed to express the hopeless state of mind of all of us, and there was a long silence. It was Heath who first came back to a practical consideration of the matter in hand.

"You spoke, Mr. Vance, about old man Greene's will. And I've been thinking that, if we knew all the terms of that will, we might find something to help us. There's millions in the estate, all of it left, I hear, to the old lady. What I'd like to know is, has she a full right to dispose of it any way she likes? And I'd also like to know what kind of a will the old lady herself has made. With all that money at stake, we might get on to a motive of some kind."

"Quite—quite!" Vance looked at Heath with undisguised admiration. "That's the most sensible suggestion that's been made thus far. I salute you, Sergeant. Yes, old Tobias's money may have some bearing on the case. Not a direct bearing, perhaps; but the influence of that money—the subterranean power it exerts—is undoubtedly tangled up in these crimes.—How about it, Markham? How does one go about finding out about other people's wills?"

Markham pondered the point.

"I don't believe there'd be any great difficulty in the present instance. Tobias Greene's will is a matter of record, of course, though it might take some little time to look it up in the Surrogate's files; and I happen to know old Buckway, the senior partner of Buckway & Aldine, the Greene solicitors. I see him here at the club occasionally, and I've done one or two small favors for him. I think I could induce him to tell me confidentially the terms of Mrs. Greene's will. I'll see what can be done to-morrow."

Half an hour later the conference broke up and we went home.

"I fear those wills are not going to help much," Vance remarked, as he sipped his high-ball before the fire late that night. "Like everything else in this harrowin' case, they'll possess some significance that can't be grasped until they're fitted into the final picture."

He rose and, going to the book-shelves, took down a small volume.

"And now I think I'll erase the Greenes from my mind *pro tempore,* and dip into the 'Satyricon.' The fusty historians pother frightfully about the reasons for the fall of Rome, whereas the eternal answer is contained in Petronius's imperishable classic of that city's decadence."

He settled himself and turned the pages of his book. But there was no concentration in his attitude, and his eyes wandered constantly from the text.

Two days later—on Tuesday, November 30—Markham telephoned Vance shortly after ten o'clock in the morning, and asked him to come at once to the office. Vance was preparing to attend an exhibition of negro sculpture at the Modern Gallery,* but this indulgence was postponed in view of the District Attorney's urgent call; and in less than half an hour we were at the Criminal Courts Building.

"Ada Greene called up this morning, and asked to see me without delay," explained Markham. "I offered to send Heath out and, if necessary, to come myself later on. But she seemed particularly anxious that I shouldn't do that, and insisted on coming here: said it was a matter she could speak of more freely away from the house. She seemed somewhat upset, so I told her to come ahead. Then I phoned you and notified Heath."

Vance settled himself and lit a cigarette.

"I don't wonder she'd grasp at any chance to shake the atmosphere of her surroundings. And, Markham, I've come to the conclusion that girl knows something that would be highly valuable to our inquiry. It's quite possible, don't y' know, that she's now reached a point where she'll tell us what's on her mind."

As he spoke the Sergeant was announced, and Markham briefly explained the situation to him.

---

* The Modern Gallery was then under the direction of Marius de Zayas, whose collection of African statuette-fetiches was perhaps the finest in America.

"It looks to me," said Heath gloomily, but with interest, "like it was our only chance of getting a lead. We haven't learned anything ourselves that's worth a damn, and unless somebody spills a few suggestions we're up against it."

Ten minutes later Ada Greene was ushered into the office. Though her pallor had gone and her arm was no longer in a sling, she still gave one the impression of weakness. But there was none of the tremulousness or shrinking in her bearing that had heretofore characterized her.

She sat down before Markham's desk, and for a while frowned up at the sunlight, as if debating how to begin.

"It's about Rex, Mr. Markham," she said finally. "I really don't know whether I should have come here or not—it may be very disloyal of me. . . ." She gave him a look of appealing indecision. "Oh, tell me: if a person knows something—something bad and dangerous—about some one very close and very dear, should that person tell, when it might make terrible trouble?"

"That all depends," Markham answered gravely. "In the present circumstances, if you know anything that might be helpful to a solution of the murder of your brother and sister, it's your duty to speak."

"Even if the thing were told me in confidence?" she persisted. "And the person were a member of my family?"

"Even under those conditions, I think." Markham spoke paternally. "Two terrible crimes have been committed, and nothing should be held back that might bring the murderer to justice—whoever he may be."

The girl averted her troubled face for a moment. Then she lifted her head with sudden resolution.

"I'll tell you. . . . You know you asked Rex about the shot in my room, and he told you he didn't hear it. Well, he confided in me, Mr. Markham; and he *did* hear the shot. But he was afraid to admit it lest you might think it funny he didn't get up and give the alarm."

"Why do you think he remained in bed silent, and pretended to every one he was asleep?" Markham attempted to suppress the keen interest the girl's information had roused in him.

"That's what I don't understand. He wouldn't tell me. But he had some reason—I know he did!—some reason that terrified him. I begged him to tell me, but the only explanation he gave was that the shot was not all he heard. . . ."

"Not all!" Markham spoke with ill-concealed excitement. "He heard something else that, you say, terrified him? But why shouldn't he have told us about it?"

"That's the strange part of it. He got angry when I asked him. But there's something he knows—some awful secret; I feel sure of it. . . . Oh, maybe I shouldn't have told you. Maybe it will get Rex into trouble. But I felt that you ought to know because of the frightful things that have happened. I thought perhaps you could talk to Rex and make him tell you what's on his mind."

Again she looked beseechingly at Markham, and there was the anxiety of a vague fear in her eyes.

"Oh, I do wish you'd ask him—and try to find out," she went on, in a pleading tone. "I'd feel—safer if—if . . ."

Markham nodded and patted her hand.

"We'll try to make him talk."

"But don't try at the house," she said quickly. "There are people—things—around; and Rex would be too frightened. Ask him to come here, Mr. Markham. Get him away from that awful place, where he can talk without being afraid that some one's listening. Rex is home now. Ask him to come here. Tell him I'm here, too. Maybe I can help you reason with him. . . . Oh, do this for me, Mr. Markham!"

Markham glanced at the clock and ran his eye over his appointment-pad. He was, I knew, as anxious as Ada to have Rex on the carpet for a questioning; and, after a momentary hesitation, he picked up the telephone-receiver and had Swacker put him through to the Greene mansion. From what I heard of the conversation that ensued, it was plain that he experienced considerable difficulty in urging Rex to come to the office, for he had to resort to a veiled threat of summary legal action before he finally succeeded.

"He evidently fears some trap," commented Markham thoughtfully, replacing the receiver. "But he has promised to get dressed immediately and come."

A look of relief passed over the girl's face.

"There's one other thing I ought to tell you," she said hurriedly; "though it may not mean anything. The other night, in the rear of the lower hall by the stairs, I picked up a piece of paper—like a leaf torn from a note-book. And there was a drawing on it of all our bedrooms up-stairs with four little crosses marked in ink—one at Julia's room, one at Chester's, one at Rex's, and one at mine. And down in the corner were several of the queerest signs, or pictures. One was a heart with three nails in it; and one looked like a parrot. Then there was a picture of what seemed to be three little stones with a line under them. . . ."

Heath suddenly jerked himself forward, his cigar half-way to his lips.

"A parrot, and three stones! . . . And say, Miss Greene, was there an arrow with numbers on it?"

"Yes!" she answered eagerly. "That was there, too."

Heath put his cigar in his mouth and chewed on it with vicious satisfaction.

"That means something, Mr. Markham," he proclaimed, trying to keep the agitation out of his voice. "Those are all symbols—graphic signs, they're called—of Continental crooks, German or Austrian mostly."

"The stones, I happen to know," put in Vance, "represent the idea of the martyrdom of Saint Stephen, who was stoned to death. They're the emblem of Saint Stephen, according to the calendar of the Styrian peasantry."

"I don't know anything about that, sir," answered Heath. "But I know that European crooks use those signs."

"Oh, doubtless. I ran across a number of 'em when I was looking up the emblematic language of the gypsies. A fascinatin' study." Vance seemed uninterested in Ada's discovery.

"Have you this paper with you, Miss Greene?" asked Markham.

The girl was embarrassed and shook her head.

"I'm so sorry," she apologized. "I didn't think it was important. Should I have brought it?"

"Did you destroy it?" Heath put the question excitedly.

"Oh, I have it safely. I put it away. . . ."

"We gotta have that paper, Mr. Markham." The Sergeant had risen and come toward the District Attorney's desk. "It may be just the lead we're looking for."

"If you really want it so badly," said Ada, "I can phone Rex to bring it with him. He'll know where to find it if I explain."

"Right! That'll save me a trip." Heath nodded to Markham. "Try to catch him before he leaves, sir."

Taking up the telephone, Markham again directed Swacker

to get Rex on the wire. After a brief delay the connection was made and he handed the instrument to Ada.

"Hello, Rex dear," she said. "Don't scold me, for there's nothing to worry about. . . . What I wanted of you is this:—in our private mail-box you'll find a sealed envelope of my personal blue stationery. Please get it and bring it with you to Mr. Markham's office. And don't let any one see you take it. . . . That's all, Rex. Now, hurry, and we'll have lunch together down-town."

"It will be at least half an hour before Mr. Greene can get here," said Markham, turning to Vance; "and as I've a waiting-room full of people, why don't you and Van Dine take the young lady to the Stock Exchange and show her how the mad brokers disport themselves.—How would you like that, Miss Greene?"

"I'd love it!" exclaimed the girl.

"Why not go along too, Sergeant?"

"Me!" Heath snorted. "I got excitement enough. I'll run over and talk to the Colonel* for a while."

Vance and Ada and I motored the few blocks to 18 Broad Street, and, taking the elevator, passed through the reception-room (where uniformed attendants peremptorily relieved us of our wraps), and came out upon the visitors' gallery overlooking the floor of the Exchange. There was an unusually active market that day. The pandemonium was almost deafening, and the feverish activity about the trading-posts resembled the riots of an excited mob. I was too familiar with the sight to be particularly impressed; and Vance, who detested noise and disorder, looked on with an air of bored annoyance. But Ada's face lighted up at once. Her eyes sparkled and the blood rushed to her cheeks. She gazed over the railing in a thrall of fascination.

---

* Colonel Benjamin Hanlon, one of the Department's greatest authorities on extradition, was then the commanding officer of the Detective Division attached to the District Attorney's office, with quarters in the Criminal Courts Building.

"And now you see, Miss Greene, how foolish men can be," said Vance.

"Oh, but it's wonderful!" she answered. "They're alive. They feel things. They have something to fight for."

"You think you'd like it?" smiled Vance.

"I'd adore it. I've always longed to do something exciting— something . . . like that. . . ." She extended her hand toward the milling crowds below.

It was easy to understand her reaction after her years of monotonous service to an invalid in the dreary Greene mansion.

At that moment I happened to look up, and, to my surprise, Heath was standing in the doorway scanning the groups of visitors. He appeared troubled and unusually grim, and there was a nervous intentness in the way he moved his head. I raised my hand to attract his attention, and he immediately came to where we stood.

"The Chief wants you at the office right away, Mr. Vance." There was an ominousness in his tone. "He sent me over to get you."

Ada looked at him steadily, and a pallor of fear overspread her face.

"Well, well!" Vance shrugged in mock resignation. "Just when we were getting interested in the sights. But we must obey the Chief—eh, what, Miss Greene?"

But, despite his attempt to make light of Markham's unexpected summons, Ada was strangely silent; and as we rode back to the office she did not speak but sat tensely, her unseeing eyes staring straight ahead.

It seemed an interminable time before we reached the Criminal Courts Building. The traffic was congested; and there was even a long delay at the elevator. Vance appeared to take the situation calmly; but Heath's lips were compressed, and he breathed heavily through his nose, like a man laboring under tense excitement.

As we entered the District Attorney's office Markham rose and looked at the girl with a great tenderness.

"You must be brave, Miss Greene," he said, in a quiet, sympathetic voice. "Something tragic and unforeseen has happened. And as you will have to be told of it sooner or later——"

"It's Rex!" She sank limply into a chair facing Markham's desk.

"Yes," he said softly; "it's Rex. Sproot called up a few minutes after you had gone. . . ."

"And he's been shot—like Julia and Chester!" Her words were scarcely audible, but they brought a sense of horror into the dingy old office.

Markham inclined his head.

"Not five minutes after you telephoned to him some one entered his room and shot him."

A dry sob shook the girl, and she buried her face in her arms.

Markham stepped round the desk and placed his hand gently on her shoulder.

"We've got to face it, my child," he said. "We're going to the house at once to see what can be done and you'd better come in the car with us."

"Oh, I don't want to go back," she moaned. "I'm afraid—*I'm afraid!* . . ."

CHAPTER XIV

FOOTPRINTS ON THE CARPET

(Tuesday, November 30; noon)

Markham had considerable difficulty in persuading Ada to accompany us. The girl seemed almost in a panic of fright. Moreover, she held herself indirectly responsible for Rex's death. But at last she permitted us to lead her down to the car.

Heath had already telephoned to the Homicide Bureau, and his arrangements for the investigation were complete when we started up Centre Street. At Police Headquarters Snitkin and another Central Office man named Burke were waiting for us, and crowded into the tonneau of Markham's car. We made excellent time to the Greene mansion, arriving there in less than twenty minutes.

A plain-clothes man lounged against the iron railing at the end of the street a few yards beyond the gate of the Greene grounds, and at a sign from Heath came forward at once.

"What about it, Santos?" the Sergeant demanded gruffly. "Who's been in and out of here this morning?"

"What's the big idea?" the man retorted indignantly. "That old bimbo of a butler came out about nine and returned in less than half an hour with a package. Said he'd been to Third Avenue to get some dog-biscuits. The family sawbones drove up at quarter past ten—that's his car across the street." He pointed to Von Blon's Daimler, which was parked diagonally opposite. "He's still inside.—Then, about ten minutes after the doc arrived, this young lady"—he indicated Ada—"came out and walked toward Avenue A, where she hopped a taxi. And that's every man, woman, or child that's passed in or out of these gates since I relieved Cameron at eight o'clock this morning."

"And Cameron's report?"

"Nobody all night."

"Well, some one got in some way," growled Heath. "Run along the west wall there and tell Donnelly to come here *pronto*."

Santos disappeared through the gate, and a moment later we could see him hurrying through the side yard toward the garage. In a few minutes Donnelly—the man set to watch the postern gate—came hurrying up.

"Who got in the back way this morning?" barked Heath.

"Nobody, Sergeant. The cook went marketing about ten o'clock, and two regular deliverymen left packages. That's every one who's been through the rear gate since yesterday."

"Is that so!" Heath was viciously sarcastic.

"I'm telling you——"

"Oh, all right, all right." The Sergeant turned to Burke. "You get up on this wall and make the rounds. See if you can find where any one has climbed over.—And you, Snitkin, look over the yard for footprints. When you guys finish, report to me. I'm going inside."

We went up the front walk, which had been swept clean, and Sproot admitted us to the house. His face was as blank as ever, and he took our coats with his usual obsequious formality.

"You'd better go to your room now, Miss Greene," said Markham, placing his hand kindly on Ada's arm. "Lie down, and try to get a little rest. You look tired. I'll be in to see you before I go."

The girl obeyed submissively without a word.

"And you, Sproot," he ordered; "come in the living-room."

The old butler followed us and stood humbly before the centre-table, where Markham seated himself.

"Now, let's hear your story."

Sproot cleared his throat and stared out of the window.

"There's very little to tell, sir. I was in the butler's pantry, polishing the glassware, when I heard the shot——"

"Go back a little further," interrupted Markham. "I understand you made a trip to Third Avenue at nine this morning."

"Yes, sir. Miss Sibella bought a Pomeranian yesterday, and she asked me to get some dog-biscuits after breakfast."

"Who called at the house this morning?"

"No one, sir—that is, no one but Doctor Von Blon."

"All right. Now tell us everything that happened."

"Nothing happened, sir—nothing unusual, that is—until poor Mr. Rex was shot. Miss Ada went out a few minutes after Doctor Von Blon arrived; and a little past eleven o'clock you telephoned to Mr. Rex. Then shortly afterward you telephoned a second time to Mr. Rex; and I returned to the pantry. I had only been there a few minutes when I heard the shot——"

"What time would you say that was?"

"About twenty minutes after eleven, sir."

"Then what?"

"I dried my hands on my apron and stepped into the dining-room to listen. I was not quite sure that the shot had been fired inside the house, but I thought I'd better investigate. So I went up-stairs and, as Mr. Rex's door was open, I looked in his room first. There I saw the poor young man lying on the floor with the blood running from a small wound in his forehead. I called Doctor Von Blon——"

"Where was the doctor?" Vance put the question.

Sproot hesitated, and appeared to think.

"He was up-stairs, sir; and he came at once——"

"Oh—up-stairs! Roaming about vaguely, I presume—a little here, a little there, what?" Vance's eyes bored into the butler. "Come, come, Sproot. Where was the doctor?"

"I think, sir, he was in Miss Sibella's room."

"*Cogito, cogito.* . . . Well, drum your encephalon a bit and try to reach a conclusion. From what sector of space did the corporeal body of Doctor Von Blon emerge after you had called him?"

"The fact is, sir, he came out of Miss Sibella's door."

"Well, well. Fancy that! And, such being the case, one might conclude—without too great a curfuffling of one's brains—that, preceding his issuing from that particular door, he was actually in Miss Sibella's room?"

"I suppose so, sir."

"Dash it all, Sproot! You know deuced well he was there."

"Well—yes, sir."

"And now suppose you continue with your odyssey . . ."

"It was more like the Iliad, if I may say so. More tragic-like, if you understand what I mean; although Mr. Rex was not exactly a Hector. However that may be, sir, Doctor Von Blon came immediately——"

"He had not heard the shot, then?"

"Apparently not, for he seemed very much startled when he saw Mr. Rex. And Miss Sibella, who followed him into Mr. Rex's room, was startled, too."

"Did they make any comment?"

"As to that I couldn't say. I came down-stairs at once and tele-phoned to Mr. Markham."

As he spoke Ada appeared at the archway, her eyes wide.

"Some one's been in my room," she announced, in a fright-ened voice. "The French doors to the balcony were partly open when I went up-stairs just now, and there were dirty snow-tracks across the floor. . . . Oh, what does it mean? Do you think——?"

Markham had jerked himself forward.

"You left the French doors shut when you went out?"

"Yes—of course," she answered. "I rarely open them in winter."

"And were they locked?"

"I'm not sure, but I think so. They must have been locked—though how could any one have got in unless I'd forgotten to turn the key?"

Heath had risen and stood listening to the girl's story with grim bewilderment.

"Probably the bird with those galoshes again," he mumbled. "I'll get Jerym himself up here this time."

Markham nodded and turned back to Ada.

"Thank you for telling us, Miss Greene. Suppose you go to some other room and wait for us. We want your room left just as you found it until we've had time to examine it."

"I'll go to the kitchen and stay with cook. I—I don't want to be alone." And with a catch of her breath she left us.

"Where's Doctor Von Blon now?" Markham asked Sproot.

"With Mrs. Greene, sir."

"Tell him we're here and would like to see him at once."

The butler bowed and went out.

Vance was pacing up and down, his eyes almost closed.

"It grows madder every minute," he said. "It was insane

enough without those foot-tracks and that open door. There's something devilish going on here, Markham. There's demonology and witchcraft afoot, or something strangely close to it. I say, is there anything in the Pandects or the Justinian Code relating to the proper legal procedure against diabolic possession or spiritism?"

Before Markham could rebuke him Von Blon entered. His usual suavity had disappeared. He bowed jerkily without speaking, and smoothed his moustache nervously with an unsteady hand.

"Sproot tells me, doctor," said Markham, "that you did not hear the shot fired in Rex's room."

"No!" The fact seemed both to puzzle and disturb him. "I can't make it out either, for Rex's door into the hall was open."

"You were in Miss Sibella's room, were you not?" Vance had halted, and stood studying the doctor.

Von Blon lifted his eyebrows.

"I was. Sibella had been complaining about——"

"A sore throat or something of the kind, no doubt," finished Vance. "But that's immaterial. The fact is that neither you nor Miss Sibella heard the shot. Is that correct?"

The doctor inclined his head. "I knew nothing of it till Sproot knocked on the door and beckoned me across the hall."

"And Miss Sibella accompanied you into Rex's room?"

"She came in just behind me, I believe. But I told her not to touch anything, and sent her immediately back to her room. When I came out into the hall again I heard Sproot phoning the District Attorney's office, and thought I'd better wait till the police arrived. After talking over the situation with Sibella I informed Mrs. Greene of the tragedy, and remained with her until Sproot told me of your arrival."

"You saw no one else up-stairs, or heard no suspicious noise?"

"No one—nothing. The house, in fact, was unusually quiet."

"Do you recall if Miss Ada's door was open?"

The doctor pondered a moment. "I don't recall—which means it was probably closed. Otherwise I would have noticed it."

"And how is Mrs. Greene this morning?" Vance's question, put negligently, sounded curiously irrelevant.

Von Blon gave a start.

"She seemed somewhat more comfortable when I first saw her, but the news of Rex's death disturbed her considerably. When I left her just now she was complaining about the shooting pains in her spine."

Markham had got up and now moved restlessly toward the archway.

"The Medical Examiner will be here any minute," he said; "and I want to look over Rex's room before he arrives. You might come with us, doctor.—And you, Sproot, had better remain at the front door."

We went up-stairs quietly: I think it was in all our minds that we should not advertise our presence to Mrs. Greene. Rex's room, like all those in the Greene mansion, was spacious. It had a large window at the front and another at the side. There were no draperies to shut out the light, and the slanting midday sun of winter poured in. The walls, as Chester had once told us, were lined with books; and pamphlets and papers were piled in every available nook. The chamber resembled a student's workshop more than a bedroom.

In front of the Tudor fireplace in the centre of the left wall—a duplication of the fireplace in Ada's room—sprawled the body of Rex Greene. His left arm was extended, but his right arm was crooked, and the fingers were tightened, as if holding some object. His dome-like head was turned a little to one side; and a thin stream of blood ran down his temple to the floor from a tiny aperture over the right eye.

Heath studied the body for several minutes.

"He was shot standing still, Mr. Markham. He collapsed in a heap and then straightened out a little after he'd hit the floor."

Vance was bending over the dead man with a puzzled expression.

"Markham, there's something curious and inconsistent here," he said. "It was broad daylight when this thing happened, and the lad was shot from the front—there are even powder marks on the face. But his expression is perfectly natural. No sign of fear or astonishment—rather peaceful and unconcerned, in fact. . . . It's incredible. The murderer and the pistol certainly weren't invisible."

Heath nodded slowly.

"I noticed that too, sir. It's damn peculiar." He bent more closely over the body. "That wound looks to me like a thirty-two," he commented, turning to the doctor for confirmation.

"Yes," said Von Blon. "It appears to have been made with the same weapon that was used against the others."

"It was the same weapon," Vance pronounced sombrely, taking out his cigarette-case with thoughtful deliberation. "And it was the same killer who used it." He smoked a moment, his troubled gaze resting on Rex's face. "But why was it done at just this time—in the daylight, with the door open, and when there were people close at hand? Why didn't the murderer wait until night? Why did he run such a needless risk?"

"Don't forget," Markham reminded him, "that Rex was on the point of coming to my office to tell me something."

"But who knew he was about to indulge in revelations? He

was shot within ten minutes of your call——" He broke off and turned quickly to the doctor. "What telephone extensions are there in the house?"

"There are three, I believe." Von Blon spoke easily. "There's one in Mrs. Greene's room, one in Sibella's room, and, I think, one in the kitchen. The main phone is, of course, in the lower front hall."

"A regular central office," growled Heath. "Almost anybody coulda listened in." Suddenly he fell on his knees beside the body and unflexed the fingers of the right hand.

"I'm afraid you won't find that cryptic drawing, Sergeant," murmured Vance. "If the murderer shot Rex in order to seal his mouth the paper will surely be gone. Any one overhearing the phone calls, d'ye see, would have learned of the envelope he was to fetch along."

"I guess you're right, sir. But I'm going to have a look."

He felt under the body and then systematically went through the dead man's pockets. But he found nothing even resembling the blue envelope mentioned by Ada. At last he rose to his feet.

"It's gone, all right."

Then another idea occurred to him. Going hurriedly into the hall, he called down the stairs to Sproot. When the butler appeared Heath swung on him savagely.

"Where's the private mail-box?"

"I don't know that I exactly understand you." Sproot's answer was placid and unruffled. "There is a mail-box just outside the front door. Do you refer to that, sir?"

"No! You know damn well I don't. I want to know where the private—get me?—*private* mail-box is, *in the house.*"

"Perhaps you are referring to the little silver pyx for outgoing mail on the table in the lower hall."

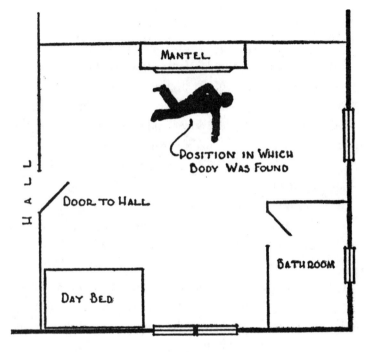

REX'S BEDROOM.

"'Pyx,' is it!" The Sergeant's sarcasm was stupendous. "Well, go down and bring me everything that's in this here pyx.—No! Wait a minute—I'll keep you company. . . . *Pyx!*" He took Sproot by the arm and fairly dragged him from the room.

A few moments later he returned, crestfallen.

"Empty!" was his laconic announcement.

"But don't give up hope entirely just because your cabalistic diagram has disappeared," Vance exhorted him. "I doubt if it would have helped you much. This case isn't a rebus. It's a complex mathematical formula, filled with moduli, infinitesimals, quantics, faciends, derivatives, and coefficients. Rex himself might have solved it if he hadn't been shoved off the earth so soon." His eyes wandered over the room. "And I'm not at all sure he hadn't solved it."

Markham was growing impatient.

"We'd better go down to the drawing-room and wait for Doctor Doremus and the men from Headquarters," he suggested. "We can't learn anything here."

We went out into the hall, and as we passed Ada's door Heath threw it open and stood on the threshold surveying the room. The French doors leading to the balcony were slightly ajar, and the wind from the west was flapping their green chintz curtains. On the light beige rug were several damp discolored tracks leading round the foot of the bed to the hall-door where we stood. Heath studied the marks for a moment, and then drew the door shut again.

"They're footprints, all right," he remarked. "Some one tracked in the dirty snow from the balcony and forgot to shut the glass doors."

We were scarcely seated in the drawing-room when there

came a knocking on the front door; and Sproot admitted Snitkin and Burke.

"You first, Burke," ordered the Sergeant, as the two officers appeared. "Any signs of an entry over the wall?"

"Not a one." The man's overcoat and trousers were smudged from top to bottom. "I crawled all round the top of the wall, and I'm here to tell you that nobody left any traces anywheres. If any guy got over that wall, he vaulted."

"Fair enough.—And now you, Snitkin."

"*I* got news for you." The detective spoke with overt triumph. "Somebody's walked up those outside steps to the stone balcony on the west side of the house. And he walked up 'em this morning after the snowfall at nine o'clock, for the tracks are fresh. Furthermore, they're the same size as the ones we found last time on the front walk."

"Where do these new tracks come from?" Heath leaned forward eagerly.

"That's the hell of it, Sergeant. They come from the front walk right below the steps to the front door; and there's no tracing 'em farther back because the front walk's been swept clean."

"I mighta known it," grumbled Heath. "And the tracks are only going one way?"

"That's all. They leave the walk a few feet below the front door, swing round the corner of the house, and go up the steps to the balcony. The guy who made 'em didn't come down that way."

The Sergeant puffed disappointedly on his cigar.

"So he went up the balcony steps, entered the French doors, crossed Ada's room to the hall, did his dirty work, and then— disappeared! A sweet case this is!" He clicked his tongue with disgust.

"The man may have gone out by the front door," suggested Markham.

The Sergeant made a wry face and bellowed for Sproot, who entered immediately.

"Say, which way did you go up-stairs when you heard the shot?"

"I went up the servants' stairs, sir."

"Then some one mighta gone down the front stairs at the same time without your seeing him?"

"Yes, sir; it's quite possible."

"That's all."

Sproot bowed and again took up his post at the front door.

"Well, it looks like that's what happened, sir," Heath commented to Markham. "Only how did he get in and out of the grounds without being seen? That's what I want to know."

Vance was standing by the window gazing out upon the river.

"There's something dashed unconvincing about those recurrent spoors in the snow. Our eccentric culprit is altogether too careless with his feet and too careful with his hands. He doesn't leave a fingerprint or any other sign of his presence except those foot-tracks—all nice and tidy and staring us in the face. But they don't square with the rest of this fantastic business."

Heath stared hopelessly at the floor. He was patently of Vance's opinion; but the dogged thoroughness of his nature asserted itself, and presently he looked up with a forced show of energy.

"Go and phone Captain Jerym, Snitkin, and tell him I wish he'd hustle out here to look at some carpet-tracks. Then make measurements of those footprints on the balcony steps.—And you, Burke, take up a post in the upper hall, and don't let any one go into the two front west rooms."

CHAPTER XV

THE MURDERER IN THE HOUSE

(Tuesday, November 30; 12.30 p. m.)

WHEN SNITKIN and Burke had gone Vance turned from the window and strolled to where the doctor was sitting.

"I think it might be well," he said quietly, "if the exact whereabouts of every one in the house preceding and during the shooting was determined.—We know, doctor, that you arrived here at about a quarter past ten. How long were you with Mrs. Greene?"

Von Blon drew himself up and gave Vance a resentful stare. But quickly his manner changed and he answered courteously:

"I sat with her for perhaps half an hour; then I went to Sibella's room—a little before eleven, I should say—and remained there until Sproot called me."

"And was Miss Sibella with you in the room all the time?"

"Yes—the entire time."

"Thank you."

Vance returned to the window, and Heath, who had been watching the doctor belligerently, took his cigar from his mouth and cocked his head at Markham.

"You know, sir, I was just thinking over the Inspector's suggestion about planting some one in the house to keep an eye on things. How would it be if we got rid of this nurse that's here now, and put in one of our own women from Headquarters?"

Von Blon looked up with eager approval.

"An excellent plan!" he exclaimed.

"Very well, Sergeant," agreed Markham. "You attend to it."

"Your woman can begin to-night," Von Blon told Heath. "I'll meet you here whenever you say, and give her instructions. There's nothing very technical for her to do."

Heath made a notation in a battered note-book.

"I'll meet you here, say, at six o'clock. How's that?"

"That will suit me perfectly." Von Blon rose. "And now, if I can be of no more service . . ."

"That's quite all right, doctor," said Markham. "Go right ahead."

But instead of immediately leaving the house Von Blon went up-stairs, and we heard him knock on Sibella's door. A few minutes later he came down again and passed on to the front door without a glance in our direction.

In the meantime Snitkin had come in and informed the Sergeant that Captain Jerym was leaving Police Headquarters at once and would arrive within half an hour. He had then gone outside to make his measurements of the footprints on the balcony steps.

"And now," suggested Markham, "I think we might see Mrs. Greene. It's possible she heard something. . . ."

Vance roused himself from apparent lethargy.

"By all means. But first let us get a few facts in hand. I long to hear where the nurse was during the half-hour preceding Rex's demise. And I could bear to know if the old lady was alone immediately following the firing of the revolver.—Why not have our Miss Nightingale on the tapis before we brave the invalid's imprecations?"

Markham concurred, and Heath sent Sproot to summon her.

The nurse came in with an air of professional detachment; but her roseate cheeks had paled perceptibly since we last saw her.

"Miss Craven"—Vance's manner was easy and business-like—"will you please tell us exactly what you were doing between half past ten and half past eleven this morning?"

"I was in my room on the third floor," she answered. "I went there when the doctor arrived a little after ten, and remained until he called me to bring Mrs. Greene's bouillon. Then I returned to my room and stayed until the doctor again summoned me to sit with Mrs. Greene while he was with you gentlemen."

"When you were in your room, was the door open?"

"Oh, yes. I always leave it open in the daytime in case Mrs. Greene calls."

"And her door was open, too, I take it."

"Yes."

"Did you hear the shot?"

"No, I didn't."

"That will be all, Miss Craven." Vance accompanied her to the hall. "You'd better return to your room now, for we're going to pay a visit to your patient."

Mrs. Greene eyed us vindictively when we entered after having knocked and been imperiously ordered to come in.

"More trouble," she complained. "Am I never to have any peace in my own house? The first day in weeks I've felt even moderately comfortable—and then all this had to happen to upset me!"

"We regret, madam—more than you do apparently—that your son is dead," said Markham. "And we are sorry for the annoyance the tragedy is causing you. But that does not relieve me from the necessity of investigating the affair. As you were awake at the time the shot was fired, it is essential that we seek what information you may be able to give us."

"What information can I give you—a helpless paralytic, lying here alone?" A smouldering anger flickered in her eyes. "It strikes me that you are the one to give *me* information."

Markham ignored her barbed retort.

"The nurse tells me your door was open this morning. . . ."

"And why shouldn't it have been? Am I expected to be entirely excommunicated from the rest of the household?"

"Certainly not. I was merely trying to find out if, by any chance, you were in a position to hear anything that went on in the hall."

"Well, I heard nothing—if that's all you want to know."

Markham persisted patiently.

"You heard no one, for instance, cross Miss Ada's room, or open Miss Ada's door?"

"I've already told you I heard nothing." The old lady's denial was viciously emphatic.

"Nor any one walking in the hall, or descending the stairs?"

"No one but that incompetent doctor and the impossible Sproot. Were we supposed to have had visitors this morning?"

"Some one shot your son," Markham reminded her coolly.

"It was probably his own fault," she snapped. Then she seemed to relent a bit. "Still, Rex was not as hard and thoughtless as the rest of the children. But even he neglected me shamefully." She appeared to weigh the matter. "Yes," she decided, "he received just punishment for the way he treated me."

Markham struggled with a hot resentment. At last he managed to ask, with apparent calmness:

"Did you hear the shot with which your son was punished?"

"I did not." Her tone was again irate. "I knew nothing of the disturbance until the doctor saw fit to tell me."

"And yet Mr. Rex's door, as well as yours, was open," said Markham. "I can hardly understand your not having heard the shot."

The old lady gave him a look of scathing irony.

"Am I to sympathize with your lack of understanding?"

"Lest you be tempted to, madam, I shall leave you." Markham bowed stiffly and turned on his heel.

As we reached the lower hall Doctor Doremus arrived.

"Your friends are still at it, I hear, Sergeant," he greeted Heath, with his usual breezy manner. Handing his coat and hat to Sproot, he came forward and shook hands with all of us. "When you fellows don't spoil my breakfast you interfere with my lunch," he repined. "Where's the body?"

Heath led him up-stairs, and after a few minutes returned to the drawing-room. Taking out another cigar he bit the end of it savagely. "Well, sir, I guess you'll want to see this Miss Sibella next, won't you?"

"We might as well," sighed Markham. "Then I'll tackle the servants and leave things to you. The reporters will be along pretty soon."

"Don't I know it! And what they're going to do to us in the papers'll be a-plenty!"

"And you can't even tell them 'it is confidently expected that an arrest will be made in the immediate future,' don't y' know," grinned Vance. "It's most distressin'."

Heath made an inarticulate noise of exasperation and, calling Sproot, sent him for Sibella.

A moment later she came in carrying a small Pomeranian.

She was paler than I had ever seen her, and there was unmistakable fright in her eyes. When she greeted us it was without her habitual gaiety.

"This thing is getting rather ghastly, isn't it?" she remarked when she had taken a seat.

"It is indeed dreadful," returned Markham soberly. "You have our very deepest sympathy. . . ."

"Oh, thanks awf'ly." She accepted the cigarette Vance offered her. "But I'm beginning to wonder how long I'll be here to receive condolences." She spoke with forced lightness, but a strained quality in her voice told of her suppressed emotion.

Markham regarded her sympathetically.

"I do not think it would be a bad idea if you went away for a while—to some friend's house, let us say—preferably out of the city."

"Oh, no." She tossed her head with defiance. "I sha'n't run away. If there's any one really bent on killing me, he'll manage it somehow, wherever I am. Anyway, I'd have to come back sooner or later. I couldn't board with out-of-town friends indefinitely— could I?" She looked at Markham with a kind of anxious despair. "You haven't any idea, I suppose, who it is that's obsessed with the idea of exterminating us Greenes?"

Markham was reluctant to admit to her the utter hopelessness of the official outlook; and she turned appealingly to Vance.

"You needn't treat me like a child," she said spiritedly. "You, at least, Mr. Vance, can tell me if there is any one under suspicion."

"No, dash it all, Miss Greene!—there isn't," he answered promptly. "It's an amazin' confession to have to make; but it's true. That's why, I think, Mr. Markham suggested that you go away for a while."

"It's very thoughtful of him and all that," she returned. "But I think I'll stay and see it through."

"You're a very brave girl," said Markham, with troubled admiration. "And I assure you everything humanly possible will be done to safeguard you."

"Well, so much for that." She tossed her cigarette into a receiver, and began abstractedly to pet the dog in her lap. "And now, I suppose, you want to know if I heard the shot. Well, I didn't. So you may continue the inquisition from that point."

"You were in your room, though, at the time of your brother's death?"

"I was in my room all morning," she said. "My first appearance beyond the threshold was when Sproot brought the sad tidings of Rex's passing. But Doctor Von shooed me back again; and there I've remained until now. Model behavior, don't you think, for a member of this new and wicked generation?"

"What time did Doctor Von Blon come to your room?" asked Vance.

Sibella gave him a faint whimsical smile.

"I'm so glad it was you who asked that question. I'm sure Mr. Markham would have used a disapproving tone—though it's quite *au fait* to receive one's doctor in one's boudoir.—Let me see. I'm sure you asked Doctor Von the same question, so I must be careful. . . . A little before eleven, I should say."

"The doc's exact words," chimed in Heath suspiciously.

Sibella turned a look of amused surprise upon him.

"Isn't that wonderful! But then, I've always been told that honesty is the best policy."

"And did Doctor Von Blon remain in your room until called by Sproot?" pursued Vance.

"Oh, yes. He was smoking his pipe. Mother detests pipes, and he often sneaks into my room to enjoy a quiet smoke."

"And what were you doing during the doctor's visit?"

"I was bathing this ferocious animal." She held up the Pomeranian for Vance's inspection. "Doesn't he look nice?"

"In the bathroom?"

"Naturally. I'd hardly bathe him in the *poudrière.*"

"And was the bathroom door closed?"

"As to that I couldn't say. But it's quite likely. Doctor Von is like a member of the family, and I'm terribly rude to him sometimes."

Vance got up.

"Thank you very much, Miss Greene. We're sorry we had to trouble you. Do you mind remaining in your room for a while?"

"Mind? On the contrary. It's about the only place I feel safe." She walked to the archway. "If you do find out anything you'll let me know—won't you? There's no use pretending any longer. I'm dreadfully scared." Then, as if ashamed of her admission, she went quickly down the hall.

Just then Sproot admitted the two finger-print experts—Dubois and Bellamy—and the official photographer. Heath joined them in the hall and took them up-stairs, returning immediately.

"And now what, sir?"

Markham seemed lost in gloomy speculation, and it was Vance who answered the Sergeant's query.

"I rather think," he said, "that another verbal bout with the pious Hemming and the taciturn Frau Mannheim might dispose of a loose end or two."

Hemming was sent for. She came in laboring under intense excitement. Her eyes fairly glittered with the triumph of the prophetess whose auguries have come to pass. But she had no information whatever to impart. She had spent most of the forenoon in the laundry, and had been unaware of the tragedy until Sproot had mentioned it to her shortly before our arrival. She was voluble, however, on the subject of divine punishment, and it was with difficulty that Vance stemmed her oracular stream of words.

Nor could the cook throw any light on Rex's murder. She had been in the kitchen, she said, the entire morning except for the hour she had gone marketing. She had not heard the shot and, like Hemming, knew of the tragedy only through Sproot. A marked change, however, had come over the woman. When she had entered the drawing-room fright and resentment animated her usually stolid features, and as she sat before us her fingers worked nervously in her lap.

Vance watched her critically during the interview. At the end he asked suddenly:

"Miss Ada has been with you in the kitchen this past half-hour?"

At the mention of Ada's name her fear was perceptibly intensified. She drew a deep breath.

"Yes, little Ada has been with me. And thank the good God she was away this morning when Mr. Rex was killed, or it might have been her and not Mr. Rex. They tried once to shoot her, and maybe they'll try again. She oughtn't to be allowed to stay in this house."

"I think it only fair to tell you, Frau Mannheim," said Vance, "that some one will be watching closely over Miss Ada from now on."

The woman looked at him gratefully.

"Why should any one want to harm little Ada?" she asked, in an anguished tone. "I also shall watch over her."

When she had left us Vance said:

"Something tells me, Markham, that Ada could have no better protector in this house than that motherly German.—And yet," he added, "there'll be no end of this grim carnage until we have the murderer safely gyved." His face darkened: his mouth was as cruel as Pietro de' Medici's. "This hellish business isn't ended. The final picture is only just emerging. And it's damnable—worse than any of the horrors of Rops or Doré."

Markham nodded with dismal depression.

"Yes, there appears to be an inevitability about these tragedies that's beyond mere human power to combat." He got up wearily and addressed himself to Heath. "There's nothing more I can do here at present, Sergeant. Carry on, and phone me at the office before five."

We were about to take our departure when Captain Jerym arrived. He was a quiet, heavy-set man, with a gray, scraggly moustache and small, deep-set eyes. One might easily have mistaken him for a shrewd, efficient merchant. After a brief hand-shaking ceremony Heath piloted him up-stairs.

Vance had already donned his ulster, but now he removed it.

"I think I'll tarry a bit and hear what the Captain has to say regarding those footprints. Y' know, Markham, I've been evolving a rather fantastic theory about 'em; and I want to test it."

Markham looked at him a moment with questioning curiosity. Then he glanced at his watch.

"I'll wait with you," he said.

Ten minutes later Doctor Doremus came down, and paused long enough on his way out to tell us that Rex had been shot with a .32 revolver held at a distance of about a foot from the forehead, the bullet having entered directly from the front and embedded itself, in all probability, in the midbrain.

A quarter of an hour after Doremus had gone Heath re-entered the drawing-room. He expressed uneasy surprise at seeing us still there.

"Mr. Vance wanted to hear Jerym's report," Markham explained.

"The Captain'll be through any minute now." The Sergeant sank into a chair. "He's checking Snitkin's measurements. He couldn't make much of the tracks on the carpet, though."

"And finger-prints?" asked Markham.

"Nothing yet."

"And there won't be," added Vance. "There wouldn't be footprints if they weren't deliberately intended for us."

Heath shot him a sharp look, but before he could speak Captain Jerym and Snitkin came down-stairs.

"What's the verdict, Cap?" asked the Sergeant.

"Those footprints on the balcony steps," said Jerym, "were made with galoshes of the same size and markings as the pattern turned over to me by Snitkin a fortnight or so ago. As for the prints in the room, I'm not so sure. They appear to be the same, however; and the dirt on them is sooty, like the dirt on the snow outside the French doors. I've several photographs of them; and I'll know definitely when I get my enlargements under the microscope."

Vance rose and sauntered to the archway.

"May I have your permission to go up-stairs a moment, Sergeant?"

Heath looked mystified. His instinct was to ask a reason for this unexpected request, but all he said was: "Sure. Go ahead."

Something in Vance's manner—an air of satisfaction combined with a suppressed eagerness—told me that he had verified his theory.

He was gone less than five minutes. When he returned he carried a pair of galoshes similar to those that had been found in Chester's closet. He handed them to Captain Jerym.

"You'll probably find that these made the tracks."

Both Jerym and Snitkin examined them carefully, comparing the measurements and fitting the rough patterns to the soles. Finally, the Captain took one of them to the window, and affixing a jeweller's glass to his eye, studied the riser of the heel.

"I think you're right," he agreed. "There's a worn place here which corresponds to an indentation on the cast I made."

Heath had sprung to his feet and stood eyeing Vance.

"Where did you find 'em?" he demanded.

"Tucked away in the rear of the little linen-closet at the head of the stairs."

The Sergeant's excitement got the better of him. He swung about to Markham, fairly spluttering with consternation.

"Those two guys from the Bureau that went over this house looking for the gun told me there wasn't a pair of galoshes in the place; and I specially told 'em to keep their eyes pealed for galoshes. And now Mr. Vance finds 'em in the linen-closet off the main hall up-stairs!"

"But, Sergeant," said Vance mildly, "the galoshes weren't there when your sleuths were looking for the revolver. On both former occasions the johnny who wore 'em had plenty of time to put 'em away safely. But to-day, d' ye see, he had no chance to sequester them; so he left 'em in the linen-closet for the time being."

"Oh, that's it, is it?" Heath growled vaguely. "Well, what's the rest of the story, Mr. Vance?"

"That's all there is to date. If I knew the rest I'd know who fired the shots. But I might remind you that neither of your *sergents-de-ville* saw any suspicious person leave here."

"Good God, Vance!" Markham was on his feet. "That means that the murderer is in the house this minute."

"At any rate," returned Vance lazily, "I think we are justified in assuming that the murderer was here when we arrived."

"But nobody's left the place but Von Blon," blurted Heath.

Vance nodded. "Oh, it's wholly possible the murderer is still in the house, Sergeant."

CHAPTER XVI

THE LOST POISONS

(Tuesday, November 30; 2 p. m.)

MARKHAM AND Vance and I had a late lunch at the Stuyvesant Club. During the meal the subject of the murder was avoided as if by tacit agreement; but when we sat smoking over our coffee Markham settled back in his chair and surveyed Vance sternly.

"Now," he said, "I want to hear how you came to find those galoshes in the linen-closet. And, damn it! I don't want any garrulous evasions or quotations out of Bartlett."

"I'm quite willing to unburden my soul," smiled Vance. "It was all so dashed simple. I never put any stock in the burglar theory, and so was able to approach the problem with a virgin mind, as it were."

He lit a fresh cigarette and poured himself another cup of coffee.

"Perpend, Markham. On the night that Julia and Ada were shot a double set of footprints was found. It had stopped snowing at about eleven o'clock, and the tracks had been made between that hour and midnight, when the Sergeant arrived on the scene. On the night of Chester's murder there was another set of footprints similar to the others; and they too had been made shortly after the weather had cleared. Here, then, were tracks in the snow, approaching and retreating from the front door, preceding each crime; and both sets had been made after the snow had stopped falling *when they would be distinctly visible and determinable*. This was not a particularly striking coincidence, but it was sufficiently arresting to create a slight strain on my *cortex cerebri*. And the strain increased perceptibly this morning when Snitkin reported his discovery of fresh footprints on the balcony steps; for once again the same meteorological conditions had accompanied our culprit's passion for leaving spoors. I was therefore driven to the irresistible inference, as you learned Solons put it, that the murderer, so careful and calculating about everything else, had deliberately made all these footprints for our special edification. In each instance, d' ye see, he had chosen the only hour of the day when his tracks would not be obliterated by falling snow or confused with other tracks.... Are you there?"

"Go ahead," said Markham. "I'm listening."

"To proceed, then. Another coincidence attached to these three sets of footprints. It was impossible, because of the dry, flaky nature of the snow, to determine whether the first set had originated in the house and returned there, or had first approached the house from the street and then retreated. Again, on the night of Chester's demise, when the snow was damp and susceptible to clear impressions, the same doubt arose. The tracks to and from the house were on opposite sides of the front walk: not a single footstep overlapped! Accidental? Perhaps. But not wholly reasonable. A person walking to and from a door along a comparatively narrow pathway would almost certainly have doubled on some of his tracks. And even if he had failed to superimpose any of his footprints, the parallel spoors would have been close together. But these two lines of prints were far apart: each clung to the extreme edge of the walk, as if the person who made them was positively afraid of overlapping. Now, consider the footprints made this morning. There was a single line of them entering the house, but none coming out. We concluded that the murderer had made his escape *via* the front door and down the neatly swept walk; but this, after all, was only an assumption."

Vance sipped his coffee and inhaled a moment on his cigarette.

"The point I'm trying to bring out is this: there is no proof whatever that all these footprints were not made by some one in the house who first went out and then returned for the express purpose of leading the police to believe that an outsider was guilty. And, on the other hand, there is evidence that the footprints actually did originate in the house; because if an outsider had made them he would have been at no pains to confuse the issue of their origin, since, in any event, they could not have been traced back farther than the street. Therefore, as a tentative starting-point, I assumed that the tracks had, in reality, been made by some one in the house.—I can't say, of course, whether or not my layman's logic adds lustre to the gladsome light of jurisprudence——"

"Your reasoning is consistent as far as it goes," cut in Markham tartly. "But it is hardly complete enough to have led you directly to the linen-closet this morning."

"True. But there were various contribut'ry factors. For instance, the galoshes which Snitkin found in Chester's clothes-closet were the exact size of the prints. At first I toyed with the idea that they were the actual instruments of our unknown's vestigial deception. But when, after they had been taken to Headquarters, another set of similar tracks appeared—to wit, the ones found this morning—I amended my theory slightly, and concluded that Chester had owned two pairs of galoshes—one that had perhaps been discarded but not thrown away. That was why I wanted to wait for Captain Jerym's report: I was anxious to learn if the new tracks were exactly like the old ones."

"But even so," interrupted Markham, "your theory that the footprints emanated from the house strikes me as being erected on pretty weak scaffolding. Were there any other indicants?"

"I was coming to them," replied Vance reproachfully. "But you *will* rush me so. Pretend that I'm a lawyer, and my summation will sound positively breathless."

"I'm more likely to pretend that I'm a presiding judge, and give you *sus. per coll.*"

"Ah, well." Vance sighed and continued. "Let us consider the hypothetical intruder's means of escape after the shooting of Julia and Ada. Sproot came into the upper hall immediately after the shot had been fired in Ada's room; yet he heard nothing—neither footsteps in the hall nor the front door closing. And, Markham old thing, a person in galoshes going down marble steps in the dark is no midsummer zephyr for silence. In the circumstances Sproot would have been certain to hear him making his escape. Therefore, the explanation that suggested itself to me was that *he did not make his escape.*"

"And the footprints outside?"

"Were made beforehand by some one walking to the front gate and back.—And that brings me to the night of Chester's murder. You remember Rex's tale of hearing a dragging noise in the hall and a door closing about fifteen minutes before the shot was fired, and Ada's corroboration of the door-shutting part of the story? The noise, please note, was heard after it had stopped snowing—in fact, after the moon had come out. Could the noise not easily have been a person walking in galoshes, or even taking them off, after having returned from making those separated tracks to and from the gate? And might not that closing door have been the door of the linen-closet where the galoshes were being temporarily cached?"

Markham nodded. "Yes, the sounds Rex and Ada heard might be explained that way."

"And this morning's business was even plainer. There were footprints on the balcony steps, made between nine o'clock and noon. But neither of the guards saw any one enter the grounds. Moreover, Sproot waited a few moments in the dining-room after the shot had been fired in Rex's room; and if any one had come down the stairs and gone out the front door Sproot would certainly have heard him. It's true that the murderer might have descended the front stairs as Sproot went up the servants' stairs. But is that likely? Would he have waited in the upper hall after killing Rex, knowing that some one was likely to step out and discover him? I think not. And anyway, the guards saw no one leave the estate. *Ergo,* I concluded that *no one came down the front stairs after Rex's death.* I assumed again that the footprints had been made at some earlier hour. This time, however, the murderer did not go to the gate and return, for a guard was there who would have seen him; and, furthermore, the front steps and the walk had been swept. So our track-maker, after having donned the galoshes, stepped out of the front door, walked round the corner of the house, mounted the balcony steps, and re-entered the upper hall by way of Ada's room."

"I see." Markham leaned over and knocked the ashes from his cigar. "Therefore, you inferred that the galoshes were still in the house."

"Exactly. But I'll admit I didn't think of the linen-closet at once. First I tried Chester's room. Then I took a look round Julia's chamber; and I was about to go up to the servants' quarters when I recalled Rex's story of the closing door. I ran my eye over all the second-story doors, and straightway tried the linen-closet—which was, after all, the most likely place for a transient occultation. And lo! there were the galoshes tucked under an old drugget. The murderer had probably hidden them there both times before, pending an opportunity of secreting them more thoroughly."

"But where could they have been concealed so that our searchers didn't run across them?"

"As to that, now, I couldn't say. They may have been taken out of the house altogether."

There was a silence for several minutes. Then Markham spoke.

"The finding of the galoshes pretty well proves your theory, Vance. But do you realize what confronts us now? If your reasoning is correct, the guilty person is some one with whom we've been talking this morning. It's an appalling thought. I've gone over in my mind every member of that household; and I simply can't regard any one of them as a potential mass-murderer."

"Sheer moral prejudice, old dear." Vance's voice assumed a note of raillery. "I'm a bit cynical myself, and the only person at the Greene mansion I'd eliminate as a possibility would be Frau Mannheim. She's not sufficiently imaginative to have planned this accumulative massacre. But as regards the others, I could picture any one of 'em as being at the bottom of this diabolical slaughter. It's a mistaken idea, don't y' know, to imagine that a murderer looks like a murderer. No murderer ever does. The only people who really look like murderers are quite harmless.

Do you recall the mild and handsome features of the Reverend Richeson of Cambridge? Yet he gave his inamorata cyanide of potassium. The fact that Major Armstrong was a meek and gentlemanly looking chap did not deter him from feeding arsenic to his wife. Professor Webster of Harvard was not a criminal type; but the dismembered spirit of Doctor Parkman doubtless regards him as a brutal slayer. Doctor Lamson, with his philanthropic eyes and his benevolent beard, was highly regarded as a humanitarian; but he administered aconitine rather cold-bloodedly to his crippled brother-in-law. Then there was Doctor Neil Cream, who might easily have been mistaken for the deacon of a fashionable church; and the soft-spoken and amiable Doctor Waite. . . . And the women! Edith Thompson admitted putting powdered glass in her husband's gruel, though she looked like a pious Sunday-school teacher. Madeleine Smith certainly had a most respectable countenance. And Constance Kent was rather a beauty—a nice girl with an engaging air; yet she cut her little brother's throat in a thoroughly brutal manner. Gabrielle Bompard and Marie Boyer were anything but typical of the *donna delinquente;* but the one strangled her lover with the cord of her dressing-gown, and the other killed her mother with a cheese-knife. And what of Madame Fenayrou——?"

"Enough!" protested Markham. "Your lecture on criminal physiognomy can go over a while. Just now I'm trying to adjust my mind to the staggering inferences to be drawn from your finding of those galoshes." A sense of horror seemed to weigh him down. "Good God, Vance! There must be some way out of this nightmare you've propounded. What member of that household could possibly have walked in on Rex Greene and shot him down in broad daylight?"

"'Pon my soul, I don't know." Vance himself was deeply affected by the sinister aspects of the case. "But some one in that house did it—some one the others don't suspect."

"That look on Julia's face, and Chester's amazed expression—that's what you mean, isn't it? They didn't suspect either. And they were horrified at the revelation—when it was too late. Yes, all those things fit in with your theory."

"But there's one thing that doesn't fit, old man." Vance gazed at the table perplexedly. "Rex died peacefully, apparently unaware of his murderer. Why wasn't there also a look of horror on his face? His eyes couldn't have been shut when the revolver was levelled at him, for he was standing, facing the intruder. It's inexplicable—mad!"

He beat a nervous tattoo on the table, his brows contracted.

"And there's another thing, Markham, that's incomprehensible about Rex's death. His door into the hall was open; but nobody up-stairs heard the shot—nobody *up-stairs*. And yet Sproot—who was down-stairs, in the butler's pantry behind the dining-room—heard it distinctly."

"It probably just happened that way," Markham argued, almost automatically. "Sound acts fantastically sometimes."

Vance shook his head.

"Nothing has 'just happened' in this case. There's a terrible logic about everything—a carefully planned reason behind each detail. Nothing has been left to chance. Still, this very systematization of the crime will eventually prove the murderer's downfall. When we can find a key to any one of the anterooms, we'll know our way into the main chamber of horrors."

At that moment Markham was summoned to the telephone. When he returned his expression was puzzled and uneasy.

"It was Swacker. Von Blon is at my office now—he has something to tell me."

"Ah! Very interestin'," commented Vance.

We drove to the District Attorney's office, and Von Blon was shown in at once.

"I may be stirring up a mare's nest," he began apologetically, after he had seated himself on the edge of a chair. "But I felt I ought to inform you of a curious thing that happened to me this morning. At first I thought I would tell the police, but it occurred to me they might misunderstand; and I decided to place the matter before you to act upon as you saw fit."

Plainly he was uncertain as to how the subject should be broached, and Markham waited patiently with an air of polite indulgence.

"I phoned the Greene house as soon as I made the—ah—discovery," Von Blon went on hesitantly. "But I was informed you had left for the office; so, as soon as I had lunched, I came directly here."

"Very good of you, doctor," murmured Markham.

Again Von Blon hesitated, and his manner became exaggeratedly ingratiating.

"The fact is, Mr. Markham, I am in the habit of carrying a rather full supply of emergency drugs in my medicine-case. . . ."

"Emergency drugs?"

"Strychnine, morphine, caffeine, and a variety of hypnotics and stimulants. I find it often convenient———"

"And it was in connection with these drugs you wished to see me?"

"Indirectly—yes." Von Blon paused momentarily to arrange his words. "To-day it happened that I had in my case a fresh tube of soluble quarter-grain morphine tablets, and a Parke-Davis carton of four tubes of strychnine—thirtieths. . . ."

"And what about this supply of drugs, doctor?"

"The fact is, the morphine and the strychnine have disappeared."

Markham bent forward, his eyes curiously animated.

"They were in my case this morning when I left my office," Von Blon explained; "and I made only two brief calls before I went to the Greenes'. I missed the tubes when I returned to my office."

Markham studied the doctor a moment.

"And you think it improbable that the drugs were taken from your case during either of your other calls?"

"That's just it. At neither place was the case out of my sight for a moment."

"And at the Greenes'?" Markham's agitation was growing rapidly.

"I went directly to Mrs. Greene's room, taking the case with me. I remained there for perhaps half an hour. When I came out——"

"You did not leave the room during that half-hour?"

"No. . . ."

"Pardon me, doctor," came Vance's indolent voice; "but the nurse mentioned that you called to her to bring Mrs. Greene's bouillon. From where did you call?"

Von Blon nodded. "Ah, yes. I did speak to Miss Craven. I stepped to the door and called up the servants' stairs."

"Quite so. And then?"

"I waited with Mrs. Greene until the nurse came. Then I went across the hall to Sibella's room."

"And your case?" interjected Markham.

"I set it down in the hall, against the rear railing of the main stairway."

"And you remained in Miss Sibella's room until Sproot called you?"

"That is right."

"Then the case was unguarded in the rear of the upper hall from about eleven until you left the house?"

"Yes. After I had taken leave of you gentlemen in the drawing-room I went up-stairs and got it."

"And also made your adieus to Miss Sibella," added Vance.

Von Blon raised his eyebrows with an air of gentle surprise.

"Naturally."

"What amount of these drugs disappeared?" asked Markham.

"The four tubes of strychnine contained in all approximately three grains—three and one-third, to be exact. And there are twenty-five tablets of morphine in a Parke-Davis tube, making six and one-quarter grains."

"Are those fatal doses, doctor?"

"That's a difficult question to answer, sir." Von Blon adopted a professorial manner. "One may have a tolerance for morphine and be capable of assimilating astonishingly large doses. But, *ceteris paribus,* six grains would certainly prove fatal. Regarding strychnine, toxicology gives us a very wide range as to lethal dosage, depending on the condition and age of the patient. The average fatal dose for an adult is, I should say, two grains, though death has resulted from administrations of one grain, or even less. And, on the other hand, recovery has taken place after as much as ten grains have been swallowed. Generally speaking, however, three and one-third grains would be sufficient to produce fatal results."

When Von Blon had gone Markham gazed at Vance anxiously. "What do you make of it?" he asked.

"I don't like it—I don't at all like it." Vance shook his head despairingly. "It's dashed queer—the whole thing. And the doctor is worried, too. There's a panic raging beneath his elegant façade. He's in a blue funk—and it's not because of the loss of his pills. He fears something, Markham. There was a strained, hunted look in his eyes."

"Doesn't it strike you as strange that he should be carrying such quantities of drugs about with him?"

"Not necessarily. Some doctors do it. The Continental M.D.s especially are addicted to the practice. And don't forget Von Blon is German-trained. . . ." Vance glanced up suddenly. "By the by, what about those two wills?"

There was a look of astonished interrogation in Markham's incisive stare, but he said merely:

"I'll have them later this afternoon. Buckway has been laid up with a cold, but he promised to send me copies to-day."

Vance got to his feet.

"I'm no Chaldean," he drawled; "but I have an idea those two wills may help us to understand the disappearance of the doctor's pellets." He drew on his coat and took up his hat and stick. "And now I'm going to banish this beastly affair from my thoughts.— Come, Van. There's some good chamber-music at Æolian Hall this afternoon, and if we hurry we'll be in time for the Mozart '*C-major*.'"

CHAPTER XVII

TWO WILLS

(Tuesday, November 30; 8 p. m.)

EIGHT O'CLOCK that night found Inspector Moran, Sergeant Heath, Markham, Vance, and me seated about a small conference-table in one of the Stuyvesant Club's private rooms. The evening papers had created a furore in the city with their melodramatic accounts of Rex Greene's murder; and these early stories were, as we all knew, but the mild forerunners of what the morning journals would publish. The situation itself, without the inevitable impending strictures of the press, was sufficient to harry and depress those in charge of the official investigation; and, as I looked round the little circle of worried faces that night, I realized the tremendous importance that attached to the outcome of our conference.

Markham was the first to speak.

"I have brought copies of the wills; but before we discuss them I'd like to know if there have been any new developments."

"Developments!" Heath snorted contemptuously. "We've been going round in a circle all afternoon, and the faster we went the quicker we got to where we started. Mr. Markham, not one damn thing turned up to give us a line of inquiry. If it wasn't for the fact that no gun was found in the room, I'd turn in a report of suicide and then resign from the force."

"Fie on you, Sergeant!" Vance made a half-hearted attempt at levity. "It's a bit too early to give way to such gloomy pessimism.—I take it that Captain Dubois found no finger-prints."

"Oh, he found finger-prints, all right—Ada's, and Rex's, and Sproot's, and a couple of the doctor's. But that don't get us anywheres."

"Where were the prints?"

"Everywhere—on the door-knobs, the centre-table, the window-panes; some were even found on the woodwork above the mantel."

"That last fact may prove interestin' some day, though it doesn't seem to mean much just now.—Anything more about the footprints?"

"Nope. I got Jerym's report late this afternoon; but it don't say anything new. The galoshes you found made the tracks."

"That reminds me, Sergeant. What did you do with the galoshes?"

Heath gave him a sly, exultant grin.

"Just exactly what you'd have done with 'em, Mr. Vance. Only—I thought of it first."

Vance smiled back.

"*Salve!* Yes, the idea entirely slipped my mind this morning. In fact, it only just occurred to me."

"May I know what was done with the galoshes?" interjected Markham impatiently.

"Why, the Sergeant returned them surreptitiously to the linen-closet, and placed them under the drugget whence they came."

"Right!" Heath nodded with satisfaction. "And I've got our new nurse keeping an eye on 'em. The minute they disappear she's to phone the Bureau."

"You had no trouble installing your woman?" asked Markham.

"A cinch. Everything went like clockwork. At a quarter to six the doc shows up; then at six comes the woman from the Central Office. After the doc has put her wise to her new duties, she gets into her uniform and goes in to Mrs. Greene. The old lady tells the doc she didn't like this Miss Craven anyway, and hopes the new nurse will show her more consideration. Things couldn't have gone smoother. I hung around until I got a chance to tip our woman off about the galoshes; then I came away."

"Which of our women did you give the case to, Sergeant?" Moran asked.

"O'Brien—the one who handled the Sitwell affair. Nothing in that house will get by O'Brien; and she's as strong as a man."

"There's another thing you'd better speak to her about as soon as possible." And Markham related in detail the facts of Von Blon's visit to the office after lunch. "If those drugs were stolen in the Greene mansion, your woman may be able to find some trace of them."

Markham's account of the missing poisons had produced a profound effect on both Heath and the Inspector.

"Good heavens!" exclaimed the latter. "Is this affair going to develop into a poisoning case? It would be the finishing touch." His apprehension went much deeper than his tone implied.

Heath sat staring at the polished table-top with futile consternation.

"Morphine and strychnine! There's no use looking for the stuff. There's a hundred places in the house where it could be hid; and we might search a month and not find it. Anyway, I'll go out there tonight and tell O'Brien to watch for it. If she's on the lookout she maybe can spot any attempt to use it."

"What astounds me," remarked the Inspector, "is the security felt by the thief. Within an hour of the time Rex Greene is shot the poison disappears from the upper hall. Good Gad! That's cold-bloodedness for you! And nerve, too!"

"There's plenty of cold-bloodedness and nerve in this case," answered Vance. "A relentless determination is back of these murders—and calculation no end. I wouldn't be surprised if the doctor's satchel had been searched a score of times before. Perhaps there's been a patient accumulation of the drugs. This morning's theft may have been the final raid. I see in this whole affair a carefully worked-out plot that's been in preparation per-haps for years. We're dealing with the persistency of an *idée fixe*, and with the demoniacal logic of insanity. And—what is even more hideous—we're confronted with the perverted imagina-tion of a fantastically romantic mind. We're pitted against a fiery, egocentric, hallucinated optimism. And this type of optimism has tremendous stamina and power. The history of nations has been convulsed by it. Mohammed, Bruno, and Jeanne d'Arc—as well as Torquemada, Agrippina, and Robespierre—all had it. It operates in different degrees, and to different ends; but the spirit of individual revolution is at the bottom of it."

"Hell, Mr. Vance!" Heath was uneasy. "You're trying to make this case something that ain't—well, natural."

"Can you make it anything else, Sergeant? Already there have been three murders and an attempted murder. And now comes the theft of the poisons from Von Blon."

Inspector Moran drew himself up and rested his elbows on the table.

"Well, what's to be done? That, I believe, is the business of to-night's conclave." He forced himself to speak with matter-of-factness. "We can't break up the establishment; and we can't assign a separate bodyguard for each remaining member of the household."

"No; and we can't give 'em the works at the police station, either," grumbled Heath.

"It wouldn't help you if you could, Sergeant," said Vance. "There's no third degree known that could unseal the lips of the person who is executing this particular *opus*. There's too much fanaticism and martyrdom in it."

"Suppose we hear those wills, Mr. Markham," suggested Moran. "We may then be able to figure out a motive.—You'll admit, won't you, Mr. Vance, that there's a pretty strong motive back of these killings?"

"There can be no doubt as to that. But I don't believe it's money. Money may enter into it—and probably does—but only as a contribut'ry factor. I'd say the motive was more fundamental—that it had its matrix in some powerful but suppressed human passion. However, the financial conditions may lead us to those depths."

Markham had taken from his pocket several legal-sized sheets of closely typed paper, and smoothed them on the table before him.

"There's no necessity to read these *verbatim*," he said. "I've gone over them thoroughly and can tell you briefly what they contain." He took up the top sheet and held it nearer to the light. "Tobias Greene's last will, drawn up less than a year before his death, makes the entire family, as you know, the residuary devisees, with the stipulation that they live on the estate and maintain it intact for twenty-five years. At the end of that time the property may be sold or otherwise disposed of. I might mention

that the domiciliary stipulation was particularly strict: the legatees must live in the Greene mansion *in esse*—no technicali-
ty will suffice. They are permitted to travel and make visits; but
such absences may not exceed three months in each respective
year. . . ."

"What provision was made in case one of them should marry?" asked the Inspector.

"None. Even marriage on the part of any of the legatees did
not vitiate the restrictions of the will. If a Greene married, he or
she had to live out the twenty-five years on the estate just the
same. The husband or wife could share the residence, of course.
In event of children the will provided for the erection of two
other small dwellings on the 52d Street side of the lot. Only one
exception was made to these stipulations. If Ada should marry,
she could live elsewhere without losing her inheritance, as she
apparently was not Tobias's own child and could not, therefore,
carry on the blood line of the Greenes."

"What penalties attached to a breaking of the domiciliary
terms of the will?" Again the Inspector put the question.

"Only one penalty—disinheritance, complete and absolute."

"A rigid old bird," murmured Vance. "But the important thing
about the will is, I should say, the manner in which he left the
money. How was this distributed?"

"It wasn't distributed. With the exception of a few minor bequests, it was left in its entirety to the widow. She was to have
the use of it during her lifetime, and could, at her death, dispose
of it to the children—and grandchildren, if any—as she saw fit.
It was imperative, however, that it all remain in the family."

"Where do the present generation of Greenes get their living
expenses? Are they dependent on the old lady's bounty?"

"Not exactly. A provision was made for them in this way: each of the five children was to receive from the executors a stipulated amount from Mrs. Greene's income, sufficient for personal needs." Markham folded up the paper. "And that about covers Tobias's will."

"You spoke of a few minor bequests," said Vance. "What were they?"

"Sproot was left a competency, for instance—enough to take care of him comfortably whenever he wished to retire from service. Mrs. Mannheim, also, was to receive an income for life beginning at the end of the twenty-five years."

"Ah! Now, that's most interestin'. And in the meantime she could, if she chose, remain as cook at a liberal salary."

"Yes, that was the arrangement."

"The status of Frau Mannheim fascinates me. I have a feeling that some day ere long she and I will have a heart-to-heart talk.—Any other minor bequests?"

"A hospital, where Tobias recovered from typhus fever contracted in the tropics; and a donation to the chair of criminology at the University of Prague. I might mention too, as a curious item, that Tobias left his library to the New York Police Department, to be turned over to them at the expiration of the twenty-five years."

Vance drew himself up with puzzled interest.

"Amazin'!"

Heath had turned to the Inspector.

"Did you know anything about this, sir?"

"It seems to me I've heard of it. But a gift of books a quarter of a century in the future isn't apt to excite the officials of the force."

Vance, to all appearances, was smoking with indolent unconcern; but the precise way he held his cigarette told me that some unusual speculation was absorbing his mind.

"The will of Mrs. Greene," Markham went on, "touches more definitely on present conditions, though personally I see nothing helpful in it. She has been mathematically impartial in doling out the estate. The five children—Julia, Chester, Sibella, Rex, and Ada—receive equal amounts under its terms—that is, each gets a fifth of the entire estate."

"That part of it don't interest me," put in the Sergeant. "What I want to know is, who gets all this money in case the others pass outa the picture?"

"The provision covering that point is quite simple," explained Markham. "Should any of the children die before a new will is drawn, their share of the inheritance is distributed equally among the remaining beneficiaries."

"Then when any one of 'em passes out, all the others benefit. And if all of 'em, except one, should die, that one would get everything—huh?"

"Yes."

"So, as it stands now, Sibella and Ada would get everything—fifty-fifty—provided the old lady croaked."

"That's correct, Sergeant."

"But suppose both Sibella and Ada, as well as the old lady, should die: what would become of the money?"

"If either of the girls had a husband, the estate would pass to him. But, in event of Sibella and Ada dying single, everything would go to the State. That is to say, the State would get it provided there were no relatives alive—which I believe is the case."

Heath pondered these possibilities for several minutes.

"I can't see anything in the situation to give us a lead," he lamented. "Everybody benefits equally by what's already happened. And there's three of the family still left—the old lady and the two girls."

"Two from three leaves one, Sergeant," suggested Vance quietly.

"What do you mean by that, sir?"

"The morphine and the strychnine."

Heath gave a start and made an ugly face.

"By God!" He struck the table with his fist. "It ain't coming to that if I can stop it!" Then a sense of helplessness tempered his outraged resolution, and he became sullen.

"I know how you feel." Vance spoke with troubled discouragement. "But I'm afraid we'll all have to wait. If the Greene millions are an actuating force in this affair, there's no way on earth to avert at least one more tragedy."

"We might put the matter up to the two girls and perhaps induce them to separate and go away," ventured the Inspector.

"That would only postpone the inevitable," Vance returned. "And besides, it would rob them of their patrimony."

"A court ruling might be obtained upsetting the provisions of the will," submitted Markham dubiously.

Vance gave him an ironical smile.

"By the time you could get one of your beloved courts to act the murderer would have had time to wipe out the entire local judiciary."

For nearly two hours ways and means of dealing with the case were discussed; but obstacles confronted nearly every line of activity advocated. Finally it was agreed that the only practicable tactics to be pursued were those of the routine police procedure. However, before the conference broke up, certain specific decisions had been taken. The guard about the Greene estate was to be increased, and a man was to be placed on the upper floor of the Narcoss Flats to keep a close watch on the front door and windows. On some pretext or other a detective was to be kept inside of the house as many hours as possible during the day; and the telephone-line of the Greenes was to be tapped.

Vance insisted, somewhat against Markham's inclination, that every one in the house and every person who called there—however seemingly remote his connection with the case—should be regarded as a suspect and watched vigilantly; and Heath was ordered by the Inspector to convey this decision to O'Brien, lest her instinctive partiality should result in the relaxation of her scrutiny of certain persons. The Sergeant, it seemed, had already instituted a thorough investigation into the private affairs of Julia, Chester, and Rex; and a dozen men were at work on their associates and activities outside of the Greene mansion, with special instructions to gather reports of conversations which might have contained some hint or reference indicating a foreknowledge or suspicion of the crimes.

Just as Markham rose to terminate the discussion Vance again leaned forward and spoke.

"In case there is to be a poisoning we should, I think, be prepared. Where overdoses of either morphine or strychnine are administered immediate action will sometimes save the victim. I would suggest that an official physician be placed in the Narcoss Flats with the man set to watch the Greene windows; and he should have at hand all the necess'ry apparatus and antidotes used in combating morphine and strychnine poisoning. Furthermore, I would suggest that we arrange some sort of signal with Sproot and the new nurse, so that, should anything happen, our doctor can be summoned without a moment's delay. If the victim of the attempted poisoning were saved, we might be able to ascertain who administered the drug."

The plan was readily agreed to. The Inspector took it upon himself to arrange the matter that night with one of the official police surgeons; and Heath went at once to the Narcoss Flats to secure a room facing the Greene mansion.

CHAPTER XVIII

IN THE LOCKED LIBRARY

(Wednesday, December 1; 1 p. m.)

VANCE, CONTRARY to his custom, rose early the next morning. He was rather waspish, and I left him severely alone. He made several desultory attempts at reading, and once, when he put his book down, I glanced at the title,—he had chosen a life of Genghis Khan! Later in the forenoon he attempted to busy himself with cataloguing his Chinese prints.

We were to have lunch with Markham at the Lawyers Club at one o'clock, and at a little after twelve Vance ordered his powerful Hispano-Suiza. He always drove himself when engaged on a problem: the activity seemed to steady his nerves and clarify his brain.

Markham was waiting for us, and it was only too plain from his expression that something of a disturbing nature had occurred.

"Unburden, old dear," invited Vance, when we were seated at our table in a corner of the main dining-room. "You look as serious as Saint John of Patmos. I'm sure something wholly to be expected has happened. Have the galoshes disappeared?"

Markham looked at him with some wonder.

"Yes! The O'Brien woman called the Bureau at nine o'clock this morning and reported that they had been removed from the linen-closet during the night. They were there, however, when she went to bed."

"And, of course, they have not been found."

"No. She made a pretty careful search before phoning."

"Fancy that. But she might have saved herself the trouble.— What does the doughty Sergeant opine?"

"Heath reached the house before ten o'clock, and made an investigation. But he learned nothing. No one admitted hearing any sound in the hall during the night. He re-searched the house himself, but without result."

"Have you heard from Von Blon this morning?"

"No; but Heath saw him. He came to the house about ten and stayed nearly an hour. He appeared very much upset over the stolen drugs, and immediately asked if any trace of them had been found. He spent most of the hour with Sibella."

"Ah, welladay! Let us enjoy our *truffes gastronome* without the intrusion of unpleasant speculations. This Madeira sauce, by the by, is very good." Thus Vance dismissed the subject.

However, that luncheon was to prove a memorable one; for toward the end of the meal Vance made a suggestion—or, rather, insisted upon an action—that was eventually to solve and explain the terrible tragedies at the Greene mansion. We had reached our dessert when, after a long silence, he looked up at Markham and said:

"The Pandora complex has seized and mastered me. I simply must get into Tobias's locked library. That sacred adytum has begun to infest my slumbers; and ever since you mentioned the legacy of those books I've had no rest. I yearn to become acquainted with Tobias's literary taste, and to learn why he should have selected the police for his beneficiaries."

"But, my dear Vance, what possible connection——?"

"Desist! You can't think of a question I have not already put to myself; and I'm unable to answer any of them. But the fact remains, I must inspect that library even if you have to get a judicial order to batter down the door. There are sinister undercurrents in that old house, Markham; and a hint or two may be found in that secret room."

"It will be a difficult proceeding if Mrs. Greene stands firm on her refusal to deliver the key to us." Markham, I could see, had already acquiesced. He was in a mood to accede to any suggestion that even remotely promised a clarification of the problem posed by the Greene murders.

It was nearly three o'clock when we reached the house. Heath had already arrived, in answer to a telephone call from Markham; and we at once presented ourselves to Mrs. Greene. Following an ocular sign from the Sergeant the new nurse left the room; and Markham went directly to the point. The old lady had eyed us suspiciously as we came in, and now sat rigidly against her pile of pillows, her gaze fixed on Markham with defensive animosity.

"Madam," he began, somewhat severely, "we regret the necessity of this call. But certain things have arisen which make it imperative that we visit Mr. Greene's library. . . ."

"You sha'n't!" she broke in, her voice rising in an infuriated *crescendo*. "You sha'n't put your foot in that room! Not for twelve years has any one passed the threshold, and no policeman now shall desecrate the place where my husband spent the last years of his life."

"I appreciate the sentiment that actuates your refusal," replied Markham; "but graver considerations have intervened. The room will have to be searched."

"Not if you kill me!" she cried. "How dare you force your way into my house——?"

Markham held up his hand authoritatively.

"I am not here to argue the matter. I came to you merely to ask for the key. Of course, if you prefer to have us break down the door. . . ." He drew a sheaf of papers from his pocket. "I have secured a search-warrant for that room; and it would cause me deep regret to have to serve it on you." (I was amazed at his aggressive daring, for I knew he had no warrant.)

Mrs. Greene broke forth with imprecations. Her anger became almost insensate, and she was changed into a creature at once repulsive and pitiful. Markham waited calmly for her paroxysm of fury to pass; and when, her vituperation spent, she beheld his quiet, inexorable bearing, she knew that she had lost. She sank back, white and exhausted.

"Take the key," she capitulated bitterly, "and save me the final infamy of having my house torn down by ruffians. . . . It's in the ivory jewel-case in the top drawer of that cabinet." She pointed weakly to the lacquered high-boy.

Vance crossed the room and secured the key—a long, old-fashioned instrument with a double bit and a filigreed bow.

"Have you always kept the key in this jewel-case, Mrs. Greene?" he asked, as he closed the drawer.

"For twelve years," she whined. "And now, after all that time, it is to be taken from me by force—and by the police, the very people who should be protecting an old, helpless paralytic like me. It's infamy! But what can I expect? Every one takes delight in torturing me."

Markham, his object gained, became contrite, and endeavored to pacify her by explaining the seriousness of the situation. But in this he failed; and a few moments later he joined us in the hall.

"I don't like this sort of thing, Vance," he said.

"You did remarkably well, however. If I hadn't been with you since lunch I'd have believed you really had a search-warrant. You are a veritable Machiavelli. *Te saluto!*"

"Get on with your business, now that you have the key," ordered Markham irritably. And we descended to the main hall.

Vance looked about him cautiously to make sure we were not observed, and led the way to the library.

"The lock works rather easily, considering its twelve years of desuetude," he remarked, as he turned the key and gently pushed open the massive oak door. "And the hinges don't even creak. Astonishin'."

Blackness confronted us, and Vance struck a match.

"Please don't touch anything," he admonished, and, holding the match high before him, he crossed to the heavy velour draperies of the east window. As he drew them apart a cloud of dust filled the air.

"These curtains, at least, have not been touched for years," he said.

The gray light of mid-afternoon suffused the room, revealing an astonishing retreat. The walls were lined with open book-shelves which reached from the floor nearly to the ceiling, leaving only space enough for a row of marble busts and squat bronze vases. At the southern end of the room was a massive flat-topped desk, and in the centre stood a long carved table laden with curious and outlandish ornaments. Beneath the windows and in the corners were piles of pamphlets and portfolios;

and along the moulding of the bookcases hung gargoyles and old prints yellow with age. Two enormous Persian lamps of perforated brass depended from the ceiling, and beside the centre-table stood a Chinese sconce eight feet high. The floor was covered with overlapping Oriental rugs laid at all angles; and at each end of the fireplace was a hideous, painted totem-pole reaching to the beams. A thick coating of dust overlay everything.

Vance returned to the door and, striking another match, closely examined the inner knob.

"Some one," he announced, "has been here recently. There's no sign of dust on this knob."

"We might get the finger-prints," suggested Heath.

Vance shook his head.

"Not even worth trying. The person we're dealing with knows better than to leave sign manuals."

He closed the door softly and threw the bolt. Then he looked about him. Presently he pointed beneath a huge geographical globe beside the desk.

"There are your galoshes, Sergeant. I thought they'd be here."

Heath almost threw himself upon them, and carried them to the window.

"They're the ones, all right," he declared.

Markham gave Vance one of his annoyed, calculating stares.

"You've got some theory," he asserted, in an accusing tone.

"Nothing more than I've already told you. The finding of the galoshes was wholly incidental. I'm interested in other things— just what, I don't know."

He stood near the centre-table and let his eyes roam over the objects of the room. Presently his gaze came to rest on a low wicker reading-chair the right arm of which was shaped into a book-rest. It stood within a few feet of the wall opposite to the fireplace, facing a narrow section of book-shelves that was surmounted by a replica of the Capitoline Museum bust of Vespasian.

"Most untidy," he murmured. "I'm sure that chair wasn't left in that position twelve years ago.

He moved forward, and stood looking down at it musingly. Instinctively Markham and Heath followed him; and then they saw the thing that he had been contemplating. On the table-arm of the chair was a deep saucer in which stood the thick stub of a candle. The saucer was almost filled with smoky wax drippings.

"It took many candles to fill that dish," commented Vance; "and I doubt if the departed Tobias did his reading by candle-light." He touched the seat and the back of the chair, and then examined his hand. "There's dust, but nowhere near a decade's accumulation. Some one has been browsing in this library rather recently; and he was dashed secretive about it. He didn't dare draw the shades or turn on the lights. He sat here with a single candle, sampling Tobias's brand of literature. And it apparently appealed to him, for this one saucer contains evidence of many bookish nights. How many other saucers of paraffin there were we don't know."

"The old lady could tell us who had a chance to put the key back this morning after hiding the galoshes," offered Heath.

"No one put the key back this morning, Sergeant. The person who was in the habit of visiting here wouldn't have stolen it and returned it on each occasion when he could have had a duplicate made in fifteen minutes."

"I guess you're right." The Sergeant was sorely perplexed. "But as long as we don't know who's got the key, we're no better off than we were."

"We're not quite through yet with our scrutiny of the library," rejoined Vance. "As I told Mr. Markham at lunch, my main object in coming here was to ascertain Tobias's taste in literature."

"A lot of good that'll do you!"

"One never can tell. Tobias, remember, bequeathed his library to the Police Department. . . . Let's see with what tomes the old boy whiled away his inactive hours."

Vance took out his monocle and, polishing it carefully, fitted it to his eye. Then he turned to the nearest book-shelves. I stepped forward and looked over his shoulder; and, as my glance ran over the dusty titles, I could scarcely suppress an exclamation of amazement. Here was one of the most complete and unusual private libraries of criminology in America—and I was familiar with many of the country's famous collections. Crime in all its phases and ramifications was represented. Rare old treatises, long out of print and now the delight of bibliophiles, shouldered one another in compact tiers on Tobias Greene's shelves.

Nor were the subjects of these books limited to a narrow interpretation of criminology. All the various allied branches of the subject were represented. There were entire sections devoted to insanity and cretinism, social and criminal pathology, suicide, pauperism and philanthropy, prison-reform, prostitution and morphinism, capital punishment, abnormal psychology, legal codes, the argot of the underworld and code-writing, toxicology, and police methods. The volumes were in many languages— English, French, German, Italian, Spanish, Swedish, Russian, Dutch, and Latin.*

* Among the volumes of Tobias Greene's library I may mention the following as typical of the entire collection: Heinroth's "De morborum animi et pathematum animi differentia," Hoh's "De maniæ pathologia," P. S. Knight's "Observations on the Causes, Symptoms, and Treatment of Derangement of the Mind," Krafft-Ebing's "Grundzüge der Kriminal-Psychologie," Bailey's "Diary of a Resurrectionist," Lange's "Om Arvelighedens Inflydelse i Sindssygedommene," Leuret's "Fragments psychologiques sur la folie," D'Aguanno's "Recensioni di antropologia giuridica," Amos's "Crime and Civilization," Andronico's "Studi clinici sul delitto," Lombroso's "Uomo Delinquente," de Aramburu's "La nueva ciencia penal," Bleakley's "Some Distinguished Victims of the Scaffold," Are-

Vance's eyes sparkled as he moved along the crowded shelves. Markham also was deeply interested; and Heath, bending here and there toward a volume, registered an expression of bewildered curiosity.

"My word!" murmured Vance. "No wonder your department, Sergeant, was chosen as the future custodian of these tomes. What a collection! Extr'ordin'ry!—Aren't you glad, Markham, you wangled the old lady into relinquishing the key——?"

Suddenly he stiffened and jerked his head toward the door, at the same time lifting his hand for silence. I, too, had heard a slight noise in the hall, like some one brushing against the woodwork of the door, but had thought nothing of it. For a few moments we waited tensely. But no further sound came to us, and Vance stepped quickly to the door and drew it open. The hall was empty. He stood on the threshold for a

nal's "Psychologie comparée du criminel," Aubry's "De l'homicide commis par la femme," Beccaria's "Crimes and Punishments," Benedikt's "Anatomical Studies upon the Brains of Criminals," Bittinger's "Crimes of Passion and of Reflection," Bosselli's "Nuovi studi sul tatuaggio nei criminali," Favalli's "La delinquenza in rapporto alla civiltà," de Feyfer's "Verhandeling over den Kindermoord," Fuld's "Der Realismus und das Strafrecht," Hamilton's "Scientific Detection of Crime," von Holtzendorff's "Das Irische Gefängnissystem insbesondere die Zwischenanstalten vor der Entlassung der Sträflinge," Jardine's "Criminal Trials," Lacassagne's "L'homme criminel comparé à l'homme primitif," Llanos y Torriglia's "Ferri y su escuela," Owen Luke's "History of Crime in England," MacFarlane's "Lives and Exploits of Banditti," M'Levy's "Curiosities of Crime in Edinburgh," the "Complete Newgate Calendar," Pomeroy's "German and French Criminal Procedure," Rizzone's "Delinquenza e punibilità," Rosenblatt's "Skizzen aus der Verbrecherwelt," Soury's "Le crime et les criminels," Wey's "Criminal Anthropology," Amadei's "Crani d'assassini," Benedikt's "Der Raubthiertypus am menschlichen Gehirne," Fasini's "Studi su delinquenti femmine," Mills's "Arrested and Aberrant Development and Gyres in the Brain of Paranoiacs and Criminals," de Paoli's "Quattro crani di delinquenti," Zuckerkandl's "Morphologie des Gesichtsschädels," Bergonzoli's "Sui pazzi criminali in Italia," Brierre de Boismont's "Rapports de la folie suicide avec la folie homicide," Buchnet's "The Relation of Madness to Crime," Calucci's "Il jure penale e la freniatria," Davey's "Insanity and Crime," Morel's "Le procès Chorinski," Parrot's "Sur la monomanie homicide," Savage's "Moral Insanity," Teed's "On Mind, Insanity, and Criminality," Worckmann's "On Crime and Insanity," Vaucher's "Système préventif des délits et des crimes," Thacker's "Psychology of Vice and Crime," Tarde's "La Criminalité Comparée," Tamassia's "Gli ultimi studi sulla criminalità," Sikes's "Studies of Assassination," Senior's "Remarkable Crimes and Trials in Germany," Savarini's "Vexata Quæstio," Sampson's "Rationale of Crime," Noellner's "Kriminal-psychologische Denkwürdigkeiten," Sighele's "La foule criminelle," and Korsakoff's "Kurs psichiatrii."

while listening. Then he closed the door, and turned again to the room.

"I could have sworn some one was listening in the hall."

"I heard a rustle of some kind," Markham corroborated him. "I took it for granted it was Sproot or the maid passing by."

"Why should anybody's hanging round the hall worry us, Mr. Vance?" Heath asked.

"I really couldn't say, don't y' know. But it bothers me, nevertheless. If some one was at the door listening, it shows that our presence here has produced a state of anxiety in the person privy to the fact. It's possible, d'ye see, that some one is desirous of ascertaining what we have found out."

"Well, I can't see that we've found out enough to make anybody lose any sleep," mumbled Heath.

"You're so discouraging, Sergeant." Vance sighed and went to the book-shelves in front of the wicker reading-chair. "There may be something in this section to cheer us. Let us see if there's a glad tiding or two written in the dust."

He struck match after match as he carefully inspected the tops of the books, beginning at the highest shelf and systematically scrutinizing the volumes of each row. He had reached the second shelf from the floor when he bent over curiously and gave a second long look at two thick gray volumes. Then, putting out the match, he took the volumes to the window.

"The thing is quite mad," he remarked, after a brief examination. "These are the only books within arm's reach of the chair that have been handled recently. And what do you think they are? An old two-volume edition of Professor Hans Gross's 'Handbuch für Untersuchungsrichter als System der Kriminalistik,' or—to claw the title loosely into the vulgate—'A Handbook on the Criminal Sciences for Examining Magistrates.'" He gave Markham a look of facetious reproach. "I say, you haven't, by any chance, been spending your nights in this library learning how to ballyrag suspects?"

Markham ignored his levity. He recognized the outward sign of Vance's inner uneasiness.

"The apparently irrelevant theme of the book," he returned, "might indicate a mere coincidence between the visits of some person to this room and the crimes committed in the house."

Vance made no answer. He thoughtfully returned the books to their place and ran his eye over the remaining volumes of the bottom shelf. Suddenly he knelt down and struck another match.

"Here are several books out of place." I detected a subdued note of eagerness in his voice. "They belong in other sections; and they've been crowded in here a little out of alignment. Moreover, they're innocent of dust. . . . 'Pon my soul, Markham, here's a coincidence for your sceptical legal mind! Lend an ear to these titles: 'Poisons: Their Effects and Detection,' by Alexander Wynter Blyth,* and 'Textbook of Medical Jurisprudence, Toxicology, and Public Health,' by John Glaister, professor of Forensic Medicine at the University of Glasgow. And here we have Friedrich Brügelmann's 'Über hysterische Dämmerzustände,' and Schwarzwald's 'Über Hystero-Paralyse und Somnambulismus.'—I say! That's deuced queer. . . ."

He rose and walked up and down agitatedly.

"No—no; absolutely not," he muttered. "It simply can't be. . . . Why should Von Blon lie to us about her?"

We all knew what was in his mind. Even Heath sensed it at once, for, though he did not speak German, the titles of the two German books—especially the latter—needed no translation to

---

* Doctor Blyth was one of the defense witnesses in the Crippen trial.

be understood. Hysteria and twilight sleep! Hysterical paralysis and somnambulism! The gruesome and terrible implication in these two titles, and their possible relation to the sinister tragedies of the Greene mansion, sent a chill of horror over me.

Vance stopped his restless pacing and fixed a grave gaze on Markham.

"This thing gets deeper and deeper. Something unthinkable is going on here.—Come, let us get out of this polluted room. It has told us its gibbering, nightmarish story. And now we will have to interpret it—find some glimmer of sanity in its black suggestions.—Sergeant, will you draw the curtains while I straighten these books? We'd best leave no evidence of our visit."

CHAPTER XIX

SHERRY AND PARALYSIS

(Wednesday, December 1; 4.30 p. m.)

WHEN WE returned to Mrs. Greene's room the old lady was apparently sleeping peacefully and we did not disturb her. Heath gave the key to Nurse O'Brien with instructions to replace it in the jewel-case, and we went down-stairs.

Although it was but a little past four o'clock, the early winter twilight had already descended. Sproot had not yet lighted the lamps, and the lower hall was in semidarkness. A ghostly atmosphere pervaded the house. Even the silence was oppressive, and seemed fraught with the spirit of commination. We went straight to the hall table where we had thrown our coats, eager to get out into the open air.

But we were not to shake the depressing influence of the old mansion so quickly. We had scarcely reached the table when there came a slight stirring of the portieres of the archway opposite to the drawing-room, and a tense, whispered voice said:

"Mr. Vance—please!"

We turned, startled. There, just inside of the reception-room, hiding behind the heavy draperies, stood Ada, her face a patch of ghastly white in the gathering gloom. With one finger placed on her lips for silence, she beckoned to us; and we stepped softly into the chill, unused room.

"There's something I must tell you," she said, in a half-whisper, "—something terrible! I was going to telephone you to-day, but I was afraid. . . ." A fit of trembling seized her.

"Don't be frightened, Ada," Vance encouraged her soothingly. "In a few days all these awful things will be over.—What have you to tell us?"

She made an effort to draw herself together, and when the tremor had passed she went on hesitantly.

"Last night—it was long after midnight—I woke, and felt hungry. So I got up, slipped on a wrap, and stole down-stairs. Cook always leaves something in the pantry for me. . . ." Again she stopped, and her haunted eyes searched our faces. "But when I reached the lower landing of the stairs I heard a soft, shuffling sound in the hall—far back, near the library door. My heart was in my mouth, but I made myself look over the banister. And just then—some one struck a match. . . ."

Her trembling began afresh, and she clutched Vance's arm with both hands. I was afraid the girl was going to faint, and I moved closer to her; but Vance's voice seemed to steady her.

"Who was it, Ada?"

She caught her breath and looked about her, her face the picture of deadly fear. Then she leaned forward.

"It was mother! . . . *And she was walking!*"

The dread significance of this revelation chilled us all into silence. After a moment a choked whistle escaped Heath; and Markham threw back his head like a man shaking himself out of an encroaching spell of hypnosis. It was Vance who first recovered himself sufficiently to speak.

"Your mother was near the library door?"

"Yes; and it seemed as though she held a key in her hand."

"Was she carrying anything else?" Vance's effort at calmness was only half successful.

"I didn't notice—I was too terrified."

"Could she, for instance, have been carrying a pair of galoshes?" he persisted.

"She might have been. I don't know. She had on her long Oriental shawl, and it fell down about her in folds. Maybe under the shawl. . . . Or she might have put them down when she struck the match. I only know I saw her—moving slowly . . . there in the darkness."

The memory of that unbelievable vision completely took possession of the girl. Her eyes stared, trance-like, into the deepening shadows.

Markham cleared his throat nervously.

"You say yourself it was dark in the hall last night, Miss Greene. Perhaps your fears got the better of you. Are you sure it might not have been Hemming or the cook?"

She brought her eyes back to Markham with sudden resentment.

"No!" Then her voice took on its former note of terror. "It was mother. The match was burning close to her face, and there was a terrible look in her eyes. I was only a few feet from her—looking straight down on her."

Her hold on Vance's arm tightened, and once more her agonized gaze turned to him.

"Oh, what does it mean? I thought—I thought mother could never walk again."

Vance ignored her anguished appeal.

"Tell me this, for it's very important: did your mother see you?"

"I—don't know." Her words were scarcely audible. "I drew back and ran softly up the stairs. Then I locked myself in my room."

Vance did not speak at once. He regarded the girl for a moment, and then gave her a slow, comforting smile.

"And I think your room is the best place for you now," he said. "Don't worry over what you saw; and keep what you have told us to yourself. There's nothing to be afraid of. Certain types of paralytics have been known to walk in their sleep under the stress of shock or excitement. Anyway, we'll arrange for the new nurse to sleep in your room to-night." And with a friendly pat on her arm he sent her up-stairs .

After Heath had given Miss O'Brien the necessary instructions we left the house and walked toward First Avenue.

"Good God, Vance!" said Markham huskily. "We've got to move quickly. That child's story opens up new and frightful possibilities."

"Couldn't you get a commitment for the old woman to some sanitarium to-morrow, sir?" asked Heath.

"On what grounds? It's a pathological case, pure and simple. We haven't a scrap of evidence."

"I shouldn't attempt it, in any event," interposed Vance. "We mustn't be hasty. There are several conclusions to be drawn from Ada's story; and if the thing that all of us is thinking should be wrong, we'd only make matters worse by a false move. We might delay the slaughter for the time being; but we'd learn nothing. And our only hope is to find out—some way—what's at the bottom of this atrocious business."

"Yeh? And how are we going to do that, Mr. Vance?" Heath spoke with despair.

"I don't know now. But the Greene household is safe for to-night anyway; and that gives us a little time. I think I'll have another talk with Von Blon. Doctors—especially the younger ones—are apt to give snap diagnoses."

Heath had hailed a taxicab, and we were headed down-town along Third Avenue.

"It can certainly do no harm," agreed Markham. "And it might bring forth something suggestive. When will you tackle him?"

Vance was gazing out of the window.

"Why not at once?" Suddenly his mood had changed. "Here we are in the Forties. And tea-time! What could be more opportune?"

He leaned over and gave the chauffeur an order. In a few minutes the taxicab drew up to the curb before Von Blon's brownstone residence.

The doctor received us apprehensively.

"Nothing wrong, I hope?" he asked, trying to read our faces.

"Oh, no," Vance answered easily. "We were passing and thought we'd drop in for a dish of tea and a medical chat."

Von Blon studied him with a slight suspicion.

"Very well. You gentlemen shall have both." He rang for his man. "But I can do even better. I've some old Amontillado sherry——"

"My word!" Vance bowed ceremoniously and turned to Markham. "You see how fortune favors her punctual children?"

The wine was brought and carefully decanted.

Vance took up his glass and sipped it. One would have thought, from his manner, that nothing in the world at that moment was as important as the quality of the wine.

"Ah, my dear doctor," he remarked, with some ostentation, "the blender on the sunny Andalusian slopes unquestionably had many rare and valuable butts with which to glorify this vintage.

There was little need for the addition of *vino dulce* that year; but then, the Spaniards always sweeten their wine, probably because the English object to the slightest dryness. And it's the English, you know, who buy all the best sherries. They have always loved their 'sherris-sack'; and many a British bard has immortalized it in song. Ben Jonson sang its praises, and so did Tom Moore and Byron. But it was Shakespeare—an ardent lover of sherry himself—who penned the greatest and most passionate panegyric to it. You remember Falstaff's apostrophe?—'It ascends me into the brain; dries me there all the foolish and dull and crudy vapors which environ it; makes it apprehensive, quick, forgetive, full of nimble, fiery and delectable shapes. . . .' Sherry, you probably know, doctor, was once regarded as a cure for gout and other malaises of faulty metabolism."

He paused and put down his glass.

"I wonder that you haven't prescribed this delicious sherry for Mrs. Greene long ago. I'm sure she would serve you with a writ of confiscation if she knew you had it."

"The fact is," Von Blon returned, "I once took her a bottle, and she gave it to Chester. She doesn't care for wine. I remember my father's telling me she objected violently to her husband's well-stocked cellar."

"Your father died, did he not, before Mrs. Greene became paralyzed?" Vance asked incuriously.

"Yes—about a year."

"And was yours the only diagnosis made of her case?"

Von Blon looked at him with an air of gentle surprise.

"Yes. I saw no necessity of calling in any of the bigwigs. The symptoms were clear-cut and conformed with the anamnesis. Furthermore, everything since then has confirmed my diagnosis."

"And yet, doctor"—Vance spoke with great deference—"something has occurred which, from the layman's point of view, tends to cast doubt on the accuracy of that diagnosis. Therefore, I feel sure you will forgive me when I ask you quite frankly if it would not be possible to place another, and perhaps less serious, interpretation on Mrs. Greene's invalidism."

Von Blon appeared greatly puzzled.

"There is," he said, "not the slightest possibility that Mrs. Greene is suffering from any disease other than an organic paralysis of both legs—a paraplegia, in fact, of the entire lower part of the body."

"If you were to see Mrs. Greene move her legs, what would be your mental reaction?"

Von Blon stared at him incredulously. Then he forced a laugh.

"My mental reaction? I'd know my liver was out of order, and that I was having hallucinations."

"And if you knew your liver was functioning perfectly—then what?"

"I'd immediately become a devout believer in miracles."

Vance smiled pleasantly.

"I sincerely hope it won't come to that. And yet so-called therapeutic miracles have happened."

"I'll admit that medical history is filled with what the uninitiated call miraculous cures. But there is sound pathology beneath all of them. In Mrs. Greene's case, however, I can see no loophole for error. If she should move her legs, it would contravert all the known laws of physiology."

"By the by, doctor"—Vance put the question abruptly—"are you familiar with Brügelmann's 'Über hysterische Dämmerzustände'?"

"No—I can't say that I am."

"Or with Schwarzwald's 'Über Hystero-Paralyse und Som-nambulismus'?"

Von Blon hesitated, and his eyes were focussed intently like those of a man who is thinking rapidly.

"I know Schwarzwald, of course," he answered. "But I'm ig-norant of the particular work you mention. . . ." Slowly a look of amazement dawned on his face. "Good heavens! You're not trying to connect the subjects of these books with Mrs. Greene's condition, are you?"

"If I were to tell you that both of these books are in the Greene mansion, what would you say?"

"I'd say their presence is no more relevant to the situation there than would be a copy of 'Die Leiden des jungen Werther' or Heine's 'Romanzero.'"

"I'm sorry I can't agree with you," returned Vance politely. "They are certainly relevant to our investigation, and I had hoped you might be able to explain the connection."

Von Blon appeared to ponder the matter, his face the picture of perplexity.

"I wish I could help you," he said, after several moments. Then he glanced up quickly: a new light had come into his eyes. "Per-mit me to suggest, sir, that you are laboring under a misapprehension as to the correct scientific connotation of the words in the titles of these two books. I have had occasion to do consid-erable reading along psychoanalytic lines; and both Freud and Jung use the terms 'Somnambulismus' and 'Dämmerzustände' in an entirely different sense from our common use of the terms 'somnambulism' and 'twilight sleep.' 'Somnambulismus,' in the ter-minology of psychopathology and abnormal psychology, is em-ployed in connection with ambivalence and dual personality: it designates the actions of the submerged, or subconscious, self in cases of aphasia, amnesia, and the like. It does not refer to one's walking in one's sleep. For instance, in psychic hysteria where one loses one's memory and adopts a new personality, the subject is called a '*Somnambule.*' It is the same as what the newspapers commonly refer to as an 'amnesia victim.'"

He rose and went to a bookcase. After a few moments' search he took down several volumes.

"Here we have, for example, an old monograph by Freud and Breuer, written in 1893 and entitled 'Über den psychischen Mechanismus der hysterischen Phenomene.' If you care to take the trouble to read it, you will see that it is an exposition of the application of the term '*Somnambulismus*' to certain temporary neurotic derangements.—And here also is Freud's 'Traumdeutung,' published in 1894, in which this terminology is explained and amplified.—In addition to these, I have here 'Nervöse Angstzustände,' by Stekel, who, though he leads one of the most important schisms in the Freudian school, uses the same nomenclature in referring to split personality." He laid the three books on the table before Vance. "You may take them along if you like. They may throw some light on the quandary you are in."

"You are inclined to believe, then, that both Schwarzwald and Brügelmann refer to waking psychic states rather than the more common type of somnambulism?"

"Yes, I am inclined to that belief. I know Schwarzwald was a former lecturer at the Psychopatisches Institut, in constant contact with Freud and his teachings. But, as I told you, I am not familiar with either of the books."

"How would you account for the term 'hysteria' in both titles?"

"Its presence there is in no way contradictory. Aphasia, amnesia, aphonia—and often anosmia and apnoea—are symptoms of hysteria. And hysterical paralysis is quite common. There are many cases of paralytics who have been unable to move a muscle for years, as a result of sheer hysteria."

"Ah, exactly!" Vance picked up his glass and drained it. "That brings me to a rather unusual request I desire to make.—As you know, the papers are waxing severe in their criticism of the police and the District Attorney's office, and are accusing of negligence every one connected with the investigation of the Greene case. Therefore Mr. Markham has decided that it might be advisable for him to possess a report of Mrs. Greene's physical condition that would carry the very highest expert authority. And I was going to suggest that, merely as a matter of formal routine, we get such a report from, let us say, Doctor Felix Oppenheimer."*

Von Blon did not speak for several minutes. He sat toying nervously with his glass, his eyes fixed with intent calculation on Vance.

"It might be well for you to have the report," he acceded at last, "if only to dispel your own doubts on the subject.—No, I have no objection to the plan. I will be very glad to make the arrangements."

Vance rose.

"That's very generous of you, doctor. But I must urge you to attend to it without delay."

"I understand perfectly. I will get in touch with Doctor Oppenheimer in the morning and explain to him the official character of the situation. I'm sure he will expedite matters."

When we were again in the taxicab Markham gave voice to his perplexity.

"Von Blon strikes me as a particularly able and trustworthy man. And yet he has obviously gone woefully astray in regard

---

* Doctor Felix Oppenheimer was then the leading authority on paralysis in America. He has since returned to Germany, where he now holds the chair of neurology at the University of Freiburg.

to Mrs. Greene's illness. I fear he's in for a shock when he hears what Oppenheimer has to say after the examination."

"Y' know, Markham," said Vance sombrely, "I'll feel infinitely bucked if we succeed in getting that report from Oppenheimer."

"Succeed! What do you mean?"

"'Pon my word, I don't know what I mean. I only know that there's a black terrible intrigue of some kind going on at the Greene house. And we don't yet know who's back of it. But it's some one who's watching us, who knows every move we make, and is thwarting us at every turn."

CHAPTER XX

THE FOURTH TRAGEDY

(Thursday, December 2; forenoon)

THE FOLLOWING day was one that will ever remain in my memory. Despite the fact that what happened had been foreseen by all of us, nevertheless when it actually came it left us as completely stunned as if it had been wholly unexpected. Indeed, the very horror that informed our anticipation tended to intensify the enormity of the event.

The day broke dark and threatening. A damp chill was in the air; and the leaden skies clung close to the earth with suffocating menace. The weather was like a symbol of our gloomy spirits.

Vance rose early, and, though he said little, I knew the case was preying on his mind. After breakfast he sat before the fire for over an hour sipping his coffee and smoking. Then he made an attempt to interest himself in an old French edition of "Till Ulenspiegel," but, failing, took down Volume VII of Osler's "Modern Medicine" and turned to Buzzard's article on myelitis. For an hour he read with despairing concentration. At last he returned the book to the shelf.

At half past eleven Markham telephoned to inform us that he

was leaving the office immediately for the Greene mansion and would stop *en route* to pick us up. He refused to say more, and hung up the receiver abruptly.

It wanted ten minutes of being noon when he arrived; and his expression of grim discouragement told us more plainly than words that another tragedy had occurred. We had on our coats in readiness and accompanied him at once to the car.

"And who is it this time?" asked Vance, as we swung into Park Avenue.

"Ada." Markham spoke bitterly through his teeth.

"I was afraid of that, after what she told us yesterday.—With poison, I suppose."

"Yes—the morphine."

"Still, it's an easier death than strychnine-poisoning."

"She's not dead, thank God!" said Markham. "That is, she was still alive when Heath phoned."

"Heath? Was he at the house?"

"No. The nurse notified him at the Homicide Bureau, and he phoned me from there. He'll probably be at the Greenes' when we arrive."

"You say she isn't dead?"

"Drumm—he's the official police surgeon Moran stationed in the Narcoss Flats—got there immediately, and had managed to keep her alive up to the time the nurse phoned."

"Sproot's signal worked all right, then?"

"Apparently. And I want to say, Vance, that I'm damned grateful to you for that suggestion to have a doctor on hand."

When we arrived at the Greene mansion Heath, who had been watching for us, opened the door.

"She ain't dead," he greeted us in a stage whisper; and then drew us into the reception-room to explain his secretive manner.

"Nobody in the house except Sproot and O'Brien knows about this poisoning yet. Sproot found her, and then pulled down all the front curtains in this room—which was the signal agreed on. When Doc Drumm hopped across Sproot was waiting with the door open, and took him up-stairs without anybody seeing him. The doc sent for O'Brien, and after they'd worked on the girl for a while he told her to notify the Bureau. They're both up in the room now with the doors locked."

"You did right in keeping the thing quiet," Markham told him. "If Ada recovers we can hush it up and perhaps learn something from her."

"That's what I was thinking, sir. I told Sproot I'd wring his scrawny neck if he spilled anything to anybody."

"And," added Vance, "he bowed politely and said 'Yes, sir.'"

"You bet your life he did!"

"Where is the rest of the household at present?" Markham asked.

"Miss Sibella's in her room. She had breakfast in bed at half past ten and told the maid she was going back to sleep. The old lady's also asleep. The maid and the cook are in the back of the house somewhere."

"Has Von Blon been here this morning?" put in Vance.

"Sure he's been here—he comes regular. O'Brien said he called at ten, sat with the old lady about an hour, and then went away."

"And he hasn't been notified about the morphine?"

"What's the use? Drumm's a good doctor, and Von Blon might blab about it to Sibella or somebody."

"Quite right." Vance nodded his approval.

We re-entered the hall and divested ourselves of our wraps.

"While we're waiting for Doctor Drumm," said Markham, "we might as well find out what Sproot knows."

We went into the drawing-room, and Heath yanked the bell-cord. The old butler came directly and stood before us without the slightest trace of emotion. His imperturbability struck me as inhuman.

Markham beckoned him to come nearer.

"Now, Sproot, tell us exactly what took place."

"I was in the kitchen resting, sir"—the man's voice was as wooden as usual—"and I was just looking at the clock and thinking I would resume my duties, when the bell of Miss Ada's room rang. Each bell, you understand, sir——"

"Never mind that! What time was it?"

"It was exactly eleven o'clock. And, as I said, Miss Ada's bell rang. I went right up-stairs and knocked on her door; but, as there was no answer, I took the liberty of opening it and looking into the room. Miss Ada was lying on the bed; but it was not a natural attitude—if you understand what I mean. And then I noticed a very peculiar thing, sir. Miss Sibella's little dog was on the bed——"

"Was there a chair or stool by the bed?" interrupted Vance.

"Yes, sir, I believe there was. An ottoman."

"So the dog could have climbed on the bed unassisted?"

"Oh, yes, sir."

"Very good. Continue."

"Well, the dog was on the bed, and he looked like he was standing on his hind legs playing with the bell-cord. But the peculiar thing was that his hind legs were on Miss Ada's face, and she didn't seem to even notice it. Inwardly I was a bit startled; and I went to the bed and picked up the dog. Then I discovered that several threads of the silk tassel on the end of the cord had got caught between his teeth; and—would you believe it, sir?—it was him who had really rung Miss Ada's bell. . . ."

"Amazin'," murmured Vance. "What then, Sproot?"

"I shook the young lady, although I had little hope of waking her after Miss Sibella's dog had been trampling over her face without her knowing it. Then I came down-stairs and drew the curtains in the reception-room as I had been instructed to do in case of an emergency. When the doctor arrived I showed him to Miss Ada's room."

"And that's all you know?"

"Everything, sir."

"Thank you, Sproot." Markham rose impatiently. "And now you might let Doctor Drumm know that we are here."

It was the nurse, however, who came to the drawing-room a few minutes later. She was a medium-sized well-built woman of thirty-five, with shrewd brown eyes, a thin mouth and a firm chin, and a general air of competency. She greeted Heath with a companionable wave of the hand and bowed to the rest of us with aloof formality.

"Doc Drumm can't leave his patient just now," she informed us, seating herself. "So he sent me along. He'll be down presently."

"And what's the report?" Markham was still standing.

"She'll live, I guess. We've been giving her passive exercise and artificial breathing for half an hour, and the doc hopes to have her walking before long."

Markham, his nervousness somewhat abated, sat down again.

"Tell us all you can, Miss O'Brien. Was there any evidence as to how the poison was administered?"

"Nothing but an empty bouillon cup." The woman was ill at ease. "I guess you'll find remains of morphine in it, all right."

"Why do you think the drug was given by means of the bouillon?"

She hesitated and shot Heath an uneasy look.

"It's this way. I always bring a cup of bouillon to Mrs. Greene a little before eleven in the morning; and if Miss Ada's around I bring two cups—that's the old lady's orders. This morning the girl was in the room when I went down to the kitchen, so I brought up two cups. But Mrs. Greene was alone when I returned, so I gave the old lady hers and put the other cup in Miss Ada's room on the table by the bed. Then I went into the hall to call her. She was down-stairs—in the living-room, I guess. Anyhow, she came up right away, and, as I had some mending to do for Mrs. Greene, I went to my room on the third floor. . . ."

"Therefore," interpolated Markham, "the bouillon was on Miss Ada's table unprotected for a minute or so after you had left the room and before Miss Ada came up from the lower hall."

"It wasn't over twenty seconds. And I was right outside the door all the time. Furthermore, the door was open, and I'd have heard any one in the room." The woman was obviously defending herself desperately against the imputation of negligence in Markham's remark.

Vance put the next question.

"Did you see any one else in the hall besides Miss Ada?"

"No one except Doctor Von Blon. He was in the lower hall getting into his coat when I called down."

"Did he leave the house at once?"

"Why—yes."

"You actually saw him pass through the door?"

"No-o. But he was putting on his coat, and he had said good-by to Mrs. Greene and me. . . ."

"When?"

"Not two minutes before. I'd met him coming out of Mrs. Greene's door just as I brought in the bouillon."

"And Miss Sibella's dog—did you notice it in the hall anywhere?"

"No; it wasn't around when I was there."

Vance lay back drowsily in his chair, and Markham again took up the interrogation.

"How long did you remain in your room, Miss O'Brien, after you had called Miss Ada?"

"Until the butler came and told me that Doctor Drumm wanted me."

"And how much later would you say that was?"

"About twenty minutes—maybe a little longer."

Markham smoked pensively a while.

"Yes," he commented at length; "it plainly appears that the morphine was somehow added to the bouillon.—You'd better return to Doctor Drumm now, Miss O'Brien. We'll wait here for him."

"Hell!" growled Heath, after the nurse had gone up-stairs. "She's the best woman for this sort of a job that we've got. And now she goes and falls down on it."

"I wouldn't say she'd fallen down exactly, Sergeant," dissented Vance, his eyes fixed dreamily on the ceiling. "After all, she only stepped into the hall for a few seconds to summon the young lady to her matutinal broth. And if the morphine hadn't found its way into the bouillon this morning it would have done so to-morrow, or the day after, or some time in the future. In fact, the propitious gods may actually have favored us this morning as they did the Grecian host before the walls of Troy."

"They will have favored us," observed Markham, "if Ada recovers and can tell us who visited her room before she drank the bouillon."

The silence that ensued was terminated by the entrance of Doctor Drumm, a youthful, earnest man with an aggressive bearing. He sank heavily into a chair and wiped his face with a large silk handkerchief.

"She's pulled through," he announced. "I happened to be standing by the window looking out—sheer chance—when I saw the curtains go down—saw 'em before Hennessey* did. I grabbed up my bag and the pulmotor, and was over here in a jiffy. The butler was waiting at the door, and took me up-stairs . Queer crab, that butler. The girl was lying across the bed, and it didn't take but one look to see that I wasn't dealing with strychnine. No spasms or sweating or *risus sardonicus,* you understand. Quiet and peaceful; shallow breathing; cyanosis. Morphine evidently. Then I looked at her pupils. Pin-points. No doubt now. So I sent for the nurse and got busy."

"A close call?" asked Markham.

"Close enough." The doctor nodded importantly. "You can't tell what would have happened if somebody hadn't got to her in a hurry. I figured she'd got all six grains that were lost, and gave her a good stiff hypo of atropine—a fiftieth. It reacted like a shot. Then I washed her stomach out with potassium permanganate. After that I gave her artificial respiration—she didn't seem to need it, but I wasn't taking any chances. Then the nurse and I got busy exercising her arms and legs, trying to keep her awake. Tough work, that. Hope I don't get pneumonia sweating there with the windows all open. . . . Well, so it went. Her breathing kept getting better, and I gave her another hundredth of atropine for good measure. At last I managed to get her on her feet. The

---

* Hennessey was the detective stationed in the Narcoss Flats to watch the Greene mansion.

nurse is walking her up and down now." He mopped his face again with a triumphant flourish of the handkerchief.

"We're greatly indebted to you, doctor," said Markham. "It's quite possible you have been the means of solving this case.— When will we be able to question your patient?"

"She'll be loggy and nauseated all day—kind of general collapse, you understand, with painful breathing, drowsiness, headache, and that sort of thing—no fit condition to answer questions. But to-morrow morning you'll be able to talk to her as much as you like."

"That will be satisfactory. And what of the bouillon cup the nurse mentioned?"

"It tasted bitter—morphine, all right."

As Drumm finished speaking Sproot passed down the hall to the front door. A moment later Von Blon paused at the archway and looked into the drawing-room. The strained silence which followed the exchange of greetings caused him to study us with growing alarm.

"Has anything happened?" he finally asked.

It was Vance who rose and, with quick decision, assumed the role of spokesman.

"Yes, doctor. Ada has been poisoned with morphine. Doctor Drumm here happened to be in the Narcoss Flats opposite and was called in."

"And Sibella—is she all right?" Von Blon spoke excitedly.

"Oh, quite."

A relieved sigh escaped him, and he sank into a chair.

"Tell me about it. When was the—the murder discovered?"

Drumm was about to correct him when Vance said quickly:

"Immediately after you left the house this morning. The poison was administered in the bouillon the nurse brought from the kitchen."

"But . . . how could that be?" Von Blon appeared unbelieving. "I was just going when she brought the bouillon. I saw her enter with it. How could the poison——?"

"That reminds me, doctor." Vance's tone was almost dulcet. "Did you, by any hap, go up-stairs again after you had donned your coat?"

Von Blon looked at him with outraged astonishment.

"Certainly not! I left the house immediately."

"That would have been just after the nurse called down to Ada."

"Why—yes. I believe the nurse did call down; and Ada went up-stairs at once—if I recall correctly."

Vance smoked a moment, his gaze resting curiously on the doctor's troubled face.

"I would suggest, without any intention of being impertinent, that your present visit follows rather closely upon your former one."

Von Blon's face clouded over, but I failed to detect any resentment in his expression.

"Quite true," he rejoined, and shifted his eyes. "The fact is, sir, that ever since those drugs disappeared from my case I've felt that something tragic was impending, and that I was in some way to blame. Whenever I'm in this neighborhood I can't resist the impulse to call here and—and see how things are going."

"Your anxiety is wholly understandable." Vance's tone was non-committal. Then he added negligently: "I suppose you will have no objection to Doctor Drumm continuing with Ada's case."

"Continuing?" Von Blon brought himself up straight in his chair. "I don't understand. You said a moment ago——"

"That Ada had been poisoned," finished Vance. "Quite. But d' ye see, she didn't die."

The other looked dumbfounded.

"Thank God for that!" he exclaimed, rising nervously.

"And," added Markham, "we are making no mention whatever of the episode. You will, therefore, be guided by our decision."

"Of course.—And is it permitted that I see Ada?"

Markham hesitated, and Vance answered.

"If you care to—certainly." He turned to Drumm. "Will you be so good as to accompany Doctor Von Blon?"

Drumm and Von Blon left the room together.

"I don't wonder he's on edge," commented Markham. "It's not pleasant to learn of people being poisoned with drugs lost through one's own carelessness."

"He wasn't worrying as much over Ada as he was over Sibella," remarked Heath.

"Observin' fella!" smiled Vance. "No, Sergeant; Ada's demise apparently bothered him far less than Sibella's possible state of health. . . . Now, I wonder what that means. It's an inveiglin' point. But—dash it all!—it everts my pet theory."

"So you have a theory." Markham spoke rebukingly.

"Oh, any number of 'em. And, I might add, they're all pets." Vance's lightness of tone meant merely that he was not ready to outline his suspicions; and Markham did not push the matter.

"We won't need any theories," declared Heath, "after we've heard what Ada's got to tell us. As soon as she talks to us to-morrow we'll be able to figure out who poisoned her."

"Perhaps," murmured Vance.

Drumm returned alone a few minutes later.

"Doctor Von Blon has stepped into the other girl's room. Said he'd be down right away."

"What did he have to say about your patient?" asked Vance.

"Nothing much. She put new energy into her walking the minute she saw him, though. Smiled at him, too, by Jove! A good sign, that. She'll come through fast. Lot of resistance in her."

Drumm had hardly ceased speaking when we heard Sibella's door close and the sound of descending footsteps on the stairs.

"By the by, doctor," said Vance to Von Blon as the latter re-entered the drawing-room, "have you seen Oppenheimer yet?"

"I saw him at eleven. The fact is, I went direct to him after leaving here this morning. He has agreed to make an examination to-morrow at ten o'clock."

"And was Mrs. Greene agreeable?"

"Oh, yes. I spoke to her about it this morning; and she made no objection whatever."

A short while later we took our departure. Von Blon accompanied us to the gate, and we saw him drive off in his car.

"We'll know more by this time to-morrow, I hope," said Markham on the way down-town. He was unwontedly depressed, and his eyes were greatly troubled. "You know, Vance, I'm almost appalled by the thought of what Oppenheimer's report may be."

No report was ever made by Doctor Oppenheimer, however. At some time between one and two the next morning Mrs. Greene died in convulsions as a result of strychnine-poisoning.

CHAPTER XXI

A DEPLETED HOUSEHOLD

(Friday, December 3; forenoon)

MARKHAM BROUGHT us the news of Mrs. Greene's death before ten o'clock the next morning. The tragedy had not been discovered until nine, when the nurse brought up her patient's morning tea. Heath had notified Markham, and Markham had stopped on his way to the Greene mansion to apprise Vance of the new development. Vance and I had already breakfasted, and we accompanied him to the house.

"This knocks out our only prop," Markham said despondently, as we sped up Madison Avenue. "The possibility that the old lady was guilty was frightful to contemplate; though all along I've been trying to console myself with the thought that she was insane. Now, however, I almost wish our suspicions had proved true, for the possibilities that are left seem even more terrible. We're dealing now with a coldblooded calculating rationality."

Vance nodded.

"Yes, we're confronted with something far worse than mania. I can't say, though, that I'm deeply shocked by Mrs. Greene's death. She was a detestable woman, Markham—a most detestable woman. The world will not bemoan her loss."

Vance's comment expressed exactly the sentiment I had felt when Markham informed us of Mrs. Greene's death. The news had of course shaken me, but I had no pity for the victim. She had been vicious and unnatural; she had thriven on hatred, and had made life a hell for every one about her. It was better that her existence was over.

Both Heath and Drumm were waiting for us in the drawing-room. Excitement and depression were mingled in the Sergeant's countenance, and the desperation of despair shone in his china-blue eyes. Drumm revealed only a look of professional disappointment: his chief concern apparently was that he had been deprived of an opportunity to display his medical skill.

Heath, after shaking hands absently, briefly explained the situation.

"O'Brien found the old dame dead at nine this morning, and told Sproot to wigwag to Doc Drumm. Then she phoned the Bureau, and I notified you and Doc Doremus. I got here fifteen or twenty minutes ago, and locked up the room."

"Did you inform Von Blon?" Markham asked.

"I phoned him to call off the examination he'd arranged for ten o'clock. Said I'd communicate with him later, and hung up before he had time to ask any questions."

Markham indicated his approval and turned toward Drumm.

"Give us your story, doctor."

Drumm drew himself up, cleared his throat, and assumed an attitude calculated to be impressive.

"I was down-stairs in the Narcoss dining-room eating breakfast when Hennessey came in and told me the curtains had gone down in the reception-room here. So I snatched my outfit and came over on the run. The butler took me to the old lady's room, where the nurse was waiting. But right away I saw I was too late to be of any good. She was dead—contorted, blue, and cold— and *rigor mortis* had set in. Died of a big dose of strychnine. Probably didn't suffer much—exhaustion and coma came inside of half an hour, I'd say. Too old, you understand, to throw it off. Old people succumb to strychnine pretty swiftly. . . ."

"What about her ability to cry out and give the alarm?"

"You can't tell. The spasm may have rendered her mute. Anyway, no one heard her. Probably passed into unconsciousness after the first seizure. My experience with such cases has taught me——"

"What time would you say the strychnine was taken?"

"Well, now, you can't tell exactly." Drumm became oracular. "The convulsions may have been prolonged before death supervened, or death may have supervened very shortly after the poison was swallowed."

"At what hour, then, would you fix the time of death?"

"There again you can't say definitely. Confusion between *rigor mortis* and the phenomenon of cadaveric spasm is a pitfall into which many doctors fall. There are, however, distinct points of dissimilarity——"

"No doubt." Markham was growing impatient with Drumm's sophomoric pedantries. "But leaving all explanation to one side, what time do you think Mrs. Greene died?"

Drumm pondered the point.

"Roughly, let us say, at two this morning."

"And the strychnine might have been taken as early as eleven or twelve?"

"It's possible."

"Anyhow, we'll know about it when Doc Doremus gets here,"

asserted Heath with brutal frankness. He was in vicious mood that morning.

"Did you find any glass or cup by which the drug might have been administered, doctor?" Markham hastened to ask, by way of covering up Heath's remark.

"There was a glass near the bed with what appeared to be sulphate crystals adhering to the sides of it."

"But wouldn't a fatal dose of strychnine make an ordin'ry drink noticeably bitter?" Vance had suddenly become alert.

"Undoubtedly. But there was a bottle of citrocarbonate—a well-known antacid—on the night-table; and if the drug had been taken with this, the taste would not have been detected. Citrocarbonate is slightly saline and highly effervescing."

"Could Mrs. Greene have taken the citrocarbonate alone?"

"It's not likely. It has to be carefully mixed with water, and the operation would be highly awkward for any one in bed."

"Now, that's most interestin'." Vance listlessly lighted a cigarette. "We may presume, therefore, that the person who gave Mrs. Greene the citrocarbonate also administered the strychnine." He turned to Markham. "I think Miss O'Brien might be able to help us."

Heath went at once and summoned the nurse.

But her evidence was unilluminating. She had left Mrs. Greene reading about eleven o'clock, had gone to her own room to make her toilet for the night, and had returned to Ada's room half an hour later, where she had slept all night, according to Heath's instructions. She had risen at eight, dressed, and gone to the kitchen to fetch Mrs. Greene's tea. As far as she knew, Mrs. Greene had drunk nothing before retiring—certainly she had taken no citrocarbonate up to eleven o'clock. Furthermore, Mrs. Greene never attempted to take it alone.

"You think, then," asked Vance, "that it was given to her by some one else?"

"You can bank on it," the nurse assured him bluntly. "If she'd wanted it, she'd have raised the house before mixing it herself."

"It's quite obvious," Vance observed to Markham, "that some one entered her room after eleven o'clock and prepared the citrocarbonate."

Markham got up and walked anxiously about the room.

"Our immediate problem boils down to finding out who had the opportunity to do it," he said. "You, Miss O'Brien, may return to your room. . . ." Then he went to the bell-cord and rang for Sproot.

During a brief interrogation of the butler the following facts were brought out:

The house had been locked up, and Sproot had retired, at about half past ten.

Sibella had gone to her room immediately after dinner, and had remained there.

Hemming and the cook had lingered in the kitchen until shortly after eleven, at which time Sproot had heard them ascend to their rooms.

The first intimation Sproot had of Mrs. Greene's death was when the nurse sent him to draw the reception-room shades at nine that morning.

Markham dismissed him and sent for the cook. She was, it appeared, unaware of Mrs. Greene's death and of Ada's poisoning as well; and what evidence she had to give was of no importance. She had, she said, been in the kitchen or in her own room practically all of the preceding day.

Hemming was interviewed next. From the nature of the questions put to her she became suspicious almost at once. Her piercing eyes narrowed, and she gave us a look of shrewd triumph.

"You can't hoodwink me," she burst out. "The Lord's been busy with his besom again. And a good thing, too! 'The Lord preserveth all them that love him: but all the wicked shall he destroy.'"

"'Will,'" corrected Vance. "And seeing that you have been so tenderly preserved, perhaps we had better inform you that both Miss Ada and Mrs. Greene have been poisoned."

He was watching the woman closely, but it took no scrutiny to see her cheeks go pale and her jaw sag. The Lord had evidently been too precipitously devastating even for this devout disciple; and her faith was insufficient to counteract her fear.

"I'm going to leave this house," she declared faintly. "I've seen enough to bear witness for the Lord."

"An excellent idea," nodded Vance. "And the sooner you go the more time you'll have to give apocryphal testimony."

Hemming rose, a bit dazed, and started for the archway. Then she quickly turned back and glared at Markham maliciously.

"But let me tell you something before I pass from this den of iniquity. That Miss Sibella is the worst of the lot, and the Lord is going to strike her down next—mark my words! There's no use to try and save her. She's—*doomed!*"

Vance lifted his eyebrows languidly.

"I say, Hemming, what unrighteousness has Miss Sibella been up to now?"

"The usual thing." The woman spoke with relish. "She's nothing but a hussy, if you ask me. Her carryings-on with this Doctor Von Blon have been scandalous. They're together, as thick as thieves, at all hours." She nodded her head significantly. "He came here again last night and went to her room. There's no telling what time he left."

"Fancy that, now. And how do you happen to know about it?"

"Didn't I let him in?"

"Oh, you did?—What time was this? And where was Sproot?"

"Mr. Sproot was eating his dinner, and I'd gone to the front door to take a look at the weather when the doctor walks up. 'Howdy-do, Hemming?' he says with his oily smile. And he brushes past me, nervous-like, and goes straight to Miss Sibella's room."

"Perhaps Miss Sibella was indisposed, and sent for him," suggested Vance indifferently.

"Huh!" Hemming tossed her head contemptuously, and strode from the room.

Vance rose at once and rang again for Sproot.

"Did you know Doctor Von Blon was here last night?" he asked when the butler appeared.

The man shook his head.

"No, sir. I was quite unaware of the fact."

"That's all, Sproot. And now please tell Miss Sibella we'd like to see her."

"Yes, sir."

It was fifteen minutes before Sibella put in an appearance.

"I'm beastly lazy these days," she explained, settling herself in a large chair. "What's the party for this morning?"

Vance offered her a cigarette with an air half quizzical and half deferential.

"Before we explain our presence," he said, "please be good enough to tell us what time Doctor Von Blon left here last night?"

"At a quarter of eleven," she answered, a hostile challenge coming into her eyes.

"Thank you. And now I may tell you that both your mother and Ada have been poisoned."

"Mother and Ada poisoned?" She echoed the words vaguely, as if they were only half intelligible to her; and for several moments she sat motionless, staring stonily out of flintlike eyes. Slowly her gaze became fixed on Markham.

"I think I'll take your advice," she said. "I have a girl chum in Atlantic City. . . . This place is really becoming too, too creepy." She forced a faint smile. "I'm off for the seashore this afternoon." For the first time the girl's nerve seemed to have deserted her.

"Your decision is very wise," observed Vance. "Go, by all means; and arrange to stay until we have settled this affair."

She looked at him in a spirit of indulgent irony.

"I'm afraid I can't stay so long," she said; then added: "I suppose mother and Ada are both dead."

"Only your mother," Vance told her. "Ada recovered."

"She would!" Every curve of her features expressed a fine arrogant contempt. "Common clay has great resistance, I've heard. You know, I'm the only one standing between her and the Greene millions now."

"Your sister had a very close call," Markham reprimanded her. "If we had not had a doctor on guard, you might now be the sole remaining heir to those millions."

"And that would look frightfully suspicious, wouldn't it?" Her question was disconcertingly frank. "But you may rest assured that if *I* had planned this affair, little Ada would not have recovered."

Before Markham could answer she switched herself out of the chair.

"Now, I'm going to pack. Enough is enough."

When she had left the room, Heath looked with doubtful inquisitiveness at Markham.

"What about it, sir? Are you going to let her leave the city? She's the only one of the Greenes who hasn't been touched."

We knew what he meant; and this spoken suggestion of the thought that had been passing through all our minds left us silent for a moment.

"We can't take the chance of forcing her to stay here," Markham returned finally. "If anything should happen . . ."

"I get you, sir." Heath was on his feet. "But I'm going to see that she's tailed—believe me! I'll get two good men up here who'll stick to her from the time she goes out that front door till we know where we stand." He went into the hall, and we heard him giving orders to Snitkin over the telephone.

Five minutes later Doctor Doremus arrived. He was no longer jaunty, and his greeting was almost sombre. Accompanied by Drumm and Heath he went at once to Mrs. Greene's room, while Markham and Vance and I waited down-stairs. When he returned at the end of fifteen minutes he was markedly subdued, and I noticed he did not put on his hat at its usual rakish angle.

"What's the report?" Markham asked him.

"Same as Drumm's. The old girl passed out, I'd say, between one and two."

"And the strychnine was taken when?"

"Midnight, or thereabouts. But that's only a guess. Anyway, she got it along with the citrocarbonate. I tasted it on the glass."*

"By the by, doctor," said Vance, "when you do the autopsy can you let us have a report on the state of atrophy of the leg muscles?"

---

* It will be remembered that in the famous Molineux poisoning case the cyanide of mercury was administered by way of a similar drug—to wit: Bromo-Seltzer.

"Sure thing." Doremus was somewhat surprised by the request. When he had gone, Markham addressed himself to Drumm. "We'd like to talk to Ada now. How is she this morning?"

"Oh, fine!" Drumm spoke with pride. "I saw her right after I'd looked at the old lady. She's weak and a bit dried up with all the atropine I gave her, but otherwise practically normal."

"And she has not been told of her mother's death?"

"Not a word."

"She will have to know," interposed Vance; "and there's no point in keeping the fact from her any longer. It's just as well that the shock should come when we're all present."

Ada was sitting by the window when we came in, her elbows on the sill, chin in hands, gazing out into the snow-covered yard. She was startled by our entry, and the pupils of her eyes dilated, as if with sudden fright. It was plain that the experiences she had been through had created in her a state of nervous fear.

After a brief exchange of amenities, during which both Vance and Markham strove to allay her nervousness, Markham broached the subject of the bouillon.

"We'd give a great deal," he said, "not to have to recall so pain- ful an episode, but much depends on what you can tell us re- garding yesterday morning.—You were in the drawing-room, weren't you, when the nurse called down to you?"

The girl's lips and tongue were dry, and she spoke with some difficulty.

"Yes. Mother had asked me to bring her a copy of a magazine, and I had just gone down-stairs to look for it when the nurse called."

"You saw the nurse when you came up-stairs?"

"Yes; she was just going toward the servants' stairway."

"There was no one in your room here when you entered?"

She shook her head. "Who could have been here?"

"That's what we're trying to find out, Miss Greene," replied Markham gravely. "Some one certainly put the drug in your bouillon."

She shuddered, but made no reply.

"Did any one come in to see you later?" Markham continued.

"Not a soul."

Heath impatiently projected himself into the interrogation.

"And say; did you drink your soup right away?"

"No—not right away. I felt a little chilly, and I went across the hall to Julia's room to get an old Spanish shawl to put round me."

Heath made a disgusted face, and sighed noisily.

"Every time we get going on this case," he complained, "something comes along and sinks us.—If Miss Ada left the soup in here, Mr. Markham, while she went to get a shawl, then almost anybody coulda sneaked in and poisoned the stuff."

"I'm so sorry," Ada apologized, almost as though she had taken Heath's words as a criticism of her actions.

"It's not your fault, Ada," Vance assured her. "The Sergeant is unduly depressed.—But tell me this: when you went into the hall did you see Miss Sibella's dog anywhere around?"

She shook her head wonderingly.

"Why, no. What has Sibella's dog to do with it?"

"He probably saved your life." And Vance explained to her how Sproot had happened to find her.

She gave a half-breathless murmur of amazement and incredulity, and fell into abstracted revery.

"When you returned from your sister's room, did you drink your bouillon at once?" Vance asked her next.

With difficulty she brought her mind back to the question.

"Yes."

"And didn't you notice a peculiar taste?"

"Not particularly. Mother always likes a lot of salt in her bouillon."

"And then what happened?"

"Nothing happened. Only, I began to feel funny. The back of my neck tightened up, and I got very warm and drowsy. My skin tingled all over, and my arms and legs seemed to get numb. I was terribly sleepy, and I lay back on the bed.—That's all I remember."

"Another washout," grumbled Heath.

There was a short silence, and Vance drew his chair nearer.

"Now, Ada," he said, "you must brace yourself for more bad news. . . . Your mother died during the night."

The girl sat motionless for a moment, and then turned to him eyes of a despairing clearness.

"Died?" she repeated. "How did she die?"

"She was poisoned—she took an overdose of strychnine."

"You mean . . . she committed suicide?"

This query startled us all. It expressed a possibility that had not occurred to us. After a momentary hesitation, however, Vance slowly shook his head.

"No, I hardly think so. I'm afraid the person who poisoned you also poisoned your mother."

Vance's reply seemed to stun her. Her face grew pale, and her eyes were set in a glassy stare of terror. Then presently she sighed deeply, as if from a kind of mental depletion.

"Oh, what's going to happen next? . . . I'm—afraid!"

"Nothing more is going to happen," said Vance with emphasis. "Nothing more *can* happen. You are going to be guarded every minute. And Sibella is going this afternoon to Atlantic City for a long visit."

"I wish I could go away," she breathed pathetically.

"There will be no need of that," put in Markham. "You'll be safer in New York. We are going to keep the nurse here to look after you, and also put a man in the house day and night until everything is straightened out. Hemming is leaving to-day, but Sproot and the cook will take care of you." He rose and patted her shoulder comfortingly. "There's no possible way any one can harm you now."

As we descended into the lower hall Sproot was just admitting Doctor Von Blon.

"Good God!" he exclaimed, hastening toward us. "Sibella just phoned me about Mrs. Greene." He looked truculently at Markham, his suavity for the moment forgotten. "Why wasn't I informed, sir?"

"I saw no necessity of bothering you, doctor," Markham returned equably. "Mrs. Greene had been dead several hours when she was found. And we had our own doctor at hand."

A quick flame leaped in Von Blon's eyes.

"And am I to be forcibly kept from seeing Sibella?" he asked coldly. "She tells me she is leaving the city to-day, and has asked me to assist with her arrangements."

Markham stepped aside.

"You are free, doctor, to do whatever you desire," he said, a perceptible chill in his voice.

Von Blon bowed stiffly, and went up the stairs.

"He's sore," grinned Heath.

"No, Sergeant," Vance corrected. "He's worried—oh, deuced worried."

Shortly after noon that day Hemming departed forever from the Greene mansion; and Sibella took the three-fifteen o'clock train for Atlantic City. Of the original household, only Ada and

Sproot and Mrs. Mannheim were left. However, Heath gave orders for Miss O'Brien to remain on duty indefinitely and keep an eye on everything that happened; and, in addition to this protection, a detective was stationed in the house to augment the nurse's watch.

CHAPTER XXII

THE SHADOWY FIGURE

(Friday, December 3; 6 p. m.)

At six o'clock that evening Markham called another informal conference at the Stuyvesant Club. Not only were Inspector Moran and Heath present, but Chief Inspector O'Brien* dropped in on his way home from the office.

The afternoon papers had been merciless in their criticism of the police for its unsuccessful handling of the investigation. Markham, after consulting with Heath and Doremus, had explained the death of Mrs. Greene to the reporters as "the result of an overdose of strychnine—a stimulant she had been taking regularly under her physician's orders." Swacker had typed copies of the item so there would be no mistake as to its exact wording; and the announcement ended by saying: "There is no evidence to show that the drug was not self-administered as the result of error." But although the reporters composed their news stories in strict accord with Markham's report, they interpolated subtle intimations of deliberate murder, so that the reader was left

---

* Chief Inspector O'Brien, who was in command of the entire Police Department, was, I learned later, an uncle of the Miss O'Brien who was acting officially as nurse at the Greene mansion.

with little doubt as to the true state of affairs. The unsuccessful attempt to poison Ada had been kept a strict official secret. But this suppressed item had not been needed to inflame the public's morbid imagination to an almost unprecedented degree.

Both Markham and Heath had begun to show the strain of their futile efforts to solve the affair; and one glance at Inspector Moran, as he sank heavily into a chair beside the District Attorney, was enough to make one realize that a corroding worry had undermined his habitual equanimity. Even Vance revealed signs of tensity and uneasiness; but with him it was an eager alertness, rather than worry, that marked any deviation from normality in his attitude.

As soon as we were assembled that evening Heath briefly epitomized the case. He went over the various lines of investigation, and enumerated the precautions that had been taken. When he had finished, and before any one could make a comment, he turned to Chief Inspector O'Brien and said:

"There's plenty of things, sir, we might've done in any ordinary case. We could've searched the house for the gun and the poison like the narcotic squad goes through a single room or small apartment—punching the mattresses, tearing up the carpets, and sounding the woodwork—but in the Greene house it would've taken a coupla months. And even if we'd found the stuff, what good would it have done us? The guy that's tearing things wide open in that dump isn't going to stop just because we take his dinky thirty-two away from him, or grab his poison.— After Chester or Rex was shot we could've arrested all the rest of the family and put 'em through a third degree. But there's too much noise in the papers now every time we give anybody the works; and it ain't exactly healthy for us to grill a family like the Greenes. They've got too much money and pull; they'd have had a whole battalion of high-class lawyers smearing us with suits and injunctions and God knows what. And if we'd just held 'em as material witnesses, they'd have got out in forty-eight hours on *habeas-corpus* actions.—Then, again, we might've planted a bunch of huskies in the house. But we couldn't keep a garrison there indefinitely, and the minute they'd have been called off, the dirty work would've begun.—Believe me, Inspector, we've been up against it good and plenty."

O'Brien grunted and tugged at his white cropped moustache.

"What the Sergeant says is perfectly true," Moran remarked. "Most of the ordinary methods of action and investigation have been denied us. We're obviously dealing with an inside family affair."

"Moreover," added Vance, "we're dealing with an extr'ordin'rily clever plot—something that has been thought out and planned down to the minutest detail, and elaborately covered up at every point. Everything has been staked—even life itself—on the outcome. Only a supreme hatred and an exalted hope could have inspired the crimes. And against such attributes, d' ye see, the ordin'ry means of prevention are utterly useless."

"A family affair!" repeated O'Brien heavily, who apparently was still pondering over Inspector Moran's statement. "It don't look to me as though there's much of the family left. I'd say, on the evidence, that some outsider was trying to wipe the family out." He gave Heath a glowering look. "What have you done about the servants? You're not scared to monkey with *them*, are you? You could have arrested one of 'em a long time ago and stopped the yapping of the newspapers for a time, anyway."

Markham came immediately to Heath's defense.

"I'm wholly responsible for any seeming negligence on the Sergeant's part in that regard," he said with a noticeable accent of cold reproach. "As long as I have anything to say about this case no arrests are going to be made for the mere purpose of quieting unpleasant criticism." Then his manner relaxed slightly. "There isn't the remotest indication of guilt in connection with any of the servants. The maid Hemming is a harmless fanatic, and is quite incapable mentally of having planned the murders. I permitted her to leave the Greenes' to-day. . . ."

"We know where to find her, Inspector," Heath hastened to add by way of forestalling the other's inevitable question.

"As to the cook," Markham went on; "she, too, is wholly outside of any serious consideration. She's temperamentally unfitted to be cast in the role of murderer."

"And what about the butler?" asked O'Brien acrimoniously.

"He's been with the family thirty years, and was even remembered liberally in Tobias Greene's will. He's a bit queer, but I think if he had had any reason for destroying the Greenes he wouldn't have waited till old age came on him." Markham looked troubled for a moment. "I must admit, however, that there's an atmosphere of mysterious reserve about the old fellow. He always gives me the impression of knowing far more than he admits."

"What you say, Markham, is true enough," remarked Vance. "But Sproot certainly doesn't fit this particular saturnalia of crime. He reasons too carefully; there's an immense cautiousness about the man, and his mental outlook is highly conservative. He might stab an enemy if there was no remote chance of detection. But he lacks the courage and the imaginative resiliency that have made possible this present gory debauch. He's too old— much too old. . . . *By Jove!*"

Vance leaned over and tapped the table with an incisive gesture. "That's the thing that's been evading me! Vitality! That's what is at the bottom of this business—a tremendous, elastic, self-confident vitality: a supreme ruthlessness mingled with audacity and impudence—an intrepid and reckless egoism—an undaunted belief in one's own ability. And they're not the components of age. There's youth in all this—youth with its ambition and venturesomeness—that doesn't count the cost, that takes no thought of risk. . . . No. Sproot could never qualify."

Moran shifted his chair uneasily, and turned to Heath.

"Whom did you send to Atlantic City to watch Sibella?"

"Guilfoyle and Mallory—the two best men we've got."* The Sergeant smiled with a kind of cruel satisfaction. "She won't get away. And she won't pull anything, either."

"And have you extended your attention to Doctor Von Blon, by any chance?" negligently asked Vance.

Again Heath's canny smile appeared.

"He's been tailed ever since Rex was shot."

Vance regarded him admiringly.

"I'm becoming positively fond of you, Sergeant," he said; and beneath his chaffing note was the ring of sincerity.

O'Brien leaned ponderously over the table and, brushing the ashes from his cigar, fixed a sullen look on the District Attorney.

"What was this story you gave out to the papers, Mr. Markham? You seemed to want to imply that the old woman took the strychnine herself. Was that hogwash, or was there something in it?"

"I'm afraid there was nothing in it, Inspector." Markham spoke with a sense of genuine regret. "Such a theory doesn't square with the poisoning of Ada—or with any of the rest of it, for that matter."

"I'm not so sure," retorted O'Brien. "Moran here has told me

---

* I recalled that Guilfoyle and Mallory were the two men who had been set to watch Tony Skeel in the Canary murder case.

that you fellows had an idea the old woman was faking her paralysis." He rearranged his arms on the table and pointed a short thick finger at Markham. "Supposing she shot three of the children, using up all the cartridges in the revolver, and then stole the two doses of poison—one for each of the two girls left; and then supposing she gave the morphine to the younger one, and had only one dose left. . . ." He paused and squinted significantly.

"I see what you mean," said Markham. "Your theory is that she didn't count on our having a doctor handy to save Ada's life, and that, having failed to put Ada out of the way, she figured the game was up, and took the strychnine."

"That's it!" O'Brien struck the table with his fist. "And it makes sense. Furthermore, it means we've cleared up the case—see?"

"Yes, it unquestionably makes sense." It was Vance's quiet, drawling voice that answered. "But forgive me if I suggest that it fits the facts much too tidily. It's a perfect theory, don't y' know; it leaps to the brain, almost as though some one had planned it for our benefit. I rather fancy that we're intended to adopt that very logical and sensible point of view. But really now, Inspector, Mrs. Greene was not the suicidal type, however murderous she may have been."

While Vance had been speaking, Heath had left the room. A few minutes later he returned and interrupted O'Brien in a long, ill-natured defense of his suicide theory.

"We haven't got to argue any more along that line," he announced. "I've just had Doc Doremus on the phone. He's finished the autopsy; and he says that the old lady's leg muscles had wasted away—gone plumb flabby—and that there wasn't a chance in the world of her moving her legs, let alone walking on 'em."

"Good God!" Moran was the first to recover from the amazement this news had caused us. "Who was it, then, that Ada saw in the hall?"

"That's just it!" Vance spoke hurriedly, trying to stem his rising sense of excitement. "If only we knew! That's the answer to the whole problem. It may not have been the murderer; but the person who sat in that library night after night and read strange books by candlelight is the key to everything. . . ."

"But Ada was so positive in her identification," objected Markham, in a bewildered tone.

"She's hardly to be blamed in the circumstances," Vance returned. "The child had been through a frightful experience and was scarcely normal. And it is not at all unlikely that she, too, suspected her mother. If she did, what would have been more natural than for her to imagine that this shadowy figure she saw in the hall long after midnight was the actual object of her dread? It is not unusual for a person under the stress of fright to distort an object by the projection of a dominating mental image."

"You mean," said Heath, "that she saw somebody else, and imagined it was her mother because she was thinking so hard of the old woman?"

"It's by no means improbable."

"Still, there was that detail of the Oriental shawl," objected Markham. "Ada might easily have mistaken the person's features, but her insistence on having seen that particular shawl was fairly definite."

Vance gave a perplexed nod.

"The point is well taken. And it may prove the Ariadne's clew that will lead us out of this Cretan labyrinth. We must find out more about that shawl."

Heath had taken out his note-book and was turning the pages with scowling concentration.

"And don't forget, Mr. Vance," he said, without looking up, "about that diagram Ada found in the rear of the hall near the library door. Maybe this person in the shawl was the one who'd dropped it, and was going to the library to look for it, but got scared off when she saw Ada."

"But whoever shot Rex," said Markham, "evidently stole the paper from him, and therefore wouldn't be worrying about it."

"I guess that's right," Heath admitted reluctantly.

"Such speculation is futile," commented Vance. "This affair is too complicated to be untangled by the unravelling of details. We must determine, if possible, who it was that Ada saw that night. Then we'll have opened a main artery of inquiry."

"How are we going to find that out," demanded O'Brien, "when Ada was the only person who saw this woman in Mrs. Greene's shawl?"

"Your question contains the answer, Inspector. We must see Ada again and try to counteract the suggestion of her own fears. When we explain that it couldn't have been her mother, she may recall some other point that will put us on the right track."

And this was the course taken. When the conference ended, O'Brien departed, and the rest of us dined at the club. At half past eight we were on our way to the Greene mansion.

We found Ada and the cook alone in the drawing-room. The girl sat before the fire, a copy of Grimm's "Fairy-Tales" turned face down on her knees; and Mrs. Mannheim, busy with a lapful of mending, occupied a straight chair near the door. It was a curious sight, in view of the formal correctness of the house, and it brought forcibly to my mind how fear and adversity inevitably level all social standards.

When we entered the room Mrs. Mannheim rose and, gathering up her mending, started to go. But Vance indicated that she was to remain, and without a word she resumed her seat.

"We're here to annoy you again, Ada," said Vance, assuming the role of interrogator. "But you're about the only person we can come to for help." His smile put the girl at ease, and he continued gently: "We want to talk to you about what you told us the other afternoon. . . ."

Her eyes opened wide, and she waited in a kind of awed silence.

"You told us you thought you had seen your mother——"

"I did see her—I did!"

Vance shook his head. "No; it was not your mother. She was unable to walk, Ada. She was truly and helplessly paralyzed. It was impossible for her even to make the slightest movement with either leg."

"But—I don't understand." There was more than bewilderment in her voice: there was terror and alarm such as one might experience at the thought of supernatural malignancy. "I heard Doctor Von tell mother he was bringing a specialist to see her this morning. But she died last night—so how could you know? Oh, you must be mistaken. I saw her—I *know* I saw her."

She seemed to be battling desperately for the preservation of her sanity. But Vance again shook his head.

"Doctor Oppenheimer did not examine your mother," he said. "But Doctor Doremus did—to-day. And he found that she had been unable to move for many years."

"Oh!" The exclamation was only breathed. The girl seemed incapable of speech.

"And what we've come for," continued Vance, "is to ask you to recall that night, and see if you cannot remember something—

some little thing—that will help us. You saw this person only by the flickering light of a match. You might easily have made a mistake."

"But how could I? I was so close to her."

"Before you woke up that night and felt hungry, had you been dreaming of your mother?"

She hesitated, and shuddered slightly.

"I don't know, but I've dreamed of mother constantly—awful, scary dreams—ever since that first night when somebody came into my room. . . ."

"That may account for the mistake you made." Vance paused a moment and then asked: "Do you distinctly remember seeing your mother's Oriental shawl on the person in the hall that night?"

"Oh, yes," she said, after a slight hesitation. "It was the first thing I noticed. Then I saw her face. . . ."

A trivial but startling thing happened at this moment. We had our back to Mrs. Mannheim and, for the time being, had forgotten her presence in the room. Suddenly what sounded like a dry sob broke from her, and the sewing-basket on her knees fell to the floor. Instinctively we turned. The woman was staring at us glassily.

"What difference does it make who she saw?" she asked in a dead, monotonous voice. "She maybe saw me."

"Nonsense, Gertrude," Ada said quickly. "It wasn't you."

Vance was watching the woman with a puzzled expression.

"Do you ever wear Mrs. Greene's shawl, Frau Mannheim?"

"Of course she doesn't," Ada cut in.

"And do you ever steal into the library and read after the household is asleep?" pursued Vance.

The woman picked up her sewing morosely, and again lapsed

into sullen silence. Vance studied her a moment and then turned back to Ada.

"Do you know of any one who might have been wearing your mother's shawl that night?"

"I—don't know," the girl stammered, her lips trembling.

"Come; that won't do." Vance spoke with some asperity. "This isn't the time to shield any one. Who was in the habit of using the shawl?"

"No one was in the habit. . . ." She stopped and gave Vance a pleading look; but he was obdurate.

"Who, then, besides your mother ever wore it?"

"But I would have known if it had been Sibella I saw——"

"Sibella? She sometimes borrowed the shawl?"

Ada nodded reluctantly. "Once in a great while. She—she admired the shawl. . . . Oh, why do you make me tell you this!"

"And you have never seen any one else with it on?"

"No; no one ever wore it except mother and Sibella."

Vance attempted to banish her obvious distress with a whimsical reassuring smile.

"Just see how foolish all your fears have been," he said lightly. "You probably saw your sister in the hall that night, and, because you'd been having bad dreams about your mother, you thought it was she. As a result, you became frightened, and locked yourself up and worried. It was rather silly, what?"

A little later we took our leave.

"It has always been my contention," remarked Inspector Moran, as we rode down-town, "that any identification under strain or excitement is worthless. And here we have a glaring instance of it."

"I'd like a nice quiet little chat with Sibella," mumbled Heath, busy with his own thoughts.

"It wouldn't comfort you, Sergeant," Vance told him. "At the end of your *tête-à-tête* you'd know only what the young lady wanted you to know."

"Where do we stand now?" asked Markham, after a silence.

"Exactly where we stood before," answered Vance dejectedly, "—in the midst of an impenetrable fog.—And I'm not in the least convinced," he added, "that it was Sibella whom Ada saw in the hall."

Markham looked amazed.

"Then who, in Heaven's name, was it?"

Vance sighed gloomily. "Give me the answer to that one question, and I'll complete the saga."

That night Vance sat up until nearly two o'clock writing at his desk in the library.

CHAPTER XXIII

THE MISSING FACT

(Saturday, December 4; 1 p. m.)

SATURDAY WAS the District Attorney's "half-day" at the office, and Markham had invited Vance and me to lunch at the Bankers Club. But when we reached the Criminal Courts Building he was swamped with an accumulation of work, and we had a tray-service meal in his private conference room. Before leaving the house that noon Vance had put several sheets of closely written paper in his pocket, and I surmised—correctly, as it turned out—that they were what he had been working on the night before.

When lunch was over Vance lay back in his chair languidly and lit a cigarette.

"Markham old dear," he said, "I accepted your invitation to-day for the sole purpose of discussing art. I trust you are in a receptive mood."

Markham looked at him with frank annoyance.

"Damn it, Vance, I'm too confounded busy to be bothered with your irrelevancies. If you feel artistically inclined, take Van here to the Metropolitan Museum. But leave me alone."

Vance sighed, and wagged his head reproachfully.

"There speaks the voice of America! 'Run along and play with your aesthetic toys if such silly things amuse you; but let me attend to my serious affairs.' It's very sad. In the present instance, however, I refuse to run along; and most certainly I shall not browse about that mausoleum of Europe's rejected corpses, known as the Metropolitan Museum. I say, it's a wonder you didn't suggest that I make the rounds of our municipal statuary."

"I'd have suggested the Aquarium——"

"I know. Anything to get rid of me." Vance adopted an injured tone. "And yet, don't y' know, I'm going to sit right here and deliver an edifying lecture on aesthetic composition."

"Then don't talk too loud," said Markham, rising; "for I'll be in the next room working."

"But my lecture has to do with the Greene case. And really you shouldn't miss it."

Markham paused and turned.

"Merely one of your wordy prologues, eh?" He sat down again. "Well, if you have any helpful suggestions to make, I'll listen."

Vance smoked a moment.

"Y' know, Markham," he began, assuming a lazy, unemotional air, "there's a fundamental difference between a good painting and a photograph. I'll admit many painters appear unaware of this fact; and when color photography is perfected—my word! what a horde of academicians will be thrown out of employment! But none the less there's a vast chasm between the two; and it's this technical distinction that's to be the burden of my lay. How, for instance, does Michelangelo's 'Moses' differ from a camera study of a patriarchal old man with whiskers and a stone tablet? Wherein lie the points of divergence between Rubens's 'Landscape with Château de Stein' and a tourist's snap-shot of a Rhine castle? Why is a Cézanne still-life an improvement on a photograph of a dish of apples? Why have the Renaissance paintings of Madonnas endured for hundreds of years whereas a mere photograph of a mother and child passes into artistic oblivion at the very click of the lens shutter? . . ."

He held up a silencing hand as Markham was about to speak.

"I'm not being futile. Bear with me a moment.—The difference between a good painting and a photograph is this: the one is arranged, composed, organized; the other is merely the haphazard impression of a scene, or a segment of realism, just as it exists in nature. In short, the one has form; the other is chaotic. When a true artist paints a picture, d'ye see, he arranges all the masses and lines to accord with his preconceived idea of composition—that is, he bends everything in the picture to a basic design; and he also eliminates any objects or details that go contr'ry to, or detract from, that design. Thus he achieves a homogeneity of form, so to speak. Every object in the picture is put there for a definite purpose, and is set in a certain position to accord with the underlying structural pattern. There are no irrelevancies, no unrelated details, no detached objects, no arbitr'ry arrangement of values. All the forms and lines are interdependent; every object—indeed, every brush stroke—takes its exact place in the pattern and fulfils a given function. The picture, in fine, is a unity."

"Very instructive," commented Markham, glancing ostentatiously at his watch. "And the Greene case?"

"Now, a photograph, on the other hand," pursued Vance, ignoring the interruption, "is devoid of design or even of arrangement in the aesthetic sense. To be sure, a photographer may pose and drape a figure—he may even saw off the limb of a tree that he intends to record on his negative; but it's quite impossible for him to compose the subject-matter of his picture to accord with a preconceived design, the way a painter does. In a photograph there are always details that have no meaning, variations of light and shade that are harmonically false, textures that create false notes, lines that are discords, masses that are out of place. The camera, d' ye see, is deucedly forthright—it records whatever is before it, irrespective of art values. The inevitable result is that a photograph lacks organization and unity; its composition is, at best, primitive and obvious. And it is full of irrelevant factors—of objects which have neither meaning nor purpose. There is no uniformity of conception in it. It is haphazard, heterogeneous, aimless, and amorphous—just as is nature."

"You needn't belabor the point." Markham spoke impatiently. "I have a rudimentary intelligence.—Where is this elaborate truism leading you?"

Vance gave him an engaging smile.

"To East 53d Street. But before we reach our destination permit me another brief amplification.—Quite often a painting of intricate and subtle design does not at once reveal its composition to the spectator. In fact, only the designs of the simpler and more obvious paintings are immediately grasped. Generally the spectator has to study a painting carefully—trace its rhythms, compare its forms, weigh its details, and fit together all its salients—before its underlying design becomes apparent. Many well-organized and perfectly balanced paintings—such as Renoir's figure-pieces, Matisse's interiors, Cézanne's water-colors, Picasso's still-lives, and Leonardo's anatomical drawings—may at first appear meaningless from the standpoint of composition; their forms may seem to lack unity and cohesion; their masses and linear values may give the impression of having been arbitrarily put down. And it is only after the spectator has related all their integers and traced all their contrapuntal activities that they take on significance and reveal their creator's motivating conception. . . ."

"Yes, yes," interrupted Markham. "Paintings and photographs differ; the objects in a painting possess design; the objects in a photograph are without design; one must often study a painting in order to determine the design.—That, I believe, covers the ground you have been wandering over desultorily for the past fifteen minutes."

"I was merely trying to imitate the vast deluge of repetitive verbiage found in legal documents," explained Vance. "I hoped thereby to convey my meaning to your lawyer's mind."

"You succeeded with a vengeance," snapped Markham. "What follows?"

Vance became serious again.

"Markham, we've been looking at the various occurrences in the Greene case as though they were the unrelated objects of a photograph. We've inspected each fact as it came up; but we have failed to analyze sufficiently its connection with all the other known facts. We've regarded this whole affair as though it were a series, or collection, of isolated integers. And we've missed the significance of everything because we haven't yet determined the shape of the basic pattern of which each of these incidents is but a part.—Do you follow me?"

"My dear fellow!"

"Very well.—Now, it goes without saying that there is a design at the bottom of this whole amazin' business. Nothing has happened haphazardly. There has been premeditation behind each act—a subtly and carefully concocted composition, as it were. And everything has emanated from that central shape. Everything has been fashioned by a fundamental structural idea. Therefore, nothing important that has occurred since the first double shooting has been unrelated to the predetermined pattern of the crime. All the aspects and events of the case, taken together, form a unity—a co-ordinated, interactive whole. In short, the Greene case is a painting, not a photograph. And when we have studied it in that light—when we have determined the interrelationship of all the external factors, and have traced the visual forms to their generating lines—then, Markham, we will know the composition of the picture; we will see the design on which the perverted painter has erected his document'ry material. And once we have discovered the underlying shape of this hideous picture's pattern, we'll know its creator."

"I see your point," said Markham slowly. "But how does it help us? We know all the external facts; and they certainly don't fit into any intelligible conception of a unified whole."

"Not yet, perhaps," agreed Vance. "But that's because we haven't gone about it systematically. We've done too much investigating and too little thinking. We've been sidetracked by what the modern painters call documentation—that is, by the objective appeal of the picture's recognizable parts. We haven't sought for the abstract content. We've overlooked the 'significant form'—a loose phrase; but blame Clive Bell for it."*

"And how would you suggest that we set about determining the compositional design of this bloody canvas? We might dub the picture, by the way, 'Nepotism Gone Wrong.'" By this facetious remark, he was, I knew, attempting to counteract the se-

---

* Vance was here referring to the chapter called "The Æsthetic Hypothesis" in Clive Bell's "Art." But, despite the somewhat slighting character of his remark, Vance was an admirer of Bell's criticisms, and had spoken to me with considerable enthusiasm of his "Since Cézanne."

rious impression the other's disquisition had made on him; for, though he realized Vance would not have drawn his voluminous parallel without a definite hope of applying it successfully to the problem in hand, he was chary of indulging any expectations lest they result in further disappointments.

In answer to Markham's question Vance drew out the sheaf of papers he had brought with him.

"Last night," he explained, "I set down briefly and chronologically all the outstanding facts of the Greene case—that is, I noted each important external factor of the ghastly picture we've been contemplating for the past few weeks. The principal forms are all here, though I may have left out many details. But I think I have tabulated a sufficient number of items to serve as a working basis."

He held out the papers to Markham.

"The truth lies somewhere in that list. If we could put the facts together—relate them to one another with their correct values—we'd know who was at the bottom of this orgy of crime; for, once we determined the pattern, each of the items would take on a vital significance, and we could read clearly the message they had to tell us."

Markham took the summary and, moving his chair nearer to the light, read through it without a word.

I preserved the original copy of the document; and, of all the records I possess, it was the most important and far-reaching in its effects. Indeed, it was the instrument by means of which the Greene case was solved. Had it not been for this recapitulation, prepared by Vance and later analyzed by him, the famous mass murder at the Greene mansion would doubtless have been relegated to the category of unsolved crimes.

Herewith is a verbatim reproduction of it:

GENERAL FACTS

1. An atmosphere of mutual hatred pervades the Greene mansion.

2. Mrs. Greene is a nagging, complaining paralytic, making life miserable for the whole household.

3. There are five children—two daughters, two sons, and one adopted daughter—who have nothing in common, and live in a state of constant antagonism and bitterness toward one another.

4. Though Mrs. Mannheim, the cook, was acquainted with Tobias Greene years ago and was remembered in his will, she refuses to reveal any of the facts in her past.

5. The will of Tobias Greene stipulated that the family must live in the Greene mansion for twenty-five years on pain of disinheritance, with the one exception that, if Ada should marry, she could establish a residence elsewhere, as she was not of the Greene blood. By the will Mrs. Greene has the handling and disposition of the money.

6. Mrs. Greene's will makes the five children equal beneficiaries. In event of death of any of them the survivors share alike; and if all should die the estate goes to their families, if any.

7. The sleeping-rooms of the Greenes are arranged thus: Julia's and Rex's face each other at the front of the house; Chester's and Ada's face each other in the centre of the house; and Sibella's and Mrs. Greene's face each other at the rear. No two rooms intercommunicate, with the exception of Ada's and Mrs. Greene's; and these two rooms also give on the same balcony.

8. The library of Tobias Greene, which Mrs. Greene believes she had kept locked for twelve years, contains a remarkably complete collection of books on criminology and allied subjects.

9. Tobias Greene's past was somewhat mysterious, and there

were many rumors concerning shady transactions carried on by him in foreign lands.

FIRST CRIME

10. Julia is killed by a contact shot, fired from the front, at 11.30 P. M.

11. Ada is shot from behind, also by a contact shot. She recovers.

12. Julia is found in bed, with a look of horror and amazement on her face.

13. Ada is found on the floor before the dressing-table.

14. The lights have been turned on in both rooms.

15. Over three minutes elapse between the two shots.

16. Von Blon, summoned immediately, arrives within half an hour.

17. A set of footprints, other than Von Blon's, leaving and approaching the house, is found; but the character of the snow renders them indecipherable.

18. The tracks have been made during the half-hour preceding the crime.

19. Both shootings are done with a .32 revolver.

20. Chester reports that an old .32 revolver of his is missing.

21. Chester is not satisfied with the police theory of a burglar, and insists that the District Attorney's office investigate the case.

22. Mrs. Greene is aroused by the shot fired in Ada's room, and hears Ada fall. But she hears no footsteps or sound of a door closing.

23. Sproot is half-way down the servants' stairs when the second shot is fired, yet he encounters no one in the hall. Nor does he hear any noise.

24. Rex, in the room next to Ada's, says he heard no shot.

25. Rex intimates that Chester knows more about the tragedy than he admits.

26. There is some secret between Chester and Sibella.

27. Sibella, like Chester, repudiates the burglar theory, but refuses to suggest an alternative, and says frankly that any member of the Greene family may be guilty.

28. Ada says she was awakened by a menacing presence in her room, which was in darkness; that she attempted to run from the intruder, but was pursued by shuffling footsteps.

29. Ada says a hand touched her when she first arose from bed, but refuses to make any attempt to identify the hand.

30. Sibella challenges Ada to say that it was she (Sibella) who was in the room, and then deliberately accuses Ada of having shot Julia. She also accuses Ada of having stolen the revolver from Chester's room.

31. Von Blon, by his attitude and manner, reveals a curious intimacy between Sibella and himself.

32. Ada is frankly fond of Von Blon.

SECOND CRIME

33. Four days after Julia and Ada are shot, at 11.30 P.M., Chester is murdered by a contact shot fired from a .32 revolver.

34. There is a look of amazement and horror on his face.

35. Sibella hears the shot and summons Sproot.

36. Sibella says she listened at her door immediately after the shot was fired, but heard no other sound.

37. The lights are on in Chester's room. He was apparently reading when the murderer entered.

38. A clear double set of footprints is found on the front walk. The tracks have been made within a half-hour of the crime.

39. A pair of galoshes, exactly corresponding to the footprints, is found in Chester's clothes-closet.

40. Ada had a premonition of Chester's death, and, when informed of it, guesses he has been shot in the same manner as Julia. But she is greatly relieved when shown the footprint patterns indicating that the murderer is an outsider.

41. Rex says he heard a noise in the hall and the sound of a door closing twenty minutes before the shot was fired.

42. Ada, when told of Rex's story, recalls also having heard a door close at some time after eleven.

43. It is obvious that Ada knows or suspects something.

44. The cook becomes emotional at the thought of any one wanting to harm Ada, but says she can understand a person having a reason to shoot Julia and Chester.

45. Rex, when interviewed, shows clearly that he thinks some one in the house is guilty.

46. Rex accuses Von Blon of being the murderer.

47. Mrs. Greene makes a request that the investigation be dropped.

THIRD CRIME

48. Rex is shot in the forehead with a .32 revolver, at 11.20 A. M., twenty days after Chester has been killed and within five minutes of the time Ada phones him from the District Attorney's office.

49. There is no look of horror or surprise on Rex's face, as was the case with Julia and Chester.

50. His body is found on the floor before the mantel.

51. A diagram which Ada asked him to bring with him to the District Attorney's office has disappeared.

52. No one up-stairs hears the shot, though the doors are open; but Sproot, down-stairs in the butler's pantry, hears it distinctly.

53. Von Blon is visiting Sibella that morning; but she says she was in the bathroom bathing her dog at the time Rex was shot.

54. Footprints are found in Ada's room coming from the balcony door, which is ajar.

55. A single set of footprints is found leading from the front walk to the balcony.

56. The tracks could have been made at any time after nine o'clock that morning.

57. Sibella refuses to go away on a visit.

58. The galoshes that made all three sets of footprints are found in the linen-closet, although they were not there when the house was searched for the revolver.

59. The galoshes are returned to the linen-closet, but disappear that night.

FOURTH CRIME

60. Two days after Rex's death Ada and Mrs. Greene are poisoned within twelve hours of each other—Ada with morphine, Mrs. Greene with strychnine.

61. Ada is treated at once, and recovers.

62. Von Blon is seen leaving the house just before Ada swallows the poison.

63. Ada is discovered by Sproot as a result of Sibella's dog catching his teeth in the bell-cord.

64. The morphine was taken in the bouillon which Ada habitually drank in the mornings.

65. Ada states that no one visited her in her room after the nurse had called her to come and drink the bouillon; but that

she went to Julia's room to get a shawl, leaving the bouillon un-guarded for several moments.

66. Neither Ada nor the nurse remembers having seen Sibel-la's dog in the hall before the poisoned bouillon was taken.

67. Mrs. Greene is found dead of strychnine-poisoning the morning after Ada swallowed the morphine.

68. The strychnine could have been administered only after 11 P.M. the previous night.

69. The nurse was in her room on the third floor between 11 and 11.30 P.M.

70. Von Blon was calling on Sibella that night, but Sibella says he left her at 10.45.

71. The strychnine was administered in a dose of citrocarbon-ate, which, presumably, Mrs. Greene would not have taken with-out assistance.

72. Sibella decides to visit a girl chum in Atlantic City, and leaves New York on the afternoon train.

DISTRIBUTABLE FACTS

73. The same revolver is used on Julia, Ada, Chester, and Rex.

74. All three sets of footprints have obviously been made by some one in the house for the purpose of casting suspicion on an outsider.

75. The murderer is some one whom both Julia and Chester would receive in their rooms, in negligé, late at night.

76. The murderer does not make himself known to Ada, but enters her room surreptitiously.

77. Nearly three weeks after Chester's death Ada comes to the District Attorney's office, stating she has important news to impart.

78. Ada says that Rex has confessed to her that he heard the

shot in her room and also heard other things, but was afraid to admit them; and she asks that Rex be questioned.

79. Ada tells of having found a cryptic diagram, marked with symbols, in the lower hall near the library door.

80. On the day of Rex's murder Von Blon reports that his medicine-case has been rifled of three grains of strychnine and six grains of morphine—presumably at the Greene mansion.

81. The library reveals the fact that some one has been in the habit of going there and reading by candle-light. The books that show signs of having been read are: a handbook of the criminal sciences, two works on toxicology, and two treatises on hysterical paralysis and sleep-walking.

82. The visitor to the library is some one who understands German well, for three of the books that have been read are in German.

83. The galoshes that disappeared from the linen-closet on the night of Rex's murder are found in the library.

84. Some one listens at the door while the library is being inspected.

85. Ada reports that she saw Mrs. Greene walking in the lower hall the night before.

86. Von Blon asserts that Mrs. Greene's paralysis is of a nature that makes movement a physical impossibility.

87. Arrangements are made with Von Blon to have Doctor Oppenheimer examine Mrs. Greene.

88. Von Blon informs Mrs. Greene of the proposed examination, which he has scheduled for the following day.

89. Mrs. Greene is poisoned before Doctor Oppenheimer's examination can be made.

90. The post mortem reveals conclusively that Mrs. Greene's leg muscles were so atrophied that she could not have walked.

91. Ada, when told of the autopsy, insists that she saw her mother's shawl about the figure in the hall, and, on being pressed, admits that Sibella sometimes wore it.

92. During the questioning of Ada regarding the shawl Mrs. Mannheim suggests that it was she herself whom Ada saw in the hall.

93. When Julia and Ada were shot there were, or could have been, present in the house: Chester, Sibella, Rex, Mrs. Greene, Von Blon, Barton, Hemming, Sproot, and Mrs. Mannheim.

94. When Chester was shot there were, or could have been, present in the house: Sibella, Rex, Mrs. Greene, Ada, Von Blon, Barton, Hemming, Sproot, and Mrs. Mannheim.

95. When Rex was shot there were, or could have been, present in the house: Sibella, Mrs. Greene, Von Blon, Hemming, Sproot, and Mrs. Mannheim.

96. When Ada was poisoned there were, or could have been, present in the house: Sibella, Mrs. Greene, Von Blon, Hemming, Sproot, and Mrs. Mannheim.

97. When Mrs. Greene was poisoned there were, or could have been, present in the house: Sibella, Von Blon, Ada, Hemming, Sproot, and Mrs. Mannheim.

When Markham had finished reading the summary, he went through it a second time. Then he laid it on the table.

"Yes, Vance," he said, "you've covered the main points pretty thoroughly. But I can't see any coherence in them. In fact, they seem only to emphasize the confusion of the case."

"And yet, Markham, I'm convinced that they only need rearrangement and interpretation to be perfectly clear. Properly analyzed, they'll tell us everything we want to know."

Markham glanced again through the pages.

"If it wasn't for certain items, we could make out a case against several people. But no matter what person in the list we may assume to be guilty, we are at once confronted by a group of contradictory and insurmountable facts. This *précis* could be used effectively to prove that every one concerned is innocent."

"Superficially it appears that way," agreed Vance. "But we first must find the generating line of the design, and then relate the subsidi'ry forms of the pattern to it."

Markham made a hopeless gesture.

"If only life were as simple as your æsthetic theories!"

"It's dashed simpler," Vance asserted. "The mere mechanism of a camera can record life; but only a highly developed creative intelligence, with a profound philosophic insight, can produce a work of art."

"Can *you* make any sense—æsthetic or otherwise—out of this?" Markham petulantly tapped the sheets of paper.

"I can see certain traceries, so to speak—certain suggestions of a pattern; but I'll admit the main design has thus far eluded me. The fact is, Markham, I have a feeling that some important factor in this case—some balancing line of the pattern, perhaps—is still hidden from us. I don't say that my résumé is insusceptible of interpretation in its present state; but our task would be greatly simplified if we were in possession of the missing integer."

Fifteen minutes later, when we had returned to Markham's main office, Swacker came in and laid a letter on the desk.

"There's a funny one, Chief," he said.

Markham took up the letter and read it with a deepening frown. When he had finished, he handed it to Vance. The letter-head read, "Rectory, Third Presbyterian Church, Stamford, Connecticut"; the date was the preceding day; and the signature was that of the Reverend Anthony Seymour. The contents of the letter, written in a small, precise hand, were as follows:

THE HONORABLE JOHN F.-X. MARKHAM,

Dear Sir: As far as I am aware, I have never betrayed a confidence. But there can arise, I believe, unforeseen circumstances to modify the strictness of one's adherence to a given promise, and indeed impose upon one a greater duty than that of keeping silent.

I have read in the papers of the wicked and abominable things that have happened at the Greene residence in New York; and I have therefore come to the conclusion, after much heart searching and prayer, that it is my bounden duty to put you in possession of a fact which, as the result of a promise, I have kept to myself for over a year. I would not now betray this trust did I not believe that some good might possibly come of it, and that you, my dear sir, would also treat the matter in the most sacred confidence. It may not help you—indeed, I do not see how it can possibly lead to a solution of the terrible curse that has fallen upon the Greene family—but since the fact is connected intimately with one of the members of that family, I will feel better when I have communicated it to you.

On the night of August 29, of last year, a machine drove up to my door, and a man and a woman asked that I secretly marry them. I may say that I am frequently receiving such requests from runaway couples. This particular couple appeared to be well-bred dependable people, and I concurred with their wishes, giving them my assurances that the ceremony would, as they desired, be kept confidential.

The names that appeared on the license—which had been secured in New Haven late that afternoon—were Sibella Greene, of New York City, and Arthur Von Blon, also of New York City.

Vance read the letter and handed it back.

"Really, y' know, I can't say that I'm astonished——"

Suddenly he broke off, his eyes fixed thoughtfully before him. Then he rose nervously and paced up and down.

"That tears it!" he exclaimed.

Markham threw him a look of puzzled interrogation.

"What's the point?"

"Don't you see?" Vance came quickly to the District Attorney's desk. "My word! That's the one fact that's missing from my tabulation." He then unfolded the last sheet and wrote:

98. Sibella and Von Blon were secretly married a year ago.

"But I don't see how that helps," protested Markham.

"Neither do I at this moment," Vance replied. "But I'm going to spend this evening in erudite meditation."

CHAPTER XXIV

A MYSTERIOUS TRIP

(Sunday, December 5)

THE BOSTON Symphony Orchestra was scheduled that afternoon to play a Bach Concerto and Beethoven's C-Minor Symphony; and Vance, on leaving the District Attorney's office, rode direct to Carnegie Hall. He sat through the concert in a state of relaxed receptivity, and afterward insisted on walking the two miles back to his quarters—an almost unheard-of thing for him.

Shortly after dinner Vance bade me good night and, donning his slippers and house-robe, went into the library. I had considerable work to do that night, and it was long past midnight when I finished. On the way to my room I passed the library door, which had been left slightly ajar, and I saw Vance sitting at his desk—his head in his hands, the summary lying before him—in an attitude of oblivious concentration. He was smoking, as was habitual with him during any sort of mental activity; and the ash-receiver at his elbow was filled with cigarette-stubs. I moved on quietly, marvelling at the way this new problem had taken hold of him.

It was half past three in the morning when I suddenly awoke, conscious of footsteps somewhere in the house. Rising quietly, I went into the hall, drawn by a vague curiosity mingled with uneasiness. At the end of the corridor a panel of light fell on the wall, and as I moved forward in the semidarkness I saw that the light issued from the partly open library door. At the same time I became aware that the footsteps, too, came from that room. I could not resist looking inside; and there I saw Vance walking up and down, his chin sunk on his breast, his hands crammed into the deep pockets of his dressing-gown. The room was dense with cigarette-smoke, and his figure appeared misty in the blue haze. I went back to bed and lay awake for an hour. When finally I dozed off it was to the accompaniment of those rhythmic foot-falls in the library.

I rose at eight o'clock. It was a dark, dismal Sunday, and I had my coffee in the living-room by electric light. When I glanced into the library at nine Vance was still there, sitting at his desk. The reading-lamp was burning, but the fire on the hearth had died out. Returning to the living-room, I tried to interest myself in the Sunday newspapers; but after scanning the accounts of the Greene case I lit my pipe and drew up my chair before the grate.

It was nearly ten o'clock when Vance appeared at the door. All night he had been up, wrestling with his self-imposed prob-lem; and the devitalizing effects of this long, sleepless concen-tration showed on him only too plainly. There were shadowed circles round his eyes; his mouth was drawn; and even his shoul-ders sagged wearily. But, despite the shock his appearance gave me, my dominant emotion was one of avid curiosity. I wanted to know the outcome of his all-night vigil; and as he came into the room I gave him a look of questioning expectancy.

When his eyes met mine he nodded slowly.

"I've traced the design," he said, holding out his hands to the warmth of the fire. "And it's more horrible than I even imagined." He was silent for some minutes. "Telephone Markham for me, will you, Van? Tell him I must see him at once. Ask him to come to breakfast. Explain that I'm a bit fagged."

He went out, and I heard him calling to Currie to prepare his bath.

I had no difficulty in inducing Markham to breakfast with us after I had explained the situation; and in less than an hour he arrived. Vance was dressed and shaved, and looked considerably fresher than when I had first seen him that morning; but he was still pale, and his eyes were fatigued.

No mention was made of the Greene case during breakfast, but when we had sought easy chairs in the library, Markham could withhold his impatience no longer.

"Van intimated over the phone that you had made something out of the summary."

"Yes." Vance spoke dispiritedly. "I've fitted all the items together. And it's damnable! No wonder the truth escaped us."

Markham leaned forward, his face tense, unbelieving.

"You know the truth?"

"Yes, I know," came the quiet answer. "That is, my brain has told me conclusively who's at the bottom of this fiendish affair; but even now—in the daylight—I can't credit it. Everything in me revolts against the acceptance of the truth. The fact is, I'm almost afraid to accept it. . . . Dash it all, I'm getting mellow. Middle-age has crept upon me." He attempted to smile, but failed.

Markham waited in silence.

"No, old man," continued Vance; "I'm not going to tell you now. I can't tell you until I've looked into one or two matters. You see, the pattern is plain enough, but the recognizable objects, set in their new relationships, are grotesque—like the shapes in an awful dream. I must first touch them and measure them to make sure that they're not, after all, mere abortive vagaries."

"And how long will this verification take?" Markham knew there was no use to try to force the issue. He realized that Vance was fully conscious of the seriousness of the situation, and respected his decision to investigate certain points before revealing his conclusions.

"Not long, I hope." Vance went to his desk and wrote something on a piece of paper, which he handed to Markham. "Here's a list of the five books in Tobias's library that showed signs of having been read by the nocturnal visitor. I want those books, Markham—immediately. But I don't want any one to know about their being taken away. Therefore, I'm going to ask you to phone Nurse O'Brien to get Mrs. Greene's key and secure them when no one is looking. Tell her to wrap them up and give them to the detective on guard in the house with instructions to bring them here. You can explain to her what section of the book-shelves they're in."

Markham took the paper and rose without a word. At the door of the den, however, he paused.

"Do you think it wise for the man to leave the house?"

"It won't matter," Vance told him. "Nothing more can happen there at present."

Markham went on into the den. In a few minutes he returned. "The books will be here in half an hour."

When the detective arrived with the package Vance unwrapped it and laid the volumes beside his chair.

"Now, Markham, I'm going to do some reading. You won't mind, what?" Despite his casual tone, it was evident that an urgent seriousness underlay his words.

Markham got up immediately; and again I marvelled at the complete understanding that existed between these two disparate men.

"I have a number of personal letters to write," he said, "so I'll run along. Currie's omelet was excellent.—When shall I see you again? I could drop round at tea-time."

Vance held out his hand with a look bordering on affection.

"Make it five o'clock. I'll be through with my perusings by then. And thanks for your tolerance." Then he added gravely: "You'll understand, after I've told you everything, why I wanted to wait a bit."

When Markham returned that afternoon a little before five Vance was still reading in the library; but shortly afterward he joined us in the living-room.

"The picture clarifies," he said. "The fantastic images are gradually taking on the aspect of hideous realities. I've substantiated several points, but a few facts still need corroboration."

"To vindicate your hypothesis?"

"No, not that. The hypothesis is self-proving. There's no doubt as to the truth. But—dash it all, Markham!—I refuse to accept it until every scrap of evidence has been incontestably sustained."

"Is the evidence of such a nature that I can use it in a court of law?"

"That is something I refuse even to consider. Criminal proceedings seem utterly irrelevant in the present case. But I suppose society must have its pound of flesh, and you—the duly elected Shylock of God's great common people—will no doubt wield the knife. However, I assure you I shall not be present at the butchery."

Markham studied him curiously.

"Your words sound rather ominous. But if, as you say, you

have discovered the perpetrator of these crimes, why shouldn't society exact punishment?"

"If society were omniscient, Markham, it would have a right to sit in judgment. But society is ignorant and venomous, devoid of any trace of insight or understanding. It exalts knavery, and worships stupidity. It crucifies the intelligent, and puts the diseased in dungeons. And, withal, it arrogates to itself the right and ability to analyze the subtle sources of what it calls 'crime,' and to condemn to death all persons whose inborn and irresistible impulses it does not like. That's your sweet society, Markham—a pack of wolves watering at the mouth for victims on whom to vent its organized lust to kill and flay."

Markham regarded him with some astonishment and considerable concern.

"Perhaps you are preparing to let the criminal escape in the present case," he said, with the irony of resentment.

"Oh, no," Vance assured him. "I shall turn your victim over to you. The Greene murderer is of a particularly vicious type, and should be rendered impotent. I was merely trying to suggest that the electric chair—that touchin' device of your beloved society—is not quite the correct method of dealing with this culprit."

"You admit, however, that he is a menace to society."

"Undoubtedly. And the hideous thing about it is that this tournament of crime at the Greene mansion will continue unless we can put a stop to it. That's why I am being so careful. As the case now stands, I doubt if you could even make an arrest."

When tea was over Vance got up and stretched himself.

"By the by, Markham," he said offhandedly, "have you received any report on Sibella's activities?"

"Nothing important. She's still in Atlantic City, and evidently intends to stay there for some time. She phoned Sproot yester-day to send down another trunkful of her clothes."

"Did she, now? That's very gratifyin'." Vance walked to the door with sudden resolution. "I think I'll run out to the Greenes' for a little while. I sha'n't be gone over an hour. Wait for me here, Markham—there's a good fellow; I don't want my visit to have an official flavor. There's a new *Simplicissimus* on the table to amuse you till I return. Con it and thank your own special gods that you have no Thöny or Gulbranssen in this country to carica-ture your Gladstonian features."

As he spoke he beckoned to me, and, before Markham could question him, we passed out into the hall and down the stairs. Fifteen minutes later a taxi-cab set us down before the Greene mansion.

Sproot opened the door for us, and Vance, with only a curt greeting, led him into the drawing-room.

"I understand," he said, "that Miss Sibella phoned you yes-terday from Atlantic City and asked to have a trunk shipped to her."

Sproot bowed. "Yes, sir. I sent the trunk off last night."

"What did Miss Sibella say to you over the phone?"

"Very little, sir—the connection was not good. She said merely that she had no intention of returning to New York for a consid-erable time and needed more clothes than she had taken with her."

"Did she ask how things were going at the house here?"

"Only in the most casual way, sir."

"Then she didn't seem apprehensive about what might hap-pen here while she was away?"

"No, sir. In fact—if I may say so without disloyalty—her tone of voice was quite indifferent, sir."

"Judging from her remarks about the trunk, how long would you say she intends to be away?"

Sproot considered the matter.

"That's difficult to say, sir. But I would go so far as to venture the opinion that Miss Sibella intends to remain in Atlantic City for a month or more."

Vance nodded with satisfaction.

"And now, Sproot," he said, "I have a particularly important question to ask you. When you first went into Miss Ada's room on the night she was shot and found her on the floor before the dressing-table, was the window open? Think! I want a positive answer. You know the window is just beside the dressing-table and overlooks the steps leading to the stone balcony. *Was it open or shut?*"

Sproot contracted his brows and appeared to be recalling the scene. Finally he spoke, and there was no doubt in his voice.

"The window was open, sir. I recall it now quite distinctly. After Mr. Chester and I had lifted Miss Ada to the bed, I closed it at once for fear she would catch cold."

"How far open was the window?" asked Vance with eager impatience.

"Eight or nine inches, sir, I should say. Perhaps a foot."

"Thank you, Sproot. That will be all. Now please tell the cook I want to see her."

Mrs. Mannheim came in a few minutes later, and Vance indicated a chair near the desk-light. When the woman had seated herself he stood before her and fixed her with a stern, implacable gaze.

"Frau Mannheim, the time for truth-telling has come. I am here to ask you a few questions, and unless I receive a straight answer to them I shall report you to the police. You will, I assure you, receive no consideration at their hands."

The woman tightened her lips stubbornly and shifted her eyes, unable to meet Vance's penetrating stare.

"You told me once that your husband died in New Orleans thirteen years ago. Is that correct?"

Vance's question seemed to relieve her mind, and she answered readily.

"Yes, yes. Thirteen years ago."

"What month?"

"In October."

"Had he been ill long?"

"About a year."

"What was the nature of his illness?"

Now a look of fright came into her eyes.

"I—don't know—exactly," she stammered. "The doctors didn't let me see him."

"He was in a hospital?"

She nodded several times rapidly. "Yes—a hospital."

"And I believe you told me, Frau Mannheim, that you saw Mr. Tobias Greene a year before your husband's death. That would have been about the time your husband entered the hospital—fourteen years ago."

She looked vaguely at Vance, but made no reply.

"And it was exactly fourteen years ago that Mr. Greene adopted Ada."

The woman caught her breath sharply. A look of panic contorted her face.

"So when your husband died," continued Vance, "you came to Mr. Greene, knowing he would give you a position."

He went up to her and touched her filially on the shoulder.

"I have suspected for some time, Frau Mannheim," he said kindly, "that Ada is your daughter. It's true, isn't it?"

With a convulsive sob the woman hid her face in her apron.

"I gave Mr. Greene my word," she confessed brokenly, "that I wouldn't tell any one—not even Ada—if he let me stay here—to be near her."

"You haven't told any one," Vance consoled her. "It was not your fault that I guessed it. But why didn't Ada recognize you?"

"She had been away—to school—since she was five."

When Mrs. Mannheim left us a little later Vance had succeeded in allaying her apprehension and distress. He then sent for Ada.

As she entered the drawing-room the troubled look in her eyes and the pallor of her cheeks told clearly of the strain she was under. Her first question voiced the fear uppermost in her mind.

"Have you found out anything, Mr. Vance?" She spoke with an air of pitiful discouragement. "It's terrible alone here in this big house—especially at night. Every sound I hear . . ."

"You mustn't let your imagination get the better of you, Ada," Vance counselled her. Then he added: "We know a lot more now than we did, and before long, I hope, all your fears will be done away with. In fact, it's in regard to what we've found out that I've come here to-day. I thought perhaps you could help me again."

"If only I could! But I've thought and thought. . . ."

Vance smiled.

"Let us do the thinking, Ada.—What I wanted to ask you is this: do you know if Sibella speaks German well?"

The girl appeared surprised.

"Why, yes. And so did Julia and Chester and Rex. Father insisted on their learning it. And he spoke it too—almost as well as he spoke English. As for Sibella, I've often heard her and Doctor Von talking in German."

"But she spoke with an accent, I suppose."

"A slight accent—she'd never been long in Germany. But she spoke very well German."

"That's what I wanted to be sure of."

"Then you do know something!" Her voice quavered with eagerness. "Oh, how long before this awful suspense will be over? Every night for weeks I've been afraid to turn out my lights and go to sleep."

"You needn't be afraid to turn out your lights now," Vance assured her. "There won't be any more attempts on your life, Ada."

She looked at him for a moment searchingly, and something in his manner seemed to hearten her. When we took our leave the color had come back to her cheeks.

Markham was pacing the library restlessly when we arrived home.

"I've checked several more points," Vance announced. "But I've missed the important one—the one that would explain the unbelievable hideousness of the thing I've unearthed."

He went directly into the den, and we could hear him telephoning. Returning a few minutes later, he looked anxiously at his watch. Then he rang for Currie and ordered his bag packed for a week's trip.

"I'm going away, Markham," he said. "I'm going to travel—they say it broadens the mind. My train departs in less than an hour; and I'll be away a week. Can you bear to be without me for so long? However, nothing will happen in connection with the Greene case during my absence. In fact, I'd advise you to shelve it temporarily."

He would say no more, and in half an hour he was ready to go.

"There's one thing you can do for me while I'm away," he told Markham, as he slipped into his overcoat. "Please have drawn up for me a complete and detailed weather report from the day preceding Julia's death to the day following Rex's murder."

He would not let either Markham or me accompany him to the station, and we were left in ignorance of even the direction in which his mysterious trip was to take him.

CHAPTER XXV

THE CAPTURE

(Monday, December 13; 4 p. m.)

It was eight days before Vance returned to New York. He arrived on the afternoon of Monday, December 13, and, after he had had his tub and changed his clothes, he telephoned Markham to expect him in half an hour. He then ordered his Hispano-Suiza from the garage; and by this sign I knew he was under a nervous strain. In fact, he had spoken scarcely a dozen words to me since his return, and as he picked his way downtown through the late afternoon traffic he was gloomy and preoccupied. Once I ventured to ask him if his trip had been successful, and he had merely nodded. But when we turned into Centre Street he relented a little, and said:

"There was never any doubt as to the success of my trip, Van. I knew what I'd find. But I didn't dare trust my reason; I had to see the records with my own eyes before I'd capitulate unreservedly to the conclusion I'd formed."

Both Markham and Heath were waiting for us in the District Attorney's office. It was just four o'clock, and the sun had already dropped below the New York Life Building which towered above the old Criminal Courts structure a block to the southwest.

"I took it for granted you had something important to tell me," said Markham; "so I asked the Sergeant to come here."

"Yes, I've much to tell." Vance had thrown himself into a chair, and was lighting a cigarette. "But first I want to know if anything has happened in my absence."

"Nothing. Your prognostication was quite accurate. Things have been quiet and apparently normal at the Greene mansion."

"Anyhow," interposed Heath, "we may have a little better chance this week of getting hold of something to work on. Sibella returned from Atlantic City yesterday, and Von Blon's been hanging round the house ever since."

"Sibella back?" Vance sat up, and his eyes became intent.

"At six o'clock yesterday evening," said Markham. "The newspaper men at the beach ferreted her out and ran a sensational story about her. After that the poor girl didn't have an hour's peace; so yesterday she packed up and came back. We got word of the move through the men the Sergeant had set to watch her. I ran out to see her this morning, and advised her to go away again. But she was pretty thoroughly disgusted, and stubbornly refused to quit the Greene house—said death was preferable to being hounded by reporters and scandalmongers."

Vance had risen and moved to the window, where he stood scanning the gray sky-line.

"Sibella's back, eh?" he murmured. Then he turned round. "Let me see that weather report I asked you to prepare for me."

Markham reached into a drawer and handed him a typewritten sheet of paper.

After perusing it he tossed it back on the desk.

"Keep that, Markham. You'll need it when you face your twelve good men and true."

"What is it you have to tell us, Mr. Vance?" The Sergeant's voice was impatient despite his effort to control it. "Mr. Markham said you had a line on the case.—For God's sake, sir, if you've got any evidence against any one, slip it to me and let me make an arrest. I'm getting thin worrying over this damn business."

Vance drew himself together.

"Yes, I know who the murderer is, Sergeant; and I have the evidence—though it wasn't my plan to tell you just yet. However"—he went to the door with grim resolution—"we can't delay matters any longer now. Our hand has been forced.—Get into your coat, Sergeant—and you, too, Markham. We'd better get out to the Greene house before dark."

"But, damn it all, Vance!" Markham expostulated. "Why don't you tell us what's in your mind?"

"I can't explain now—you'll understand why later——"

"If you know so much, Mr. Vance," broke in Heath, "what's keeping us from making an arrest?"

"You're going to make your arrest, Sergeant—inside of an hour." Though he gave the promise without enthusiasm, it acted electrically on both Heath and Markham.

Five minutes later the four of us were driving up West Broadway in Vance's car.

Sproot as usual admitted us without the faintest show of interest, and stood aside respectfully for us to enter.

"We wish to see Miss Sibella," said Vance. "Please tell her to come to the drawing-room—alone."

"I'm sorry, sir, but Miss Sibella is out."

"Then tell Miss Ada we want to see her."

"Miss Ada is out also, sir." The butler's unemotional tone sounded strangely incongruous in the tense atmosphere we had brought with us.

"When do you expect them back?"

"I couldn't say, sir. They went out motoring together. They probably won't be gone long. Would you gentlemen care to wait?"

Vance hesitated.

"Yes, we'll wait," he decided, and walked toward the drawing-room.

But he had barely reached the archway when he turned suddenly and called to Sproot, who was retreating slowly toward the rear of the hall.

"You say Miss Sibella and Miss Ada went motoring together? How long ago?"

"About fifteen minutes—maybe twenty, sir." A barely perceptible lift of the man's eyebrows indicated that he was greatly astonished by Vance's sudden change of manner.

"Whose car did they go in?"

"In Doctor Von Blon's. He was here to tea——"

"And who suggested the ride, Sproot?"

"I really couldn't say, sir. They were sort of debating about it when I came in to clear away the tea things."

"Repeat everything you heard!" Vance spoke rapidly and with more than a trace of excitement.

"When I entered the room the doctor was saying as how he thought it would be a good thing for the young ladies to get some fresh air; and Miss Sibella said she'd had enough fresh air."

"And Miss Ada?"

"I don't remember her saying anything, sir."

"And they went out to the car while you were here?"

"Yes, sir. I opened the door for them."

"And did Doctor Von Blon go in the car with them?"

"Yes. But I believe they were to drop him at Mrs. Riglander's, where he had a professional call to make. From what he said as he went out I gathered that the young ladies were then to take a drive, and that he was to call here for the car after dinner."

"What!" Vance stiffened, and his eyes burned upon the old butler. "Quick, Sproot! Do you know where Mrs. Riglander lives?"

"On Madison Avenue in the Sixties, I believe."

"Get her on the phone—find out if the doctor has arrived."

I could not help marvelling at the impassive way in which the man went to the telephone to comply with this astonishing and seemingly incomprehensible request. When he returned his face was expressionless.

"The doctor has not arrived at Mrs. Riglander's, sir," he reported.

"He's certainly had time," Vance commented, half to himself. Then: "Who drove the car when it left here, Sproot?"

"I couldn't say for certain, sir. I didn't notice particularly. But it's my impression that Miss Sibella entered the car first as though she intended to drive——"

"Come, Markham!" Vance started for the door. "I don't like this at all. There's a mad idea in my head. . . . Hurry, man! If something devilish should happen . . ."

We had reached the car, and Vance sprang to the wheel. Heath and Markham, in a daze of incomprehension but swept along by the other's ominous insistence, took their places in the tonneau; and I sat beside the driver's seat.

"We're going to break all the traffic and speed regulations, Sergeant," Vance announced, as he manoeuvred the car in the narrow street; "so have your badge and credentials handy. I may be taking you chaps on a wild-goose chase, but we've got to risk it."

We darted toward First Avenue, cut the corner short, and turned up-town. At 59th Street we swung west and went toward Columbus Circle. A surface car held us up at Lexington Avenue; and at Fifth Avenue we were stopped by a traffic officer. But Heath showed his card and spoke a few words, and we struck across Central Park. Swinging perilously round the curves of the driveways, we came out into 81st Street and headed for Riverside Drive. There was less congestion here, and we made between forty and fifty miles an hour all the way to Dyckman Street.

It was a nerve-racking ordeal, for not only had the shadows of evening fallen, but the streets were slippery in places where the melted snow had frozen in large sheets along the sloping sides of the Drive. Vance, however, was an excellent driver. For two years he had driven the same car, and he understood thoroughly how to handle it. Once we skidded drunkenly, but he managed to right the traction before the rear wheels came in contact with the high curbing. He kept the siren horn screeching constantly, and other cars drew away from us, giving us a fairly clear road.

At several street intersections we had to slow down; and twice we were halted by traffic officers, but were permitted to proceed the moment the occupants of the tonneau were recognized. On North Broadway we were forced to the curb by a motorcycle policeman, who showered us with a stream of picturesque abuse. But when Heath had cut him short with still more colorful vituperation, and he had made out Markham's features in the shadows, he became ludicrously humble, and acted as an advance-guard for us all the way to Yonkers, clearing the road and holding up traffic at every cross-street.

At the railroad tracks near Yonkers Ferry we were obliged to wait several minutes for the shunting of some freight-cars, and Markham took this opportunity of venting his emotions.

"I presume you have a good reason for this insane ride, Vance," he said angrily. "But since I'm taking my life in my hands by accompanying you, I'd like to know what your objective is."

"There's no time now for explanations," Vance replied brusquely. "Either I'm on a fool's errand, or there's an abominable tragedy ahead of us." His face was set and white, and he looked anxiously at his watch. "We're twenty minutes ahead of the usual running time from the Plaza to Yonkers. Furthermore, we're taking the direct route to our destination—another ten minutes' saving. If the thing I fear is scheduled for to-night, the other car will go by the Spuyten Duyvil Road and through the back lanes along the river——"

At this moment the crossing-bars were lifted, and our car jerked forward, picking up speed with breathless rapidity.

Vance's words had set a train of thought going in my mind. The Spuyten Duyvil Road—the back lanes along the river. . . . Suddenly there flashed on my brain a memory of that other ride we had taken weeks before with Sibella and Ada and Von Blon; and a sense of something inimical and indescribably horrifying took possession of me. I tried to recall the details of that ride—how we had turned off the main road at Dyckman Street, skirted the palisades through old wooded estates, traversed private hedge-lined roadways, entered Yonkers from the Riverdale Road, turned again from the main highway past the Ardsley Country Club, taken the little-used road along the river toward Tarrytown, and stopped on the high cliff to get a panoramic view of the Hudson. . . . That cliff overlooking the waters of the river!—Ah, now I remembered Sibella's cruel jest—her supposedly satirical suggestion of how a perfect murder might be committed there. And on the instant of that recollection I knew where Vance was heading—I understood the thing he feared! He believed that another car was also heading for that lonely precipice beyond Ardsley—a car that had nearly half an hour start. . . .

We were now below the Longue Vue hill, and a few moments later we swung into the Hudson Road. At Dobbs Ferry another officer stepped in our path and waved frantically; but Heath, leaning over the running-board, shouted some unintelligible words, and Vance, without slackening speed, skirted the officer and plunged ahead toward Ardsley.

Ever since we had passed Yonkers, Vance had been inspecting every large car along the way. He was, I knew, looking for Von Blon's low-hung yellow Daimler. But there had been no sign of it, and, as he threw on the brakes preparatory to turning into the narrow road by the Country Club golf-links, I heard him mutter half aloud:

"God help us if we're too late!"*

We made the turn at the Ardsley station at such a rate of speed that I held my breath for fear we would upset; and I had to grip the seat with both hands to keep my balance as we jolted over the rough road along the river level. We took the hill before us in high gear, and climbed swiftly to the dirt roadway along the edge of the bluff beyond.

Scarcely had we rounded the hill's crest when an exclamation broke from Vance, and simultaneously I noticed a flickering red light bobbing in the distance. A new spurt of speed brought us perceptibly nearer to the car before us, and it was but a few moments before we could make out its lines and color. There was no mistaking Von Blon's great Daimler.

"Hide your faces," Vance shouted over his shoulder to

---

* This was the first and only time during my entire friendship with Vance that I ever heard him use a Scriptural expletive.

Markham and Heath. "Don't let any one see you as we pass the car ahead."

I leaned over below the panel of the front door, and a few seconds later a sudden swerve told me that we were circling about the Daimler. The next moment we were back in the road, rushing forward in the lead.

Half a mile further on the road narrowed. There was a deep ditch on one side and dense shrubbery on the other. Vance quickly threw on the brakes, and our rear wheels skidded on the hard frozen earth, bringing us to a halt with our car turned almost at right angles with the road, completely blocking the way.

"Out, you chaps!" called Vance.

We had no more than alighted when the other car drove up and, with a grinding of brakes, came to a lurching halt within a few feet of our machine. Vance had run back, and as the car reached a standstill he threw open the front door. The rest of us had instinctively crowded after him, urged forward by some undefined sense of excitement and dread foreboding. The Daimler was of the sedan type with small high windows, and even with the lingering radiance of the western sky and the dashboard illumination I could barely make out the figures inside. But at that moment Heath's pocket flash-light blazed in the semidarkness.

The sight that met my straining eyes was paralyzing. During the drive I had speculated on the outcome of our tragic adventure, and I had pictured several hateful possibilities. But I was wholly unprepared for the revelation that confronted me.

The tonneau of the car was empty; and, contrary to my suspicions, there was no sign of Von Blon. In the front seat were the two girls. Sibella was on the further side, slumped down in the corner, her head hanging forward. On her temple was an ugly cut, and a stream of blood ran down her cheek. At the wheel sat Ada, glowering at us with cold ferocity. Heath's flash-light fell directly on her face, and at first she did not recognize us. But as her pupils became adjusted to the glare her gaze concentrated on Vance, and a foul epithet burst from her.

Simultaneously her right hand dropped from the wheel to the seat beside her, and when she raised it again it held a small glittering revolver. There was a flash of flame and a sharp report, followed by a shattering of glass where the bullet had struck the wind-shield. Vance had been standing with one foot on the running-board leaning into the car, and, as Ada's arm came up with the revolver, he had snatched her wrist and held it.

"No, my dear," came his drawling voice, strangely calm and without animosity; "you sha'n't add me to your list. I was rather expecting that move, don't y' know."

Ada, frustrated in her attempt to shoot him, hurled herself upon him with savage fury. Vile abuse and unbelievable blasphemies poured from her snarling lips. Her wrath, feral and rampant, utterly possessed her. She was like a wild animal, cornered and conscious of defeat, yet fighting with a last instinct of hopeless desperation. Vance, however, had secured both her wrists, and could have broken her arms with a single twist of his hands; but he treated her almost tenderly, like a father subduing an infuriated child. Stepping back quickly he drew her into the roadway, where she continued her struggles with renewed violence.

"Come, Sergeant!" Vance spoke with weary exasperation. "You'd better put handcuffs on her. I don't want to hurt her."

Heath had stood watching the amazing drama in a state of bewilderment, apparently too nonplussed to move. But Vance's voice awakened him to sharp activity. There were two metallic clicks, and Ada suddenly relaxed into a listless attitude of sullen tractability. She leaned panting against the side of the car as if too weak to stand alone.

Vance bent over and picked up the revolver which had fallen to the road. With a cursory glance at it he handed it to Markham.

"There's Chester's gun," he said. Then he indicated Ada with a pitying movement of the head. "Take her to your office, Markham—Van will drive the car. I'll join you there as soon as I can. I must get Sibella to a hospital."

He stepped briskly into the Daimler. There was a shifting of gears, and with a few deft manipulations he reversed the car in the narrow road.

"And watch her, Sergeant!" he flung back, as the car darted away toward Ardsley.

I drove Vance's car back to the city. Markham and Heath sat in the rear seat with the girl between them. Hardly a word was spoken during the entire hour-and-a-half's ride. Several times I glanced behind me at the silent trio. Markham and the Sergeant appeared completely stunned by the surprising truth that had just been revealed to them. Ada, huddled between them, sat apathetically with closed eyes, her head forward. Once I noticed that she pressed a handkerchief to her face with her manacled hands; and I thought I heard the sound of smothered sobbing. But I was too nervous to pay any attention. It took every effort of my will to keep my mind on my driving.

As I drew up before the Franklin Street entrance of the Criminal Courts Building and was about to shut off the engine, a startled exclamation from Heath caused me to release the switch.

"Holy Mother o' God!" I heard him say in a hoarse voice. Then he thumped me on the back. "Get to the Beekman Street Hospital—as quick as hell, Mr. Van Dine. Damn the traffic lights! Step on it!"

Without looking round I knew what had happened. I swung the car into Centre Street again, and fairly raced for the hospital. We carried Ada into the emergency ward, Heath bawling loudly for the doctor as we passed through the door.

It was more than an hour later when Vance entered the District Attorney's office, where Markham and Heath and I were waiting. He glanced quickly round the room and then looked at our faces.

"I told you to watch her, Sergeant," he said, sinking into a chair; but there was neither reproach nor regret in his voice.

None of us spoke. Despite the effect Ada's suicide had had on us, we were waiting, with a kind of conscience-stricken anxiety, for news of the other girl whom all of us, I think, had vaguely suspected.

Vance understood our silence, and nodded reassuringly.

"Sibella's all right. I took her to the Trinity Hospital in Yonkers. A slight concussion—Ada had struck her with a box-wrench which was always kept under the front seat. She'll be out in a few days. I registered her at the hospital as Mrs. Von Blon, and then phoned her husband. I caught him at home, and he hurried out. He's with her now. Incidentally, the reason we didn't reach him at Mrs. Riglander's is because he stopped at the office for his medicine-case. That delay saved Sibella's life. Otherwise, I doubt if we'd have reached her before Ada had run her over the precipice in the machine."

He drew deeply on his cigarette for a moment. Then he lifted his eyebrows to Markham.

"Cyanide of potassium?"

Markham gave a slight start.

"Yes—or so the doctor thinks. There was a bitter-almond odor on her lips." He shot his head forward angrily. "But if you knew——"

"Oh, I wouldn't have stopped it in any case," interrupted Vance. "I discharged my wholly mythical duty to the State when I warned the Sergeant. However, I didn't know at the time. Von Blon just gave me the information. When I told him what had happened I asked him if he had ever lost any other poisons—you see, I couldn't imagine any one planning so devilish and hazard-ous an exploit as the Greene murders without preparing for the eventuality of failure. He told me he'd missed a tablet of cyanide from his dark-room about three months ago. And when I jogged his memory he recalled that Ada had been poking round there and asking questions a few days before. The one cyanide tablet was probably all she dared take at the time; so she kept it for herself in case of an emergency."*

"What I want to know, Mr. Vance," said Heath, "is how she worked this scheme. Was there any one else in on the deal?"

"No, Sergeant. Ada planned and executed every part of it."

"But how, in God's name——?"

Vance held up his hand.

"It's all very simple, Sergeant—once you have the key. What misled us was the fiendish cleverness and audacity of the plot. But there's no longer any need to speculate about it. I have a printed and bound explanation of everything that happened. And it's not a fictional or speculative explanation. It's actual criminal history, garnered and recorded by the greatest expert on

---

* As I learned later, Doctor Von Blon, who was an ardent amateur photographer, often used half-gramme tablets of cyanide of potassium; and there had been three of them in his darkroom when Ada had called. Several days later, when preparing to redevelop a plate, he could find only two, but had thought little of the loss until questioned by Vance.

the subject the world has yet known—Doctor Hans Gross, of Vienna."

He rose and took up his coat.

"I phoned Currie from the hospital, and he has a belated dinner waiting for all of us. When we have eaten, I'll present you with a reconstruction and exposition of the entire case."

CHAPTER XXVI

THE ASTOUNDING TRUTH

(Monday, December 13; 11 p. m.)

"As you know, Markham," Vance began, when we were seated about the library fire late that night, "I finally succeeded in
putting together the items of my summary in such a way that I
could see plainly who the murderer was.* Once I had found the
basic pattern, every detail fitted perfectly into a plastic whole.
The technic of the crimes, however, remained obscure; so I asked
you to send for the books in Tobias's library—I was sure they
would tell me what I wanted to know. First, I went through
Gross's 'Handbuch für Untersuchungsrichter,' which I regarded
as the most likely source of information. It is an amazing treatise,
Markham. It covers the entire field of the history and science
of crime; and, in addition, is a compendium of criminal technic,
citing specific cases and containing detailed explanations and diagrams. Small wonder it is the world's standard cyclopaedia on

---

* I later asked Vance to rearrange the items for me in the order of his final sequence. The
distribution, which told him the truth, was as follows: 3, 4, 44, 92, 9, 6, 2, 47, 1, 5, 32, 31,
98, 8, 81, 84, 82, 7, 10, 11, 61, 15, 16, 93, 33, 94, 76, 75, 48, 17, 38, 55, 54, 18, 39, 56, 41,
42, 28, 43, 58, 59, 83, 74, 40, 12, 34, 13, 14, 37, 22, 23, 35, 36, 19, 73, 26, 20, 21, 45, 25, 46,
27, 29, 30, 57, 77, 24, 78, 79, 51, 50, 52, 53, 49, 95, 80, 85, 86, 87, 88, 60, 62, 64, 63, 66, 65,
96, 89, 67, 71, 69, 68, 70, 97, 90, 91, 72.

its subject. As I read it, I found what I was looking for. Ada had copied every act of hers, every method, every device, every detail, from its pages—*from actual criminal history!* We are hardly to be blamed for our inability to combat her schemes; for it was not she alone who was deceiving us; it was the accumulated experience of hundreds of shrewd criminals before her, plus the analytic science of the world's greatest criminologist—Doctor Hans Gross."

He paused to light another cigarette.

"But even when I had found the explanation of her crimes," he continued, "I felt that there was something lacking, some fundamental *penchant*—the thing that made this orgy of horror possible and gave viability, so to speak, to her operations. We knew nothing of Ada's early life or of her progenitors and inherited instincts; and without that knowledge the crimes, despite their clear logic, were incredible. Consequently, my next step was to verify Ada's psychological and environmental sources. I had had a suspicion from the first that she was Frau Mannheim's daughter. But even when I verified this fact I couldn't see its bearing on the case. It was obvious, from our interview with Frau Mannheim, that Tobias and her husband had been in shady deals together in the old days; and she later admitted to me that her husband had died thirteen years ago, in October, at New Orleans after a year's illness in a hospital. She also said, as you may recall, that she had seen Tobias a year prior to her husband's death. This would have been fourteen years ago—just the time Ada was adopted by Tobias.* I thought there might be some connection between Mannheim and the crimes, and I even toyed with the idea

---

* We later learned from Mrs. Mannheim that Mannheim had once saved Tobias from criminal prosecution by taking upon himself the entire blame of one of Tobias's shadiest extra-legal transactions, and had exacted from Tobias the promise that, in event of his own death or incarceration, he would adopt and care for Ada, whom Mrs. Mannheim had placed in a private institution at the age of five, to protect her from Mannheim's influence.

that Sproot was Mannheim, and that a dirty thread of blackmail ran through the situation. So I decided to investigate. My mysterious trip last week was to New Orleans; and there I had no difficulty in learning the truth. By looking up the death records for October thirteen years ago, I discovered that Mannheim had been in an asylum for the criminally insane for a year preceding his death. And from the police I ascertained something of his record. Adolph Mannheim—Ada's father—was, it seems, a famous German criminal and murderer, who had been sentenced to death, but had escaped from the penitentiary at Stuttgart and come to America. I have a suspicion that the departed Tobias was, in some way, mixed up in that escape. But whether or not I wrong him, the fact remains that Ada's father was homicidal and a professional criminal. And therein lies the explanat'ry background of her actions. . . ."

"You mean she was crazy like her old man?" asked Heath.

"No, Sergeant. I merely mean that the potentialities of criminality had been handed down to her in her blood. When the motive for the crimes became powerful, her inherited instincts asserted themselves."

"But mere money," put in Markham, "seems hardly a strong enough motive to inspire such atrocities as hers."

"It wasn't money alone that inspired her. The real motive went much deeper. Indeed, it was perhaps the most powerful of all human motives—a strange, terrible combination of hate and love and jealousy and a desire for freedom. To begin with, she was the Cinderella in that abnormal Greene family, looked down upon, treated like a servant, made to spend her time caring for a nagging invalid, and forced—as Sibella put it—to earn her livelihood. Can you not see her for fourteen years brooding over this treatment, nourishing her resentment, absorbing the poison about her, and coming at length to despise every one in that household? That alone would have been enough to awaken her congenital instincts. One almost wonders that she did not break forth long before. But another equally potent element entered the situation. She fell in love with Von Blon—a natural thing for a girl in her position to do—and then learned that Sibella had won his affections. She either knew or strongly suspected that they were married; and her normal hatred of her sister was augmented by a vicious and eroding jealousy. . . .

"Now, Ada was the only member of the family who, according to the terms of old Tobias's will, was not compelled to live on the estate in event of marriage; and in this fact she saw a chance to snatch all the things she craved and at the same time to rid herself of the persons against whom her whole passionate nature cried out in deadly hatred. She calculated to get rid of the family, inherit the Greene millions, and set her cap for Von Blon. There was vengeance, too, as a motivating factor in all this; but I'm inclined to think the amatory phase of the affair was the prim'ry actuating force in the series of horrors she later perpetrated. It gave her strength and courage; it lifted her into that ecstatic realm where anything seemed possible, and where she was willing to pay any price for the desired end. And there is one point I might recall parenthetically—you remember that Barton, the younger maid, told us how Ada sometimes acted like a devil and used vile language. That fact should have given me a hint; but who could have taken Barton seriously at that stage of the game? . . .

"To trace the origin of her diabolical scheme we must first consider the locked library. Alone in the house, bored, resentful, tied down—it was inevitable that this pervertedly romantic child should play Pandora. She had every opportunity of securing the key and having a duplicate made; and so the library became her retreat, her escape from the gruelling, monotonous routine of her existence. There she ran across those books on criminology. They appealed to her, not only as a vicious outlet for her smouldering, repressed hatred, but because they struck a responsive chord in her tainted nature. Eventually she came upon Gross's great manual, and thus found the entire technic of crime laid out before her, with diagrams and examples—not a handbook for examining magistrates, but a guide for a potential murderer! Slowly the idea of her gory orgy took shape. At first perhaps she only imagined, as a means of self-gratification, the application of this technic of murder to those she hated. But after a time, no doubt, the conception became real. She saw its practical possibilities; and the terrible plot was formulated. She created this horror, and then, with her diseased imagination, she came to believe in it. Her plausible stories to us, her superb acting, her clever deceptions—all were part of this horrible fantasy she had engendered. That book of Grimm's 'Fairy-Tales'!—I should have understood. Y' see, it wasn't histrionism altogether on her part; it was a kind of demoniac possession. She lived her dream. Many young girls are like that under the stress of ambition and hatred. Constance Kent completely deceived the whole of Scotland Yard into believing in her innocence."

Vance smoked a moment thoughtfully.

"It's curious how we instinctively close our eyes to the truth when history is filled with substantiating examples of the very thing we are contemplating. The annals of crime contain numerous instances of girls in Ada's position who have been guilty of atrocious crimes. Besides the famous case of Constance Kent, there were, for example, Marie Boyer, and Madeleine Smith, and Grete Beyer.* I wonder if we'd have suspected them——"

"Keep to the present, Vance," interposed Markham impatiently. "You say Ada took all her ideas from Gross. But Gross's handbook is written in German. How did you know she spoke German well enough——?"

"That Sunday when I went to the house with Van I inquired of Ada if Sibella spoke German. I put my questions in such a way that she could not answer without telling me whether or not she, too, knew German well; and she even used a typical German locution—'Sibella speaks very well German'—showing that that language was almost instinctive with her. Incidentally, I wanted her to think that I suspected Sibella, so that she would not hasten matters until I returned from New Orleans. I knew that as long as Sibella was in Atlantic City she was safe from Ada."

"But what I want to know," put in Heath, "is how she killed Rex when she was sitting in Mr. Markham's office."

"Let us take things in order, Sergeant," answered Vance. "Julia was killed first because she was the manager of the establishment. With her out of the way, Ada would have a free hand. And, another thing, the death of Julia at the start fitted best into the scheme she had outlined; it gave her the most plausible setting for staging the attempted murder on herself. Ada had undoubtedly heard some mention of Chester's revolver, and after she had secured it she waited for the opportunity to strike the first blow. The propitious circumstances fell on the night of November 8; and at half past eleven, when the house was asleep, she knocked on Julia's door. She was admitted, and doubtless sat

---

* An account of the cases of Madeleine Smith and Constance Kent may be found in Edmund Lester Pearson's "Murder at Smutty Nose"; and a record of Marie Boyer's case is included in H. B. Irving's "A Book of Remarkable Criminals." Grete Beyer was the last woman to be publicly executed in Germany.

on the edge of Julia's bed telling some story to explain her late visit. Then she drew the gun from under her dressing-gown and shot Julia through the heart. Back in her own bedroom, with the lights on, she stood before the large mirror of the dressing-table, and, holding the gun in her right hand, placed it against her left shoulder-blade at an oblique angle. The mirror and the lights were essential, for she could thus see exactly where to point the muzzle of the revolver. All this occupied the three-minute interval between the shots. Then she pulled the trigger——"

"But a girl shooting herself as a fake!" objected Heath. "It ain't natural."

"But Ada wasn't natural, Sergeant. None of the plot was natural. That was why I was so anxious to look up her family history. But as to shooting herself; that was quite logical when one considers her true character. And, as a matter of fact, there was little or no danger attaching to it. The gun was on a hair-trigger, and little pressure was needed to discharge it. A slight flesh wound was the worst she had to fear. Moreover, history is full of cases of self-mutilation where the object to be gained was far smaller than what Ada was after. Gross is full of them. . . ."

He took up Volume I of the "Handbuch für Untersuchungsrichter," which lay on the table beside him, and opened it at a marked page.

"Listen to this, Sergeant. I'll translate the passage roughly as I read: *'It is not uncommon to find people who inflict wounds on themselves; such are, besides persons pretending to be the victims of assaults with deadly weapons, those who try to extort damages or blackmail. Thus it often happens that, after an insignificant scuffle, one of the combatants shows wounds which he pretends to have received. It is characteristic of these voluntary mutilations that most frequently those who perform them do not quite complete the operation, and that they are for the most part people who manifest excessive piety, or lead a solitary life."* . . . And surely, Sergeant, you are familiar with the self-mutilation of soldiers to escape service. The most common method used by them is to place their hand over the muzzle of the gun and blow their fingers off."

Vance closed the book.

"And don't forget that the girl was hopeless, desperate, and unhappy, with everything to win and nothing to lose. She would probably have committed suicide if she had not worked out the plan of the murders. A superficial wound in the shoulder meant little to her in view of what she was to gain by it. And women have an almost infinite capacity for self-immolation. With Ada, it was part of her abnormal condition.—No, Sergeant; the self-shooting was perfectly consistent in the circumstances. . . ."

"But in the back!" Heath looked dumbfounded. "That's what gets me. Whoever heard——?"

"Just a moment." Vance took up Volume II of the "Handbuch" and opened it to a marked page. "Gross, for instance, has heard of many such cases—in fact, they're quite common on the Continent. And his record of them indubitably gave Ada the idea for shooting herself in the back. Here's a single paragraph culled from many pages of similar cases: *'That you should not be deceived by the seat of the wound is proved by the following two cases. In the Vicuna Prater a man killed himself in the presence of several people by shooting himself in the back of the head with a revolver. Without the testimony of several witnesses nobody would have accepted the*

---

* "Selbstverletzungen kommen nicht selten vor; abgesehen von solchen bei fingierten Raubanfällen, stösst man auf sie dann, wenn Entschädigungen erpresst werden sollen; so geschieht es, dass nach einer harmlosen Balgerei einer der Kämpfenden mit Verletzungen auftritt, die er damals erlitten haben will. Kenntlich sind solche Selbstverstümmelungen daran, dass die Betreffenden meistens die Operation wegen der grossen Schmerzen nicht ganz zu Ende führen, und dass es meistens Leute mit übertrieben pietistischer Färbung und mehr einsamen Lebenswandels sind."—H. Gross, "Handbuch für Untersuchungsrichter als System der Kriminalistik," I, pp. 32-34.

*theory of suicide. A soldier killed himself by a shot with his military
rifle through the back, by fixing the rifle in a certain position and then
lying down over it. Here again the position of the wound seemed to
exclude the theory of suicide.'"* *

"Wait a minute!" Heath heaved himself forward and shook
his cigar at Vance. "What about the gun? Sproot entered Ada's
room right after the shot was fired, and there wasn't no sign of a
gun!"

Vance, without answering, merely turned the pages of Gross's
"Handbuch" to where another marker protruded, and began
translating:

" *'Early one morning the authorities were informed that the corpse
of a murdered man had been found. At the spot indicated the body
was discovered of a grain merchant, A. M., supposed to be a well-
to-do man, face downward with a gunshot wound behind the ear.
The bullet, after passing through the brain, had lodged in the frontal
bone above the left eye. The place where the corpse was found was in
the middle of a bridge over a deep stream. Just when the inquiry was
concluding and the corpse was about to be removed for the post mortem, the investigating officer observed quite by chance that on the de-
cayed wooden parapet of the bridge, almost opposite to the spot where
the corpse lay, there was a small but perfectly fresh dent which appeared to have been caused by a violent blow on the upper edge of the
parapet of a hard and angular object. He immediately suspected that
the dent had some connection with the murder. Accordingly he determined to drag the bed of the stream below the bridge, when almost
immediately there was picked up a strong cord about fourteen feet*

---

* "Dass man sich durch den Sitz der Wunde niemals täuschen lassen darf, beweisen zwei
Fälle. Im Wiener Prater hatte sich ein Mann in Gegenwart mehrerer Personen getötet,
indem er sich mit einem Revolver in den Hinterkopf schoss. Wiären nicht die Aussagen
der Zeugen vorgelegen, hätte wohl kaum jemand an einen Selbstmord geglaubt. Ein Sol-
dat tötete sich durch einen in den Rücken gehenden Schuss aus einem Militärgewehr,
über das er nach entsprechender Fixierung sich gelegt hatte; auch hier wäre aus dem Sitz
der Wunde wohl kaum auf Selbstmord geschlossen worden."—*Ibid.*, II, p. 843.

*long with a large stone at one end and at the other a discharged pistol,
the barrel of which fitted exactly the bullet extracted from the head of
A. M. The case was thus evidently one of suicide. A. M. had hung the
stone over the parapet of the bridge and discharged the pistol behind
his ear. The moment he fired he let go the pistol, which the weight of
the stone dragged over the parapet into the water."* ... Does that answer your question, Sergeant?"

Heath stared at him with gaping eyes.

"You mean her gun went outa the window the same like that guy's gun went over the bridge?"

"There can be no doubt about it. There was no other place for the gun to go. The window, I learned from Sproot, was open a foot, and Ada stood before the window when she shot herself. Returning from Julia's room she attached a cord to the revolver with a weight of some kind on the other end, and hung the weight out of the window. When her hand released the weapon it was simply drawn over the sill and disappeared in the drift

* "Es wurde zeitlich morgens dem UR. die Meldung von der Auffindung eines 'Ermordeten' überbracht. An Ort und Stelle fand sich der Leichnam eines für wohlhabend geltenden Getreidehändlers M., auf dem Gesichte liegend, mit einer Schusswunde hinter dem rechten Ohre. Die Kugel war über dem linken Auge im Stirnknochen steeken geblieben, nachdem sie das Gehirn durchdrungen hatte. Die Fundstelle der Leiche befand sich etwa in der Mitte einer über einen ziemlich tiefen Fluss führenden Brücke. Am Schlusse der Lokalerhebungen und als die Leiche eben zur Obduktion fortgebracht werden sollte, fiel es dem UR. zufällig auf, dass das (hölzerne und wettergraue) Brückengeländer an der Stelle, wo auf dem Boden der Leichnam lag, eine kleine und sichtlich ganz frische Beschädigung aufwies, so als ob man dort (am oberen Rande) mit einem harten, kantigen Körper heftig angestossen wäre. Der Gedanke, dass dieser Umstand mit dem Morde in Zusammenhang stehe, war nicht gar von der Hand zu weisen. Ein Kahn war bald zur Stelle und am Brückenjoche befestigt; nun wurde vom Kahne aus (unter der fraglichen Stelle) der Flussgrund mit Rechen an langen Stielen sorgfältig abgesucht. Nach kurzer Arbeit kam wirklich etwas Seltsames zutage: eine etwa 4 *m* lange starke Schnur, an deren einem Ende ein grosser Feldstein, an deren anderem Ende eine abgeschossene Pistole befestigt war, in deren Lauf die später aus dem Kopfe des M. genommene Kugel genau passte. Nun war die Sache klarer Selbstmord; der Mann hatte sich mit der aufgefundenen Vorriclhtung auf die Brilcke begeben, den Stein über das Briückengeländer gehängt und sich die Kugel hinter dem rechten Ohre ins Hirn gejagt. Als er getroffen war, liess er die Pistole infolge des durch den Stein bewirkten Zuges aus und diese wurde von dem schweren Steine an der Schnur über das Geländer und in das Wasser gezogen. Hierbei hatte die Pistole, als sie das Geländer passierte, heftig an dieses angeschlagen und die betreffende Verletzung erzeugt."—*Ibid.*, II, pp. 834-836.

of soft snow on the balcony steps. And there is where the importance of the weather came in. Ada's plan needed an unusual amount of snow; and the night of November 8 was ideal for her grisly purpose."

"My God, Vance!" Markham's tone was strained and unnatural. "This thing begins to sound more like a fantastic nightmare than a reality."

"Not only was it a reality, Markham," said Vance gravely, "but it was an actual duplication of reality. It had all been done before and duly recorded in Gross's treatise, with names, dates, and details."

"Hell! No wonder we couldn't find the gun." Heath spoke with awed disgust. "And what about the footprints, Mr. Vance? I suppose she faked 'em all."

"Yes, Sergeant—with Gross's minute instructions and the footprint forgeries of many famous criminals to guide her, she faked them. As soon as it had stopped snowing that night, she slipped down-stairs, put on a pair of Chester's discarded galoshes, and walked to the front gate and back. Then she hid the galoshes in the library."

Vance turned once more to Gross's manual.

"There's everything here that one could possibly want to know about the making and detection of footprints, and—what is more to the point—about the manufacturing of footprints in shoes too large for one's feet.—Let me translate a short passage: *"The criminal may intend to cast suspicion upon another person, especially if he foresees that suspicion may fall upon himself. In this case he produces clear footprints which, so to speak, leap to the eyes, by wearing shoes which differ essentially from his own. One may often in this way, as has been proved by numerous experiments, produce footprints which deceive perfectly."* . . . And here at the end of the paragraph

* "Die Absicht kann dahin gehen, den Verdacht von sich auf jemand anderen zu wälzen, was namentlich dann Sinn hat, wenn der Täter schon im voraus annehmen durfte, dass

Gross refers specifically to galoshes[*]—a fact which very like-ly gave Ada her inspiration to use Chester's overshoes. She was shrewd enough to profit by the suggestions in this passage."

"And she was shrewd enough to hoodwink all of us when we questioned her," commented Markham bitterly.

"True. But that was because she had a *folie de grandeur*, and lived the story. Moreover, it was all based on fact; its details were grounded in reality. Even the shuffling sound she said she heard in her room was an imaginative projection of the actual shuf-fling sound she made when she walked in Chester's huge ga-loshes. Also, her own shuffling, no doubt, suggested to her how Mrs. Greene's footsteps would have sounded had the old lady regained the use of her legs. And I imagine it was Ada's original purpose to cast a certain amount of suspicion on Mrs. Greene from the very beginning. But Sibella's attitude during that first interview caused her to change her tactics. As I see it, Sibella was suspicious of little sister, and talked the situation over with Chester, who may also have had vague misgivings about Ada. You remember his *sub-rosa* chat with Sibella when he went to summon her to the drawing-room. He was probably informing her that he hadn't yet made up his mind about Ada, and was ad-vising her to go easy until there was some specific proof. Sibella evidently agreed, and refrained from any direct charge until Ada, in telling her grotesque fairy-tale about the intruder, rather im-plied it was a woman's hand that had touched her in the dark. That was too much for Sibella, who thought Ada was referring to her; and she burst forth with her accusation, despite its seem-

sich der Verdacht auf ihn lenken werde. In diesem Falle crzeugt er recht auffallencde. deutliche Spuren und zwar mit angezogenen Schuhen, die von den seinigen sich wesen-tlich unterscheiden. Man kann, wie angestellte Versuche beweisen, in dieser Weise recht gute Spuren erzeugen."—*Ibid.*, II, p. 667.

[*] "Über Gummiüberschuhe und Galoschen s. Loock; Chem. u. Phot. bei Krim. Forschungen: Düsseldorf, II, p. 56."—*Ibid.*, II, p. 668.

ing absurdity. The amazing thing about it was that it happened to be the truth. She named the murderer and stated a large part of the motive before any of us remotely guessed the truth, even though she did back down and change her mind when the inconsistency of it was pointed out to her. And she really did see Ada in Chester's room looking for the revolver."

Markham nodded.

"It's astonishing. But after the accusation, when Ada knew that Sibella suspected her, why didn't she kill Sibella next?"

"She was too canny. It would have tended to give weight to Sibella's accusation. Oh, Ada played her hand perfectly."

"Go on with the story, sir," urged Heath, intolerant of these side issues.

"Very well, Sergeant." Vance shifted more comfortably into his chair. "But first we must revert to the weather; for the weather ran like a sinister motif through all that followed. The second night after Julia's death it was quite warm, and the snow had melted considerably. That was the night chosen by Ada to retrieve the gun. A wound like hers rarely keeps one in bed over forty-eight hours; and Ada was well enough on Wednesday night to slip into a coat, step out on the balcony, and walk down the few steps to where the gun lay hidden. She merely brought it back and took it to bed with her—the last place any one would have thought to look for it. Then she waited patiently for the snow to fall again—which it did the next night, stopping, as you may remember, about eleven o'clock. The stage was set. The second act of the tragedy was about to begin. . . .

"Ada rose quietly, put on her coat, and went down to the library. Getting into the galoshes, she again walked to the front gate and back. Then she went directly up-stairs so that her tracks would show on the marble steps, and hid the galoshes temporarily in the linen-closet. That was the shuffling sound and the clos-ing door that Rex heard a few minutes before Chester was shot. Ada, you recall, told us afterward she had heard nothing; but when we repeated Rex's story to her she became frightened and conveniently remembered having heard a door close. My word! That was a ticklish moment for her. But she certainly carried it off well. And I can now understand her obvious relief when we showed her the pattern of the footprints and let her think we believed the murderer came from outside. . . . Well, after she had removed the galoshes and put them in the linen-closet, she took off her coat, donned a dressing-gown, and went to Ches-ter's room—probably opened the door without knocking, and went in with a friendly greeting. I picture her as sitting on the arm of Chester's chair, or the edge of the desk, and then, in the midst of some trivial remark, drawing the revolver, placing it against his breast, and pulling the trigger before he had time to recover from his horrified astonishment. He moved instinctively, though, just as the weapon exploded—which would account for the diagonal course of the bullet. Then Ada returned quickly to her own room and got into bed. Thus was another chapter writ-ten in the Greene tragedy."

"Did it strike you as strange," asked Markham, "that Von Blon was not at his office during the commission of either of the crimes?"

"At first—yes. But, after all, there was nothing unusual in the fact that a doctor should have been out at that time of night."

"It's easy enough to see how Ada got rid of Julia and Chester," grumbled Heath. "But what stops me is how she murdered Rex."

"Really, y' know, Sergeant," returned Vance, "that trick of hers shouldn't cause you any perplexity. I'll never forgive myself for not having guessed it long ago,—Ada certainly gave us enough clews to work on. But, before I describe it to you, let me recall a certain architectural detail of the Greene mansion. There is a Tudor fireplace, with carved wooden panels, in Ada's room, and another fireplace—a duplicate of Ada's—in Rex's room; and these two fireplaces are back to back on the same wall. The Greene house, as you know, is very old, and at some time in the past—perhaps when the fireplaces were built—an aperture was made between the two rooms, running from one of the panels in Ada's mantel to the corresponding panel in Rex's mantel. This miniature tunnel is about six inches square—the exact size of the panels—and a little over two feet long, or the depth of the two mantels and the wall. It was originally used, I imagine, for private communication between the two rooms. But that point is immaterial. The fact remains that such a shaft exists—I verified it to-night on my way down-town from the hospital. I might also add that the panel at either end of the shaft is on a spring hinge, so that when it is opened and released it closes automatically, snapping back into place without giving any indication that it is anything more than a solid part of the woodwork——"

"I get you!" exclaimed Heath, with the excitement of satisfaction. "Rex was shot by the old man-killing safe idea: the burglar opens the safe door and gets a bullet in his head from a stationary gun."

"Exactly. And the same device has been used in scores of murders. In the early days out West an enemy would go to a rancher's cabin during the tenant's absence, hang a shotgun from the ceiling over the door, and tie one end of a string to the trigger and the other end to the latch. When the rancher returned—perhaps days later—his brains would be blown out as he entered his cabin; and the murderer would, at the time, be in another part of the country."

"Sure!" The Sergeant's eyes sparkled. "There was a shooting like that in Atlanta two years ago—Boscomb was the name of the murdered man. And in Richmond, Virginia——"

"There have been many instances of it, Sergeant. Gross quotes two famous Austrian cases, and also has something to say about this method in general."

Again he opened the "Handbuch."

"On page 943 Gross remarks: '*The latest American safety devices have nothing to do with the safe itself, and can in fact be used with any receptacle. They act through chemicals or automatic firing devices, and their object is to make the presence of a human being who illegally opens the safe impossible on physical grounds. The judicial question would have to be decided whether one is legally entitled to kill a burglar without further ado or damage his health. However, a burglar in Berlin in 1902 was shot through the forehead by a self-shooter attached to a safe in an exporting house. This style of self-shooter has also been used by murderers. A mechanic, G. Z., attached a pistol in a china-closet, fastening the trigger to the catch, and thus shot his wife when he himself was in another city. R. C., a merchant of Budapest, fastened a revolver in a humidor belonging to his brother, which, when the lid was opened, fired and sent a bullet into his brother's abdomen. The explosion jerked the box from the table, and thus exposed the mechanism before the merchant had a chance to remove it.*'* . . . In

* "Die neuesten amerikanischen Schutzvorrichtungen haben direkt mit der Kasse selbst nichts zu tun und können eigentlich an jedem Behältnisse angebracht werden. Sie bestehen aus chemischen Schutzmitteln oder Selbstschüssen, und wollen die Anwesenheit eines Menschen, der den Schrank unbefugt geöffnet hat, aus sanitären oder sonst physischen Gründen unmöglich machen. Auch die juristische Seite der Frage ist zu erwägen, da man den Einbrecher doch nicht ohne weiteres töten oder an der Gesundheit schädigen darf. Nichtsdestoweniger wurde im Jahre 1902 ein Einbrecher in Berlin durch einen solchen Selbstschuss in die Stirne getötet, der an die Panzertüre einer Kasse befestigt war. Derartige Selbstschüsse wurden auch zu Morden verwendet; der Mechaniker G. Z. stellte einen Revolver in einer Kredenz auf, verband den Drücker mit der Türe durch eine Schnur und erschoss auf diese Art seine Frau, während er tatsächlichvon seinem Wohnorte abwesend war. R. C., ein Budapester Kaufmann, befestigte in einem, seinem Bruder gehörigen Zigarrenkasten, eine Pistole, die beim Öffnen des Deckels seinen Bruder durch einen Unterleibsschuss tötlich verletzte. Der Rückschlag warf die Kiste von

both these latter cases Gross gives a detailed description of the mechanisms employed. And it will interest you, Sergeant—in view of what I am about to tell you—to know that the revolver in the china-closet was held in place by a *Stiefelknecht*, or boot-jack."

He closed the volume but held it on his lap.

"There, unquestionably, is where Ada got the suggestion for Rex's murder. She and Rex had probably discovered the hidden passageway between their rooms years ago. I imagine that as children—they were about the same age, don't y' know—they used it as a secret means of correspondence. This would account for the name by which they both knew it—'our private mailbox.' And, given this knowledge between Ada and Rex, the method of the murder becomes perfectly clear. To-night I found an old-fashioned bootjack in Ada's clothes-closet—probably taken from Tobias's library. Its width, overall, was just six inches, and it was a little less than two feet long—it fitted perfectly into the communicating cupboard. Ada, following Gross's diagram, pressed the handle of the gun tightly between the tapering claws of the bootjack, which would have held it like a vise; then tied a string to the trigger, and attached the other end to the inside of Rex's panel, so that when the panel was opened wide the revolver, being on a hair-trigger, would discharge straight along the shaft and inevitably kill any one looking into the opening. When Rex fell with a bullet in his forehead the panel flapped back into place on its spring hinge; and a second later there was no visible evidence whatever pointing to the origin of the shot. And here we also have the explanation for Rex's calm expression of unawareness. When Ada returned with us from the District Attorney's office, she went directly to her room, removed the gun

ihrem Standort, sodass der Mördermechanismus zu Tage trat, ehe R. C. denselben bei Seite schaffen konnte."—*Ibid.*, II, p. 943.

and the bootjack, hid them in her closet, and came down to the drawing-room to report the foot-tracks on her carpet—foot-tracks she herself had made before leaving the house. It was just before she came down-stairs, by the way, that she stole the morphine and strychnine from Von Blon's case."

"But, my God, Vance!" said Markham. "Suppose her mechanism had failed to work. She would have been in for it then."

"I hardly think so. If, by any remote chance, the trap had not operated or Rex had recovered, she could easily have put the blame on some one else. She had merely to say she had secreted the diagram in the chute and that this other person had prepared the trap later on. There would have been no proof of her having set the gun."

"What about that diagram, sir?" asked Heath.

For answer Vance again took up the second volume of Gross and, opening it, extended it toward us. On the right-hand page were a number of curious line-drawings, which I reproduce here.

"There are the three stones, and the parrot, and the heart, and even your arrow, Sergeant. They're all criminal graphic symbols; and Ada simply utilized them in her description. The story of her finding the paper in the hall was a pure fabrication, but she knew it would pique our curiosity. The truth is, I suspected the paper of being faked by some one, for it evidently contained the signs of several types of criminal, and the symbols were meaninglessly jumbled. I rather imagined it was a false clew deliberately placed in the hall for us to find—like the footprints; but I certainly didn't suspect Ada of having made up the tale. Now, however, as I look back at the episode it strikes me as deuced queer that she shouldn't have brought so apparently significant a paper to the office. Her failure to do so was neither logical nor reasonable; and I ought to have been suspicious. But—my word!—what was one illogical item more or less in such a melange of inconsistencies? As it happened, her decoy worked beautifully, and gave her the opportunity to telephone Rex to look into the chute. But it didn't really matter. If the scheme had fallen through that morning, it would have been successful later on. Ada was highly persevering."

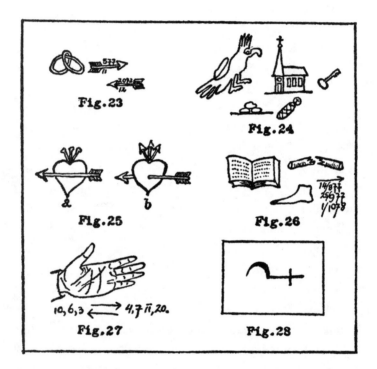

"You think then," put in Markham, "that Rex really heard the shot in Ada's room that first night, and confided in her?"

"Undoubtedly. That part of her story was true enough. I'm inclined to think that Rex heard the shot and had a vague idea Mrs. Greene had fired it. Being rather close to his mother temperamentally, he said nothing. Later he voiced his suspicions to

Ada; and that confession gave her the idea for killing him—or, rather, for perfecting the technic she had already decided on; for Rex would have been shot through the secret cupboard in any event. But Ada now saw a way of establishing a perfect alibi for the occasion; although even her idea of being actually with the police when the shot was fired was not original. In Gross's chapter on alibis there is much suggestive material along that line."

Heath sucked his teeth wonderingly.

"I'm glad I don't run across many of her kind," he remarked.

"She was her father's daughter," said Vance. "But too much credit should not be given her, Sergeant. She had a printed and diagrammed guide for everything. There was little for her to do but follow instructions and keep her head. And as for Rex's murder, don't forget that, although she was actually in Mr. Markham's office at the time of the shooting, she personally engineered the entire *coup*. Think back. She refused to let either you or Mr. Markham come to the house, and insisted upon visiting the office. Once there, she told her story and suggested that Rex be summoned immediately. She even went so far as to plead with us to call him by phone. Then, when we had complied, she quickly informed us of the mysterious diagram, and offered to tell Rex exactly where she had hidden it, so he could bring it with him. And we sat there calmly, listening to her send Rex to his death! Her actions at the Stock Exchange should have given me a hint; but I confess I was particularly blind that morning. She was in a state of high nervous excitement; and when she broke down and sobbed on Mr. Markham's desk after he had told her of Rex's death, her tears were quite real—only, they were not for Rex; they were the reaction from that hour of terrific tension."

"I begin to understand why no one up-stairs heard the shot," said Markham. "The revolver detonating in the wall, as it were, would have been almost completely muffled. But why should Sproot have heard it so distinctly down-stairs?"

"You remember there was a fireplace in the living-room directly beneath Ada's—Chester once told us it was rarely lighted because it wouldn't draw properly—and Sproot was in the butler's pantry just beyond. The sound of the report went downward through the flue and, as a result, was heard plainly on the lower floor."

"You said a minute ago, Mr. Vance," argued Heath, "that Rex maybe suspected the old lady. Then why should he have accused Von Blon the way he did that day he had a fit?"

"The accusation primarily, I think, was a sort of instinctive effort to drive the idea of Mrs. Greene's guilt from his own mind. Then again, as Von Blon explained, Rex was frightened after you had questioned him about the revolver, and wanted to divert suspicion from himself."

"Get on with the story of Ada's plot, Vance." This time it was Markham who was impatient.

"The rest seems pretty obvious, don't y' know. It was unquestionably Ada who was listening at the library door the afternoon we were there. She realized we had found the books and galoshes; and she had to think fast. So, when we came out, she told us the dramatic yarn of having seen her mother walking, which was sheer moonshine. She had run across those books on paralysis, d' ye see, and they had suggested to her the possibility of focussing suspicion on Mrs. Greene—the chief object of her hate. It is probably true, as Von Blon said, that the two books do not deal with actual hysterical paralysis and somnambulism, but they no doubt contain references to these types of paralysis. I rather think Ada had intended all along to kill the old lady last and have it appear as the suicide of the murderer. But the proposed examination by Oppenheimer changed all that. She learned of the examination when she heard Von Blon apprise Mrs. Greene of it on his morning visit; and, having told us of that mythical midnight promenade, she couldn't delay matters any longer. The old lady had to die—*before Oppenheimer arrived*. And half an hour later Ada took the morphine. She feared to give Mrs. Greene the strychnine at once lest it appear suspicious. . . ."

"That's where those books on poisons come in, isn't it, Mr. Vance?" interjected Heath. "When Ada had decided to use poison on some of the family, she got all the dope she needed on the subject outa the library."

"Precisely. She herself took just enough morphine to render her unconscious—probably about two grains. And to make sure she would get immediate assistance she devised the simple trick of having Sibella's dog appear to give the alarm. Incidentally, this trick cast suspicion on Sibella. After Ada had swallowed the morphine, she merely waited until she began to feel drowsy, pulled the bell-cord, caught the tassel in the dog's teeth, and lay back. She counterfeited a good deal of her illness; but Drumm couldn't have detected her malingering even if he had been as great a doctor as he wanted us to believe; for the symptoms for all doses of morphine taken by mouth are practically the same during the first half-hour. And, once she was on her feet, she had only to watch for an opportunity of giving the strychnine to Mrs. Greene. . . ."

"It all seems too cold-blooded to be real," murmured Markham.

"And yet there has been any number of precedents for Ada's actions. Do you recall the mass murders of those three nurses,

Madame Jegado, Frau Zwanzigger, and Vrouw Van der Linden? And there was Mrs. Belle Gunness, the female Bluebeard; and Amelia Elizabeth Dyer, the Reading baby-farmer; and Mrs. Pearcey. Cold-blooded? Yes! But in Ada's case there was passion too. I'm inclined to believe that it takes a particularly hot flame—a fire at white heat, in fact—to carry the human heart through such a Gethsemane. However that may be, Ada watched for her chance to poison Mrs. Greene, and found it that night. The nurse went to the third floor to prepare for bed between eleven and eleven-thirty; and during that half-hour Ada visited her mother's room. Whether she suggested the citrocarbonate or Mrs. Greene herself asked for it, we'll never know. Probably the former, for Ada had always given it to her at night. When the nurse came downstairs again Ada was already back in bed, apparently asleep, and Mrs. Greene was on the verge of her first— and, let us hope, her only—convulsion."

"Doremus's *post-mortem* report must have given her a terrific shock," commented Markham.

"It did. It upset all her calculations. Imagine her feelings when we informed her that Mrs. Greene couldn't have walked! She backed out of the danger nicely, though. The detail of the Oriental shawl, however, nearly entangled her. But even that point she turned to her own advantage by using it as a clew against Sibella."

"How do you account for Mrs. Mannheim's actions during that interview?" asked Markham. "You remember her saying it might have been she whom Ada saw in the hall."

A cloud came over Vance's face.

"I think," he said sadly, "that Frau Mannheim began to suspect her little Ada at that point. She knew the terrible history of the girl's father, and perhaps had lived in fear of some criminal outcropping in the child."

There was a silence for several moments. Each of us was busy with his own thoughts. Then Vance continued:

"After Mrs. Greene's death, only Sibella stood between Ada and her blazing goal; and it was Sibella herself who gave her the idea for a supposedly safe way to commit the final murder. Weeks ago, on a ride Van and I took with the two girls and Von Blon, Sibella's venomous pique led her to make a foolish remark about running one's victim over a precipice in a machine; and it no doubt appealed to Ada's sense of the fitness of things that Sibella should thus suggest the means of her own demise. I wouldn't be at all surprised if Ada intended, after having killed her sister, to say that Sibella had tried to murder *her*, but that she had suspected the other's purpose and jumped from the car in time to save herself; and that Sibella had miscalculated the car's speed and been carried over the precipice. The fact that Von Blon and Van and I had heard Sibella speculate on just such a method of murder would have given weight to Ada's story. And what a neat ending it would have made—Sibella, the murderer, dead; the case closed; Ada, the inheritor of the Greene millions, free to do as she chose! And—'pon my soul, Markham!—it came very near succeeding."

Vance sighed, and reached for the decanter. After refilling our glasses he settled back and smoked moodily.

"I wonder how long this terrible plot had been in preparation. We'll never know. Maybe years. There was no haste in Ada's preparations. Everything was worked out carefully; and she let circumstances—or, rather, opportunity—guide her. Once she had secured the revolver, it was only a question of waiting for a chance when she could make the footprints and be sure the gun would sink out of sight in the snow-drift on the balcony steps. Yes, the most essential condition of her scheme was the snow. . . . Amazin'!"

There is little more to add to this record. The truth was not given out, and the case was "shelved." The following year Tobias's will was upset by the Supreme Court in Equity—that is, the twenty-five-year domiciliary clause was abrogated in view of all that had happened at the house; and Sibella came into the entire Greene fortune. How much Markham had to do with the decision, through his influence with the Administration judge who rendered it, I don't know; and naturally I have never asked. But the old Greene mansion was, as you remember, torn down shortly afterward, and the estate sold to a realty corporation.

Mrs. Mannheim, broken-hearted over Ada's death, claimed her inheritance—which Sibella generously doubled—and returned to Germany to seek what comfort she might among the nieces and nephews with whom, according to Chester, she was constantly corresponding. Sproot went back to England. He told Vance before departing that he had long planned a cottage retreat in Surrey where he could loaf and invite his soul. I picture him now, sitting on an ivied porch overlooking the Downs, reading his beloved Martial.

Doctor and Mrs. Von Blon, immediately after the court's decision relating to the will, sailed for the Riviera and spent a belated honeymoon there. They are now settled in Vienna, where the doctor has become a *Privatdocent* at the University—his father's Alma Mater. He is, I understand, making quite a name for himself in the field of neurology.

DISCUSSION QUESTIONS

- Did any aspects of the plot date the story? If so, which?

- Would the story be different if it were set in the present day? If so, how?

- Did the social context of the time play a role in the narrative? If so, how?

- If you were one of the main characters, would you have acted differently at any point in the story?

- Did you identify with any of the characters? If so, which?

- What skills or qualities make Philo Vance such an effective sleuth?

- What do you think made the Philo Vance books so successful in their time? How have audiences changed between then and now?

- Did this book remind you of any present day authors? If so, which?

PHILO VANCE'S FIRST OUTING

THE BENSON
MURDER CASE

IS ALSO AVAILABLE FROM

AMERICAN MYSTERY CLASSICS

OTTO PENZLER PRESENTS
AMERICAN MYSTERY CLASSICS

All titles are available in hardcover and in trade paperback.

Order from your favorite bookstore or from
The Mysterious Bookshop, 58 Warren Street, New York, N.Y. 10007
(www.mysteriousbookshop.com).

Charlotte Armstrong, *The Chocolate Cobweb*. When Amanda Garth was born, a mix-up caused the hospital to briefly hand her over to the prestigious Garrison family instead of to her birth parents. The error was quickly fixed, Amanda was never told, and the secret was forgotten for twenty-three years … until her aunt revealed it in casual conversation. But what if the initial switch never actually occurred? **Introduction by A. J. Finn.**

Charlotte Armstrong, *The Unsuspected*. First published in 1946, this suspenseful novel opens with a young woman who has ostensibly hanged herself, leaving a suicide note. Her friend doesn't believe it and begins an investigation that puts her own life in jeopardy. It was filmed in 1947 by Warner Brothers, starring Claude Rains and Joan Caulfield. **Introduction by Otto Penzler.**

Anthony Boucher, *The Case of the Baker Street Irregulars*. When a studio announces a new hard-boiled Sherlock Holmes film, the Baker Street Irregulars begin a campaign to discredit it. Attempting to mollify them, the producers invite members to the set, where threats are received, each referring to one of the original Holmes tales, followed by murder. Fortunately, the amateur sleuths use Holmesian lessons to solve the crime. **Introduction by Otto Penzler.**

Anthony Boucher, *Rocket to the Morgue*. Hilary Foulkes has made so many enemies that it is difficult to speculate who was responsible for stabbing him nearly to death in a room with only one door through which no one was seen entering or leaving. This classic locked room mystery is populated by such thinly disguised science fiction legends as Robert Heinlein, L. Ron Hubbard, and John W. Campbell. **Introduction by F. Paul Wilson.**

Fredric Brown, *The Fabulous Clipjoint*. Brown's outstanding mystery won an Edgar as the best first novel of the year (1947). When Wallace

Hunter is found dead in an alley after a long night of drinking, the police don't really care. But his teenage son Ed and his uncle Am, the carnival worker, are convinced that some things don't add up and the crime isn't what it seems to be. **Introduction by Lawrence Block.**

John Dickson Carr, *The Crooked Hinge*. Selected by a group of mystery experts as one of the 15 best impossible crime novels ever written, this is one of Gideon Fell's greatest challenges. Estranged from his family for 25 years, Sir John Farnleigh returns to England from America to claim his inheritance but another person turns up claiming that he can prove he is the real Sir John. Inevitably, one of them is murdered. **Introduction by Charles Todd.**

John Dickson Carr, *The Eight of Swords*. When Gideon Fell arrives at a crime scene, it appears to be straightforward enough. A man has been shot to death in an unlocked room and the likely perpetrator was a recent visitor. But Fell discovers inconsistencies and his investigations are complicated by an apparent poltergeist, some American gangsters, and two meddling amateur sleuths. **Introduction by Otto Penzler.**

John Dickson Carr, *The Mad Hatter Mystery*. A prankster has been stealing top hats all around London. Gideon Fell suspects that the same person may be responsible for the theft of a manuscript of a long-lost story by Edgar Allan Poe. The hats reappear in unexpected but conspicuous places but, when one is found on the head of a corpse by the Tower of London, it is evident that the thefts are more than pranks. **Introduction by Otto Penzler.**

John Dickson Carr, *The Plague Court Murders*. When murder occurs in a locked hut on Plague Court, an estate haunted by the ghost of a hangman's assistant who died a victim of the black death, Sir Henry Merrivale seeks a logical solution to a ghostly crime. A spiritual medium employed to rid the house of his spirit is found stabbed to death in a locked stone hut on the grounds, surrounded by an untouched circle of mud. **Introduction by Michael Dirda.**

John Dickson Carr, *The Red Widow Murders.* In a "haunted" mansion, the room known as the Red Widow's Chamber proves lethal to all who spend the night. Eight people investigate and the one who draws the ace of spades must sleep in it. The room is locked from the inside and watched all night by the others. When the door is unlocked, the victim has been poisoned. Enter Sir Henry Merrivale to solve the crime. **Introduction by Tom Mead.**

Frances Crane, *The Turquoise Shop.* In an arty little New Mexico town, Mona Brandon has arrived from the East and becomes the subject of gossip about her money, her influence, and the corpse in the nearby desert who may be her husband. Pat Holly, who runs the local gift shop, is as interested as anyone in the goings on—but even more in Pat Abbott, the detective investigating the possible murder. **Introduction by Anne Hillerman.**

Todd Downing, *Vultures in the Sky.* There is no end to the series of terrifying events that befall a luxury train bound for Mexico. First, a man dies when the train passes through a dark tunnel, then it comes to an abrupt stop in the middle of the desert. More deaths occur when night falls and the passengers panic when they realize they are trapped with a murderer on the loose. **Introduction by James Sallis.**

Mignon G. Eberhart, *Murder by an Aristocrat.* Nurse Keate is called to help a man who has been "accidentally" shot in the shoulder. When he is murdered while convalescing, it is clear that there was no accident. Although a killer is loose in the mansion, the family seems more concerned that news of the murder will leave their circle. *The New Yorker* wrote than "Eberhart can weave an almost flawless mystery." **Introduction by Nancy Pickard.**

Erle Stanley Gardner, *The Case of the Baited Hook.* Perry Mason gets a phone call in the middle of the night and his potential client says it's urgent, that he has two one-thousand-dollar bills that he will give him as a retainer, with an additional ten-thousand whenever he is called on to represent him. When

Mason takes the case, it is not for the caller but for a beautiful woman whose identity is hidden behind a mask. **Introduction by Otto Penzler.**

Erle Stanley Gardner, *The Case of the Borrowed Brunette.* A mysterious man named Mr. Hines has advertised a job for a woman who has to fulfill very specific physical requirements. Eva Martell, pretty but struggling in her career as a model, takes the job but her aunt smells a rat and hires Perry Mason to investigate. Her fears are realized when Hines turns up in the apartment with a bullet hole in his head. **Introduction by Otto Penzler.**

Erle Stanley Gardner, *The Case of the Careless Kitten.* Helen Kendal receives a mysterious phone call from her vanished uncle Franklin, long presumed dead, who urges her to contact Perry Mason. Soon, she finds herself the main suspect in the murder of an unfamiliar man. Her kitten has just survived a poisoning attempt—as has her aunt Matilda. What is the connection between Franklin's return and the murder attempts? **Introduction by Otto Penzler.**

Erle Stanley Gardner, *The Case of the Rolling Bones.* One of Gardner's most successful Perry Mason novels opens with a clear case of blackmail, though the person being blackmailed claims he isn't. It is not long before the police are searching for someone wanted for killing the same man in two different states—thirty-three years apart. The confounding puzzle of what happened to the dead man's toes is a challenge. **Introduction by Otto Penzler.**

Erle Stanley Gardner, *The Case of the Shoplifter's Shoe.* Most cases for Perry Mason involve murder but here he is hired because a young woman fears her aunt is a kleptomaniac. Sarah may not have been precisely the best guardian for a collection of valuable diamonds and, sure enough, they go missing. When the jeweler is found shot dead, Sarah is spotted leaving the murder scene with a bundle of gems stuffed in her purse. **Introduction by Otto Penzler.**

Erle Stanley Gardner, *The Bigger They Come.* Gardner's first novel using the pseudonym A.A. Fair starts off a series featuring the large and loud Bertha Cool and her employee, the small and meek Donald Lam. Given the job of delivering divorce papers to an evident crook,

Lam can't find him—but neither can the police. The *Los Angeles Times* called this book: "Breathlessly dramatic ... an original." Introduction by Otto Penzler.

Frances Noyes Hart, *The Bellamy Trial*. Inspired by the real-life Hall-Mills case, the most sensational trial of its day, this is the story of Stephen Bellamy and Susan Ives, accused of murdering Bellamy's wife Madeleine. Eight days of dynamic testimony, some true, some not, make headlines for an enthralled public. Rex Stout called this historic courtroom thriller one of the ten best mysteries of all time. Introduction by Hank Phillippi Ryan.

H.F. Heard, *A Taste for Honey*. The elderly Mr. Mycroft quietly keeps bees in Sussex, where he is approached by the reclusive and somewhat misanthropic Mr. Silchester, whose honey supplier was found dead, stung to death by her bees. Mycroft, who shares many traits with Sherlock Holmes, sets out to find the vicious killer. Rex Stout described it as "sinister ... a tale well and truly told." Introduction by Otto Penzler.

Dolores Hitchens, *The Alarm of the Black Cat*. Detective fiction aficionado Rachel Murdock has a peculiar meeting with a little girl and a dead toad, sparking her curiosity about a love triangle that has sparked anger. When the girl's great grandmother is found dead, Rachel and her cat Samantha work with a friend in the Los Angeles Police Department to get to the bottom of things. Introduction by David Handler.

Dolores Hitchens, *The Cat Saw Murder*. Miss Rachel Murdock, the highly intelligent 70-year-old amateur sleuth, is not entirely heartbroken when her slovenly, unattractive, bridge-cheating niece is murdered. Miss Rachel is happy to help the socially maladroit and somewhat bumbling Detective Lieutenant Stephen Mayhew, retaining her composure when a second brutal murder occurs. Introduction by Joyce Carol Oates.

Dorothy B. Hughes, *Dread Journey*. A bigshot Hollywood producer has worked on his magnum opus for years, hiring and firing one beautiful starlet after another. But Kitten Agnew's contract won't allow her to be fired, so she fears she might be terminated more permanently. Together with the producer on a train journey from Hollywood to Chicago, Kitten becomes more terrified with each passing mile. Introduction by Sarah Weinman.

Dorothy B. Hughes, *Ride the Pink Horse*. When Sailor met Willis Douglass, he was just a poor kid who Douglass groomed to work as a confidential secretary. As the senator became increasingly corrupt, he knew he could count on Sailor to clean up his messes. No longer a senator, Douglass flees Chicago for Santa Fe, leaving behind a murder rap and Sailor as the prime suspect. Seeking vengeance, Sailor follows. Introduction by Sara Paretsky.

Dorothy B. Hughes, *The So Blue Marble*. Set in the glamorous world of New York high society, this novel became a suspense classic as twins from Europe try to steal a rare and beautiful gem owned by an aristocrat whose sister is an even more menacing presence. *The New Yorker* called it "Extraordinary ... [Hughes'] brilliant descriptive powers make and unmake reality." Introduction by Otto Penzler.

W. Bolingbroke Johnson, *The Widening Stain*. After a cocktail party, the attractive Lucie Coindreau, a "black-eyed, black-haired Frenchwoman" visits the rare books wing of the library and apparently takes a head-first fall from an upper gallery. Dismissed as a horrible accident, it seems dubious when Professor Hyett is strangled while reading a priceless 12th-century manuscript, which has gone missing. Introduction by Nicholas A. Basbanes

Baynard Kendrick, *Blind Man's Bluff*. Blinded in World War II, Duncan Maclain forms a successful private detective agency, aided by his two dogs. Here, he is called on to solve the case of a blind man who plummets from the top of an eight-story building, apparently with no one present except his dead-drunk son. Introduction by Otto Penzler.

Baynard Kendrick, *The Odor of Violets*. Duncan Maclain, a blind former intelligence officer, is asked to investigate the murder of an actor in his Greenwich Village apartment. This would cause a stir at any time but, when the actor possesses secret government plans that then go missing, it's enough to interest the local police as well as the American government and Maclain, who suspects a German spy plot. Introduction by Otto Penzler.

C. Daly King, *Obelists at Sea*. On a cruise ship traveling from New York to Paris, the lights of the smoking room briefly go out, a gunshot crashes through the night, and a man is dead. Two detectives are on board but so are four psychiatrists who believe their professional knowledge can solve the case by understanding the psyche of the killer—each with a different theory. **Introduction by Martin Edwards.**

Jonathan Latimer, *Headed for a Hearse*. Featuring Bill Crane, the booze-soaked Chicago private detective, this humorous hard-boiled novel was filmed as *The Westland Case* in 1937 starring Preston Foster. Robert Westland has been framed for the grisly murder of his wife in a room with doors and windows locked from the inside. As the day of his execution nears, he relies on Crane to find the real murderer. **Introduction by Max Allan Collins**

Lange Lewis, *The Birthday Murder*. Victoria is a successful novelist and screenwriter and her husband is a movie director so their marriage seems almost too good to be true. Then, on her birthday, her happy new life comes crashing down when her husband is murdered using a method of poisoning that was described in one of her books. She quickly becomes the leading suspect. **Introduction by Randal S. Brandt.**

Frances and Richard Lockridge, *Death on the Aisle*. In one of the most beloved books to feature Mr. and Mrs. North, the body of a wealthy backer of a play is found dead in a seat of the 45th Street Theater. Pam is thrilled to engage in her favorite pastime—playing amateur sleuth—much to the annoyance of Jerry, her publisher husband. The Norths inspired a stage play, a film, and long-running radio and TV series. **Introduction by Otto Penzler.**

John P. Marquand, *Your Turn, Mr. Moto*. The first novel about Mr. Moto, originally titled *No Hero*, is the story of a World War I hero pilot who finds himself jobless during the Depression. In Tokyo for a big opportunity that falls apart, he meets a Japanese agent and his Russian colleague and the pilot suddenly finds himself caught in a web of intrigue. Peter Lorre played Mr. Moto in a series of popular films. **Introduction by Lawrence Block.**

Stuart Palmer, *The Penguin Pool Murder*. The

first adventure of schoolteacher and dedicated amateur sleuth Hildegarde Withers occurs at the New York Aquarium when she and her young students notice a corpse in one of the tanks. It was published in 1931 and filmed the next year, starring Edna May Oliver as the American Miss Marple—though much funnier than her English counterpart. **Introduction by Otto Penzler.**

Stuart Palmer, *The Puzzle of the Happy Hooligan*. New York City schoolteacher Hildegarde Withers cannot resist "assisting" homicide detective Oliver Piper. In this novel, she is on vacation in Hollywood and on the set of a movie about Lizzie Borden when the screenwriter is found dead. Six comic films about Withers appeared in the 1930s, most successfully starring Edna May Oliver. **Introduction by Otto Penzler.**

Otto Penzler, ed., *Golden Age Bibliomysteries*. Stories of murder, theft, and suspense occur with alarming regularity in the unlikely world of books and bibliophiles, including bookshops, libraries, and private rare book collections, written by such giants of the mystery genre as Ellery Queen, Cornell Woolrich, Lawrence G. Blochman, Vincent Starrett, and Anthony Boucher. **Introduction by Otto Penzler.**

Otto Penzler, ed., *Golden Age Detective Stories*. The history of American mystery fiction has its pantheon of authors who have influenced and entertained readers for nearly a century, reaching its peak during the Golden Age, and this collection pays homage to the work of the most acclaimed: Cornell Woolrich, Erle Stanley Gardner, Craig Rice, Ellery Queen, Dorothy B. Hughes, Mary Roberts Rinehart, and more. **Introduction by Otto Penzler.**

Otto Penzler, ed., *Golden Age Locked Room Mysteries*. The so-called impossible crime category reached its zenith during the 1920s, 1930s, and 1940s, and this volume includes the greatest of the great authors who mastered the form: John Dickson Carr, Ellery Queen, C. Daly King, Clayton Rawson, and Erle Stanley Gardner. Like great magicians, these literary conjurors will baffle and delight readers. **Introduction by Otto Penzler.**

Ellery Queen, *The Adventures of Ellery Queen*. These stories are the earliest short works to feature Queen as a detective and are among the best of the author's fair-play mysteries. So many of the elements that comprise the gestalt of Queen may be found in these tales: alternate solutions, the dying clue, a bizarre crime, and the author's ability to find fresh variations of works by other authors. **Introduction by Otto Penzler.**

Ellery Queen, *The American Gun Mystery*. A rodeo comes to New York City at the Colosseum. The headliner is Buck Horne, the once popular film cowboy who opens the show leading a charge of forty whooping cowboys until they pull out their guns and fire into the air. Buck falls to the ground, shot dead. The police instantly lock the doors to search everyone but the offending weapon has completely vanished. **Introduction by Otto Penzler.**

Ellery Queen, *The Chinese Orange Mystery*. The offices of publisher Donald Kirk have seen strange events but nothing like this. A strange man is found dead with two long spears alongside his back. And, though no one was seen entering or leaving the room, everything has been turned backwards or upside down: pictures face the wall, the victim's clothes are worn backwards, the rug upside down. Why in the world? **Introduction by Otto Penzler.**

Ellery Queen, *The Dutch Shoe Mystery*. Millionaire philanthropist Abagail Doorn falls into a coma and she is rushed to the hospital she funds for an emergency operation by one of the leading surgeons on the East Coast. When she is wheeled into the operating theater, the sheet covering her body is pulled back to reveal her garroted corpse—the first of a series of murders **Introduction by Otto Penzler.**

Ellery Queen, *The Egyptian Cross Mystery*. A small-town schoolteacher is found dead, headed, and tied to a T-shaped cross on December 25th, inspiring such sensational headlines as "Crucifixion on Christmas Day." Amateur sleuth Ellery Queen is so intrigued he travels to Virginia but fails to solve the crime. Then a similar murder takes place on New York's Long Island—and then another. **Introduction by Otto Penzler.**

Ellery Queen, *The Siamese Twin Mystery*. When Ellery and his father encounter a raging forest fire on a mountain, their only hope is to drive up to an isolated hillside manor owned by a secretive surgeon and his strange guests. While playing solitaire in the middle of the night, the doctor is shot. The only clue is a torn playing card. Suspects include a society beauty, a valet, and conjoined twins. **Introduction by Otto Penzler.**

Ellery Queen, *The Spanish Cape Mystery*. Amateur detective Ellery Queen arrives in the resort town of Spanish Cape soon after a young woman and her uncle are abducted by a gun-toting, one-eyed giant. The next day, the woman's somewhat dicey boyfriend is found murdered—totally naked under a black fedora and opera cloak. **Introduction by Otto Penzler.**

Patrick Quentin, *A Puzzle for Fools*. Broadway producer Peter Duluth takes to the bottle when his wife dies but enters a sanitarium to dry out. Malevolent events plague the hospital, including when Peter hears his own voice intone, "There will be murder." And there is. He investigates, aided by a young woman who is also a patient. This is the first of nine mysteries featuring Peter and Iris Duluth. **Introduction by Otto Penzler.**

Clayton Rawson, *Death from a Top Hat*. When the New York City Police Department is baffled by an apparently impossible crime, they call on The Great Merlini, a retired stage magician who now runs a Times Square magic shop. In his first case, two occultists have been murdered in a room locked from the inside, their bodies positioned to form a pentagram. **Introduction by Otto Penzler.**

Craig Rice, *Eight Faces at Three*. Gin-soaked John J. Malone, defender of the guilty, is notorious for getting his culpable clients off. It's the innocent ones who are problems. Like Holly Inglehart, accused of piercing the black heart of her well-heeled aunt Alexandria with a lovely Florentine paper cutter. No one who knew the old battle-ax liked her, but Holly's prints were found on the murder weapon. **Introduction by Lisa Lutz.**

Craig Rice, *Home Sweet Homicide*. Known as the Dorothy Parker of mystery fiction for her memorable wit, Craig Rice was the first detective writer to appear on the cover of *Time* magazine. This comic mystery features two kids who are trying to find a husband for their widowed mother while she's engaged in sleuthing. Filmed with the same title in 1946 with Peggy Ann Garner and Randolph Scott. **Introduction by Otto Penzler.**

Mary Roberts Rinehart, *The Album*. Crescent Place is a quiet enclave of wealthy people in which nothing ever happens—until a bedridden old woman is attacked by an intruder with an ax. *The New York Times* stated: "All Mary Roberts Rinehart mystery stories are good, but this one is better." **Introduction by Otto Penzler.**

Mary Roberts Rinehart, *The Haunted Lady*. The arsenic in her sugar bowl was wealthy widow Eliza Fairbanks' first clue that somebody wanted her dead. Nightly visits of bats, birds, and rats, obviously aimed at scaring the dowager to death, was the second. Eliza calls the police, who send nurse Hilda Adams, the amateur sleuth they refer to as "Miss Pinkerton," to work undercover to discover the culprit. **Introduction by Otto Penzler.**

Mary Roberts Rinehart, *Miss Pinkerton*. Hilda Adams is a nurse, not a detective, but she is observant and smart and so it is common for Inspector Patton to call on her for help. Her success results in his calling her "Miss Pinkerton." *The New Republic* wrote: "From thousands of hearts and homes the cry will go up: Thank God for Mary Roberts Rinehart." **Introduction by Carolyn Hart.**

Mary Roberts Rinehart, *The Red Lamp*. Professor William Porter refuses to believe that the seaside manor he's just inherited is haunted but he has to convince his wife to move in. However, he soon sees evidence of the occult phenomena of which the townspeople speak. Whether it is a spirit or a human being, Porter accepts that there is a connection to the rash of murders that have terrorized the countryside. **Introduction by Otto Penzler.**

Mary Roberts Rinehart, *The Wall*. For two decades, Mary Roberts Rinehart was the second-best-selling author in America (only Sinclair Lewis outsold her) and was beloved for her tales of suspense. In a magnificent mansion, the ex-wife of one of the owners turns up making demands and is found dead the next day. And there are more dark secrets lying behind the walls of the estate. **Introduction by Otto Penzler.**

Joel Townsley Rogers, *The Red Right Hand*. This extraordinary whodunnit that is as puzzling as it is terrifying was identified by crime fiction scholar Jack Adrian as "one of the dozen or so finest mystery novels of the 20th century." A deranged killer sends a doctor on a quest for the truth—deep into the recesses of his own mind—when he and his bride-to-be elope but pick up a terrifying sharp-toothed hitch-hiker. **Introduction by Joe R. Lansdale.**

Roger Scarlett, *Cat's Paw*. The family of the wealthy old bachelor Martin Greenough cares far more about his money than they do about him. For his birthday, he invites all his potential heirs to his mansion to tell them what they hope to hear. Before he can disburse funds, however, he is murdered, and the Boston Police Department's big problem is that there are too many suspects. **Introduction by Curtis Evans**

Vincent Starrett, *Dead Man Inside*. 1930s Chicago is a tough town but some crimes are more bizarre than others. Customers arrive at a haberdasher to find a corpse in the window and a sign on the door: *Dead Man Inside! I am Dead. The store will not open today.* This is just one of a series of odd murders that terrorizes the city. Reluctant detective Walter Ghost leaps into action to learn what is behind the plague. **Introduction by Otto Penzler.**

Vincent Starrett, *The Great Hotel Murder*. Theater critic and amateur sleuth Riley Blackwood investigates a murder in a Chicago hotel where the dead man had changed rooms with a stranger who had registered under a fake name. *The New York Times* described it as "an ingenious plot with enough complications to keep the reader guessing." **Introduction by Lyndsay Faye.**

Vincent Starrett, *Murder on 'B' Deck*. Walter Ghost, a psychologist, scientist, explorer, and former intelligence officer, is on a cruise ship and his friend novelist Dunsten Mollock, a Nigel Bruce-like Watson whose role is to offer occasional comic relief, accommodates when he fails to leave the ship before it takes off. Although they make mistakes along the way, the amateur sleuths solve the shipboard murders. **Introduction by Ray Betzner.**

Phoebe Atwood Taylor, *The Cape Cod Mystery*. Vacationers have flocked to Cape Cod to avoid the heat wave that hit the Northeast and find their holiday unpleasant when the area is flooded with police trying to find the murderer of a muckraking journalist who took a cottage for the season. Finding a solution falls to Asey Mayo, "the Cape Cod Sherlock," known for his worldly wisdom, folksy humor, and common sense. **Introduction by Otto Penzler.**

S. S. Van Dine, *The Benson Murder Case.* The first of 12 novels to feature Philo Vance, the most popular and influential detective character of the early part of the 20th century. When wealthy stockbroker Alvin Benson is found shot to death in a locked room in his mansion, the police are baffled until the erudite flaneur and art collector arrives on the scene. Paramount filmed it in 1930 with William Powell as Vance. **Introduction by Ragnar Jónasson.**

Cornell Woolrich, *The Bride Wore Black.* The first suspense novel by one of the greatest of all noir authors opens with a bride and her new husband walking out of the church. A car speeds by, shots ring out, and he falls dead at her feet. Determined to avenge his death, she tracks down everyone in the car, concluding with a shocking surprise. It was filmed by Francois Truffaut in 1968, starring Jeanne Moreau. **Introduction by Eddie Muller.**

Cornell Woolrich, *Deadline at Dawn.* Quinn is overcome with guilt about having robbed a stranger's home. He meets Bricky, a dime-a-dance girl, and they fall for each other. When they return to the crime scene, they discover a dead body. Knowing Quinn will be accused of the crime, they race to find the true killer before he's arrested. A 1946 film starring Susan Hayward was loosely based on the plot. **Introduction by David Gordon.**

Cornell Woolrich, *Waltz into Darkness.* A New Orleans businessman successfully courts a woman through the mail but he is shocked to find when she arrives that she is not the plain brunette whose picture he'd received but a radiant blond beauty. She soon absconds with his fortune. Wracked with disappointment and loneliness, he vows to track her down. When he finds her, the real nightmare begins. **Introduction by Wallace Stroby.**